Blood Father

by Tessa Dawn

A Blood Curse Novel
Book Six
In the Blood Curse Series

Published by Ghost Pines Publishing, LLC
http://www.ghostpinespublishing.com

Volume VI of the Blood Curse Series by Tessa Dawn
First Edition Trade Paperback Published June 12, 2014
10 9 8 7 6 5 4 3 2 1

ISBN-13: 978-1-937223-12-0
Printed in the United States of America

Author may be contacted at: http://www.tessadawn.com

Ghost Pines Publishing, LLC

Acknowledgments

Chad Jones, *Artistic Design*

Ghost Pines Publishing, LLC., *Publishing & Design*

GreenHouse Design, Inc., *Cover Art*

Lidia Bercea, *Romanian Translations*

Mercedes Arnold, *Reading & Critique*

Reba Hilbert, *Editing*

Credits

"*To Make You Feel My Love*," written by Bob Dylan.

Dedication

To all those who have struggled with inner demons or fought to achieve personal freedom. (Tara, you are my hero!)

And for Carrie C ~ you know why!

The Blood Curse

In 800 BC, Prince Jadon and Prince Jaegar Demir were banished from their Romanian homeland after being cursed by a ghostly apparition: *the reincarnated Blood of their numerous female victims*. The princes belonged to an ancient society that sacrificed its females to the point of extinction, and the punishment was severe.

They were forced to roam the earth in darkness as creatures of the night. They were condemned to feed on the blood of the innocent and stripped of their ability to produce female offspring. They were damned to father twin sons by human hosts who would die wretchedly upon giving birth; and the firstborn of the first set would forever be required as a sacrifice of atonement for the sins of their forefathers.

Staggered by the enormity of *The Curse*, Prince Jadon, whose own hands had never shed blood, begged his accuser for leniency and received *four small mercies*—four exceptions to the Curse that would apply to his house and his descendants, alone.

Ψ Though still creatures of the night, they would be allowed to walk in the sun.

Ψ Though still required to live on blood, they would not be forced to take the lives of the innocent.

Ψ While still incapable of producing female offspring, they would be given *one opportunity and thirty days* to obtain a mate, a human *destiny* chosen by the gods, following a sign that appeared in the heavens.

Ψ While they were still required to sacrifice a firstborn son, their twins would be born as one child of darkness and one child of light, allowing them to sacrifice the former while keeping the latter to carry on their race.

And so...forever banished from their homeland in the Transylvanian mountains of Eastern Europe, the descendants of

BLOOD FATHER

Jaegar and the descendants of Jadon became the Vampyr of legend: roaming the earth, ruling the elements, living on the blood of others…forever bound by an ancient curse. They were brothers of the same species, separated only by degrees of light and shadow.

Prologue

Kagen Silivasi reclined in an elegant, rust-colored armchair, staring up at the ceiling in his twin's vaulted Great Room. He was waiting, along with the other members of his family, to welcome Nathaniel's guests. Well, in truth, Vanya Demir and Saber Alexiares were hardly what one could call *guests,* and they weren't so much coming to see Nathaniel as all of the Silivasi brothers at once: It was more than just a little bit cryptic, this urgent, impromptu meeting.

Unsettling to say the least.

He glanced out the floor-to-ceiling windows, taking in the magnificent mountain view, before regarding his eldest brother Marquis inquisitively. "And you have no idea what this is about?"

"None," Marquis responded. He shuffled restlessly in his own armchair. "To tell you the truth, I'm still a bit shocked that the male had the brass to ask for this meeting, to step foot in this house"—he regarded Nachari's mate Deanna as well as their newly acquired little sister Kristina with deference—"to show his face around either of these females, willingly, after what he did to them."

"Agreed," Nachari Silivasi said, leaning back against the wall beside the fireplace. "It does seem like a bold move." He crossed his arms over his chest. "On the other hand, I also have to concede that the male is trying."

"Hmm," Marquis grumbled, refusing to say any more.

"It seems like only yesterday when we went through Vanya's conversion at the clinic," Kagen commented.

"Hell, it seems like only yesterday when the bastard didn't burn in the sun," Marquis retorted.

"Marquis," Kagen chastised. "At some point, we may have to let bygones be bygones."

Nachari shrugged. "The way I see it: If Vanya wants to be with him—and it's pretty evident she does—then that's her call; and we all have to get used to it."

"The way you see it," Marquis growled. "Who asked you how you saw it?"

Nachari winked at the burly Ancient Master Warrior. "Love you, too, bro."

"Whatever," Marquis grumbled.

Kagen sat forward then. "I just don't understand what this is about—what could Saber possibly have to say to all of us that is this important?"

Nathaniel, who was sitting next to his mate on the sofa, shrugged with indifference. "Perhaps, there's an apology coming."

Jocelyn rubbed her temples. "Maybe."

Deanna shifted uneasily in her seat next, sharing a knowing glance with Kristina, who was nestled on the soft beige sofa beside Jocelyn. "I hope not," she said wearily. "I'm not sure I'm quite as *forgiving* as my mate."

Nachari strolled languidly to her side and sat on the arm of her chair. He took her hand in his and softly kissed her knuckles. "Not forgiving, love. Just…evolving."

Deanna nodded and squeezed his hand.

As far as Kagen could tell, something important had passed between his little brother and the newly redeemed vampire not so long ago in the Red Canyons. Saber's dark brother Diablo, along with two soldiers from the Dark Ones' colony, had tried to kill Saber; and Nachari and Ramsey had shown up to defend the recalcitrant male, to try and save Saber despite the bad blood that existed between them. Whatever had taken place in that valley had quenched some of Nachari's anger and begun to forge at least a tentative truce between the two males. As far as Kagen was concerned, Nachari was a wise and intuitive wizard. If he was beginning to see things in a different light, then perhaps a different light existed. He was just about to make a comment to that effect when Alejandra, Nathaniel's live-in housekeeper, stepped into the living room.

"Mr. Silivasi," she said in her thick Latin accent. "Your guests have arrived. Should I show them in?"

Nathaniel stretched fluidly in his seat to relieve some tension, and then he placed a protective arm around Jocelyn's shoulders. Jocelyn had her own history with Saber Alexiares, and none of the males seemed too keen on allowing their women to face the dangerous vampire alone. "Of course, Alejandra," Nathaniel drawled in his typical, laid-back fashion. "Show them in."

The maid retreated, and everyone in the room waited with bated breath.

Vanya appeared first, the regal beauty commanding instant attention as always. Saber was not far behind, his hand resting conspicuously, if not possessively, on the small of Vanya's back. Now that was one visually jarring sight if Kagen had ever seen one: the devil in blue jeans staking claim to an angel of light.

Kagen watched the ensuing interaction unfold with interest: The moment Nathaniel and Saber's eyes met, an undeniable spark of tension flashed between them, and the temperature in the room rose a couple of degrees.

"Dark One," Nathaniel spoke in greeting.

The term *Dark One* was a bit confusing as Saber was no longer a Dark One, at least, not technically. In truth, he never really had been. He was a son of Jadon who had been stolen by the Dark Ones at birth, raised as a member of the house of Jaegar, and only recently returned to his true lineage. Still, he had been one obstinate nut to crack; and with all his defiance, rebellion, and just plain meanness, the term *Dark One* had stuck to him like glue. It might be years before the sons of Jadon stopped referring to him that way.

If ever.

Saber seemed to take it in stride, maybe even wear it like a badge of honor. With a gait as weighted in stealth as it was in swagger, he sauntered toward Nathaniel and inclined his head. "Nathaniel."

Nathaniel rose like vapor from a steaming cauldron, all at once ascending to his feet; and Jocelyn immediately took a place at his side. "Sweetheart," she murmured, placing a gentle hand on his arm. She turned to face their guest. "Hello, Saber."

Nathaniel couldn't help it. He sidestepped between them and growled in warning, his watchful eyes darting back and forth between the pair. In truth, it wasn't meant as a challenge: It was simply an unconscious signal—a way of saying, *Caution!*—from one male predator to another. In other words: *Back up. You're too close.*

Kagen held his breath, waiting to see what would happen next. Both Jocelyn and Saber stepped back, their collective response so perfectly timed it almost appeared to be choreographed, a primordial waltz.

Nathaniel visibly relaxed, his powerful chest rising and falling with deeper breaths.

Peeking from behind the barrier of Nathaniel's shoulder, Jocelyn forced an uneasy smile and tried again. "Hello, Saber."

Saber looked her over with more than a small measure of scrutiny. He obviously remembered her. "You," he whispered. "How have you been?"

Seemingly surprised, Jocelyn's eyebrows shot up. "I've been…good."

Saber nodded. "Still jumping into your mate's battles?"

Jocelyn smiled then. "Not so much." She smirked at him. "Avoiding guillotines?"

Saber laughed without restraint, and the sound seemed almost alien coming from such a ruthless male, bizarre in its unexpected nature.

Deanna Silivasi rose softly from her seat, placed her hand on her lower stomach, and quietly announced, "I can't do this." Her stately five-foot-ten frame seemed to fold inward, constricting in Saber's presence. "I thought I could, but I can't." She was just about to leave the room when Nachari slid effortlessly behind her and placed both arms firmly around her waist.

"You *can* do this," he whispered in her ear. When she started to shake her head, Saber stepped forward, and she visibly flinched, drawing back in surprise. When he descended to one knee in front of her, Deanna looked at him like he had grown a second head. She glanced over her shoulder at Nachari and frowned. "What is he doing?"

"He is trying to appear as nonthreatening as he can," Saber answered for the Master Wizard. He bowed his head and shook it slowly back and forth. "Deanna, you have nothing to fear from me. Not now. Not ever again."

Deanna tried to take a cautious step back but ran into the brick wall of Nachari's chest. "I have much to…*remember* with you," she said bitterly.

Saber stood slowly then. He reached as gingerly as he could, as slowly as he was able, and retrieved a burnished dagger with serrated edges from the waistband of his jeans. He flipped it deftly in his hand and extended the grip to Deanna.

Marquis stirred restlessly. His eyes flashed red, but he didn't rise or interfere.

"In the house of Jaegar," Saber said, "when someone has a wrong to redress, it's done in blood, and then the matter is closed…forever."

Deanna blanched. She shook her beautiful head, her exotic bluish-gray eyes clouding with distaste. "I…I can't cut you, Saber."

Kristina Silivasi rose from the sofa, took four long strides across the room, her hips swaying in an effort to balance her petite frame above her three-inch stilettos, and snatched the blade from Saber's hand. She swung it neatly across his face, slicing from his left ear to the corner of his mouth, then, once again, from his right cheek to his temple, cutting deep into the bone. "I can," she snapped.

Saber didn't flinch, although Vanya did. "Should I leave it as it is, unhealed?" he asked.

Vanya sighed in exasperation. "Please, Kristina. I have to look at him for the rest of my life."

Kristina stared at Vanya and frowned. "Fine. He can heal it

later."

Saber nodded. "Very well. Later then."

Kristina looked startled by his compliance, more than a little off balance. Searching for a way to regain control, she smirked. "How are your flat tires, Dark One?"

Vanya dropped her head in shame.

"No longer flat," Saber said. The corners of his mouth turned up in a smile, or a predatory scowl, depending on how one looked at it, and he winked at her.

Kristina drew back in surprise, and a tiny glint of respect registered in her eyes. "Cool." She turned to face Deanna. "Are we good now, Dee? The second one was for you."

Deanna nodded tentatively at Kristina. She forced herself to meet the vampire's eyes once more, and something unspoken passed between them. "I don't want your blood, Saber. I just want to know *why*."

Again, Saber stood strong against the scrutiny. "I was a soldier in the Dark Ones' colony. I was ordered to hurt the enemy, and I obeyed. I didn't think; I didn't feel; I didn't reason. It may not be what you want to hear, but it's the truth."

Deanna frowned. "And now?"

Saber glanced at Vanya. "And now I am learning how to think and feel…and reason. Or at least I'm trying." He shrugged then. "It's all I've got."

Nachari tightened his arms around his mate and waited. When she still didn't speak, he whispered, "Deanna?"

"I'm still—"

"For what it's worth," Saber offered, "I am sorry."

Deanna nodded and Marquis snorted. "Enough!" He waved his hand through the air, as if to dismiss the whole silly scene, and scowled. "You were a soulless bastard who deserved to die. We tried to kill you, but you wouldn't burn. And now you're in love with the princess. So you've come here to talk to us about something: Get on with it."

Kagen rolled his eyes. Leave it to Marquis to put things in perspective. Of course, the Ancient Master Warrior did conveniently leave out the part where he almost removed Saber's heart for getting his mate's sister pregnant; but all in all, it was a fairly good summary.

Saber regarded Marquis thoughtfully and inclined his head. "Very well." He eyed an empty chair next to the fireplace and sat down. "May I?"

"Looks like you already did," Marquis snorted. He gestured at the chair. "Sit, stand, hang upside down if you like. Just talk."

Saber leaned forward and braced his arms on his elbows, looking as if he were bracing himself for the conversation. When Vanya made her way to his side, placed a supportive hand on his shoulder, and squeezed it reassuringly, Kagen tensed with anticipation.

What in the world was this all about?

Saber cleared his throat. "I don't want to take up any more of your time than is necessary, and I really don't know how to start, how to say this, so I'll just put it out there as succinctly as I can."

Nathaniel leaned forward, looking both leery and intense. "Go on."

Saber drew a deep breath. "In the colony, I did a lot of things other than fight, for the house of Jaegar. Mostly woodwork, iron work, shit with my hands." He eyed the females apologetically. "*Stuff* with my hands." When Marquis gave him an impatient stare, he hurried on. "And on a few occasions, I put data into our computers for the council—I fed the historic annals." He glanced upward as if searching for a better way to put it. "The historic annals are kind of like the colony's version of an electronic library, where we keep our important records, demographic information, our history." He sighed, frustrated by the recurring slip. "Where *they* keep *their* history."

Vanya stroked his shoulder with her hand as if to say, *You're doing fine*, and the whole thing made Kagen restless, uneasy deep down in the pit of his stomach.

Where in Hades was this going?

He shifted anxiously in his seat. "So?"

"So, about 480 years ago, when the lycans attacked the valley, there were about thirty Dark Ones killed."

Marquis's jaw stiffened and he clenched his fists, cracking all ten of his knuckles at once, before relaxing once again and staring blankly at Saber.

Kagen inhaled deeply: The Silivasis had intimate knowledge of the lycan attack—how could they not? They had lost their own mother at the hands of the werewolves, and their father had been lost soon after.

Nathaniel cleared his throat, and Nachari pursed his brows. "Continue," the Master Wizard said, his voice lacking its usual charisma.

Saber made eye contact with Vanya, and the princess nodded.

"At the time," Saber said, "Salvatore and the other sorcerers spent an enormous amount of time and energy trying to locate our common enemy. Needless to say, we wanted revenge pretty badly. But more so, we wanted to find out where they lived so we could eliminate them once and for all."

"They live all over the planet," Nachari said thoughtfully. "Embedded in their Council of Nations; disguised as national headhunters; meeting on occasion with human militia leaders."

"That's true," Saber agreed, "but there's more to it than that. A lot more to it."

"Like what?" Marquis asked.

"The sorcerers were able to discover something new, something really odd, something previously unheard of." He took a deep breath and just put it out there. "Another dimension."

"Another dimension?" Kagen asked.

"Yes," Saber replied. "A world apart from our own, the origin of the werewolves."

The entire room inhaled as one.

"What do you mean?" Nathaniel asked.

Saber looked off into the distance for a moment as if trying to *see* the right words. "I mean another dimension, a realm parallel to this one, but apart. A place called Mhier." Before one of the Silivasis could interrupt him again, he explained: "There's a reason none of us have ever been able to locate anything more than a regional headhunter here or there, a reason why we've never been able to ferret out an entire community or civilization of lycans and exterminate them. It's because they're not here. Not the majority of them, anyhow. Not in this dimension." He sat back in his chair, apparently deep in concentration. "The sorcerers said that Mhier was like, I don't know, a lost civilization from somewhere back in time, complete with salt mines, slaves, and some pretty gnarly animals. And from what I could garner from Salvatore's entries in the annals, any Dark Ones that had been taken by the Lycanthrope were long dead, and the challenge of trying to get there was a greater risk than it was worth—it was better to just wait for their periodic attacks and fight them here."

Marquis exhaled slowly then. "Okay, so no one is going to deny this is important information. *Very important information.* You should be sharing it with Napolean. Why did you come to us?"

Saber scrubbed his face with his hand and swallowed hard. "Because it affects your family more than most."

Kagen did not like the sound of that...wherever this was going.

Not one bit.

"How so?" he asked, his heart beginning to beat rapidly with a brash, resounding thud.

"Indeed, how so?" Marquis repeated.

Saber closed his eyes briefly. When he reopened them, they were dark with regret and deathly serious. "Because of a small entry I came across, written as no more than a footnote in the text."

"Well?" Marquis Silivasi bit out impatiently.

Saber met the Ancient Master Warrior's stare head-on. "It was the name of a vampire, a slave still living in Mhier, at least at the time of Salvatore's last entry."

"And?" Nathaniel Silivasi demanded, his voice growing harsh with anticipation.

"And the name was Keitaro Silivasi."

Nachari released his hold on Deanna and took two steps back, his stunning features flushing absent of color. He ran a rigid hand through his thick, wavy hair, and shook it out in disbelief. The wizard had only been twenty-one years old when their father disappeared; he had barely had a chance to know him.

Nathaniel's fangs slowly extended in his mouth, and his eyes burned a deep crimson red; yet he said nothing. For centuries, he had believed Keitaro was still alive, and he had searched from one end of the globe to the other before finally giving up and laying the male's memory to rest.

Marquis sat back in his chair, far too casually.

His piercing eyes dimmed from deep phantom blue to eerie shark black, the depths going vacant with barely concealed anguish *and rage*, and then he began to tremble.

Uncontrollably.

Kagen sat forward on the edge of his seat, watching Marquis carefully, fully expecting him to plunge over the edge of sanity at any moment: Marquis and Keitaro had been the best of friends, bar none. And their father's loss had affected Marquis more tragically than any of the others, hardening his heart, changing his personality, molding him into the brutal, impassive male he was today. Kagen couldn't help but wish Ciopori had come with him, that the other females had found someone else to watch their kids, because by the look on Marquis's stony face, the male was slipping further and further away by the second, perhaps going somewhere from which he would never return.

To Kagen's immense surprise, the huge male seemed to simply snap out of it. That is, in a truly creepy, *five-faces-of-Eve* kind of way. It was almost as if another personality had simply taken over for him, run his emotions through a paper-shredder, and discarded them in a bin on the other side, leaving him free to process the information. "That was almost five centuries ago," Marquis grumbled in irritation. "Even if he was alive then, he's unlikely to be alive now. Especially if he was surviving as a…a slave." He stumbled over the last word despite his self-control.

Vanya took a deep breath then. "I don't believe that to be true, brother-in-law," she said. "I have reason to believe he might yet be living."

"What reason, Princess?" Nachari asked, his tone also carefully controlled.

Vanya swallowed hard. "Before I met Saber, I had a dream about him, a dream that vexed me horribly and would not give me a moment's peace. I dreamed that there was a fire-breathing dragon in the house of Jadon, and that our paths would cross inexorably. In the dream, he always burned me when I approached him; yet I couldn't stay away. *I simply couldn't.* Because he was guarding something so precious, so valuable to the house of Jadon. A treasure. One that had to be returned to the people." She sat back and sighed. "Last night, I told Saber about the dream, and it sparked his memory. He believes—and I agree—that the treasure he was guarding was not his own return to the house of Jadon, but his knowledge of that single footnote: that marginalized entry. Your father's name."

Whatever…*whoever*…was guarding Marquis Silivasi's emotions stepped aside. He shot out of his chair like a rocket, fueled by highly combustible energy, ready to launch to the sky, and roared like an angry lion. "Son of a bitch!"

Nathaniel and Nachari immediately flanked him on either side, both males placing a firm hand on his shoulders. "Settle down, Marquis," Nathaniel warned, alluding to the powerful impact a male vampire's emotions had on the earth around them. The last thing they wanted was to trigger an electrical storm or create a flash flood.

"Be calm," Nachari said, immediately weaving an intricate pattern over the male's head, no doubt some spell or another to catch his rage.

Kagen stood to face Saber then, his own heart practically

beating out of his chest. "Do you know where the portal is, the entrance to this…this other dimension?"

Saber shook his head. "No, I never saw that information."

Nachari's expression grew intense. "Perhaps not, but if Salvatore Nistor could divine it with his sorcery, then I can find it using wizardry."

Saber held up his hands in question. "I don't know if that's true or not, but I do know this: If you guys can find the portal, I can draw you a map of the territory."

one

Dark Moon Vale ~ four weeks later

Kagen Silivasi strolled onto the rooftop terrace of Nachari and Deanna's lavish brownstone, located at the northern face of the forest cliffs, and smiled warmly at Deanna. "Sister."

"Hi, Kagen." Deanna's rich, bluish-gray eyes brightened. "How are you tonight?"

Kagen shrugged his broad shoulders. There was no point in answering—all of the Silivasi brothers were wound as tight as drums, and they had been for the last four weeks, ever since Saber had shared his shocking news with them. He glanced up at the sky, making note of the crystalline stars and the shimmering moon. "Beautiful night," he commented, trying to find something positive to focus on.

"Very beautiful," Deanna said. She turned to face Nachari and frowned, the slightest downward curve of her heart-shaped lips. The Master Wizard was sitting at a modern drafting table, beside a series of expensive, intimidating-looking telescopes, scribbling wildly on a piece of paper, his brow furrowed in concentration. "He's still at it."

"I see," Kagen said. He was just about to walk in Nachari's direction when Deanna took a step back and smiled.

"You cut your hair." She sounded genuinely pleased with the outcome.

Kagen chuckled lightly. "Yeah, just a little."

She appraised him thoughtfully. "No, I think it looks great." She took a step forward to assess it more closely. "Chin length suits you." She reached out to smooth her hand through a mass of his thick brown locks. "And these subtle layers, the way the waves lie so smoothly away from your face, it's...stunning, really."

Kagen placed his hand on his heart. "Stop, sister. You're going to make me blush."

She laughed then. "Well, I think it suits you very well. Your natural highlights really bring out your eyes now."

Kagen averted his eyes. He turned to appraise Nachari and frowned. "Wow, he really is concentrating if he missed that exchange. Otherwise, I would expect to have all six feet, 180 pounds of possessive male all over me about now."

Deanna rolled her eyes. "Nachari doesn't get jealous. Not really." She gave Kagen a knowing glance then. "Not like Marquis or Nathaniel."

"He *is* a vampire," Kagen said, his tone laced with caution. "Don't ever forget that."

"Yes," Deanna agreed, "but a very arrog—*self-assured*—vampire."

Kagen smiled. "Well put."

"Still," Deanna said, eyeing her mate suspiciously, "perhaps I've grown old hat already."

Kagen shook his head, dismissing the comment offhand, as he eyed the exotically beautiful female appreciatively. There was nothing *old hat* about Deanna Dubois-Silivasi, and there never would be. "Never," he reassured her, meaning it emphatically.

Deanna cleared her throat and raised her voice. "I mean your hair is really *gorgeous*." She put a strong emphasis on the last word.

Kagen cut his eyes at her and stared at Nachari.

Nothing.

The wizard was still deep in thought.

"In fact, I would have to say it's *sexy as hell*," Deanna added, whistling at her brother for effect.

"Stop it!" Kagen whispered. When Nachari still didn't look up, he shrugged.

"Ah well," Deanna said, feigning disappointment. "I suppose I'll go check on our son then. I imagine Sebastian is still in love with me." She laughed, making it clear she was only teasing. Despite all the recent turmoil surrounding Keitaro Silivasi,

Nachari and Deanna were still like newlyweds, always gazing into each other's eyes, utterly incapable of keeping their hands to themselves, even in public. They were a match made in the heavens, quite literally.

"Your mate will step away from that desk soon enough," Kagen said. "Count on it." He gave her a conspiratorial wink. "In the meantime, I'm going to go see what he's working on so intently."

"Please do," Deanna said. "See if you can't get him to at least stand up and stretch his legs."

Kagen nodded. He watched as Deanna headed for the rooftop staircase and made her way back inside the brownstone, and then he took three long strides, sidled up to Nachari, and glanced over the wizard's shoulder to study his drawings. "So, how's it—"

"Back off, already!" Nachari snarled, leveling a severe glower at the Master Healer.

Kagen stepped back and threw up both hands. "Whoa, brother. I haven't even said anything."

Nachari sighed. "Sorry. It's going the same way it's been going. I'm making progress. It's just slow. Way too slow."

Kagen eyed the map on the desk, the one Saber Alexiares had drawn for the Silivasi brothers, the one that outlined the territories, tributaries, and passageways of Mhier, the realm of the Lycanthrope; and then he eyed the haphazard drawing Nachari was working on. It was a series of circles drawn with a compass, with one plot-point after another stressed in red ink. There were lines dissecting the circles and arrows connecting the lines. It looked like a frenzied maze. "The warriors are ready," Kagen said cautiously, referring to Marquis, Nathaniel, and Ramsey Olaru, the three other males who would accompany Kagen and Nachari into Mhier, to begin searching for their father, as soon as Nachari located the portal.

"Yeah, they've been ready," Nachari snapped defensively. The stress of the whole situation was really taking a toll on the otherwise laid-back male.

"I don't mean mentally, emotionally," Kagen said. "I mean we have the tents packed, the weapons cleaned and sharpened, the silver ammunition cached in carriers, and the ability to haul it all now. We have enough blood bagged to *feed* for six months to a vampire if necessary. I mean, everything is finally *ready*."

Nachari dropped his pencil and splayed his large hands flat over the page he had been scribbling on. "Everything except the one thing we need: to pinpoint the entrance to Mhier."

Kagen was just about to reply, to try and say something supportive and encouraging, even though the delay was killing him every bit as much as Nachari, when Braden Bratianu rounded the corner. The boy had just turned sixteen eight days ago, on May 10th, and Kagen could've sworn he had grown two inches in the last month alone. He now stood about five-foot-ten, and his once thin, underdeveloped frame was beginning to fill out nicely; his body was adjusting quickly to its ever-evolving vampiric state.

"What's up, Kagen," Braden said. Did his voice sound just a little bit deeper?

Kagen took a scrutinizing look at the youngster: His chestnut brown hair, interspersed with occasional blond highlights, had darkened just a bit; and it appeared as if the boy was growing it out, even as Kagen had shortened his. It fell just beyond Braden's shoulders now, and whether it was the longer hair or the rapid development, his features seemed just a little bit sharper, more masculine. More adult. "Hey, Braden. How have you been, son?"

Braden's smile was exuberant. "Cool…cool. I'm hanging in there."

Kagen chuckled beneath his breath. *Still Braden.*

"Hey, Nachari," Braden said cautiously, not wanting to disturb him but eager to say something useful.

"What do you need?" Nachari asked. His voice was even, a paternal attempt at exercising patience.

"Um, yeah. I just…" Braden bit his bottom lip and wrinkled up his nose. "I just thought of something that might help."

Nachari looked up from his work and raised his eyebrows. "What's that?"

Braden stepped forward and pointed at the cluttered page of dizzying circles and crisscrossed lines, circling a red dot in the middle with his forefinger. "So I was thinking that the nucleus—you know, the center of the map that represents the portal—might not be a place so much as an energy field."

Nachari sat up straighter. "Meaning?"

"Well, you've already defined the coordinates, right?"

"Right," Nachari said, his voice perking up with interest.

"The north represents—"

"The edge of the valley," Nachari supplied. "The thick of the Dark Moon Forest."

"Right," Braden replied. "And the south represents the winding Snake Creek River."

"As well as the Dark Moon Lake," Nachari said, "the element of water."

"*Right*," Braden said, his own voice mounting with enthusiasm. Apparently, they were already on the same page.

"The east represents the steepest cliffs, and the west represents the meadow and the Red Canyons—"

"A hallow or a void."

"I'm already with you," Nachari said, swiveling around in his chair to meet the youngster's eyes. "But the lines don't intersect in a way that makes sense. I can't divine the energy of anything close to a portal at the center of the four points."

"Yeah, yeah, I know." Braden took a step closer to the drawing, placed his fingers on the edge of the paper, and raised his brows. "May I?" he asked, sounded far more grown-up than usual.

"Please do." Nachari leaned back in his chair and waited as Braden lifted the paper off the desk and began to appraise it thoughtfully.

"So, what if it's not supposed to? What if it's not a place but an energy?"

"Elaborate," Nachari said.

Braden sighed. He narrowed his eyes and furrowed his brows, deep in thought. "What if you were to go to the highest point in the northern forest and gather bark from a tree? You know, just to recreate the energy. Then do it again in the south, collect some water from the river and the lake. Then—"

"Take a chunk out of the Red Canyons in the west and some stones from the cliffs in the east," Nachari supplied.

"Arrange them in a circle where the four lines meet—"

"In the center of the valley…and create our own portal?" Nachari shook his head in wonderment. "It's not a place but an energy."

"Maybe," Braden said, his eager eyes brightening with anticipation.

"It's worth a shot," Nachari said, "but there's still something missing."

"What's that?" Kagen interjected, chiming in on the conversation, his own hope beginning to rise.

"The energy of the lycans," Nachari and Braden answered in unison. Their eyes met and a look of understanding, of mutual pride and admiration, passed between them.

Nachari stood up, appearing all at once to be all business, no nonsense. "Brother, do you remember when Nathaniel *eliminated* Tristan Hart? Do you know whether or not he kept anything that belonged to the lycan? Before he incinerated his body?"

Kagen scrunched up his face. "You don't mean—"

"No. *No*! Not *that*." Nachari winced, immediately grasping the reference to the unfortunate appendage Nathaniel Silivasi had removed from Tristan Hart, in effect making him a eunuch, before he ripped his heart out by way of his throat for trying to assault Jocelyn. "That's disgusting, Kagen."

Kagen sniffed. "Well, you're the one asking."

"I meant a trophy," Nachari said. "You know, Nathaniel and his…creativity. He doesn't just kill his enemies in unique, inventive ways; he often keeps a souvenir, for whatever reason."

"Yeah," Kagen said, grimacing. "He is a bit of a warped bastard, that twin of mine."

"No doubt," Nachari said. "So maybe…just maybe?"

Nathaniel… Kagen immediately reached out telepathically to his twin on the familiar family bandwidth. No need to involve the entire house of Jadon in the communication.

Kagen, Nathaniel replied immediately.

I'm with Nachari, and we have a question for you, Kagen said, getting right to the point.

Ask away, Nathaniel said.

Do you remember Tristan Hart, the lycan?

Nathaniel's answering growl said it all: Of course he remembered the worthless bastard.

Kagen sighed. *Did you take anything…save anything…as a token of your kill?*

Of course not, Nathaniel said slyly, his voice taking on a dark, perilous edge. *That would be demented.*

No one is going to tell Jocelyn, Nachari added. *It's important, Nathaniel.*

The connection grew quiet.

Perhaps…a lock of that wild mass of unruly hair, Nathaniel said. *Why?*

Thank the gods, Nachari said. *We need it. To conjure a spell.*

Nathaniel hissed like a rattlesnake, sounding far more vampiric than civilized.

For Auriga's sake, Kagen barked. *He won't be any less dead if you turn it over, and you won't be any less the male who sent him to the afterlife.*

Why would you want to remember something like that, anyhow? Nachari cut in, incredulous. Apparently, he couldn't help it. *Hold onto a souvenir like that?*

Nathaniel harrumphed. *You have your telescopes; I have my museum. Don't worry about it, Wizard. It's a warrior thing.*

Nachari looked at Kagen and rolled his eyes, shaking his head back and forth as if to say, *cuckoo…cuckoo. Fine*, he responded. *How quickly can you get it to me, Warrior?*

Five or ten minutes, Nathaniel said.

"And I can have all of the objects, the energetic catalysts you need to work your spell, back to you in less than an hour."

Kagen spoke aloud. He had already released his silken brown wings, preparing to launch into flight, before Nachari could reply. "Bark from a northern tree, water from the south, stones from the eastern cliffs, and a piece of the Red Canyons? Do containers matter?"

"Not at this point," Nachari said.

Braden swelled up with pride. "Then we're going to try it?"

"Yes," Nachari said emphatically. "We are definitely going to try it." *Nathaniel, we will see you on the rooftop in five minutes then?*

Very well, Nathaniel replied. *I'll be there.*

Thank you, Kagen added, knowing his twin hated to relinquish the trophy, no matter how compliant he sounded…for whatever demented reason.

Yep, Nathaniel drawled in acknowledgment.

Kagen chuckled then. *We'll see you soon. Be well, brother.*

Be well, Kagen. With that formal exit, the Ancient Master Warrior closed the communication, and Nachari turned to Braden.

"Braden, I have to start working on a spell to conjure and open the portal. Would you do me a favor in the meantime?"

Braden's handsome face positively lit up with excitement. "Yeah. *Yeah, of course.* What?"

"Bring Marquis up to speed with what we're doing."

Braden nodded his assent. "Most definitely." By the self-satisfied look on his face, he clearly felt important. He started to say something else, but Kagen didn't hear him. He had already launched into the sky, leaving the roof and soaring into the brilliant night, his large glossy wings spread out like an angel's cloak behind him. He turned sharply to the right, toward the North Star, and then headed for the highest point in the Dark Moon Forest to retrieve the first mystic object.

two

Mhier

Arielle Nightsong waited in the shadows until the last of King Thane's guards had left the meadow. As one of Thane's four trusted alpha generals, it was Xavier Matista's duty to patrol Thane's private grounds each night before heading back to his own clan, the western pack of the Lycanthrope. She was careful to stand downwind as Xavier, the cruelest and most brutal of Thane's inner circle, passed by, singing a vile, dissonant tune in his harsh, arrogant voice.

She shivered as she watched Xavier stroll into the night, and then she said a prayer to the gods of her ancestors as she gathered her leather pouch under her arm and prepared to slip into Keitaro's hut. She had no doubt that the slave had been treated horrendously that day, for no other reason than Tyrus Thane, the king of the Lycanthrope, was still enraged as a result of his human wife's recent adultery; and being a miscreant bully as well as a sadistic animal, he had to take it out on someone. Keitaro Silivasi was as good a choice as any. After all, he was Thane's favorite prisoner—*favorite* meaning the one he hated the most—and Thane always kept Keitaro in a weakened, defenseless state by bleeding him out on a daily basis, constantly injecting intravenous poisons into the vampire's veins, some cruel combination of saline solution and liquefied diamond dust, and keeping his ankles chained and his wrists shackled at all times. Whenever Keitaro wasn't working or fighting, he was drugged so he couldn't run away or heal himself with his venom.

It was unthinkable.

Barbaric.

And it had gone on for hundreds of years.

Arielle had no doubt that Keitaro would be in need of her

various healing herbs and tonics tonight, and that was why she had snuck away from the Rebel Camp.

Holding her breath, she tiptoed silently to the entrance of the small lean-to hut and quickly ducked inside the bearskin flap. Keitaro was lying on a threadbare blanket, the worn skin of a mule deer that had been killed what looked like decades ago, and never properly tanned or cured. His skin was covered in open sores and raised welts that looked like a mixture of a leopard's spots and a zebra's stripes, marring every inch of his otherwise immortal flesh. As usual, he had experienced a toxic reaction to the poisonous concoction that always flowed like acid through his veins. Even from ten feet away, Arielle could sense his agony.

Keitaro groaned as he turned on his side, and then he caught sight of Arielle from the corner of his eye. Raising his head and yanking on his chains—both arms were staked in cross-like fashion to the ground; it was how they always made him sleep—he met her gaze with a cautionary stare of his own. "Rielle, you shouldn't be here." His voice was calm and paternal, despite his torment.

"Shh, Keitaro," she whispered. "You know I could not stay away."

The ancient vampire simply shook his head, his dark, intelligent eyes brimming with regret. "I'm fine, Rielle. I will survive." He grimaced from the pain of speaking. "I always do."

Arielle sighed. "Yes, you do, and my wonderful healing herbs have a lot to do with it." It was a pitiful attempt at cheering him up. At cheering herself up.

Keitaro forced a smile then, however slight, his mature features framing his darkly tanned, handsome face. "Rielle," he chastised, "one of these days you're going to get caught, and I'll never be able to live with myself when that happens."

"It won't happen," Arielle reassured him. "I'm always careful." She dug into her pouch and removed a pain-relieving poultice of valerian root, skullcap, nettle, and cloves. As she stirred the mixture with a knotty stick, combining the herbs to activate their healing properties before beginning the treatment, she smiled brightly. "I'll have you fixed up in no time, Mr. Silivasi."

Keitaro frowned. "Mr. Silivasi? You really are in a formal mood today."

She chuckled softly. "No, I just need to get in and out quickly." Her eyes darted back and forth around the dimly lit, circular space, and she shivered. "I'm well aware of the increased danger of being here tonight."

Keitaro rolled back over. He settled onto his back once more and tried to stifle a moan, unsuccessfully. "Then you should also know that it's much too risky. Not worth the chance. I'm serious, Rielle." His already gravelly voice deepened with concern. "You can't keep coming back here, not just for me, especially not now, considering what's about to happen to Queen Cassandra."

Arielle removed a damp white cloth, pretreated with herbal antiseptic from her medicine bag, and began gently dabbing Keitaro's wounds, cleaning them carefully, one at a time, preparing them for the ointment. When he grimaced beneath her touch, she frowned in apology. "I'm sorry…*I am*…this won't take long." She continued to dab at the wounds, taking extra care not to further irritate his already inflamed skin. "And yes," she added, "I have heard about Cassandra, the fact that she cheated on the king and is soon to be executed for adultery. I can't say I feel sorry for her, the evil witch."

Keitaro inclined his head in a serious nod. "Nor can I, but that doesn't mean I'm anxious to witness the foul event, to see what manner of torture Thane has cooked up for bride number nine."

Arielle cringed. Every one of Thane's young brides eventually met with a gruesome fate: If he didn't accidentally kill them in a murderous rage, he grew tired of them and passed them on to his generals, who already had wives—*correction*, slaves—of their own. And if they managed to escape that horrific fate, he usually had them executed for one flimsy excuse or another. The bottom line was plain: Thane was utterly heartless, needlessly violent, and insanely evil. And as far as the lycan was concerned, women were nothing more than property to be used, abused, and discarded at will. "Hopefully, he will do it cleanly, *swiftly*, this time. Show some mercy for once."

Keitaro chuckled low in his throat, and the humorous sound was distinctly predatory and raw. "Mercy? From Thane?" He sank further back into the roughened deerskin. "Then you really haven't heard the latest news."

Arielle raised her eyebrows in question. She tucked the white cloth back into her bag, scooped a large gob of ointment onto the pads of her index and middle fingers, and began to smooth the healing liniment on Keitaro's abraded skin. "What news?"

"Thane has decided to execute Cassandra *in the arena* on Sunday."

Arielle momentarily stopped dressing his wounds and clenched her eyes shut. "In the auditorium?" She blew out an anxious breath. "So he intends to make sport of it for all the other slaves and lycans to see?"

Keitaro nodded. "Yes."

"And that means—"

"That he will want to use me as the opening act, part of the day's entertainment."

Arielle bristled inside and out. She ground her teeth together and continued applying the ointment. Why couldn't Thane just leave Keitaro alone, just once? By all that was holy, he had played with the male like a prized toy for nearly four hundred years, or at least that's how legend had it. One would think the king would tire of him eventually, perhaps find a new distraction in one of his human servants, one of the captured rebels, or even an insubordinate lycan. "One of these days, someone is going to kill that evil bastard, and I hope I'm there with a front row seat when it happens."

Keitaro chuckled despite his pain. "Not as badly as I'd like to be the one to do it." She pressed too hard on a wound, and he involuntarily jerked his leg in pain.

"Sorry," she whispered, making a concerted effort to be

more gentle.

Keitaro ignored the slip. "If only I could find a way to get to him." He nodded at the intravenous bag of poisonous fluid, flowing steadily into his veins even as they spoke, and heaved a sigh. "If only I could break free of this poison…for just one night." His eyes flashed a dangerous crimson red, and Arielle regarded him cautiously. Despite his station and his condition, Keitaro Silivasi was a dangerous predator and an unparalleled warrior; if the male were to ever be given a clean shot at Tyrus Thane, well, it would be hell's fire and the devil's vengeance unleashed in one fell swoop. She shuddered at the thought. She stared at the intravenous bag hanging above them, attached securely to a thick lodge pole, and wished like hell she could just disconnect it for him. But it was far too risky. The small monitor was connected to a trigger device of some sort, a detonator. One false move, and everyone would go up in smoke. Besides, the lycans didn't just booby-trap their apparatus, they also relied heavily on curses and wards to protect their maniacal contraptions—it wasn't like she could just disable the device or disarm the explosive. It took magic to disarm magic, and Arielle was only human. No one in the Rebel Camp had the skill to unravel a lycanthropic ward. Not to mention, the lycans had one other distinct and profound advantage over the humans born in Mhier: Because they could travel in and out of other dimensions, they had access to modern devices and technologies that the Mhieridians could not even hope to understand or manipulate, like the intravenous apparatus and whatever booby-trap accompanied it. "I'm sorry, Keitaro," she whispered sadly. "I wish I could do more for you."

Keitaro shook his head sympathetically. Even in his suffering, he sought to reassure Arielle, and didn't that just make him one of the most endearing beings she had ever known. "You didn't create this hell," he said. "It isn't your responsibility to fix it."

Arielle chewed on her bottom lip, wishing she had something useful to say, something truly encouraging, not just lip service. After several pregnant moments had passed, she finally returned to the previous subject. "So, if Thane is planning to make a public sport of his latest wife—to execute her at high-noon, so to speak—and if he's planning to use you as the opening act for his sadistic games, then who, or what, will you be fighting this time?"

Keitaro seemed to actually perk up, if that was even possible. His tortured yet handsome face grew rigid with anticipation. "Cain Armentieres."

Arielle's eyes opened wide in surprise. "*Cain*? Thane's top alpha general? His closest ally?"

Keitaro nodded. "You really don't know what happened, do you?"

Arielle shook her head. "Rumor has it that wife number nine, Cassandra Villanosa, was caught cheating on the king, as if that crazy werewolf needs an incentive to go off the deep end *again*. They say Thane walked in on her in the throne-room, of all places, and caught her with—" Her mouth dropped open as she put two and two together. "*Cain* was her lover?"

"None other," Keitaro agreed, and then he frowned. "Although I think *lover* might be too civilized a word." He winced as she applied another dollop of ointment to his skin and began to rub it into a welt, this time, on his battered chest.

"I can't believe that the king's best friend, his right-hand Alpha, would do something so stupid…so dangerous."

Keitaro actually smiled then, his dark, intelligent eyes alighting with titillation. "At least there is justice now and then."

"So that's why you're going to be paired in battle with Cain—Thane is planning to use you to punish him."

"To kill him," Keitaro supplied, "because there's probably no one else in Mhier, outside of Thane himself, who can do it."

"And Thane's too proud—and self-important—to get his hands dirty," she said.

Despite himself, Keitaro snarled.

"Then you think Thane should do it himself?" Arielle asked, hardly believing her ears. "Kill a female, no matter who she is?"

The thought made her queasy inside: Keitaro was far too noble, far too reasoned, to casually sanction a male killing a female, not unless the circumstances were truly dire.

"That's not what I'm saying," Keitaro said. "But a real male attends to his own house. He handles his own business."

Arielle shivered, and then she began to think about the upcoming battle, to picture Keitaro, an ancient vampire, legendary for his fighting skills, going up against an ancient lycan, legendary for his brutality and lack of fair play. "This isn't a sure win for you, is it?" The moment the words left her mouth, she regretted them: Keitaro Silivasi was a legend for a reason, a rare, calculated killer, captured from the house of Jadon and forced to work as a slave in the salt mines for two hundred years, before Thane realized he was a prized, undefeatable combatant. He was one of the best warriors the lycans had ever seen: brutal, exacting, and lethal in his swift execution. He didn't need a human female questioning his prowess, casting doubt on the outcome of the upcoming battle. "I'm sorry," she whispered. "I didn't mean—"

"That I could die in this battle?" His vivid eyes softened. "It is only truth, Rielle. Cain is one of the oldest werewolves in Mhier, and he's a vicious son of a bitch with nothing left to lose."

"No," Arielle insisted, refusing to even consider Keitaro's death as a potential outcome. "He isn't your equal—*no one is*—I just meant that you are always in danger when you step into the arena. That's all."

Her hand slipped quietly into his, and he squeezed it softly before reluctantly letting go. "It's okay, Rielle." He shut his eyes and took several deep breaths as the healing ointment began to work on his wounds, to gently ease the pain. "I know what you meant, and honestly? I have never been more eager to regain my strength, to drink the rancid blood the king will give me right before the battle, no matter how foul and abhorrent, in order to dispatch my opponent." He tightened his chained hands into fists instinctively. "I have been waiting 480 years to murder Cain

Armentieres. It will be a sweet victory, one I will not relinquish to fear of death. Not when it will free us both."

Before Arielle could respond, a set of heavy footsteps approached outside the door, rustling a pile of dry leaves on the ground. Arielle stuffed all of her healing supplies beneath Keitaro's blanket, even as the vampire drew to immediate attention.

"Take my hand again, *now*. And. Don't. Even. Breathe," he commanded.

The moment Keitaro snatched Arielle's hand, she felt a visceral infusion of power transfer from his body into hers; and then just like that, she was rendered invisible by the powerful being beside her—and just how had he drawn upon such power in his weakened, compromised state, anyhow? With all the diamond that was flowing through his veins, he should have been incapable of hearing the lycan's approach, let alone doing something about it. Rielle wept inside. She knew the cost of performing such a feat would cost Keitaro dearly: physically, mentally, and energetically. His pain would return with a vengeance.

Xavier stuck his head inside the tent and scowled angrily. "Who are you speaking with, vampire?"

Keitaro snarled, his face a virulent mask of hatred. "The ghostly apparition of the jackal who birthed you, lycan." His fangs elongated in his mouth. "Unchain me, and let's talk it over."

Xavier raised a clenched fist and held it in the air, obviously wishing he could pummel Keitaro's face in. "Haven't you had enough pain for one day, slave?"

Despite his weakened state, Keitaro Silivasi hissed, his midnight eyes heating in his skull until they shone bloodred. "You've been torturing me for centuries, you useless bastard. I don't even notice it anymore."

Xavier laughed then, the sound both guttural and harsh. "You're lying, vampire."

"And you're inferior, lycan. So now, we both know where

we stand."

"One of these days," Xavier grit out between clenched teeth.

"Yeah, whatever," Keitaro snarled. "Either do something about it or get out."

Xavier spat on Keitaro's chest and stormed out in a fury; no doubt, he was struggling to restrain himself from acting on his threats. When he was finally gone, Keitaro released Arielle's hand and glared at the deposit of spittle running down his chest. "Wipe that shit off," he growled.

Arielle dug out her white cloth and immediately wiped the saliva away, crumpling the dirty rag in her hand. "That wasn't very smart, Keitaro. You have to stop—"

Keitaro leveled a cautionary glare at her, cutting her off mid-sentence. Although Arielle knew it was not meant to be threatening—the vampire had meant it as a gentle warning—it put chills down her spine just the same: She should have known better by now, to challenge Keitaro's pride or his anger when they were all the vampire had left. Keitaro Silivasi was not afraid of death, and he sure as hell was not afraid of Xavier Matista.

Arielle sighed, feeling all at once remorseful and out of place. If Keitaro Silivasi could have taken his own life before then, he would have. As it stood, his existence was a long, endless repetition of suffering and slavery, a hell on Mhier, without his wife, without his beloved sons, without any hope for an end…without a reprieve. He wanted to provoke one or the other: a chance to exact vengeance or a chance to die as he wished.

If it hadn't been for Arielle's own captivity—she had only escaped Thane's clutches ten years prior, just before her eighteenth birthday—she would have never met Keitaro Silivasi, and the vampire would have been virtually alone. No, Keitaro Silivasi survived because King Tyrus Thane wanted him to survive, and it was a cruel, prolonged torment for the Ancient Master Warrior at best, a twisted joke at the least. But Keitaro would never back down to a werewolf, and Arielle knew that, if one day, Keitaro provoked one of the vulgar beasts into killing him, it would only be another victory. Still, she couldn't bear to see him take such chances. Keitaro was like the father she had never known. The rebel she had never met.

"Penny for your thoughts?" Keitaro said, interrupting her inner monologue. Before she could reply, he grasped her hand. "Promise me, you won't come back, Arielle; I mean it."

Arielle recoiled at his words. Not only had he snatched her hand a bit too brusquely, but he had called her Arielle, as opposed to the shortened version of Rielle, and that meant the vampire was deathly serious. "I won't promise that. I can't just leave you to the wolves." She winked at him, hoping to underscore the twisted humor in her words. "I will not, Keitaro."

Keitaro's jaw stiffened. "Look at me, Rielle, and listen to what I'm telling you."

Arielle met his gaze reluctantly.

"If the generals had not gotten drunk that night, if the sentry posted outside your hut had not passed out…" His voice trailed off, and he shook his head to dismiss the memory. "If Thane had gotten his way, if you hadn't escaped ten years ago, when you were still seventeen years old, you would have been wife number seven, not Leah. And after her death, he would have chosen you over Paulina as wife number eight. After her, you would have been victim number nine, not Cassandra. The king has always wanted you, and you, slipping through his fingers, humiliated him. Made a mockery of his manhood…and his throne. This is not a game, sweet girl. We both know that all nine of his previous wives have been executed or murdered at his hands: If he doesn't beat them to death, he eventually tires of them and has them killed." He glanced at her long and hard before softening his voice. "Even with your rare, incomparable beauty, you wouldn't stand a chance, long term. Every time Thane loses a wife, he sends his guard to search for *you*…again. This time will be no different. You need to go into hiding for as long as you can, and you need stay there until he has found another wife. I am not free, Rielle. I cannot protect you. He has never forgotten you. Do you understand what I'm saying?"

Arielle nodded, understanding fully just what was at stake, what kind of risk she took every time she entered the encampment to see to Keitaro's needs, to try and ease his endless suffering. "I do understand, and I will go into hiding again. But I can't leave you at his mercy, not indefinitely. I just can't, Keitaro. It's hard to explain. I just…*can't*."

"By all the celestial gods, you are a pure soul, Rielle, and I love you like a daughter. Please, I have already lost my wife and my sons. Do not force me to lose you, too."

Arielle's eyes filled with tears, but she held back the ensuing river. "You are unspeakably dear to me, Keitaro."

"Then promise me you will not come back."

Arielle sat back on her heels and slowly shook her head. "I'm sorry, Mr. Silivasi. I just can't make that promise." She pressed her forefinger gently to his mouth to silence any protest. "Sleep well. Regain your strength for Sunday. I will light a prayer-fire for you in the Rebel Camp."

Keitaro shook his head sadly, clearly wishing he could change her mind. "Go, now. I wish I could change your mind, but I know that you are as stubborn as an ox. Just be careful."

"I will," she promised.

"You better be," he warned.

She smiled then and pressed a gentle kiss on his forehead. "Father of my heart," she whispered.

"Daughter of mine," he replied. "Be well, Arielle."

She averted her eyes and bowed her head, ever so slightly, in the way he had taught her, in the way of the Vampyr. "Be well, Keitaro."

Keitaro Silivasi sank deeper into the damnable blanket, the threadbare deerskin chafing his back, and tried to relax as the healing ointments began to work their magic on his raw, inflamed skin. He watched the bearskin flap over the doorway rustle, sway, and then settle into its normal position, as darkness, once again, enveloped the tiny hut. And then he closed his eyes.

Arielle Nightsong was truly the daughter of his heart, the one bright light he had in an otherwise miserable, endless existence. And her charitable visits, which she took at great risk to her health and her future—Thane would give *anything* to make her wife number ten—were more deeply appreciated than she could ever know. What point would there have been in telling her the upcoming games were rigged? That Thane would stack the approaching match heavily in Cain's favor, even though the arrogant king had every intention of seeing to it that Cain never made it out alive. As it stood, Cain would be equipped with the weapon of his choice, not to mention a lethal entourage of three vicious rhino-beasts, all trained from birth to kill on command, while Keitaro would be forced to fight with his bare hands, still in a weakened state. There had been no point in telling Arielle that the chances of him making it out of the match alive were slim to none. No, Keitaro had done the right thing. She would find out soon enough.

He sighed and struggled to find a more comfortable position, such as it were.

It didn't matter.

It was time.

Long past time, really, to finally exit this gods-forsaken realm and reunite with his wife Serena in the afterlife. A bare hint of a smile crossed his chapped lips as he, once and for all, accepted his fate.

At least he would have the ultimate satisfaction of taking Cain Armentieres out with him, murdering the vile alpha general of the Northern Clan of the Lycanthrope—the same one who had murdered his wife Serena so many centuries ago in Dark Moon Vale—on his way to the afterlife.

Perhaps this was why the gods had allowed him to live in such a barren purgatory for so long.

Of course…

"Sa razbun moartea nevestei mele, as mai suferii inca o mie

de ani." The words rolled off his tongue in his native Romanian language:

To avenge my wife in death, I would suffer a thousand years more.

three

Dark Moon Vale

Kagen Silivasi could hardly believe it: Nachari had completed the spell.

Using the materials Kagen had brought back from the four outermost directions of Dark Moon Vale, Nachari had managed to capture their essence, reconstruct their energy into an interwoven pattern that contained a portal at the center, and manufacture a spiritual doorway into another realm. There was nothing left to do but activate it in the valley, once they were ready to enter Mhier.

Well, that, and to go over their plans *and the map* one last time.

Unwilling to waste another second, Kagen and Nachari had called Saber Alexiares, asking him to bring his latest version of the map to the rooftop. To their surprise, the male had obliged them at once.

Nathaniel had returned to his sprawling cliff-side estate, right after dropping off the morbid trophy he had saved from Tristan's kill—he had wanted to spend his last night home with Jocelyn and Storm. And Marquis was still at his traditional three-story farmhouse, hunkered down with Ciopori, which was fine. The princess wanted to take full advantage of Marquis's last night in the vale, spending every waking moment with her mate, before the Silivasi clan ventured into the great unknown, perhaps never to return again.

Besides, Marquis really needed to center, to get his head on straight.

He was like a lit fuse ready to go off at any moment. He needed this time with Ciopori even more than she needed it with him. And, in truth, the impromptu meeting with Saber was only cursory—they had all gone over the map of Mhier at least twelve times already—they just wanted to *be sure…*

Of what?

Kagen couldn't really say.

Now, as he aimed a Maglite flashlight at the drawing, shining the luminescent beam on a ternary group of tributaries that flowed just southeast of a steep, perilous mountain range, he could feel his temperature rising, his stomach tying up in knots.

It wasn't as if it hadn't all been real before…

It was all *too* real, to coin a phrase, but somehow, now that Nachari had made it not only real but *possible*, it was also all too much. Too overwhelming.

Too close to home.

Kagen stared at the heavy black flashlight resting squarely in his palm—and didn't that just bring it all home?—it wasn't as if a vampire needed a flashlight to see in the dark. Heck, it wasn't as if Nachari's rooftop wasn't already lit up like a freakin' evergreen on Christmas. It was just that they wanted this to turn out right *so badly*.

They needed Keitaro to be alive.

Everything, *absolutely everything*, was riding on the outcome of this voyage, and Kagen didn't know how to control the variables: how to be any more prepared, any more deliberate, or any more careful than he was.

How to be any more strategic.

Like Marquis, he was also wound too tight for comfort, ready to splinter into pieces at the slightest provocation. It was almost as if something buried deep inside of him was stirring, a long-forgotten ember still glowing in the fires of his soul, and the slightest amount of kindling could set the coals ablaze.

Needing to get a grip on his emotions, to wrap his mind around concrete details instead of obscure possibilities, Kagen turned to regard Saber and Nachari. They were sitting side-by-side in front of Nachari's adjustable drafting table, which was a remarkable occurrence in and of itself, considering that just under three months ago, the two had been bitter enemies; and they were tracing the various diagrams on the page with their fingers, pointing, fine-tuning, and adding important notations to the page. Surely, the fact that they could work together like this had to be a good omen, a sign of even better things to come.

Kagen shook his head, once again trying to dismiss the incessant rambling in his mind. He stepped up to the drawing, maneuvered his body just slightly to the side of the table—he did not want to disturb Saber and Nachari—and pointed at the upper right quadrant, just below an area marked *The Arena*, just to the right of a large, fenced-in parcel of land, denoted *The Royal District*. "The slave quarters, the huts, how many are there? And how many lycans act as guards on a typical night?" he asked.

Saber shrugged his broad shoulders, his characteristic scowl tugging the right corner of his top lip upward. "I don't know. Salvatore drew seven in his original plat, but there could be more…maybe less."

Kagen frowned. He pointed to a vast area of high-peaked mountains that divided the realm in half, north from south, giving way to two distinct valleys: On the northern side, the *Mystic Mountain Valley* housed the slave quarters, the place they expected to find Keitaro, and on the southern end, the valley became a rocky ravine, the *Mystic Mountain Gorge*, nestled beyond both banks of an enormous, turbulent tributary called the *Lykos River*. "The mountains are treacherous?" he asked, not really expecting an answer. "Subzero temperatures and steep, unexpected cliffs—are there strange animals, prehistoric beasts, that dwell here as well?"

Saber shook his head, studying the region more closely. "Mmm…don't know that, either."

Kagen shifted his weight from one foot to the other. He pointed to another quadrant, located just left of center on the map. "And this, the *Wolverine Woods*; are they as dense as they appear?"

Saber shrugged.

"They clearly separate two very large districts, the dwellings of the western pack, about ten miles above, and the domain of the southern pack, about fifteen miles below. What are these communes like? Are they townships, cities, or fortresses? Do they have modern amenities, or will we be walking into some medieval time warp?"

"Sorry," Saber said evenly.

Kagen sighed in frustration. "And the king of the realm—you said his name was Tyrus Thane—is he still living?"

Saber glanced at Kagen through the corner of his eye. Instead of speaking, he simply held up his hands, the gesture saying it all for him: *I honestly don't know.*

Kagen felt his alter ego stir, the character his brothers jokingly called Mr. Hyde, the counterpart to his rational Dr. Jekyll, and he wondered where all this intensity was coming from. Now was not the time to lose his cool. He pinched his nose at the bridge, trying to maintain his composure, and then he pointed once again at the map, his finger tracing the outline of the lower *Lykos River*, where it curved at the base of the *Mystic Mountains*, began to head east, and provided a natural barrier to the lower gorge and the *Skeleton Swamps*, just beyond a rocky crevice. "And the animals, the prehistoric beasts that inhabit the realm; you say we'll find the majority of them here? Are any of them *supernatural*? Like lycans or vampires, something we should really be concerned about…prepared for?"

Saber didn't respond this time. He simply pursed his lips together and looked off into the distance.

"Well?" Kagen persisted.

Saber met his eyes once more and frowned. "*Kagen…*"

"*You don't know.*"

Saber raised his brows and shook his head. His eyes heated with insolence, but to his credit, he didn't say anything rude or defensive. He didn't say anything at all.

And this just made Kagen angrier. "Well, what the hell *do* you know, *Dark One*?"

Nachari leveled a heated glare at his brother, his chastening green eyes reflecting his disapproval. "No need to go there, Kagen. He's telling us everything he knows."

Saber rolled his shoulders and popped his neck to release some tension. "Nah, it's cool. I've been called worse."

"I bet you have," Kagen snarled beneath his breath.

Saber clenched and released his fist, inadvertently snapping the pencil he was holding in two. He flicked it off the easel and gently picked up another one from the tabletop container, his shadowy eyes remaining fixed on the drawing. "Watch yourself, healer." It was an icy warning: low, calculated, and laced with lethal intention.

Nachari gave Saber a sideways glance, beseeching him with his eyes. "Just leave him be. He'll work it out soon enough. It's not about you." He turned his attention to Kagen. "You need to check your beast, Dr. J—he's riding dangerously close to the surface." His voice neither rose nor fell.

Saber licked his lips, and Kagen took a deep breath.

Work it out, indeed.

He needed to stay calm, focused.

After all, none of this was Saber's fault. Saber hadn't done anything to warrant this abuse, yet the knowledge, the very idea that the male had carried this information around for however many hundreds of years before sharing it with their family was sticking in Kagen's craw like a burr beneath a saddle: irritating, stabbing, and constantly provoking. Just the same, Saber's allegiance had been to the house of Jaegar—not the house of Jadon—there was no reason for the male to have approached the Silivasis, his sworn enemy, and divulged such a vital secret. At least not before he found out that he was truly one of them.

Not before his relationship with Vanya had changed him, at least to some degree.

Besides, Saber hadn't invaded the valley 480 years ago, killed Kagen's mother, or enslaved his father. Saber had not taken Keitaro to Mhier and done *gods-know-what* to him out of spite, cruelty, and vengeance. And none of that mattered anyway.

That was then.

This was now.

"Look," Kagen finally said, his voice at least steady, if not altogether friendly, "I know you're telling us everything you can. *I do.*" He turned to regard Nachari then, and his tone softened a bit more. "It's just…*damn.* There's so much we don't know. Will it be day or night when we emerge? Will we retain all of our powers? Can we still function as we do in this dimension? Can we communicate telepathically with each other in Mhier *or* with Napolean and our warriors back here in Dark Moon Vale? How many lycans are we potentially facing—a few, a dozen, *a thousand*? Can we get out the same way we get in?" His voice began to rise with concern. "What are the odds that Keitaro is even—"

"Kagen!" Nachari interrupted. "Saber doesn't know. *I* don't know. None of us know *anything* yet."

Just then, Nathaniel Silivasi shimmered into view on the rooftop terrace, materializing just behind his twin. More than likely, he had come in response to Kagen's increasingly erratic emotions. He placed a steadying hand on his twin's shoulder and inclined his head gracefully. "Brother."

The greeting was met with respect. "Nathaniel."

Nathaniel's touch was as light as a feather, nothing intimidating or intrusive, just a symbolic gesture of solidarity, as if he was trying to say, *I'm here.*

Kagen glanced at Nathaniel's hand and willed his muscles to relax. "I'm fine," he whispered, hoping to reassure the vampire.

Are you? Nathaniel asked on a private telepathic bandwidth. He turned his attention to Nachari and Saber and stoically regarded them both: "Brother…soldier." He tightened the pressure of his hand on Kagen's shoulder. "Is all going well this night?"

Nachari gave Nathaniel a knowing glance. "As well as can be expected, under the circumstances."

Saber smirked. "Just peachy."

Kagen clenched his eyes shut and tried to devise an internal plan to ratchet things down a notch. He opened his eyes, angled his body ever so slightly toward Saber, and bowed his head, infinitesimally. "Apologies." He tried to stop the next words from rolling off his tongue, but they spewed out anyway. "*Son of Jaegar.*"

Hell—now that was uncalled for, he thought. *Not to mention untrue.*

Saber chuckled in response to the glib apology, cloaked in a fresh, new jab, and slowly ran his tongue over his teeth, over his fangs. "Forget it. You're obviously on edge."

"Forgot," Kagen clipped, clearly taking offense at the appraisal as he shrugged his shoulder abruptly to dislodge Nathaniel's hand.

Nathaniel glided forward in an instant, placing his large muscular frame between Kagen's chest and Saber's back, before the newest member of the house of Jadon could get up and offer Kagen exactly what he was itching for: a fight. He eyed Saber intently and spoke as plainly as he could. "He's trying to provoke you, Saber. Why? I don't know. Don't let him." He spun around to face Kagen then and gestured toward the far end of the terrace. "Take a walk, healer."

Kagen linked his hands behind his back, cracked his knuckles, one at a time, and took several paces back to gain some space. There was a reason why he lived in borderline isolation at the end of a winding dirt road, on the other side of a stony bridge that crossed a rushing stream; and it wasn't so he could socialize on a daily basis. "*Yeah*, fine." He strolled away, brooding, taking several measured strides in the opposite direction of the other males, until he stood at the far end of the terrace, at the edge of the iron railing, alone.

Stopping to stare at the ground, he couldn't help but notice a particularly ugly pine cone on the terrace floor. It had fallen from the low branch of an overhanging Ponderosa, one that had grown right out of the rocky face of the canyon wall, and the oblong thing was half brown and half black, oddly rotting from the inside out. Somehow, Kagen found the presence of the hideous pine cone disturbingly ironic, and then he booted the misshapen thing over the side of the ledge, watching as it soared like a rocket, traveling so fast and so far that it was impossible to tell where it landed.

And just like that, the fuse was extinguished.

The growing rage…was gone.

Strolling back to join the others, he sighed. "Saber…"

"Yeah?"

"I…"

The hot-blooded male held his gaze, waiting.

"I don't know what my problem is, okay? But you're not it." It was as close to an *authentic* apology as Kagen was going to come.

Saber shrugged it off. "Been there a time or two, myself."

Kagen smirked. "Yeah, I imagine so." He took several deep breaths in a row before continuing to speak. "There is something *else*, a little less petty, that I wanted to talk to you about." He gestured toward Nachari and Nathaniel with his open hand. "That *we* wanted to talk to you about."

"And that is?" Saber asked.

Kagen sighed. "It's about your offer to come with us to Mhier, to help us navigate the territory…utilize the map." He ran his fingers through his hair, feeling suddenly weary. "It's just…we all talked it over, and we're not prepared to let you do that. You're not coming with us on this one."

Saber didn't react. He didn't snarl or flinch or even cut his eyes. He simply chuckled in three clipped bursts and then grinned, the derisive sound a paradoxical mixture of acceptance and contempt. "Ah'ight."

"Ah'ight?" Nachari echoed, looking at the male who sat beside him through the corner of his eye. "That's it?"

"What the hell do you expect me to say?" Saber replied. "That's jacked up? That's typical? *Whatever*. You don't want me with you—it's all good."

Kagen frowned, feeling unexpectedly burdened. "No, soldier"—the term was at least better than *Dark One*—"it's not *all good*. It's all necessary."

"Necessary for whom?" Saber asked.

"For everyone involved," Kagen said. He set his jaw and met

Saber's steely gaze head-on.

"Look," Nachari intervened, setting down his pen on the easel and swiveling in his chair to face Saber directly. "This isn't some sort of prejudice or malice. This isn't about the past or any unresolved issues between you and us."

Saber raised his brows. "So you're saying that all those *issues*—what I did to your women, what I put Vanya through—they've all been resolved?" He eyed Nachari, Kagen, and Nathaniel in turn, his wary eyes awaiting a reply.

Nathaniel whistled low beneath his breath. "You offered your blood to settle the score. Kristina drew it, Deanna refused it, and Vanya forgave you. On some level, Jocelyn owes you her life; so yes, I am willing to call the scales balanced, at least as far as my household is concerned."

Saber nodded, accepting Nathaniel's words. "And you, healer?" He stared pointedly at Kagen. "You didn't try to pick a fight with your brothers this night—you tried to pick one with me. Can you honestly stand there and tell me you aren't still harboring a grudge?"

Kagen considered Saber's words carefully. "I've picked more fights over the centuries with my brothers than I can count, so don't flatter yourself, Saber." He smiled faintly. "Honestly, I haven't even had time to think about it since you told us about Keitaro: It's been the furthest thing from my mind, Dark—" He caught himself before he said *Dark One* again. "*Dragon*," he offered, making polite reference to Vanya's pet name for the hot-tempered male.

Nachari chuckled beneath his breath, partly because—well, he was *Nachari*—and partly because he was trying to ease the tension. "I like that better anyhow. It suits you." He rolled the word off his tongue in a deliberate Romanian accent: "*Dragon…*"

Saber rolled his eyes, but there was nothing playful in the gesture. "All right; that's fair." He angled his head to acknowledge Nachari directly. "Nicknames aside, *wizard*, you still haven't answered my question: Have you also resolved what happened…between me and your *destiny*?"

Nachari's jaw tightened, and his expression grew all at once stern. "What happened *between* you and Deanna?" he echoed, his voice dropping to a cautionary tone. "What you *did* to Deanna," he clarified.

"What *I did* to your *destiny*?" Saber repeated.

Nachari shrugged, and the gesture was guilelessly honest. "Maybe—maybe not—point is: You're one of us, Saber. I don't know how many ways we can tell you that, *show you that.* And as far as we're all concerned, you're here to stay." He stared at the vampire with penetrating eyes, and then he gestured with his head, indicating the familiar, concealed pouch in Saber's front right pocket. "I will say this: You could help things along quite a bit by putting that damn Crest Ring on your finger—oh, maybe before the next millennium." He held up both hands for emphasis. "Just sayin'."

Saber tapped his hip pocket and nodded. "I'm working on it."

"And *we're* working on it," Nathaniel said candidly.

"Point is…" Nachari picked up where he had left off. "None of that has anything to do with what we discussed about going into Mhier, our decision to do it alone."

"Alone?" Saber said. "Just the Silivasis *and* Ramsey Olaru." It was clearly a rhetorical question.

Kagen frowned. "Look, Saber; the fact that you even offered to take such an enormous risk—just to help us find our *father*?" His voice faltered on the last word, but he pushed through it. "We all know what that means to a male like you."

"A *proud* male," Nachari clarified. "Independent."

"Obstinate," Nathaniel said, apparently trying to keep it real.

Saber snarled at the Ancient Master Warrior, but his eyes were smiling this time.

Nathaniel took a step back, chuckling.

"We know what that took," Kagen repeated. "It's not a small thing. But us, accepting your offer, that's not a small thing, either."

"You have a two-and-a-half-month-old son," Nachari said.

"And you're mated to an original princess, one who has been through more than enough in the past year," Kagen added.

"We can't risk it," Nathaniel chimed in.

"No way, no how," Kagen said. "There's a good chance, a *very* good chance, that none of us are going to come out of this alive, that none of us are coming back. Keitaro is our father. We owe him *everything*. But you? You owe your *destiny* and that child. You owe Lorna and Rafael, at least a chance to get to know you. The stakes are too high. We can't gamble with the lives of so many who have already suffered so much."

Saber nodded slowly, carefully considering Kagen's words. "And Ramsey?" He obviously had to ask. "How is that different?"

"Ramsey doesn't have a *destiny* or a son," Kagen said bluntly. "If you were unencumbered, if things were different—well, things might be different."

"Even Braden is staying home on this one," Nachari said. "It is what it is."

Before Saber could reply, Braden Bratianu sauntered up to the circle of vampires. Since he lived at the brownstone with Nachari, Deanna, and Sebastian, it wasn't unusual for the curious youngster to try and eavesdrop on adult conversations, and he had obviously overheard the tail end of this one. He threw his hands up in the air, huffed with indignation, and stomped his foot on the deck, looking for all intents and purposes like a spoiled brat, a recalcitrant boy in a man's body. "Dang, Nachari!" He glared at the wizard in defiance. "So when were you going to tell me?"

Nachari rubbed his brow with his thumb and forefinger, belying his frustration. "Braden…"

"No…*no*! That is *so* messed up!"

Nachari shook his head then. "We so don't have time for this, Braden," he muttered beneath his breath. Turning to face the youngster head-on, he lowered his voice and spoke in a measured, paternal tone: "I'm going to make this real short and simple: Since your parents placed you in my care, you have been kidnapped by lycans and nailed to a cross, where you ended up getting your *neck broken,* I might add. You erased the memory of a twelve-year-old girl and got so sick when you merged with Napolean, after the Dark Lord Ademordna tried to possess him, that you threw up your guts and broke several of your ribs. Not to mention, you recently got into a *confrontation* with Ramsey Olaru over Kristina." He paused to amend his last comment. "Okay, well, it wasn't much of a confrontation, really. More like—"

"More like some half-crazed, rock-throwing, chest-thumping display of insanity," Nathaniel added, smiling. He glanced at Braden and grimaced. "Yeah, Ramsey described it to me. You're lucky he didn't snap your little confrontational neck." He shrugged. "Just making an observation."

Nachari cut his eyes at Nathaniel and quickly rushed his next words before Braden could take offense, which was the last thing they needed. "Point is: You weren't placed in my care so I could use you as I see fit, whenever the need arises. I'm supposed to be your teacher, your mentor, your protector. And you are *not* going into the completely unknown world of the lycans with us. You're just *not.*"

Braden slowly sucked his teeth, smacked his lips, and crossed his arms over his chest, taking a judicious step back. "Ah, okay. So it's like that, then?"

Nachari narrowed his gaze, about to lose his patience. "Yes, Braden. It's *exactly* like that."

"Fine," Braden snapped. "I'll just go find my woman, then—leave you all to it." He threw up his hands in frustration and stomped away.

"His woman?" Nathaniel asked, his bottomless black eyes narrowing in question.

Nachari shook his head and sighed in exasperation. "Kristina."

"Oh," Nathaniel said, apparently hesitant to pry any further. "Does Kristina know this?"

"He never lets her forget," Nachari said, his voice thick with exhaustion.

Kagen smiled, thinking about Braden's latest antics: Ever since Napolean had shared Nachari's secret with the flighty youngster, the secret the demoness Noiro had told him during his captivity in the Abyss—the fact that he was not beholden to the Curse; he would never have a Blood Moon; and he could, in fact, sire female children one day and was, consequently, promised to Kristina—Braden had become like a blowfish, swollen with self-importance and masculine pride. "If she doesn't kill him before he turns twenty-one," Kagen told his twin, "I don't think Napolean is going to leave her a choice."

Nachari shrugged. "Female children…pretty valuable."

Nathaniel nodded in assent. "Indeed."

And then they all turned back to regard Saber. "Sorry about the interruption," Kagen said. "At this point, I don't know what else to add to what we've told you, only to say *thank you* for offering." He made a profound gesture of respect then, by holding out his hand in an offer of friendship. He only half expected Saber to take it.

Saber stood, stared at the extended palm, and took a reflexive step back, moving away from the healer. "Despite what you might think, I can reason objectively…*sometimes*." His mouth turned up in that wicked, scowl-laced grin so characteristic of the male. "And I understand your reasoning. It's cool. Honestly. No need to get too formal."

Nachari pushed back his chair and stood up brusquely. He took one determined stride in Saber's direction and, without hesitating, punched him right in the bicep. His eyes flashed red, and his fangs extended of their own accord. "Damn, Dragon," he snarled, inclining his head at Kagen's outstretched hand. "Take his hand already. *Shit.* See, that's why you're still having trouble fitting in."

"Damn," Saber snarled, "and I thought it was because my mom only packs bologna sandwiches in my lunch."

Nathaniel burst into laughter, clearly amused by the all-too-human reference.

Saber threw up both hands and laughed, surprising the heck out of all of them. "I was going to, wizard," he said. Stepping confidently forward, he clasped Kagen's forearm instead, and both of their palms instantly linked around each other's wrists before sliding forward into a firm, finger-clasping grasp. "Be careful," he said next, his tone betraying the seriousness behind his otherwise playful demeanor. "The beta lycans are no match for our kind, but the Alphas are deadly. And Mhier is their world."

Kagen nodded solemnly. "We understand our enemy, and we have a score of our own to settle." He relaxed a little then. "Just take care of Vanya and Lucien."

"Always," Saber replied, finally releasing Kagen's grip. He turned to regard Nachari. "When are you leaving?"

"Tomorrow morning," the wizard answered, "around six AM."

Saber's posture straightened reflexively. "Well, may the dark lords be with—" His eyes grew wide as he caught the inexcusable slip and immediately ducked out of Nachari's reach, covering his exposed bicep with a palm. "May the *gods* be with you," he quickly amended, laughing.

"Dude," Nachari barked. "You are so *incredibly* jacked up. You do know this, right?"

Saber cringed, and then he smiled.

And his smile gave Kagen hope.

If the celestial deities could take a lost, soulless monster like Saber Alexiares, give him to a princess, and bring him back into the light, even just a little, enough to actually *smile* and mean it, then they could also lead the Silivasi brothers to their father.

To Keitaro.

After all these years.

They had to.

Kagen paced to the other end of the terrace, once again, needing to clear his mind, to find solace in isolation. As he glanced at the vast night sky, he felt oddly connected to the dark, expansive void; he couldn't help but wonder what the future held, just what were they about to embark upon; and he had to reassure himself once more:

They were ready.

At least he hoped they were.

They had the map. They had packed everything they needed to track, to fight…to survive. And Nachari knew how to open the portal, how to usher them into the strange new world of Mhier, the native home of the Lycanthrope.

Now all they needed was a little luck.

And a lot of courage.

And a chance, *just one chance*, to atone for the unforgiveable sins of the past: a healer who couldn't save his mother; a son who no longer knew his father; a vampire who walked with one foot in both worlds because he never truly felt worthy of existing in either one.

Although just why, he couldn't say.

Kagen Silivasi had been a faithful servant to the house of Jadon, a loyal brother to his beloved siblings, and a consummate healer to his noble race, the Vampyr. He had tended broken bones, mended wounded flesh, and always, *always*, saved lives.

At any cost.

It was the least he could do.

Yet, it was never enough…not even close.

And therein lay the rub: that unidentifiable ember that burned at the center of his soul, masking, if not outright hiding, something so combustible and profound that he didn't dare confront it, let alone try and name it.

It just was.

And his carefully controlled life—indeed, his seemingly perfect persona—concealed it like a pile of cooled gray ash, cleverly masking whatever lay beneath the slag, cloaking the nameless pain, concealing the anonymous rage.

Disguising the red-hot coals glowing just beneath the surface.

For reasons he couldn't name or even comprehend, Kagen Silivasi worked tirelessly to remain detached from his past, to stay ahead of a memory he didn't even possess, and he healed fervently in an attempt to avoid that mysterious, marginal part of his soul that frightened him the most, the part that wasn't a healer at all.

The part that, given half a chance, would seek to take life rather than sustain it.

The part that wanted to hunt…and claim…and devour.

And kill.

Until all the rivers ran crimson with blood.

Until somehow, those same *blood rivers*—those sanguine pools of righteous retribution—eventually swept away the original sin.

four

Mhier

Although it was late, nearly midnight, when Arielle Nightsong finally made her way out of the Mystic Mountains, traveling the well-worn path that snaked between Thane's valley and the rebel camp, she stopped at the second of three streams that branched off the Lykos River to get a drink of water and refill her canteen. She intended to circle back once more, just in case she had been followed, before crossing the remaining two streams, traversing the rocky gorge, and entering the Rebel Camp on the other side of the final tributary. She dipped a near-frozen hand into the frigid water and watched as the clear, icy liquid washed over her skin, causing instant frost to form on her flesh, before seeping through her open fingers as it slowly rejoined the stream. Luckily, each subsequent river would grow warmer as she moved further away from the base of the mountains and closer to the camp.

Ignoring the chill, she dipped her hand in the water once more, and this time, she drank heartily.

The water may have been cold, but it was also refreshing; and she was grateful that the *resistance* had chosen to hide their camp in such a remote yet hospitable place. Not only was the encampment hard to locate—it was flanked on one side by the gorge and required passing through the formidable Mystic Mountains; and it was bordered on the other side by the Skeleton Swamps, a place no one dared to go, lest they never escape alive—but it forced its inhabitants to cross three fast-flowing streams before they arrived as well. And unlike the tainted, muddy waters that flowed like coagulated blood through Mhier's central waterway, the ternary streams were crystal and clear: pure enough to bathe in, drink from, and irrigate for crops.

Not to mention, the rivers washed away the scent of travelers, a definite bonus when your enemies were wolves.

Arielle rocked back on her heels and glanced at the peaceful river before her. She thought about her mother and her biological father, wondering if the infamous Ryder Nightsong, the founder of the resistance, had ever dipped his hands into this same stream. She wondered if her mother had ever stolen away in the night to make love to the handsome rebel when she was yet Arielle's age.

But that had been eons ago, or at least it seemed like it had been:

Arielle's mother had been slain by Teague Verasachi, the alpha general of the southern pack, nearly eighteen years ago, when Arielle was only ten years old. It had happened during an ill-advised raid on Teague's encampment: At the time, the rebels had not yet learned how to grow their own food, how to live as a self-sufficient unit; and desperately needing to restock their supplies for the winter, they had risked entering the Alpha's district in order to steal from the general's food caches. The decision had been as foolish as it was deadly. And Alina Page, Arielle's mother, had paid with her life.

Arielle shivered, remembering the horrific autumn of her tenth year. Not only had her mother been brutally beaten and killed, but Arielle had been captured as well and given to King Thane as a gift from Teague. She had spent seven long years in the slave encampment before finally escaping just prior to her eighteenth birthday, the year Thane would have taken her as wife number seven.

Arielle dipped her hands in the river and scrubbed her cheeks until they stung, as if shocking herself with the cold could alter the path of her thoughts. She quickly turned her attention to Ryder, instead, wondering if the topic wasn't just as unwise: Legend had it that the founder of the human resistance, *her biological father*, had been killed trying to rescue Arielle from Thane's clutches, but Arielle didn't know if the rumors were true. She had never met her father. She had never even seen her father, and she had a hard time believing that after seventeen years of life, he had suddenly taken an interest in his bastard offspring.

Although the man was reputed to be an unparalleled fighter, he was also renowned as a shameless lover, an unapologetic seducer of women. Alina Page had only been one of many, but she had been the only one to bear him a child. She had loved the infamous warrior deeply, never speaking an ill word of him, and always reminding Arielle that she, proudly, came from his formidable stock.

Now, gazing at the icy stream before her and the beautiful valley beyond, Arielle couldn't help but hope that her mother had, at least once, stood on these banks with the man she adored, that, together, they had admired the valley.

She was just about to fill her canteen when she heard a faint noise coming from the gorge, just beyond a grouping of birch trees, the unmistakable rustling of leaves beneath heavy, approaching footsteps. Nimbly spinning around, she drew an arrow from her quiver and notched it against her bow. She crouched down low behind a large, rounded boulder and held her breath. *Dearest Ancestors, please tell me I wasn't followed. Please tell me Thane hasn't found me.*

She looked off to the side and tilted her head, as if aligning her ears with the sound might sharpen her hearing.

"Arielle?" The masculine voice was hushed and urgent. "Arielle!" It came again, and she struggled to identify the caller.

"*Arielle? Is that you?*" The voice belonged to Walker Alencion, one of the five men still fighting for the resistance.

"Walker!" she exclaimed, fisting her hand around the upper limb of her bow in anger. She placed her arrow back in the quiver, hoisted the bow over her shoulder, and brushed the dirt off her animal-hide skirt.

"Yeah," he whispered, his voice coming closer. "It's me." He stepped out of the brush, made his way down the riverbank, and stopped a few feet in front of her. "What are you doing out so late?"

"Hell's fire, Walker! You almost scared the daylights out of me."

Walker winced. "Sorry." He reached out to take the heavy bow from her shoulder, and then he reached behind his back and retrieved a wilted bouquet of red-and-yellow wild flowers. "I picked these for you."

"At *midnight*?" Arielle protested, practically seething. This was the last thing she needed to deal with right now: Walker, and his never-ending advances.

"No, not at midnight," he said defensively, sounding curiously immature for a twenty-nine-year-old male. "Earlier today. But you weren't around, so I had to wait to give them to you."

Arielle frowned. She reached out and took the flowers, pausing to give them a cursory sniff out of kindness.

"Where were you?" he asked.

Arielle sighed. "We don't have time to talk right now." She immediately regretted the clipped tone of her voice—she had to be patient with Walker; he was far too sensitive for his own good—still, she needed to set firm boundaries. "I mean, thank you for the flowers, but we should be getting back to camp." She started walking briskly in the direction of the rebel encampment, and then she held out the flowers to demonstrate her objection. "I really wish you would stop doing these kinds of things for me, Walker. It's…well…it's kind of awkward." Arielle had tried in a dozen different ways to softly rebuke Walker's advances. She had tried to show him with her actions and her words that she was a loyal, trustworthy friend, but nothing more…and she never would be. At times, it became more than just a little bit frustrating; it became downright maddening, how avid he was about winning her affections, something that was never going to happen…

For a dozen different reasons.

Walker frowned, shuffling to keep up with Arielle's brisk pace. "I don't mind, Arielle. I like doing nice things for you."

She tucked her unruly hair behind her ears and pressed on.

"I know you do, but"—she almost said, *I don't like it*, then thought better of it—"never mind." She glanced at a thick group of bushes, just shy of the second waterway, and scanned the area for the presence of others before pushing back a cluster of branches in order to expose a rustic, hidden canoe. The behavior was instinctive. It was one thing to take chances with one's own life, to sneak into Thane's encampment to see Keitaro, to risk leading someone back to the Rebel Camp, but it was another thing to reveal one of the Rebels' hidden treasures: a food cache, a concealed armament of weapons, or one of the secret water vessels they kept at hand to cross the ternary rivers. Arielle, along with every other member of the resistance, had grown up learning how to watch, look, and listen at every turn, along every leg of the journey home. "Would you mind grabbing that oar?" she said, pointing to a chipped, timeworn paddle. "How's everything in camp?"

"Everything is fine," Walker said, reaching for the oar. He hefted it easily from the boat and helped her drag the canoe from the brush into the water. She automatically sat in front, and he automatically began rowing in the back, his strong, lean arms flexing from the strength of the water's resistance.

Arielle took a deep breath and stared out over the fast-moving river. She understood how much work it was to keep the vessel upright and heading in the right direction in such a rapidly flowing stream, but all the men and women were adept at doing it by now. She watched Walker as he rowed faster and faster, dipping the oar deeper and deeper, wishing that she could return his romantic feelings. Though flushed with color from exertion, his narrow face was handsome enough, and his flame-red hair was soft and curly, not wild and unruly like her long, bronze-colored locks. He was a gentle man, most of the time, and a fine warrior. He was dangerous with a battle-axe, and he could take down a gamma lycan from twenty yards away, using only a bola with two silver balls; but he was just, somehow, awkward, gangly, unseemly, even beneath all that sinewy muscle. And his insecurity didn't help matters much. Just the same, he was a loyal friend and a die-hard rebel, and he hated the lycans with every ounce of his being. On that front, he and Arielle had scores in common.

"Where were you earlier?" he asked again, angling the oar in the stream to guide the boat around an impending log.

When Arielle didn't answer, he frowned immediately, the gesture causing deep lines of disappointment to appear between his brows. "Keitaro…the slave…*again*?"

Arielle sat up straight on the bench at the back of the boat. She unfastened the extra oar from beneath the rear deck and began to paddle, needing something else to look at, something else to do, other than to sit and stare at Walker. "Shh!" she warned him. "There are some things you shouldn't even speak out loud. Don't even think them."

Walker jerked back then, his mouth turning down in a scowl. "What's with you and that *vampire*?" He said the last word with clear disdain.

Arielle took offense, backing him up as she leaned angrily toward him. "You are not my father, Walker. I don't have to explain myself to—"

"I know!" he practically shouted, holding his right hand up so high in front of him, he almost dropped the oar. He bent over and caught it quickly, before it fell into the water. "I'm just saying that I don't understand…I really don't get it…you just shouldn't go out of your way"—his eyes darted upward and to the left like he was searching for a plausible explanation, or perhaps concocting a lie—"I'm just saying that you should probably take me with you next time." He quickly amended the statement: "I mean, at least take *someone* with you, one of the men. I just don't think it's safe for you to sneak into the quarters of a vampire, slave or not, all alone. And that's to say nothing of the danger you put yourself in every time you enter King Thane's district." He sighed in exasperation. "It's almost as if you want to get caught. It's insane, Arielle." His voice thickened as he stood his ground. "The risk isn't worth it."

Arielle looked down at her lap in sudden contrition. "You

wouldn't understand, Walker." She spoke softly, hoping to appeal to his compassion. "You *had* a father."

"Is that what he is to you?" His tone was mildly accusatory, and maybe even a little bit jealous. "A father?"

"What is that supposed to mean?"

He shrugged. "Do you *feed* him? Your blood?"

Arielle refused to answer that question. Not only was it highly personal, but the way Walker had said it, it sounded almost vulgar. "What do you want from me, Walker?" She took her left hand off the oar and held it up in exasperation. "I care for him. He's a prisoner, and I know very well what that's like. I don't ask you *or anyone else* to take the risk with me. Why do you care so much?"

It was the wrong question.

Walker stopped rowing then, and she instinctively did the same. They got out of the boat, pulled it to shore, and tucked it beneath another grouping of thick, wild brush. And then, they headed for the third and final stream. Once they were safely in the last canoe, both seated and about to push off from the bank, he reached out to touch her face, to softly stroke her cheek, and she drew back reflexively.

"Don't touch me like that," she whispered, turning her face away.

"Like what?" he responded, his pale gray eyes brimming with hurt from the reprisal. "Like this?" He reached out and touched her again.

Arielle gasped and batted his hand away.

Instinctively, he reached out and grasped her jaw, squeezing her cheeks in a pincer grasp, tighter than he surely intended. "Could I touch you if I were a vampire?" He leaned in closer, and his lips hovered just above hers. "Could I kiss you?"

Arielle was stunned.

Speechless.

Both by his words and his actions.

While Walker had always been known to have an odd, awkward way about him, he had never acted like this before, at least not with her. She planted her palms squarely on his chest and shoved him back, thrusting hard enough to let him know she meant business. "How dare you!"

Walker shot back in his seat, nearly falling off the narrow, wooden plank. "I'm sorry, Arielle." He rushed the words. "I don't know what got into me. I just…I…I didn't mean to frighten you."

"Well, you did." Arielle stared at him like he had fish guts on his face, and she was just about to give him a firm tongue-lashing when a white owl flew across the river toward the embankment, and dipped its wings so low to the boat that its outstretched feathers nearly clipped her cheek. She ducked and pressed a hand to her chest. "Did you see that, Walker?" The sudden appearance of the ominous bird of prey distracted her from her imminent rant; after all, white owls were extremely rare in Mhier, and their presence had always portended a bad omen.

Walker drew in a sharp intake of breath and slowly shook his head. "Yeah, I wonder what it means."

Arielle cringed. "I don't know, but whatever it is, it isn't good."

"Change is coming," Walker said absently. "Change…and death."

Arielle stared at him then, wondering where the cryptic words were coming from. "Could it have something to do with King Thane or Queen Cassandra?" she asked, not believing that it did.

"When the white owl soars in a midnight sky, friends and foes alike will die. When the white owl dips his snow-tipped wing—"

"Hearts will weep and tongues will sing," she interjected.

"A song of grief, lives lost too soon—"

"A song of blood, beneath the moon." Arielle finished the refrain, and Walker slowly nodded.

"It was a childhood refrain," he said. "I remember singing it around the campfire as a kid."

"Yeah, me, too," she said. "Only we sang it in the slave

camp."

Walker shivered. "What do you think it means? I mean, specifically?"

Arielle reached for an oar and glanced up at the moon. "I have no idea," she said, pushing off the embankment to launch the canoe.

Walker stood to help her, placing his own oar deep into the sandy riverbed to gain enough leverage to propel the boat forward. "I hope it didn't happen because I scared you. I'm not a threat to you, Arielle. I hope you know that. *Never.*"

Arielle shook her head. "No, Walker. I don't think it has anything to do with you." She stared at the water then, noticing how blue it looked in the haunting moonlight, how effortlessly her oar sliced through the rippling current, and the way the water sloshed off the blade of her paddle, dissipating into the river as if it had never crossed her path to begin with. One moment, it was there, an integral part of the resistance. The next, it was just *gone.*

She sat up straight, her spine stiffening, and recalled the words of the song once more.

Despite herself, she got the chills. After all, the white owl had almost touched her.

Her.

Not Walker.

Whatever it was, whatever it meant, the omen was *for her.*

And *Ancestors be merciful*, she prayed it wasn't Tyrus Thane Montego, the ruthless king of the Lycanthrope, coming to claim her at last.

five

Dark Moon Vale ~ the next morning

Kagen Silivasi stood in the meadow, the valley that divided Dark Moon Vale from the bordering Red Canyons, the place where the house of Jadon's civilized society began to merge into the forest, the wilderness, and beyond. He watched as Ramsey Olaru approached, a thin reed of grass protruding from his taut lips, his arms markedly empty of baggage or traveling gear.

"Sentinel," Kagen called in greeting, eyeing the massive warrior suspiciously. "Where's your pack, your weapons?"

Ramsey shrugged. He spit the reed out on the ground and brought his hand to his face, rubbing his jaw with his thumb and forefinger. "Bad news," Ramsey said. "The king says it's a no-go."

Kagen's eyes grew wide in alarm. "What do you mean a *no-go*?" Surely, Napolean Mondragon would not try to stop the Silivasis from entering Mhier, from going on the dangerous mission to try and find their father. It was their right as sons, their duty as vampires. It was their *imperative* as males of honor.

Ramsey shook his head and made a pacifying gesture with his hands as he spoke. "Not you guys," he said, as if reading Kagen's thoughts. "Me. My going with you. It's a no-go."

Kagen took an unwitting step back and stared at the Ancient Master Warrior, the sentinel, his light hazel eyes reflecting disappointment in their depths. "Can I ask why?"

Ramsey knitted his brow. "It's pretty much all the unknowns…and the potential sacrifice."

Kagen remained quiet, waiting for Ramsey to elaborate.

Ramsey angled his head to the side as if to say, *What can you do*? "As it stands, Marquis and Nathaniel are two of our strongest warriors. The loss of either one would be a devastating blow to the house of Jadon." Leave it to Ramsey to get straight to the point, without mincing words.

"You," he continued, "are our strongest healer." He sniffed reflexively. "Oh, we have other acolytes, those who are training to become Master Healers, and a few who already practice the craft; but you are by far the most skilled of the lot. And Nachari? Is there a finer wizard among us? Especially since he spent all that time…" To his credit, he left out *in hell*—there was no need to say the words when the point was clear—Nachari had not only obtained and read the Blood Canon, the ancient book of Black Magic, but he had lived among the demon lords in the Valley of Death and Shadows for over four months. His knowledge, as well as his skill, was irreplaceable to the house of Jadon: The mission the Silivasis were about to embark upon was more than a family crusade, a personal vendetta, or an inter-species war; it was an incalculable risk to the house of Jadon. Napolean Mondragon was sending four of his best masters—centuries-trained warriors, a healer, and an accomplished wizard—into harm's way with no guarantee, whatsoever, that any of them would return.

Kagen stood silently, contemplating Ramsey's words. He was disappointed to say the least, but he understood the wise king's reasoning. "So," he finally said, "our Sovereign is not willing to risk one of the valley's three revered sentinels as well, not even for Keitaro."

Ramsey frowned, clearly understanding the implication. "It's not like that, Kagen." He glanced over his shoulder and inclined his head toward the gathering of vampires about twenty yards away in the thicket: Marquis and Ciopori; Nathaniel and Jocelyn; Nachari and Deanna; even Braden and Kristina were all convening in the grove, moving in and out of the pine trees, checking packs, sharing last-minute instructions, and trying to make peace with the imminent departure. "It's not just a matter of who's going. It's a matter of who's being left behind."

Kagen breathed out a sigh of growing appreciation.

"You have to understand, Ciopori is still an original princess, a rare and precious treasure to the house of Jadon. Napolean isn't willing to leave her with anyone other than himself or me; and Jocelyn and Deanna? Saxson is going to be staying at Nathaniel's estate while the warrior is gone, and Santos is going to be staying at Nachari's brownstone—there was no room for debate on either issue. Our lord thought about bringing the women to the manse or the lodge, but he didn't want to disrupt the kids' routines. As it stands, his own house will be…less protected."

Kagen cringed, wrinkling up his nose in reaction to the news. He had been so busy concentrating on the trip to Mhier, he hadn't considered what life might look like after they left, here in Dark Moon Vale. Yet, it all made sense. Of course, Napolean would not take any unnecessary chances—that wasn't his way—but the thought of Nathaniel Silivasi, hell, Nachari, too, for that matter, sitting comfortably with the idea of other vampires, alpha males, living in their homes, with their mates and their sons, while they were away? Well, that was another matter entirely.

Ramsey laughed. "Oh yeah, I feel you, Chief." He leaned in closer. "And I get to be the one to tell Marquis that I'm staying in his well-appointed homestead with Ciopori and Nikolai." He grimaced, flashing his fangs for effect.

"Wouldn't want to be you," Kagen remarked, meaning it.

Ramsey chuckled low and deep. "Yeah, tell me about it." He rolled his shoulders, as if to dismiss the repercussions. "There's also another factor at play, something Napolean would be remiss not to consider."

"And that is?" Kagen asked.

"Fallout," Ramsey said. He crossed his arms over his broad chest. "Let's say you do find your father"—he quickly extended his palm toward Kagen's chest as if to say, *Don't overreact, healer; I believe that you will*—"are the lycans just going to give him up at this point, after all these years? Are they just going to lay down their weapons, let a band of vampires come into their territory—hell, their hidden, protected *world*—and march out with a coveted prize, having rubbed their noses in their inherent inferiority?" The last statement was an added dig against the enemy, Ramsey's way of saying, *Screw the mangy bastards.* "Who's to say they won't follow you out of Mhier, back into Dark Moon Vale, and wage a full-scale war once and for all?" His posture remained nonchalant, but his top lip twitched ever so slightly. "It's not about Keitaro, Kagen, or how much our king reveres your father. He's willing to take the risk of an all-out war for your family, for your sire. He's just not willing to do it without *lining everything up back here*, without being prepared in the event that all hell breaks loose. You know what I'm saying?"

"Yeah," Kagen said astutely. "He's not willing to take the risk…without you."

Ramsey tilted his head to the side and shrugged. He held up both hands in apology. "I'm sorry, healer. I truly wanted to go."

Kagen placed his hand on Ramsey's shoulder and gave it a firm clasp. "Thank you, Ramsey—that means a lot."

Ramsey relaxed his bearing. "Eh," he snorted, "you know me. When do I get a chance to kill on a large scale, indiscriminately? Blood spurting, guts spilling, and heads rolling? *Shit*, I hate to miss this one."

Kagen chuckled then. He rubbed his hands together. "Shall we break it to the others?"

Ramsey inclined his head in the direction of the gathering, gesturing toward his own twin, Saxson. "I think my brother already broke the news to Nathaniel." By the look on Nathaniel's face, the sudden expansion of his chest, and the tension gathering in his shoulders, it was clear the male had just been told about Saxson residing at the cliff-side estate with Jocelyn. And Nathaniel was *this close* to losing his cool.

Kagen cringed. "On second thought, let's wait a minute or two before we catch up with the others."

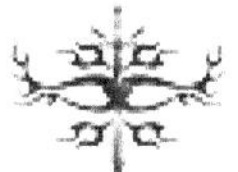

"Did you hear this bullshit!" Marquis snarled, flashing a hint of fang at Kagen before crouching to drop a heavy pack full of silver ammunition on the ground at his feet.

"It's not bullshit, brother," Kagen said, his own voice steady and calm, if not mildly amused. "And yes, I've heard. Ramsey told me."

Just then, Nachari Silivasi sauntered up to join Marquis and Kagen. He was decked out in loose-fitting jeans and a knee-length trench coat, his trusty scabbard and beloved sword sheathed neatly at his side, and the various bulges and pouches, concealed beneath the jacket, betrayed the presence of ancient weapons forged in silver: a curved scythe, a serrated dagger, and a well-concealed Beretta Px4 Storm. He looked far more like a warrior than a wizard. "Nathaniel bit Saxson," Nachari said, his blasé tone at odds with his lethal appearance, as if he were merely commenting on the weather.

"What?" Kagen asked, incredulous.

"Bit him. Right beneath his ear. He was trying to go for his throat."

Kagen recoiled, staring at Nachari like he wasn't sure he was telling the truth. "And Saxson? What did he do?"

"He bit him back," Nachari said in a matter-of-fact tone. He raised his left arm and pointed toward his armpit, moving his finger slightly to the right to indicate the heart region. "Right here, I think."

Kagen shook his head. "Damn." What else could he say? He turned to regard Marquis then. "Honestly, I thought it would be you, attacking Ramsey, if anyone was going to lose it."

Marquis harrumphed, a low growl rumbling in his throat. "Pshaw," he said dismissively, and then he waved a glib hand through the air. "*Ramsey*." He spoke the word with feigned derision. "That crazy bastard stood there the entire time he was telling me about *the living arrangements* with his trident in his hand, that crazy, medieval pitchfork he insists upon fighting with." Marquis's voice rose an octave, yet it was still harshly deep and laced with menace. "He was daring me to react poorly. I think he *wanted* to stab me."

Nachari fingered the top of the scabbard, nestled snugly over his left hip, and patted his beloved sword. "I want to stab you, Marquis—I've always wanted to stab you—but I won't because you're my brother." He chuckled heartily then. "I'm glad you didn't provoke him."

Marquis narrowed his gaze at Nachari, glaring at him with feigned contempt. Kagen wasn't quite sure what he mouthed to the vampire, but it looked something like, *I would kick your wizardly butt from one end of Dark Moon Vale to the other.*

Nachari grinned for all he was worth. "You would try."

"Okay...okay," Kagen said, suddenly growing serious. They had a mission to embark upon, a foreign world to enter, and a father to rescue. "Are you guys ready? Do you have everything you need?"

Marquis stiffened, growing instantly somber. "We're ready."

Nachari followed suit, indicating a shallow metal bin with two handles on either side, resting at his feet. It contained all the objects the Silivasis would need to open the portal—*gods be merciful.*

"Then you should probably say your good-byes," Kagen added.

As if on cue, Nathaniel and Jocelyn, along with Princess Ciopori, strolled over to the circle of vampires. Ciopori instantly sidled up to Marquis's side, slipped her long, elegant arm around his back, and leaned her head lovingly into the crook of his arm. "It is time then?" she whispered.

Marquis drew her close. "It is, my love."

Ciopori clenched her golden eyes shut and slowly nodded. She ducked out from beneath the warrior's arm and stood directly in front of him, grasping his long black trench coat by the lapels with both hands. "You be careful, warrior." She patted his chest, smoothing out the wrinkles she had just made. "I will petition the celestial god Perseus on your behalf, but you—" Her voice began to falter, and her eyes filled with pressing tears. "You come home to me, Marquis. Your son and I will be waiting."

Marquis enfolded her in his arms and held her so close to his heart that it seemed he might just squeeze the breath right out of her. His arms were steady; he didn't tremble, and neither did she, but the truth of their apprehension was written all over their faces.

Kagen turned away. The moment was far too personal, far too intimate, for his intruding eyes. When he noticed Nathaniel doing the same with Jocelyn, he took a measured step back, wanting to allow them some privacy as well.

Nachari and Deanna were locked in a passionate embrace, kissing each other as if the world might just end at any moment, as if their souls would only survive if they were interwoven, as one, and their mouths, their very breath, were the ties that would bind them together.

Kagen looked down at the ground.

His brothers had so much to lose, yet they also had so much to gain.

They had to succeed in their mission.

They had to.

When at last, Nachari and Deanna pulled apart, Nachari whispered in her ear: "It can't be worse than hell, Deanna, and I survived that. I will come home to you. "

Deanna nodded bravely.

"No tears, *Draga mea.* Never tears," Nathaniel crooned to Jocelyn as she clung to his broad shoulders, careful to avoid the heavy belt of silver ammunition draped about his neck and hanging to his side.

"I wish I could go with you," she said, a stubborn glint of frustration in her eyes. "Support you. Fight with you."

"Ah, yes," Nathaniel drawled softly, "but then, who would fight for our son?"

Jocelyn stuck out her bottom lip in a playful pout, and then she smiled, just a little, mischievously. "Saxson?" she said, pitching her voice just a tad bit higher.

Nathaniel growled deep in his throat. "I do not find this humorous, *destiny* of mine. The male is hardly six feet tall."

"I think he's six foot two," Jocelyn said, laughing.

Nathaniel nipped at her ear. "Do not anger me before I leave, woman."

Kagen laughed out loud, feeling a bit voyeuristic for listening to their intimate banter, but appreciating his sister's sense of humor just the same. He was just about to walk away, put some *real* distance between himself, his brothers, and their mates, when Kristina Silivasi came storming into the clearing, stomping her delicate feet, which were strapped into three-inch heels, with Braden Bratianu following close behind her, his own confident stride laced with arrogant bravado and swagger.

"Ah, baby, don't do me like that," Braden called after Kristina.

Kristina threw her hands up in the air and marched directly over to Nachari and Deanna, interrupting another round of passionate lip play. "Nachari!" Kristina howled. "Tell him. Tell him now."

Nachari pulled away from his mate, regarded Kristina with mild annoyance, and frowned. "Tell him what, sister?" he said, his striking eyes alight with sudden intrigue.

Kristina huffed. She planted her feet shoulder-length apart and side by side on the ground. She placed her hands on her hips and snorted. "Tell him that kissing is *not* a good luck charm." She turned up her nose in disgust. "Tell him that a twenty-nine-year-old woman *kissing* a sixteen-year-old-boy is disgusting. *Wrong*. Pedophilia!"

Nachari laughed. "Technically, pedophilia refers to someone at or over the age of sixteen who has a…prurient…interest in someone thirteen or younger, and since you're actually Vampyr, not human, the term doesn't really—"

"Damnit, Nachari!" Kristina snapped. "I'm not playing with you. Tell him!"

"Braden, she doesn't want to kiss you," Nachari said, suppressing a slight, devilish grin.

Braden swelled up like a peacock. He drew back his shoulders, puffed out his chest, and flexed his biceps, before dropping his arms to his sides. In truth, the kid was growing taller, stronger, and more muscular by the day, so the blatant show of masculinity was not as unimpressive as it might have been, say, a month ago. "Ask her who she's calling *boy*."

Kagen bit his tongue to keep from laughing, too. He watched Nachari, waiting to see how the wizard would handle the situation now.

"I'm calling *you* a boy, Braden Bratianu!" Kristina sniffed, angling her petite frame to square off with him, vampire to vampire.

Braden flipped his chestnut-brown, shoulder-length hair out of his eyes with a proud toss of his head; and then he smiled roguishly, the barest hint of fangs gleaming beneath his full, teasing lips. "I tell you what, kiss me, and we'll see if you still think I'm a boy then."

Kristina turned the color of ripe, pink-lady apples just before the fall harvest. Her hands curled into fists, her pupils narrowed, and her mouth dropped open in astonishment.

Undaunted, Braden bent down to taste the proffered offering.

And Nachari caught him around the waist and yanked him back, tugging his feet a good twelve inches off the ground, just before his lips met Kristina's. "Whoa there, cowboy," he said. "You can't take a woman who's unwilling. There are *rules*, Braden. Etiquette."

Braden shrugged out of Nachari's grasp and shook out his shoulders, landing gracefully, if not quite stealthily, on the ground. "Yeah, well, tell my future *mate* that it's inevitable. I'm her male, and she's my female, so she may as well submit to me now." He slowly licked his lips for effect. "And while you're at it, tell her that I'm getting stronger every day. Bigger. And in more places than one."

"Eww!" Kristina moaned.

Nachari recoiled, and his hands shot up in the air defensively, as if the boy had just brandished a dagger. "Whoa! *Damn*. Way too much Neanderthal, Braden! And *way too much* information." He cringed and shook his head. "That's…that's just not okay. None of it. No woman wants to hear that."

"Oh, I don't know," Deanna teased, leveling a sideways glance at her mate, a gaze that was heated with innuendo. "Some of us like to know our men…are men."

Ciopori giggled and took Marquis's hand. "Indeed."

Jocelyn laughed out loud. "What say you, warrior?" She winked at Nathaniel, who practically purred in response.

"You think this is funny?" Kristina said to no one in particular, wringing her hands in frustration. She turned to glare at Nachari. "He just tried to molest me. You saw it! Make him stop, Nachari."

Nachari nodded. He planted a large hand on Braden's shoulder, squeezed tightly enough to make him wince in pain, and then shoved him away from the crowd. "Come here for a second, son. We need to have a quick talk."

Kristina stood there seething, rolling her eyes and smacking her gum as they all waited for the two vampires to return. When at last Nachari and Braden strolled back to the group, Braden lowered his head in a gesture of respect and then sheepishly eyed the angry redhead. "I'm sorry, Kristina."

Kristina huffed and leveled a sidelong glance at him, churlishly.

"It won't happen again," he added. "At least not until you want it. And then"—he did a little hip-hop dance move and rolled his hips in a circle—"and then *it's on*."

Nachari rolled his beleaguered eyes and shrugged. "Progress comes in little steps," he told Kristina. "Take what you can get. He won't molest you again." He glared daggers at Braden then. "You *won't* molest her again. Hear me?"

Braden rolled his eyes in turn, and the entire group laughed.

Kagen had to admit: The humor was undeniably welcome. At least for one moment, no one was thinking about the upcoming voyage, the danger, or the uncertainty, the unspoken but ever-present high stakes.

At least not until Kagen glanced at the sky and cleared his

throat.

Fixing his gaze squarely on Nachari, he said, "We do have to go, wizard. It's time to open the portal."

Nachari bent to retrieve the necessary objects from a large leather pouch on the ground and slowly nodded his head. Turning to regard his mate with tenderness, he whispered, "Deanna…" He glanced at each of the other women in turn and said, "Sisters, the energy for the spell has to be pure. There can be no doubt, worry, or conflicting desires present when I conjure the portal."

"In other words," Kagen said, "you can't want it to open and hope that it doesn't, all at the same time." He smiled then, his soft demeanor radiating warmth. "You can't love your mate so much that you support him in this journey, while needing him so badly that you wish he wouldn't go. The intentions are…conflicting. And they have to be pure."

"Precisely," Nachari said. "We have to do this part alone."

Braden's playful manner grew all at once serious, his childish antics evaporating like a droplet of water in the sun. The silly adolescent, the would-be suitor without any manners, both were instantly gone, and a determined vampire from the house of Jadon stood in the child's place. "Do you want me to stay?"

"We need you to stay," Nachari replied. "Not only can you help conjure the spell, but there are other things we need from you, just in case."

"Just in case of what?" Ciopori asked, her tone dripping with authority and malaise. She wanted to know the whole of it, and she wanted to know now.

"We don't know how the portal is going to *behave*, my love," Marquis said solemnly. "That is all."

"We don't know if the doorway is going to remain open, if it's going to vanish altogether, or if it's going to close the moment we enter Mhier," Nathaniel added for clarity. "And we don't know if we can reopen it from the other side."

Deanna nearly swayed on her feet, but she quickly caught herself and righted her posture. "And even if you can, reopen it from the other side, that is," she said quietly, "you can't guarantee that Nachari will still be with you to do it when you return."

Nachari reached out to take her hand. "Sweetie…" His voice trailed off. What could he really say? None of their fates were certain.

If silence could be felt as a vibration in the concert of the soul, reverberating as a clashing symbol or a deafening roar, then the entire valley became one sustained note in that solitary moment, a virtual amphitheater of comprehension and dread.

Kristina finally pierced the silence. "And that's the *real* reason why Bray isn't going, isn't it?"

The term of endearment, the shortened version of Braden's name, was not lost on anyone, least of all Kagen. The volatile redhead, with all her hot-tempered protests and understandable misgivings about her future, being promised to a teenage vampire, cared more deeply about the silly boy than she let on. It was written all over her face: the fact that she felt the awesome weight of Braden's responsibility on her own shoulders, the fact that she was infinitely relieved that he wouldn't be accompanying the Silivasis on their mission.

"One of the reasons," Kagen said, answering her question as honestly as he could. Braden was also far too young and inexperienced as a warrior to embark upon a journey into the land of the Lycanthrope, but Kagen wasn't about to say that out loud.

"It's only wise to make sure that more than one *practitioner* knows how to open this door," Nathaniel added, winking at Kristina. "Just a precaution."

Kristina nodded, and Deanna turned away. Clearly, the implication was too much for her to handle.

"Braden," Nachari said softly. "You remember what we discussed, right? For the next thirty days, no matter what, you will return to this meadow, every hour on the hour, *to this exact spot*, and you will reopen this portal. Understood?" He turned toward Deanna then. "Baby?"

She bit her bottom lip and nodded.

"It's just a precaution," Nachari reiterated.

She nodded more emphatically.

Braden drew back his shoulders and raised his head. "I understand. Starting at twelve o'clock noon until twelve o'clock midnight, I need to open the portal twelve times each day—if only for a minute or two—and then close it." His eyes narrowed with intensity. "I'll be here, Nachari. I swear, *I will*." He turned to look at all the males and placed his right hand over his heart in an unspoken pledge. "I'll be here."

"Good," Marquis said. "Because we're counting on it."

"And what happens after the thirty days?" Deanna asked. Her voice rose with angst despite her best effort to remain stoic.

Nachari's luminous eyes softened with compassion. "Then Braden will begin opening the portal twice each day: at noon and at midnight."

Deanna's face grew pale. "For how long?"

Nachari shook his head in an attempt to dismiss her worry. "We'll be back by then, my love. Have faith."

Before Deanna could reply, Kagen cleared his throat. "Very well," he said, hoping to move things along. What point was there in hashing over all the morbid, unspoken possibilities? They all needed to believe things would unfold exactly as planned, that everything would work out, and quickly. He gestured toward the distant grove of trees, indicating that it was time for the women to go. After all, he couldn't expect Marquis, Nachari, or Nathaniel to do it—the parting was just too hard, and their first instinct, their foremost duty, was always to see to their *destinies'* comfort. "It is time, sisters," he reiterated. "We will see you soon."

Watching as the women hugged and kissed their mates one last time before turning to amble from the meadow, Kagen added silently, "*And if the celestial gods are willing, our Blood Father will be with us.*"

six

Kagen watched in rapt fascination, the methodical, scientific part of his mind that sought to unravel puzzles observing every step Nachari and Braden took with objective curiosity. The two vampires laid out the contents of the leather pouch in a perfect circle in the center of the meadow: the bark from a northern tree placed in the north; stones from the eastern cliffs placed in the east; a sealed container of water from the Winding Snake River set gently in the south; and a chunk of stone, removed from the Red Canyons, positioned in the west. With each placement, Nachari spoke a rhythmic phrase in Latin, and then he placed Tristan's *remains*, Nathaniel's grisly trophy from his brutal kill, in the center and buried it just below the surface. He ushered each of the males forward, beckoning them to stand within the circle, and Braden stepped out, placing a wide berth between him and the other vampires.

"Marquis, as firstborn, you need to stand in the north. Nathaniel, you will stand in the east. Kagen, stay as you are, in the south, and I will take the west." Nachari shuffled to the side, about three or four feet, and then held out his hands.

The males linked arms, each brother grasping the wrist of the brother next to him in an unbroken loop. Nachari took a deep breath and turned toward Braden. "Bring the supplies," he said.

They waited, a million unspoken words passing between them, as Braden hefted and dragged the heavy backpacks full of supplies—the tents and the medicine, the extra, cached ammunition and venom, and the stored, bagged blood—into the center of the circle, being careful not to bump any of the Silivasis' arms, not to break their link. "That's everything," the youngster muttered.

Nachari nodded his approval and gestured toward a far-off

tree, at least thirty yards away, with his chin. "Stand back, way beyond the circle," he said.

Braden started to walk away, and then he stopped, turned around, and stared at Nachari, almost as if he was afraid to look away. "I just…I mean…you're like a…" For whatever reason, he stopped just shy of saying the last word.

"I know," Nachari said softly, his stark green eyes deepening with affection. "And you are like a son." Neither male actually said the word *cherished*, but it was clearly spoken just the same.

Braden raised his head, drew back his shoulders, and tried to appear brave. "Be well, Master Wizard."

"Be well, young acolyte," Nachari said, winking at the kid affectionately.

Braden cleared his throat. "Marquis, Nathaniel, Kagen…be well."

The brothers didn't answer him with words. They simply inclined their heads in the manner of warriors, of vampires, and Braden walked away, continuing to take long, measured strides, until he stood far off, beneath the branches of a limber pine.

Nachari looked at Marquis. "Are you ready, warrior?"

Marquis snorted. "I was born ready."

Nachari chuckled. "And you, Nathaniel?"

"I'm ready."

"Kagen?"

The healer nodded in consent.

"For our Blood Father then," Nachari whispered. His voice was barely audible.

"For our Blood Father," all three replied in unison.

With that, Nachari shut his eyes and began to chant. As his mystical words drifted up toward the heavens, the lyrical intonation of his speech grew more and more fluid until his words, unwittingly, reverted from English to Romanian and flowed like an ancient, mystic wind, eddying to the ears of the gods, and the circle began to take form.

Blue and violet light began to rise from the ground, the soft, incandescent beams radiating outward like a halo, beyond the circular boundary; and the center began to glow a fiery red. It emerged from the soil like an otherworldly geyser, a stream of conical light, spinning in tapering waves of sight and sound—and ethereal substance—shimmering as the portal began to open.

Nachari spoke more rapidly then, the words flowing off his tongue as if someone else was speaking them: They were as haunting as they were beguiling. And just like that, the gateway opened.

The entrance to Mhier emerged.

The Silivasi brothers broke their link, drew back their arms, each one reaching for a different hoard of supplies, and then, without hesitation, they stepped through the portal and entered the land of the Lycanthrope.

The landscape was inexplicably vivid in Mhier. The blues were bluer; the greens were greener; and the yellows were so endless in variation and texture that it was like a virtual explosion of color everywhere one looked. One glimpse at the Mhieridian sunrise was like sampling a honeycomb, a dozen sunflowers, and a golden goblet all at once. Yet the strangest omen of all was the sun's shadow: A full timber wolf moon stood directly behind the sun's emerging rays, even at 6:45 in the morning. The soil was rich in texture and minerals, and the vegetation—the trees, bushes, and grass—were as lush as they were tall and bountiful. It was like stepping into a prehistoric Garden of Eden. Everything was inexpressibly beautiful and larger than life.

Kagen immediately set down his pack and reached for the map in order to determine their whereabouts. The rolled-up scroll was tucked like a cherished keepsake into the top, most easily accessible compartment of his backpack, and he laid it out on the ground, placing several stones atop the parchment to keep it flat. He immediately began comparing the drawing to their new surroundings.

Nachari squatted down beside him, placing both hands flat, palms down, against the earth, in order to start divining the native energy—he was taking the spiritual temperature of the land, so to speak.

Marquis and Nathaniel took on a different role, entirely.

The role of Master Warriors.

They stood back to back like Vikings of old, guardians of an ancient treasure, each one hovering protectively over the healer and the wizard as they sent all *six* senses outward, seeking, in all four directions. They listened for danger; sniffed for the scent of an enemy; tasted the faintest vibrations in the air with their tongues, all the while, feeling for subtle variations in the atmosphere with their skin as they also scanned the skies, the ground, and the countryside in order to detect any imminent threats.

Like astronauts running through a final checklist before launching a rocket into space, they tested their vampiric powers, one by one.

"Hearing?" Marquis grunted.

Nathaniel grew deathly quiet for a moment. "There's a deer running in the woods about fifteen miles northwest, a snake sunning at the edge of a swamp ten miles due east, and I can hear two streams—no, three—about forty miles northeast."

"Sight," Marquis barked.

Nathaniel's eyes grew narrow, and the pupils constricted ever so slightly as he turned his head to the left and the right, snaking it back and forth in an eerily serpentine motion. He was scanning the area using infrared vision. "There's a family of squirrels in that nearby tree, a large colony of ants with an intricate system of chambers directly beneath our feet. I don't detect anything human or Lycanthrope in the immediate vicinity." He cringed then. "But there's a hell of a lot of motion going on in those Skeleton Swamps nearly fifteen miles away—large, lumbering movement, like that of gigantic beasts."

"Speed and flight," Marquis said, ignoring the last comment.

Just like that, Nathaniel shot into the air like the

aforementioned rocket. He released his glorious, raven-black wings and soared effortlessly through the sky, dipping, spinning, and tunneling downward with dizzying speed in an effort to test each of his aviation skills. When at last he headed for the ground, his feet took purchase with a soft, graceful landing; his wings fluttered softly, then flashed in and out of view; and the silky black annexes retreated once again into the smooth, even musculature of his back. "Everything seems to be fine," he said, rolling his shoulders to realign his muscles.

"Strength?" Marquis asked, moving immediately to the next item on the list.

Nathaniel dematerialized from their watchful position. He reappeared at the trunk of a nearby tree—the ancient redwood was nearly thirty feet in diameter at the base, at least three hundred feet high from trunk to tip, and it had to be at least a thousand years old. Nathaniel wrapped his arms around as much of the base as he could and proceeded to rip it out of the ground as if it were nothing more than a dandelion cluttering a pristine garden. He stepped back swiftly and let it hit the ground with a resounding thump, careful to remain clear of the falling timber. "Feels the same," he said, returning to Marquis's side.

Telepathy? Marquis asked next, speaking on the family bandwidth.

I can hear you just fine, Nathaniel replied.

Marquis nodded with satisfaction. "Mind reading?"

Nathaniel reached out to touch his twin on the shoulder and bowed his head with respect. "Forgive me, Kagen." With that, he burrowed into Kagen's mind and retrieved his last several thoughts, recounting them to Marquis. "He believes we are somewhere near the southern border of the realm, perhaps ten or fifteen miles east of the southern pack's territory, perhaps fifteen or twenty miles southwest of the Skeleton Swamps. Thane's castle and the slave territory are much further away, on the northern end of the territory, perhaps one to two days' travel by foot." He placed the tip of one finger on Nachari's shoulder next, even though the touch was not necessary to garner the information. "Nachari agrees. However, he also believes that we are no less than ten miles away, as the crow flies, from the lowest convergence of the Lykos River, where the main waterway curves sharply to the right, coming out of the Mystic Mountains before it heads back into the rocky gorge. However, it is his judgment that, even if we lose a little time, we should take a back route to the slave encampment, travel through the cover of the swamps, along the ternary rivers, and over the Mystic Mountains. We should avoid the most direct, exposed route. "

"Get out of my head, Nathaniel," Nachari said quietly. "I can't concentrate."

Kagen rubbed his brow and grunted. "Tell me about it."

"Very well," Marquis said. "I'm satisfied with your report, Nathaniel."

Just then, Nachari shrugged his right shoulder brusquely and frowned. "I mean it, Nathaniel. *Get out.* And stop touching me."

Nathaniel took a judicious step back, his eyes widening in alarm.

Nachari's shoulder jerked again. *"Stop."* He reached up to swat Nathaniel's hand away and drew back in sudden distress when his fingers came in contact with something black, wiry, and furry. "What the hell!" Nachari shouted, leaping to his feet. He began to dance an undignified jig, his deep green eyes nearly bulging out of his head, even as he began to squeal like a teenage girl. "Get it off! Get it off! Kagen, get it off me!"

The humongous, man-sized spider reacted to the vampire's frenzied emotion and erratic movement by leaping onto Nachari's chest and trying to bite him in the forehead.

"Shit!" Nachari yelped, backpedaling furiously.

Kagen leapt to his feet and grabbed the spider by two of its spindly hind legs, the hairy limbs closest to the spider's abdomen, and yanked for all he was worth. The legs dislodged from the body, but the spider kept attacking with the remaining six members.

Nachari reached hastily for his sword. He withdrew it from the scabbard in a whistling chime of steel and brandished it so wildly he almost sliced himself in the nose before dropping the sword on the ground with a reverberating clang.

"Calm down!" Nathaniel bellowed, approaching the frantic melee with mild amusement.

Nachari gulped, beginning to turn pale. "You calm down!" He reached inside his cloak to withdraw his next weapon of choice, a shiny, curved sickle. He grasped the spider with his left hand, right between the thorax and the abdomen, and squeezed for dear life, even as he wielded the sickle deftly with his right hand, cropping half the head off in his first swing.

Poison dripped out of the angry spider's fangs, and its four remaining eyes focused on Nachari with deadly, laser-like precision. "Oh, hell no!" Nachari snarled, his teeth clenched as tight as a vise. "Somebody get it off! *Now*!"

Nathaniel was just about to step up and unload his military grade AK-47 into the body of the spider when Marquis shoved him aside, rolled his phantom blue-black eyes in disgust, and focused a pure red beam of fire at the dark, spindly creature, instantly reducing it to ash.

"Really?" Marquis barked, angrily. "Really!" He turned to glare at Nathaniel. "You would fire your weapon in this strange new land, alert everyone within a dozen miles of our presence, warrior?" He glared at Nachari next. The vampire was stomping the remains of the smoking bug into the dirt with a fury unbecoming of a wizard. "Is this what we can expect on our journey, Nachari? The wizard who survived three months in hell, brought to his knees by a little black bug."

Nachari fumed. "*Little* black bug?"

Nathaniel whistled low beneath his breath. "Not so little, warrior," he said to Marquis. "And I already placed a custom-made silencer on the end of my weapon, so focus your ire elsewhere."

Kagen chuckled then, watching as Nachari danced on the spider's metaphorical grave. "He's dead, Nachari." He looked at the upturned ground and the sticky black goo adhering to the bottom of Nachari's steel-toed boots. "I don't think he's coming back, wizard."

Nachari frowned. He stomped the spider a few more times just for good measure and then began to brush off his clothing in short, quick bursts, just in case some…spider parts?…got stuck on his threads. "Yeah, well…" His voice trailed off.

"Well, you better get a grip, wizard!" Marquis snorted crossly, his voice brooking no argument. "You have a dozen defenses in your arsenal, all of them lethal and exacting, and all you could do was scream like a girl. Unacceptable, Nachari."

Nachari spun around in annoyance. He took three measured strides toward Marquis and pointed in the vampire's face. "Yeah, well, don't worry about it! I can do demons and dark vampires—and even lycans if I have to." He glanced over his shoulder to eye the gooey, smoldering mess in the dirt one last time and shuddered. "But I don't do spiders. I just…*don't*."

"Spiders or porcupines," Nathaniel added with humor, making reference to an unfortunate childhood incident that had left Nachari scarred with an unnatural fear of the prickly little animals.

Nachari snarled. "Sue me."

Kagen laughed out loud. "Clearly, little woodland creatures are not your friends." He winked good-naturedly.

Nachari shrugged and set about cleaning the bottom of his boots.

Kagen watched with amusement, even as he let out a deep breath: He knew Nachari had never been in any real danger, at least not this time. The vampire would have triumphed over the arachnid eventually. Hell, the wizard would have conjured a spell before allowing the eight-eyed monster to bite him, perhaps even shape shifted into the form of a panther to hightail it out of there, but still, they all needed to be a bit more careful. This was their first unpleasant encounter in Mhier, and by the look of the strange, prehistoric land, there might be many more to come—they all needed to remain on their toes from this point forward. "So, you'll be all right if we run into a T. rex in the Skeleton Swamps then?" Kagen asked, just to be sure.

Nachari looked up and smiled that breathtaking grin of his. "Hey, as far as I'm concerned, bigger is better. At least a T. rex can't crawl up the leg of your pants or shoot you in the ankle with a quill."

"Indeed," Nathaniel said, nodding his head as if considering Nachari's words seriously. "He just eats you in one bite."

All four of the brothers laughed then.

"Not if Marquis bites him first," Nachari added, finally beginning to soften.

They laughed again, and then, as if the reality of their situation *and the seriousness of their purpose* descended upon each of them in turn, the air grew densely quiet, and the laughter faded into mist.

"So we're one to two days out from the slave encampment?" Marquis asked, the solemn tone of his voice reflecting the brothers' collective change of mood. "Possibly two to three if we take Nachari's preferred back route?"

"Assuming we travel swiftly without any major delays," Kagen said, absently glancing at the map tucked into the outer pocket of his pack. "If we run into any *distractions*, then of course, it could take longer."

Nathaniel sighed long and deep. "Then time is of the essence."

"Agreed," Kagen said. "As far as I'm concerned, this journey isn't about the Lycanthrope or their gods-forsaken land, however beautiful it might appear on the outside. It's not even about vengeance—*necessarily*—although I'll take it if it comes." He felt his eyes heat with lethal purpose and chose to forego any further dialogue.

"It's about bringing our father home," Nachari added quietly, "at any cost."

Marquis drew back his shoulders, expanding to his full, intimidating height. His harshly masculine features grew hard with purpose, and his voice took on a savage, malignant edge. "By all the gods in the heavens—or the dark lords of the underworld—I will not leave this land without my father. And I will lay ruin to every village, encampment, or citizen of this cursed realm if that is what it takes to bring him out alive. Innocent or guilty. It makes no difference to me." His words resounded like the clash of a symbol, and the branches on a nearby tree shook in reaction to the virulent vibration.

Nathaniel whistled low beneath his breath, but he didn't speak.

Nachari nodded his head in agreement and donned his pack.

Kagen did the same, allowing Marquis's words to wash over him like the icy fingers of a cool mountain stream, caressing his ferocity into utter resolve. As he felt his own inner demon stir, his hand trembled:

Indeed, the Silivasis were coming for their father.

And hell was coming with them.

seven

King Tyrus Thane Montego stepped onto the sandy floor of the arena and began to pace in large, purposeful strides around the ancient, circular dome. He wanted to make sure everything was in order, that all preparations were being carried out meticulously, to the letter, for the upcoming weekend's event.

After all, it was his pride, his throne, and his name on the line.

He had to make a clear and unequivocal statement to the entire realm, lest anyone begin to question his authority or his supreme, unqualified rule: Treachery of an alpha general would not go unpunished. Adultery, at least as far as the king's wife was concerned, was a sin beyond reparation.

Unforgivable.

Punishable by death.

As a warm wind whipped through his long, curly locks, tossing the unruly mass back into his eyes, he quickly shoved it aside and tucked it into the collar of his golden robe, determined to see with clear vision. "Teague," he called brusquely to one of his three remaining loyal generals, ushering him forward with a slight bend of his hand.

The fierce, stalwart lycan rushed to his side. He lowered his head, averted his eyes, and kept his torso exposed as a subordinate should. "My king."

Thane waved his hand through the air with impatience. "Dispense with the formalities, Teague. We are old friends, are we not?"

Teague leveled his pale, opal eyes at the king and smiled a wolfish grin. "Of course, Thane. I just…with what recently happened…*with Cain*…" His voice trailed off, and he shrugged. "We are all a little bit on edge at the moment."

Thane squared his shoulders to the alpha general of the

southern pack and narrowed his gaze. "Did you also sleep with Cassandra?" he asked, beneath a snarl.

Teague visibly recoiled. "No! *Hell no.*"

Thane frowned then. "Is she that ugly?"

Teague seemed utterly bewildered and more than just a little bit flustered. "No, my king. She is…she was…beautiful. But, she is yours."

"Was mine," Thane corrected, throwing up both hands and patting Teague playfully on the shoulders. "I'm only teasing you, Teague. My point is: You have nothing to fear from me as long as you remain loyal."

Teague nodded his head. "Of course." He forced an awkward laugh. "*Of course.*"

Thane took a judicious step forward and gestured toward a raised circular platform at the southwestern corner of the arena. It was topped with two enormous jutting posts, each sporting a matching pair of rawhide straps, two straps along the top and two straps along the bottom; and right below the center of the platform, there was a shallow, hollowed-out fire pit, constructed in the shape of a V in order to generate the swiftest uprising blaze possible. "So, this is where the wench will burn?"

Teague nodded emphatically. "Yes." He pointed at the two protruding columns at the top of the platform. "Her wrists will be bound up there, to the tops of the posts"—he pointed next at two oval loops toward the bottom— "and her feet will be fettered down there."

Thane studied the setup carefully, slowly nodding his head. "She will be naked…humiliated?"

"Of course," Teague said. "Except for the accelerant."

Thane nodded more brusquely in approval. "And you are to use—"

"Pitch…*tar*…she should burn as intended. Hot and quick."

Thane took a step toward the platform, trying to imagine the ghoulish scene in his mind. "I want the tar placed only on her breasts and her…nether regions. Understood?"

"The executioner is well aware of your instructions," Teague replied. He pointed toward the base of the platform then, the V beneath the soon-to-be victim's feet. "We will use softwoods with flammable resins in the shape of a tepee in order to keep the fire burning strong."

"Mmm," Thane intoned. "Good." He turned toward the center of the arena then. "And that monstrous distraction will be going on in the background while Keitaro murders Cain on the sands?"

Teague's keen blue eyes lit up with amusement. "Yes, sire"—he quickly amended the address—"yes, *Thane*. Cassandra will provide the background…*music*…for Cain and Keitaro's battle." He chuckled at his own analogy. "Her screams should be a melodious addition to the festivities."

Thane laughed heartily then. "I expect so. And since the battle should take no more than two to five minutes, I assume you are prepared to release the rhino beasts with impeccable timing." He narrowed his gaze and interlaced his fingers at his back. "I don't want the vampire to live through this, Teague." He angled his body toward the general. "While Cain is a traitor and deserves the fate that awaits him, he is also Lycanthrope, *a superior species*, and his death must be meted out with honor. The bitch for amusement; the vampire for the general; two debts—*and three deaths*—on Sunday."

Teague listened with rapt attention. He walked out to the middle of the ring and turned around, gesturing broadly in a wide arc. "The beasts are being starved leading up to the battle. They are being goaded and abused every hour on the hour. They should be murderous by the time combat begins, and Keitaro should be…*will be*…already wounded. I think they will dispatch the slave in record time."

Thane frowned. He hated to lose his most prized possession, the vampire slave that drew such large crowds to the arena, but what else could he do? Cain had committed an inconceivable wrong, an unforgivable sin, and this heinous slight, this inexcusable act of treason, had to be redressed in flamboyant fashion. And Keitaro was just the male to do it. The need for proper vengeance trumped the need to keep the slave. He wrung his hands together behind his back before pulling them apart. "Very well, it would appear that everything is in order." He glanced up at the empty stands and gestured in earnest. "I want this arena packed, Teague. This is a *very* important event."

"It is," Teague agreed. "And it will be, my king." Pausing, as if deep in thought, he reached into the pocket of his bright blue tunic and pulled out a rolled-up piece of paper. "By the way, there is still the matter of our next queen."

Thane spat on the ground in disgust. "I'm hardly interested at the moment."

Teague nodded cautiously. "I understand, Your Grace. Nevertheless, your subjects expect you to sire royal offspring, to take another bride. And since female lycans are extremely rare, and almost always infertile, it's imperative that you choose another human wife. Besides, if you hesitate, they might *misinterpret* your behavior. They might assume that you actually *cared* for Cassandra, after all."

Thane threw back his head and shook out his hair, exasperated. "Bring the list here."

Teague immediately complied. He strolled swiftly to his king's side, handed him the ten potential names, all virgins who had been born or kept in captivity since a very early age, and took a judicious step back to await Thane's reply.

Thane gave the page a cursory glance. He sneered as he perused the names, and then he quickly pointed to the three on top. "Sorah, Tawni, or Janelle. I suppose one of them will do as well as the next."

Teague blanched and then quickly recovered. Clearing his throat, he said, "Very well. Do you wish to have the women brought to your bedchamber individually or together, prior to making your final choice?" He leaned forward in a gesture of collusion. "Do you wish to try them out before you make a final selection?"

At first, Thane shrugged with indifference, but then his brows furrowed as he considered it more carefully. "Are all three willing?"

Teague laughed aloud. "Sorah is an ambitious sort. I think the idea of becoming your queen sits well with her. She will be only too willing to please. Tawni, on the other hand, is still fairly childlike: She will fear you and resist, but in the end, she will comply."

Thane pursed his lips. "And Janelle?"

"She will fight you every step of the way. She's headstrong and proud. She wishes to have nothing to do with the royal court. Ah, but her beauty is legendary throughout the realm, and she is a virgin."

Thane capitulated. "Mm, then bring Janelle first. Tonight." He waved a dismissive hand through the air. "And bind her wrists to the bedpost. I neither have the time nor the inclination to wrestle with a recalcitrant wench at the moment, just to take what is my due. I will make sure she understands *clearly* who it is that mounts her, and I will see if she is worth keeping."

Teague bowed his head in obedience. "Of course. And the girls you discard?"

"Give one to Gavin and the other to Xavier. Let them propagate their packs on the finest stock in the land." When Teague hesitated, Thane added, "Do you want one for yourself?"

"No," Teague answered quickly. "I prefer my meat…unsalted." He laughed conspiratorially, and Thane chuckled with him. "Is there anything else?"

Thane stood erect then, his mind instantly shifting to *the one that got away*, the rebellious, beautiful teenager who had eluded him so many years ago. "Always, Teague. There is *always* something else. Always someone else. Have you or the other generals had any luck locating Arielle Nightsong or the resistance?"

Teague frowned as he shook his head. He took an inadvertent step back, just in case the legendary king lost his composure, decided to shift into his wolverine form and tear his general's throat out. "We're searching, Thane. By all the gods in the lykoi heavens, we are scouring this land from one end to the other."

"Keep trying," Thane bit out, his voice a harsh, clipped command. "I want Arielle—not Sorah, Tawni, or Janelle. Do you understand?"

Teague nodded emphatically. "I do, but just in case—"

"Yes, yes," Thane cut him off. "I will try them all…just in case. But you must swear to me that you are making this your number one priority. I don't care if you have to scorch the land to burn her out, just *find her* this time."

Teague bowed low and practically whimpered like a pup, trying to placate his master. Despite his own powerful bearing—and his god-like position in the realm—the general knew better than to argue with his king on this one bedeviling point.

Tyrus Thane Montego wanted Arielle Nightsong more than he wanted to draw his next breath.

He always had.

And the longer she eluded him, the greater the desire became, until it had almost grown into an obsession, a desperate, gnawing hunger that ate at his gut day in and day out like a parasite lodged in his belly. It was a hunger he could no longer deny.

At this point, he wasn't sure if he would claim her as his bride, murder her as his enemy, or take her innocence, violently, on a raised dais in the arena for the entire realm to see, just to make a point: He was Tyrus Thane Montego, king of the lycan, imperial ruler of Mhier, and he would not be denied the most coveted treasure in the land. Not behind the stubborn will of a disobedient girl, one who had managed to elude him for ten long years. No matter how he turned it, he had to find her.

He had to have her.

Just once.

She had always been his due: his to claim, his to command, his to destroy…if he chose to do so.

eight

Arielle Nightsong approached the steep, sandy banks of the Skeleton Swamps, nearest to the Rebel Camp, careful not to get too close to the actual water. The swamps covered a ten-mile swath of land, stretching from the eastern bend of the Lykos River to the southernmost edge of the Rebel Camp, and while the southern end was dangerous—the center, positively lethal—the bank that Arielle explored was often peaceful, enchanting, and rich with healing plants and herbs.

Adding another bushel of river sage to her pouch, Arielle cast a furtive glance at the sparkling sun, paying little attention to the ever-present timber wolf moon. She decided to sit down on the bank and rest for a while before returning to camp—she needed to clear her mind—at the least, she hoped to replenish her energy before heading back.

She gathered her belongings and thought about her present circumstances: the unique challenges confronting her life, how she had come to this junction, this crossroads, this particular moment in time:

She was living like a refugee in a camp of rebel warriors, always afraid, always on the run, in a land fraught with danger and corruption. She was hiding from Tyrus Thane—always and again—in order to avoid the unspeakable, a life as his glorified sex slave.

Or worse…

She noticed an unusually bright orange-and-blue swallow hopping about the riverbank, meandering behind a thick bushel of reeds while pecking at insects on the ground, and it catapulted her back to her childhood. As much as she hated to relive the past, she couldn't help but return to her years in the slave camp, years when the swallows and the squirrels had been her only friends. Well, the woodland animals, and Keitaro Silivasi.

She shivered as the memories came rushing back like water released from a dam: At ten years old, Thane had forced her to help bring food and water to his troops, to trudge back and forth across the royal district, the brutal slave encampment, with a platter of bread and cheese in her hands or a wooden carrying pole draped across her slender shoulders, both buckets balanced precariously over her narrow frame. The buckets had been filled to the brim with sloshing water from the well, a burden that felt more like a yoke of bricks, and the vulgar catcalls from the lycans had been obscene, things no innocent little girl should have ever been forced to hear, let alone be exposed to on a daily basis.

And the water?

Ancestors have mercy…

Those cursed buckets had been so damn heavy, *so painfully, unbearably heavy.* The rough wooden shaft had bit into her shoulders and chafed her skin—at times, her legs had given way under the substantial burden—yet she had pressed on, always pressed on, as nothing more than a servant to a diabolical king.

By age twelve, Arielle had grown a much thicker skin. The lecherous propositions from the soldiers had ceased to bother her—she hardly even heard them—and she could hoist nearly half her weight in water with unusual strength and dexterity. She could deliver the platters in half the time. She had already become a rebel in her heart, a tomboy by necessity, and an alchemist by nature. She had worn her hair in a simple braid that snaked down her back and fell to her hips; she had taken every opportunity to collect plants and healing herbs during her frequent explorations outdoors; and she had affixed a permanent satchel to a band around her waist in order to have easy access to her herbal specimens. In truth, Thane had given her a *small* amount of freedom, as long as she never abused it, and she had quickly become adept at patching up her own skinned knees, treating her frequently bruised elbows, curing her own sporadic illnesses.

Arielle had already begun to dream of providing curative

services for the other slaves, somehow making a difference in an otherwise barren world.

It hadn't been a happy time, but it hadn't been as bad as when she was first taken, either.

She had adapted to her life, such as it was, and she'd had hopes and dreams, like any other human, perhaps of one day becoming a great healer for the resistance, or maybe just a shaman for the slave encampment. One way or another, she had hoped to serve others, to be for them what no one had ever been for her: a bastion of safety, a symbol of security, and a temporary haven of peace, if only for a fleeting moment.

Arielle frowned. Perhaps it wasn't true that *no one* had *ever* provided that for her. It was just…the one thing that had always been missing from her life was the presence of loving parents. Sure, her mother had tended to her basic needs when she was young. She had provided food, water, and shelter, such as it was—she had even taught her how to read and write—but Alina Page had been so busy with the resistance, so busy surviving, *so obsessed with Ryder Nightsong*, that she hadn't had time to nurture her little girl. She hadn't had time to play or to linger or to touch, beyond what was required for grooming and instruction.

She hadn't had time to show Arielle *love*.

And when she had been killed during the raid on Teague's encampment, Arielle had buried that need along with her mother. In all honesty, it was the only way she had been able to deal with the tragedy, the unimaginable loss, the only way she had managed to stay sane in her new, untenable circumstances. After all, there was little hope—no hope, really—that her father would somehow save the day.

And wasn't that just the understatement of the decade…

Ryder Nightsong's absence had left a hole in Arielle's heart the size of the Mystic Mountains.

She had grown up hearing stories of his gallant exploits, as well as his bravery and courage: how he had taught the rebels to hide from the lycans, given them the knowledge to fend for themselves, shown them when and where to go underground.

He had inspired them to live free, as neither slaves nor subjects, in spite of the Lycanthrope's rule. And over time, he had become *larger than life* in Arielle's mind, a legend in her heart, a hero for her soul…

But never, *ever,* a father.

The lycans had hated Ryder with a passion that bordered on irrational, and that, in and of itself, had made Arielle revere him even more, but he was nothing at all in her life on a personal level, just the pollen that had seeded the flower. And somehow, somewhere deep inside, where little girls are sewn together and made into the tapestry that will one day unfold as a woman, Ryder's ability to fight for every cause, *but her,* to challenge the invincible Lycanthrope on behalf of the resistance, *but never on behalf of her,* had sent a message to her little mind that even Thane's soldiers could not have imparted with all their crude, misogynic taunts and gestures: Arielle was a child without value. She wasn't just a slave to a vile creature; she was an afterthought in her father's mind.

Arielle hugged her knees to her chest, bit down on her bottom lip, and then quickly dismissed the memory: What was the point of all of this reflection?

Her mother was gone, and so was Ryder.

And the fact that he had never come for her, checked on her, counted her among his worthy accomplishments, was just a fact of life, one she had long ago resolved.

Still, it sometimes continued to niggle: If she didn't matter to the one who had created her, why should she matter to the ones who had enslaved her, to those who reviled her for being a subordinate species and gender?

If only…

Just once…

Her father could have loved her…

Arielle wiped an unexpected tear from her eye, wishing she could just let it go, once and for all. As it stood, she had learned how to live with the hole in her heart; she had stopped longing for a savior that was never going to come; and she had found her place among the other slaves, soothed by the paternal affection of Keitaro Silivasi.

And that had been enough.

It had to be.

Besides, she was no longer ten years old, and while she was still often alone, she was rarely afraid. And most important, she was no longer King Thane's slave, no matter how badly the evil monarch desired to make that happen. Arielle Nightsong was by no means free, but at least she was free of Tyrus-the-god-forsaken-tyrant-Thane.

The sun beat down upon her brow with unusual intensity, and she plucked a large leaf from a nearby tree and set it on her forehead in an effort to block the piercing rays. Her spine literally stiffened as she, at last, recalled the night of her sixteenth birthday and just how close she had come to being claimed by the evil monarch:

Teague Verasachi had entered her humble dwelling with a wicked grin on his face and a glow of pure devilish elation radiating in his eyes. The timber wolf moon had been full, pale yellow, and unusually bright; and it had cast a luminous shadow about the domed straw-and-mud hut like a muted torch being raised in a cave. And then the general had fixed his gaze on

Arielle with such malice, such hatred, such spite in his eyes that Arielle had begun to shiver on the cold earthen floor. "You have two years, my sweet, untouchable little minx." He had winked at her in a way that made her skin crawl. "Two years of freedom, and then you will know only pain, degradation, and sorrow."

Arielle hadn't understood.

Sure, she had known that Teague despised her—when it really came down to it, he had always hated the fact that she was *off-limits*, that the generals couldn't touch her, break her, or force submission into her eyes—all they could do was taunt, tease, and threaten. Arielle belonged to Thane.

But this?

It had been something entirely different.

Something sinister and cruel.

Teague had wanted to humiliate and terrify her. "Are you even the least bit curious?" he had drawled.

Arielle had wanted to defy him; even then, as a teenager, she had almost said *no*. But she had understood the consequences—it would have only egged him on. "Why?" she had whispered instead.

"Up until now," he had snarled, "you have been Thane's prized possession, his wind-up toy, his cute little puppy, but when you turn eighteen, you will become his *wife*." He had let the last word linger, knowing that nothing more needed to be said.

Arielle had doubled over, as if he had physically kicked her, and then she had spilled the contents of her stomach on the ground. She knew the games Thane played with his wives: the whips, the chains, the implements of torture…the public displays for his guards. And the idea that she would belong to him *in that manner* was more than she could bear.

It had jolted her.

Destroyed her.

Left her feeling terrified and alone.

Teague had finally managed to break her, to take all of her hopes and dreams and crush them in one fateful blow: The king's wife would never be a healer. She would never be more than an object or a blatant tool for breeding. She would never have a life of her own.

Arielle shifted nervously on the ground, digging her fingers into the sand. By all that was sacred, why was she reliving this now? She had escaped. She had managed to avoid such a horrific fate, and she wasn't going back. She would die first—even if it had to be by her own hand—so why was she still so haunted?

Arielle fisted a handful of sand and watched as the grains sifted through her fingers, falling in random patterns to the ground. Perhaps it was because the ghosts of the past still haunted her today—they lived in the shadows of her soul. While her life was free, it had become a daily exercise of duty and purpose. Sure, she believed in the resistance, but truth be told, they would never rid Mhier of the lycans or find a place of equal footing among them. At best, they would fight to maintain a token of liberation, to live as vagabonds, forever on the run. They would survive, hand-to-mouth, from one season to the next, and even with all her skills as a warrior—her healing arts—it wasn't a *life* at all.

Arielle was ultimately and always…alone, even when she was surrounded by friends.

She had learned to live with the death of her mother and the absence of her father, but the ghosts of her past were like unrelenting hounds from hell, always stalking their prey, forever nipping at her heels.

They were too ethereal to destroy.

Too corporeal to banish.

And too ever-constant to outrun.

Kagen Silivasi waded slowly into the murky waters of the Skeleton Swamp, turning his lip up in disgust as his boots sank deeper into the muck. They had been at it all day, slowly trudging along, making slow but steady progress.

Marquis had insisted that the swamp was the safest route to take north, at least initially. It gave them added protection, obscured them from sight, and masked them from smell. Not to mention, they needed to sustain as wide a berth as possible from the southern lycan camp and the Wolverine Woods. They simply could not march up the center of Mhier and follow the Lykos River, not when they were carrying so many accoutrements, subsisting on subpar, bottled blood. They needed to maintain their precious energy, not waste it on cloaking objects or trying to remain invisible. And, honestly, who was he to argue with a Master Warrior?

As a one-eyed snake slithered across the top of the water, he reached out, snatched it by the tail, and sent it spiraling across the surface, far too close to Nachari, which earned him a bone-chilling glare. *Sorry, brother*, he said telepathically, before shrugging in apology.

Nachari simply rolled his intense green eyes.

As they waded further into the waist-deep waters, Kagen began to study all the fauna. He couldn't help it. It was an integral part of who he was. Laughing inwardly, he flashed back to a time when he was seven years old and he and Nathaniel had waded into a similar swamp—well, minus all the enormous creepy-crawly creatures and the bizarre, otherworldly land—in what was now Ouray County, Colorado. Even then, Kagen had been intrigued by nature and its inner workings. He'd had an unquenchable thirst for knowledge about science and mystics, how the two forces intermingled, worked so seamlessly together. True, he was the descendant of powerful celestial gods and their human mates, so possessing an inner commune with nature, sensing the subtle biorhythms all around him, was as natural as breathing for his kind. But for Kagen, it had always been something more.

He wanted to know *why* it worked as it did, *how* it all came about, *when* it originated, and *what* made it true. He had always needed to understand the life beyond the life, so he could manipulate it at will. And Nathaniel had found that very funny at seven years old, especially when Kagen lost his truly ridiculous, *and wholly unnecessary*, magnifying globe in that same hidden swamp. He had invented the magnifying device from a 424 B.C. prototype of a globe filled with water, used to magnify specimens, and he had carried it with him everywhere he went, even though he had beyond-perfect vision, including the ability to amplify objects with his naked eye. Just the same, he had believed it made him look more *scientific*, and Nathaniel had ribbed him beyond endurance, time and time again. Marquis had threatened to bounce the globe off Kagen's "scientific head" and smash it to smithereens beneath his boot, but Keitaro had intervened on his curious son's behalf, warning both boys to leave the inquisitive vampire, claiming he was just exploring his interests.

Kagen chuckled out loud. Funny how memories popped up at the oddest times.

By age twelve, the difference in Nathaniel and Kagen's personalities was pretty much set in stone. Nathaniel had a smooth, devious edge, even back then, always staging pranks and trying to best the other vampires in feats of prowess: flying, telekinesis, and mind control. Whereas, Kagen had emerged as more of a loner, content to go on long forays through the forest, endless hikes through the canyon, and to spend countless hours in his makeshift labs. He just had to be hands-on with the elements, to actually touch them, feel them, and taste them on a regular basis. His curiosity by that age was insatiable, and Keitaro had journeyed from one civilization to the next in order to collect the latest human contraptions, scientific innovations, and crude investigative kits so Kagen could conduct his endless experiments. And Serena, his mother, brought every written text she could find into the house to encourage Kagen's burgeoning interests: tablets, scripts, and the mad writings of deceased alchemists, anything that would keep the young vampire occupied. Kagen had devoured everything he could get his hands on, memorizing it instantly with his innate photographic ability.

It wasn't like Kagen had been a nerd.

Not really.

He had enjoyed playing the *sporting* games with the other vampires as much as the next kid, especially psychic fishing, where the vampires sat on the edge of a stream, covered their eyes with a loose leather tie, and felt for the psychic vibration of a fish moving through the water before them. The first vampire to toss a stone with enough accuracy to score the fish, stun it, and then retrieve it from the water, using only telekinesis, won the game.

And then Kagen got to dissect the carcass, of course, at least until Serena had finally put a stop to it. She had insisted that the stench was too vile to tolerate in the house.

Kagen smiled at the memory.

Okay, he had to admit—at least if he was being honest—he had been a fairly nerdy child, especially for a vampire. But luckily for him, by age sixteen, the young males had discovered human girls, and more importantly, the human girls had discovered the vampire males. True, the mortal females had no idea what the Silivasis were—the vampires attended a wholly separate private academy, and any true romantic interaction between the species was strictly prohibited by Napolean Mondragon, not to mention Keitaro and Serena. Just the same, the natural magnetism of the species had done wonders for Kagen's self-esteem, and frankly, now that he was a thousand years old as of last July, he was somewhat ashamed to admit to some of the games he and his twin had invented to amuse themselves back in 1025 A.D.

Alas, true maturity only came with age, *with living*, and none of the unsuspecting females he and Nathaniel had *toyed with* had truly been harmed in any way by their silly teenage pranks. So, why then did he suddenly feel so morose? Why had all this reflection, this innocent recollection of the past, left him feeling oddly disconnected, if not a bit restless and discontent?

He came across a hollowed-out log in the water, draped in moss and covered with bugs, and he slowly moved it aside, cringing at the sight of the strange, ugly creatures. He needed to redirect his thoughts, to focus on a memory that made him feel settled and confident, something that reminded him that all was truly well.

It wasn't like his childhood had been anything other than pleasant.

And nurturing.

In fact, it was only later in life that true tragedy had visited the Silivasi household, that Kagen had lost Serena, his mother, then Keitaro, his father, and at last, Shelby, his beloved younger brother, each cherished family member in turn.

It wasn't until later in life that he had begun to recognize the true dual nature of his being, the fact that the gentle, consummate healer concealed a wild, dangerous beast within. The fact that Kagen had somehow become a loner—and perhaps even a bit of a haunted predator—in his own confusing way. It wasn't that he had a desire to hurt the innocent—*never, absolutely not*—it was just that he had an insatiable desire to see *blood*, a yearning to cause destruction on an epic scale, something that went beyond the normal vampiric instincts.

And gods be compassionate, none of it was intentional.

Kagen Silivasi was a caring male, a loving soul by nature, but he had survived the unthinkable, time and time again, by retreating into that solitary place inside of his soul that no one else could touch; hell, that he himself could no longer even define. And he had built a life, a way of *being*, inside a cocoon, a safe, hemmed-in shell that kept the shadows at bay, the demons barred at the gate, and any true potential for intimacy rendered impossible.

Perhaps Kagen was simply being honest with himself for the first time in decades.

Because if the truth were ever to be spoken aloud, Kagen would have to admit that his internal demons, those enigmatic ghosts of the past, still haunted him today. They lived in the shadows of his soul. While his life was one of meaning and purpose, it had also become a monotonous exercise of duty and service as well, lacking whatever intrinsic curiosity and joy had once driven him to get up each night as a child. To be sure, he believed in the mastery of healing with all his heart, in the sacred oath he had sworn to the house of Jadon, but he had walked this path in such utter solitude for so long that perhaps he no longer recognized the ache for what it was: *loneliness*.

All Kagen knew was that the seasons blended into years; the years blended into decades; and the decades had become an endless repetition of monotony at best.

Was this really a *life* at all, when the ghosts of the past were like unrelenting hounds from hell, always stalking their prey, forever nipping at his heels? When his beast was too ethereal to destroy, too corporeal to banish, and too ever-constant to outrun?

Kagen dismissed his thoughts as he picked up his pace,

falling into closer step behind Nathaniel. Perhaps this journey would put an end to the ghosts, once and for all.

As if sensing his unease, perhaps even detecting his inner conflict, Nathaniel glanced over his shoulder and met the healer's gaze. *Brother?* he asked, telepathically. There was no need for further words.

All is well, Kagen assured him. *I'm fine, Nathaniel.*

Nathaniel stared at him for a few seconds too long and then spoke on a private bandwidth: *If it helps at all, know that I am here. You are* never *alone.*

Kagen stopped in his tracks, shook off the vulnerable moment, and moved on.

nine

Just before nightfall

Arielle grew instantly alert as she listened to the approaching sound of water sloshing in the swamp and then heavy, prodding footsteps steadily coming her way.

Dearest ancestors!

She immediately snatched her belongings, scrambled from the edge of the bank to a nearby grove of trees, and took cover behind a thick cluster of bushes. She drew an arrow from her quiver, notched her bow, and held her breath...waiting.

She hadn't been wrong!

There were several large, intimidating males coming her way.

And unlike the typical gold-and-russet-haired lycans, all but one of these males had dark black locks. In fact, one of them had hair so black it shimmered with a kaleidoscope of bottomless, reflective blue. An uneasy knot twisted in her gut, and her palms grew sweaty as she studied them more closely. Their gait was smooth and predatory, like that of wild cats, and the seamless way they moved as one, each disarming male functioning as a separate limb on a singular body, stole her very breath. They were magnificent as soldiers, vulturine as a species, *terrifying as men.*

And somehow she just knew that death followed in their wake.

Clutching her bow more tightly, she trembled in her boots, wishing for all intents and purposes that she could just blend into the landscape and disappear.

These males were dangerous in a way that not even Thane's generals could match. They didn't appear to be Lycanthrope, and they definitely were not human. *By all the ancestors, what were they?*

Who were they?

And why were they here, within five hundred yards of the Rebel Camp?

She pressed her belly lower into the dirt and shimmied further back beneath the prickly bush, hoping to remain undetected as their approach grew nearer. She glanced anxiously to the left and then the right, eyeing the inconspicuous trail that led to the Rebel Camp and the large mossy trees that dotted the northern banks of the Skeleton Swamps, and then it just occurred to her: *Great ancestors*, these men had traveled from the south, *through the Skeleton Swamps,* and they had all lived to tell about it!

They had survived the ferocious beasts.

But how?

Of all the days to venture out alone to the edge of the forbidden swamp, to collect plants for her healing tonics and poultices, why had she chosen today?

Arielle felt like she was going to be sick.

Of all the ways she had imagined her death, this wasn't it. She absently wondered what Walker would think when she didn't return. What everyone in the camp would do—would they ever find her body?

Just then, the lightest-haired male turned his head in her direction and lightly scented the air, his exquisite, chiseled features tightening with recognition. His intense brown eyes reflected silvery light from the centers, even as they narrowed in focus, homing in on the bush where she crouched.

She felt like a sitting duck.

One of those idiotic rabbits that tried to freeze in place right out in the middle of a field, even though it was clear to everyone except the rabbit that the gig was up, as if the predator could no longer see its prey if it stopped moving or avoided eye contact. And like a cornered rabbit, she wanted to scamper away, run like the wind from the alarming male who was staring right at her—or was he?—but the lot of them were too close now. She would never get away. She couldn't hope to outrun them.

Arielle bit her bottom lip and steeled her resolve. Unlike a rabbit, she wasn't stupid or defenseless. Slowly removing two more silver-tipped arrows from her quiver, she prepared to do the only thing she knew how: to fight to the death if necessary.

And, hopefully, to die with her honor *and her virtue* still intact.

The Silivasi brothers emerged from the Skeleton Swamps like crusaders emerging from months of battle. They shook off the foul, prehistoric experience even as they shook out the musty water from their clothes and their hair, immediately utilizing their vampiric powers to dry their packs and reset their body temperatures.

Kagen shuddered as he fell back into place to the left of Nathaniel, and to the right of Nachari, essentially bringing up the rear—and just what had that last creature been anyway? The one with the giant, ten-foot wingspan and two globular heads protruding out of its neck like some kind of carnival freak? He glanced appreciatively at Nachari and smiled. The wizard had been true to his word: He had brandished his beloved sword, as well as his curved sickle, with expert ease and precision, taking on one monstrous predator after another without flinching. He had even used his magic on several precarious occasions, an impressive display of mysticism to say the least, and it wasn't until they had run into the fifty-foot-long snake that he had become squeamish.

Kagen chuckled inwardly.

This was a strange land indeed.

As beautiful on the outside as it was ugly and distorted on the inside, just like the lycans that inhabited the realm.

Now, moving forward at a brisk place, his eyes and ears alert for the impending presence of another enemy—beast, human, or werewolf—he thought he detected the outline of a person about one hundred yards ahead, a shadow ducking beneath a large, thorny bush. He didn't register a reaction—the last thing he wanted to do was alert an enemy to their presence—rather, he reached out to his brothers on a telepathic wavelength: *Marquis, fifty yards ahead. Three o'clock. Beneath the bush.*

I see it, the fearsome warrior grumbled.

It…is a her, Nachari offered, his psychic voice even yet alert.

Indeed, Nathaniel chimed in. *The heart is smaller and the rhythm is faster, and not just because she's afraid. And by the familiar aroma of the hormones being released into her bloodstream, it would appear that* she *is a human.*

And alone, Nachari said.

Are you sure? Marquis asked. *That she's alone?* There was no room for error in such calculations.

Nachari paused only for a moment. *She's alone*, he reiterated.

And scared to death, Nathaniel added.

Kagen turned his gaze in the female's direction and lightly scented the air. *Adrenaline*, he commented to no one in particular. *Fight or flight response. She's getting ready to do…something.*

Yes, Nathaniel agreed, *and by the acrid scent of her fear, the sudden constriction in her veins, my guess is that she's preparing to fight. Not run.*

Kagen nodded in agreement. *What say you, warrior*? he asked Marquis. *Is it time to meet the natives? Find out a bit more about this oddly picturesque yet repulsive land?*

Marquis grunted his permission, and it was all Kagen needed to proceed.

He instantly teleported from where he stood and reappeared just as suddenly about two feet in front of the bush. Reaching down to extend a hand, he gave the woman a quiet command. "Come out from underneath the bush, sweeting."

The woman moved incredibly fast for a human. She sprang to her knees, rocked back on her heels, and immediately released an arrow from a crude, makeshift bow, the missile heading straight for Kagen's heart.

Kagen caught the arrow in his right hand and crushed it on impact, but before he could reach out to stop her, she released two more arrows, each in quick succession. *By all the gods, she was skilled with that weapon.* Kagen swatted the last two arrows away and reached for the bow. He snatched it out of her hand, flung it over his right shoulder, and scooped her up by the crook of her arm before she could even register what had happened.

And then he let go of her and took a measured step back.

The female was literally quaking in her animal-hide boots, her stunning aquamarine eyes as wide as saucers. Her impossibly thick, wavy hair was the color of burnt copper with fiery red highlights interspersed throughout, and it stood up in several places—no doubt, mussed by the prickly branches of the bush—so that she looked like a wild-thing from the nearby swamps, fiercely beautiful, inconceivably rare, and despite her obvious fear, angry as a rattlesnake.

She was dressed in some primitive outfit from a time long gone, the hide of some native beast wrapped around her torso, from the left side of her neck to the right side of her waist, leaving one shoulder bare. The garment clung to her midriff and descended to her thighs, before dividing into two long flaps that covered an equally crude pair of leggings. The leggings were tucked inside a thick pair of boots, and the entire visage practically screamed *Amazon, queen of the jungle*. She was fairly tall and unmistakably lean, with all the right curves in all the right places, and the clear definition of the muscles in her arms belied the fact that she was in spectacular shape: She was a warrior of some standing.

Kagen held up both hands in a defensive posture. "I mean you no harm, little warrior." He eyed the quiver at her back and tapped the bow, the one he had taken just moments before, with respect. "As long as you make no further attempts to harm me."

The woman's eyes darted frantically from one end of the clearing to the next—she was obviously trying to map out an escape, to determine whether or not she could get away.

"You won't get far," Kagen said softly, trying to relax the rasp in his voice. "What is your name?"

Her aquamarine eyes grew even bigger—if that was possible—and by the tortured look on her exquisite face, one would have sworn the healer had just asked her to remove her clothes. She pursed her lips together in defiance and angled her jaw upward, refusing to answer.

Kagen pushed gently into her mind. "Arielle Nightsong…that's an unusual name."

She staggered backward. "What? How? Who are you?"

Just then, Marquis, Nathaniel, and Nachari approached, and the terrified woman bolted in fear. She shoved at Kagen's chest, barely moving him an inch, and then tried to duck around his wide shoulders before tearing off to the left and running straight into Marquis's implacable girth.

She screamed like a cougar, twisting this way and that, trying to break out of his hold.

Marquis instantly stole her voice—he blocked all sound from emerging—lest she alert an enemy to their presence.

She reached up for her throat and stroked her larynx impulsively, her hand quivering with barely concealed panic. She tried several times to speak before falling to her knees and cowering on the ground.

Back up a bit, Marquis, Kagen suggested on the family bandwidth. *We don't want her to die of fright before we have a chance to question her.* He bent to address the cowering woman at eye level. "My brother would be happy to return your voice, but you must agree to stop screaming." He held her gaze with one of compassion. "Do I have your word?"

Arielle nodded slowly, staring blankly at each male before her like a deer staring into a pair of blinding headlights.

"Very well," Kagen said. He nodded at Marquis.

The Ancient Master Warrior released her voice and harrumphed. "You are wasting our precious time, female. The sooner you answer our questions, the sooner we can scrub your memory of this unfortunate event and get on about our business. So just be quiet and cooperate."

"Tactful, Marquis," Nachari said.

The warrior leveled a warning glance at the wizard.

Tears filled Arielle's eyes, and she shivered uncontrollably. "Please," she whimpered, "I don't want any trouble. I just…I just…"

Her cowering was a ruse.

As she stammered before them, she reached into her tunic and withdrew a hidden short-sword from a thin leather sheath, gripping it like one who knew how to wield it. *Great celestial gods, she was going to fight them to the death, even though she stood no chance, whatsoever, of prevailing in the battle.* With a sudden burst of speed, she slashed sideways at Kagen's chest, managing to draw the tip of the blade across his right pectoral muscle. Although the clever maneuver failed to draw blood, she didn't appear daunted. She leapt to her feet with amazing dexterity and lunged at Marquis in one fluid motion, placing the full weight of her body into the stab.

Marquis flew back, moving instantly out of her reach, and then he held out a hand to keep her at bay. "Stop this, at once," he grumbled. "Are you daft?" And then he reached out slowly to grab her arm.

She spun around in a circle, crouching as she revolved in order to evade his hold, and then she leapt backward like a gazelle, landing with both legs and one arm braced against the ground, the short-sword still brandished in her free hand, her proud jaw tilted upward to meet the warrior's stare head-on.

Marquis's typically stoic features registered surprise at the female's audacity, and then he rolled his dark eyes in annoyance and took a single step forward to end the battle, once and for all. By the way he raised his hand and angled it toward her head, he intended to paralyze her where she stood, reduce her to a granite statue—perhaps one of bravery and courage—but a statue nonetheless.

The woman jolted, almost as if Marquis had struck her, and then she slowly stood to her full height and glared at him, open mouthed, as she instinctively lowered her sword to her side.

Perhaps she has chosen to acquiesce after all, Marquis said telepathically, sounding relieved.

Her eyelids fluttered rapidly several times, as if a small butterfly had taken possession of the frail skin, and then she tilted her head at a peculiar angle and nearly gawked at Nachari. *Surely the male's striking good looks had not halted a warrior such as she in the midst of a life-and-death struggle, but then again, Kagen had seen stronger reactions to the wizard's good looks before…*

She cleared her throat.

Twice.

As if all at once testing her voice.

And then she took an unwitting step forward toward Nachari. "Did you just call him *Marquis*?"

Nachari's eyes opened wide with curiosity. "I did. Why?"

"*Marquis*?" she repeated. "Like the angular cut of a diamond?" She didn't wait for an answer. Rather, she stared at Nachari like he had just descended from the heavens and walked on water, measuring every little nuance of his features with scrutinizing interest: his eyes, his nose, his jaw, even the shape of his lips. Then she turned and did the same to Nathaniel and Kagen, each male in turn. "You're vampires, aren't you?" she murmured, her voice reflecting a considerable measure of awe in its depth.

"And what do you know of our kind?" Marquis asked. He was beginning to grow wary.

Arielle slowly released her breath. She lifted her free hand tentatively, almost like she was going to touch Nachari softly on the cheek, and then she quickly pulled it away and tucked it beneath her arm. "Your eyes…they're so green…like the forest trees in a moonlit valley. Woodland emeralds wrapped in celestial light." She turned toward Marquis and winced, clearly afraid to provoke him but obviously compelled to continue. "And yours; they're so black they're nearly blue." She spoke the words with reverence. "And you're built like a mountain." She almost laughed then, but caught herself before the mirth sprang forth. She turned to Nathaniel and gently cocked her head to the other side—she was staring so intently it was unnerving. "And this one is devious to his soul, his gaze as dark and enchanting as the ocean floor."

Her eyes misted with tears, and that's when Marquis lost his patience. He shifted nervously in his heavy boots. "What is your malfunction?" he jeered. "Are you touched in the head or something, woman?"

Ignoring his comment, Arielle turned to Kagen. "And one has brown hair, the color of milk chocolate with almond swirls lightly intermixed, and his eyes are just as rich, only they shimmer with an unspoken depth in the centers, silver, like the autumn moon." She took a careful step back then, sheathed her short-sword, and brought her hands to her face, where she grasped her cheeks in disbelief. "The one called Kagen."

Kagen swallowed his surprise. *Now this was getting freaky.* "How do you know my name?"

She arched her brows, displaying a bit of her inner fire. "How do you know mine?"

"Don't play games, woman!" Marquis growled. He was clearly not in the mood for banter.

She shook her head. "Sorry, I didn't mean to…" Her voice trailed off, and she grinned. And when she did, the entire clearing smiled with her: The sun was brighter, the timber wolf moon was lighter, and the surrounding vegetation seemed to sharpen with intensity.

Kagen tried again. "How do you know my name?"

She giggled unabashedly. "Then you *are* Kagen…*Silivasi*?"

Kagen raised his shoulders and nodded his head slowly. "Yes."

She turned to the wizard next. "And you are Nachari?"

Nachari furrowed his brow. "I am."

When she turned to Nathaniel, their eyes met in a knowing glance, and both of them spoke the word as one: "Nathaniel."

Marquis seemed positively dumbfounded. He cleared his throat and tried to speak, but no words came out.

Arielle placed her hand on her heart. "I know you…because I know your father."

Kagen's entire body shook. He could hardly contain his hope. "You know our father, or you *knew* our father?"

Arielle nodded emphatically. "I *know* your father…I know Keitaro."

Marquis staggered backward; Nathaniel swayed to the side;

and Nachari placed an unsteady hand on Kagen's arm, trying to maintain his own equilibrium. "Don't lie to us," the wizard whispered. His voice was thick with desperation.

Arielle shook her head. "I would never do such a thing. By all the ancestors, Keitaro has suffered like no other. He has waited hundreds of years for this day. And yet, he never thought it would come. *I* never thought it would come."

The words made Kagen ecstatic, and then they made him queasy—*Keitaro has suffered like no other*—but he couldn't let his mind go there. Not now. Not when they were so close to learning about their father's whereabouts, perhaps even learning how to rescue him, after 480 years. "Who are you to Keitaro?" Kagen asked, unashamed of the raw emotion that surfaced in his voice.

Arielle's eyes softened with compassion, and her voice intensified with sincerity. "I am the daughter of his heart." She spoke proudly. "And he is the father of mine."

Kagen and Nathaniel traded an intimate glance, in the way that only twins could, and the depth of emotion, their shared relief, was as palpable as the bond between them. Kagen could not believe their good fortune—what were the odds that the first person they met in Mhier would know Keitaro…and be his friend? Surely, the gods were with them.

Nachari took Arielle's hand in his and squeezed it eagerly. "Tell us. Please. Tell us *everything*."

Marquis finally gathered his composure. He glanced around the clearing and frowned. "Not here. Not now. We should retreat someplace safe."

"Of course," Arielle agreed, albeit reluctantly. "Yes." She eyed a nearly concealed path just beyond the bank of the swamp, approaching a grove of trees. "The warriors in the Rebel Camp will not be happy to learn that there are new vampires in the land, and Thane's men"—she shivered as she spoke the name—"well, needless to say, we need to avoid them at all costs."

"Is there someplace we can go?" Nathaniel asked, hurriedly. It was clear that he was growing impatient.

Arielle glanced over her shoulder absently as if expecting to find someone there. "I suppose we could try to conceal ourselves in the Skeleton Swamps, but that's—"

"Hell no!" Nachari interrupted. "I'm not going back in there."

Marquis held up his hand to silence the wizard. "Anywhere else?"

"If we make it to the gorge, there are some very large rocks and boulders."

"But it's still not entirely safe?" Nathaniel asked.

Arielle nodded. "No place in Mhier is safe. Well…except…there is a small system of caves at the base of the Mystic Mountains. As far as we know, the lycans have no idea the caves are there. It should be safe *enough* for however long it takes." She grimaced as she gave it further thought. "But the caves are a good eight hours away."

Marquis considered her words carefully. "Flying is out," he said, to no one in particular. "Too risky."

Kagen knew exactly what the Ancient Master Warrior was referring to—invisibility was always tricky: While most vampires could render themselves invisible, it took a great deal of concentration to hold an additional object in an unseen state for a significant period of time…let alone another person. At best, the Silivasis might be able to cloak their packs and their munitions for a couple of minutes, over a couple of miles. Add Arielle to the mix, and the whole thing was an accident waiting to happen.

Marquis shrugged as if his mind was made up. "I guess we're walking."

"That's fine," Nachari said. "If it means being safe, it's better to wait."

All at once, Arielle began to turn a pale shade of blue. Her eyes grew dim, and her hands began to tremble at her sides. "*Oh gods*," she muttered, frantically, "but we don't have much time."

"What do you mean?" Marquis asked.

"Today is already Wednesday," Arielle explained. "On

Sunday, your father may be killed in the arena."

Kagen's heart stopped beating in his chest. *Killed in the arena?* "What does that mean?"

To her credit, Arielle didn't mince words. "King Thane scheduled a public execution in the arena—he intends to kill his wife while all the realm looks on. Your father is being used as an opening act for the games. He'll be fighting Cain Armentieres, one of Thane's alpha generals, but not in a fair match. I just know the king intends to see them both killed before it's all over."

Nathaniel sucked in a harsh, ragged breath, and Nachari rocked back on his heels.

Kagen grew eerily calm, yet something inside of him stirred, dangerously.

"How far away is this *arena*?" Marquis barked, practically spitting the last word.

"Two or three days' travel, if you don't run into any of Thane's guards," Arielle answered. She looked positively ill.

"We can get there much sooner if we have to," Kagen insisted, no longer addressing the female warrior: Time was too critical, and he and his brothers needed to devise a plan…

Yesterday.

"But not without a plan," Marquis said gravely; clearly, they were on the same page. "Not without knowing all that Arielle knows first." He leveled a brutally honest gaze at his brothers. "We may only have one chance to get this right, and only the gods know what kind of odds we are facing. We need to go to these caves, and we need to get there *now*."

"We can make it in half the time if we jog…an hour if we run," Nachari offered.

"Agreed," Nathaniel said. He shared a knowing glance with Kagen, and his eyes heated with the intensity of his telepathic words: *This woman's well-being and our father's are intertwined. While we must keep her safe at all costs, we have* much *to learn in a small amount of time.*

Kagen nodded, understanding the unspoken implication:

There was no time for niceties.

He turned to face the clearly distraught human and smiled placidly to distract her. "Where are the caves, Arielle?"

She started to answer, but Kagen didn't wait—he didn't dare waste a single moment.

He burrowed into her mind and took the information, trying to be as gentle as possible. "I've got it," he told his brothers, and then he met Arielle's startled expression head-on. "Sleep, little one," he commanded, and she fell into his arms.

"I'll take the cache of ammo," Marquis said gruffly.

"And I'll take your pack with the blood, venom, and meds," Nathaniel said. He slid the heavy pack off the warrior's shoulders, even as Marquis reached down to heft the large chest of ammo and balance it on his back.

"I've got everything else," Nachari chimed in, referring to the excess tents and bedrolls, which he quickly detached from the other packs and tethered to his own.

Kagen transferred Arielle's bow to his left arm, adjusted his own pack, and hefted the slumbering woman, along with her quiver, over his remaining, dominant shoulder, shifting her into the most comfortable position possible. "I'm ready."

"Lead the way," Marquis barked.

And just like that, Kagen Silivasi and his brothers began to jog with their heavy burdens in tow…and then, they began to sprint.

As they became nothing more than a coursing blur, blazing across the landscape, an *impression* of light, sound, and speed, Kagen couldn't help but think about the sudden turn of events: the incredible good fortune and the imminent, unspeakable threat.

And all the while, Arielle slept…

Peacefully.

Unknowing.

The cornered queen in a high-stakes game of chess.

She was like a captive bird in the healer's hands, a rare, invaluable treasure, and Kagen Silivasi had no intention of letting the native Mhieridian go.

ten

Arielle struggled to contain her emotions, to conceal her mounting fear, and to process all the vampires had told her, *and done to her*, thus far. On one hand, this was more than she had ever hoped for, the first real opportunity to help Keitaro Silivasi significantly—in fact, a real chance to save him from his endless captivity and torture—but on the other hand, the fearsome creatures had put her to sleep without her permission, carried her to the cave as if she were nothing more than a sack of potatoes, and now, they were asking things of her that left her quaking in her boots.

An offering of her blood, for starters.

She drew the blanket Nachari had given her more tightly around her shoulders, scooted closer to the crackling fire, situated at the cave's center, for warmth—and just how had the healer started it with his hand, anyhow?—and she tried to quiet her mind. The healer—*Kagen*—had explained that the blood exchange was necessary: The brothers could use it to track her at will if the need arose. In other words, no matter where she went in Mhier, they could find her as long as they had taken her blood.

Arielle wasn't sure if that fact was reassuring or terrifying. They were Keitaro's sons, after all, and this gave her more than just a small measure of comfort: Keitaro would not have raised a male without nobility at his core, yet a supernatural creature was a supernatural creature; and Arielle knew all too well what males could do when their power remained unchecked. No parents could ensure that their offspring never made a wrong choice or went down an errant path, no matter how well they were raised.

"Are you okay?" Kagen's silky voice interrupted her thoughts. He seemed to be the one taking the lead most of the time, and it only made sense, in a way. Considering that both she and Kagen were healers, they had a natural connection, a host of things in common outside of their love for Keitaro.

And that last truth was self-evident, the fact that all of Keitaro's sons clearly revered him, that they were practically desperate to get him back.

"I'm fine," she answered meekly, turning her attention back to the vampires' second enormous request: They wanted to read her memories, every last one, starting from the day she was born. As the healer had explained, there was just too much information in her head to garner it all in a day. There were things that might be important, things that might get overlooked, and there were details that a human might not think to relay—scents, impressions, background information—things that might prove invaluable in a critical moment. And every moment from this point forward was as critical as critical could be. In short, they wanted to know everything there was to know about the lycans, everything there was to know about Mhier, and everything Arielle knew about Keitaro. And they wanted to know it all *right now*.

Since Arielle's mind was a ripe treasure chest full of more information than they could ever hope to obtain by listening to her stories or her firsthand accounts, they expected her to share the booty, without hesitation.

Arielle sighed, feeling as lost as she was overwhelmed.

Unfortunately, there was a lot more in her mind than memories of the realm and Keitaro: There were feelings about her father, Ryder, the one who had never loved her or claimed her. There were Walker's embarrassing advances and her own girlish hopes and dreams. She wasn't sure just how much they could take from her psyche, but she figured if she had once thought it, wished it, or dreamed it, it would surely be there. Open to their perusal.

"Is it the blood…or the memories?" Kagen asked, his soft voice washing over her skin like a gentle ray of sunshine. *Bless the Ancient Ones*; these vampires were too powerful for their own good. And Kagen, he had a way about him that was especially dangerous, particularly to the female persuasion. The way all that rugged brown hair hung loose about his eyes, the way he modulated his voice to make sure it seeped beneath one's skin, and the way he flirted, however unintentionally, with his eyes and his gestures, that powerful, masculine frame; all of it was deadly. And Arielle had no doubt that he used *all* his assets on purpose.

"The blood." She led with the scariest proposition first. "It won't hurt, right?"

"And even if it did?" Marquis cut in from across the fire. The huge, surly vampire was quickly growing impatient, and although he scared the wits right out of her, Arielle couldn't help but feel compassion for his situation. After all, Marquis was exactly as Keitaro had described him, and that made his rough demeanor a little easier to take.

"Of course, I would endure pain for Keitaro," Arielle said, understanding the Ancient Master Warrior's true question. "I'm just trying to understand—"

Kagen waved his hand through the air to silence her, and then he leveled a heated gaze at Marquis. "You don't have to answer every question, just because he asks." He winked at her, and her stomach did an odd little flip.

"Of course she does," Marquis grumbled. And then, blessedly, he turned his attention back to a map of Mhier and the side-conversation he was having with Nathaniel.

Kagen appraised her thoughtfully. "So if it isn't the blood, then it's the memories. The intimate nature of your thoughts."

Arielle felt abominable.

Selfish.

Beyond reprehensible.

"I'm sorry," she whispered.

Kagen shrugged and rotated his hands, turning both palms up in a gesture of forbearance. "Feelings aren't necessarily right or wrong, sweeting. They simply are." He smiled, a gentle, reassuring grin. "But it's what we choose to do with them that defines our character."

She groaned, feeling even worse, and he reached out and took her hand, rotating his thumb in soft but firm caresses over the inside of her wrist. Over her pulse and her median vein.

"Stop," she whispered in a rush, pulling her hand away. "You're using your powers to influence me."

"I am," Kagen admitted, unapologetically. He leaned in closer and held her gaze in an unblinking stare. "Arielle, you must know that we are trying to approach this situation with as much diplomacy as possible…*for your sake.*" He looked off into the distance before returning to her eyes. "That we don't wish to cause you pain or discomfort…*or fear.* But that these questions have already been answered." He sighed, as if the words weighed heavily on his shoulders. "Your permission is a formality, beautiful warrior. *Keitaro is our father.* We would oppose the gods themselves to save him, and we will leave no stone unturned in our attempt. We may only get one try." He paused to modulate his voice, to try to make it softer. "Tell me then, how can we make the taking of your blood *and your memories* easier on you? Since it really isn't a question as to whether or not it will happen."

Marquis looked up from the map, measured the two of them, and then nodded his head in approval. And didn't that just make Arielle feel like jumping up and running. She chose to muster her courage instead. "Which one of you has the most experience?" she asked, getting straight to the point. "I mean with each one."

Kagen's perfectly arched brows shot up, and a sly smile crossed his sultry mouth. "Mmm, well, when it comes to *feeding*, taking blood"—he corrected himself—"we are Vampyr, sweeting, so all of us have a wealth of experience. I assure you, you won't experience any discomfort. If anything, you may experience a slight euphoria."

Arielle eyed him sideways and grimaced, clutching the blanket more closely to her chest. That was the last thing she wanted: to experience a *slight euphoria* while one of Keitaro's sons had their fangs lodged in her neck. She had no desire to act a fool or a besotted dolt in front of these powerful creatures. She nervously licked her lips and shuddered. "And taking memories?"

"It's painless, Arielle. We don't even need to touch you." He leaned in a little bit closer. "Although, considering that we wish to…procure them all…it would probably be more expedient, easier for the one who takes your blood, to absorb your memories as well, at the same time. Whoever takes them can share them with the others, so you only have to experience it once."

Arielle nodded with understanding. "And all of you are equal at doing this?"

Kagen appeared to consider her words carefully. "No, not really." He seemed to be searching for just the right way to explain things. "I am a healer, so I can enter your mind with more precision—and more speed—than most, but Nachari is a wizard. He is not only adept at absorbing one's thoughts, but he is expertly trained in all matters of the mind, in manipulation. He can retract memories or implant them. He can read the finest nuances of *thought* as well as the soul of the one he is reading, so that his *work* is a masterpiece of both pragmatic skill and intuition. I would say Nachari is our most advanced practitioner."

The Master Wizard looked up from his lone perch, cattycorner from Kagen and Arielle, and smiled that warm, breathtaking grin of his, and Arielle's mind was immediately placed at ease. "Nachari then," she said, deciding to just hurry up and get it over with. "The sooner this is behind us, the sooner you can all begin to ask your many questions."

"Very well," Kagen said, rising gracefully from his seat on the cave floor, almost as if his body didn't rise at all, but unfolded in an upward, fluid motion. "Wizard," he called, glancing at Nachari and nodding.

Nachari rose with the same graceful ease and poise, and as he padded across the cave, approaching them from behind, his soft gait had the unmistakable stealth of a wildcat about it.

Kagen quickly stepped aside, and Nachari closed the distance, sidling up to Arielle's back, dropping into an effortless crouch behind her, and immediately encircling her shoulders with one large arm. "Be at ease, sister," he whispered in her ear, at once imparting her with both peace and tranquility. He tightened his hold on her shoulders and ran the backs of his fingers along the nape of her neck, just below her hairline, as if he had done it a thousand times before.

Despite the fact that she hated to lose control, Arielle felt her lashes flutter, her eyelids grow heavy, and her muscles begin to relax, even as her body sank back against his. "Nachari," she whispered in alarm, afraid of what was happening.

"Shh," he whispered dreamily, continuing to stroke her neck. "Lean into me and just…let…go."

Arielle, indeed, felt euphoric, and he hadn't even pierced her skin yet. His warm presence, his hypnotic voice—even his powerful stature—somehow commanded submission and coaxed trust. She moaned softly as he drew his fangs along her jugular, and her breathing grew shallow the moment he nicked the outer layer of her skin.

And that's when Kagen growled.

Not like a brother.

Not like a healer.

Not like a vampire simply clearing his throat—if that's what vampires did—but like a wild, hungry animal defending a piece of raw meat.

Through the corner of her hooded eyes, Arielle watched as Kagen's supple lips grew taut and retracted from his gums, as they drew back to expose a lethal set of elongating fangs. His eyes burned suddenly crimson, and his skin seemed to practically glow with ferocity.

Nachari froze in mid-bite.

"Healer?" Marquis's voice resounded from across the cave. "What are you doing?"

Kagen snarled, and he dropped into a low crouch, almost as if he were about to pounce—*on Nachari.*

Nathaniel flew to his feet. "Whoa there, Dr. J. *What the hell?*"

Kagen's head tilted slowly to the side, and the motion was eerily serpentine in nature. His lips twitched in feral spasms, and he had trouble forming his next word: "*Mine.*" He spoke in a harsh, guttural rasp.

"Excuse me?" Nathaniel said softly, his tone a measured, even drawl.

Kagen rocked on his heels, the powerful muscles in his thighs flexing with the desire to spring forward, and by the savage look on his face, it was evident that the vampire was beyond reasoning or control.

Nathaniel caught the healer just as he pounced.

He wrapped him up in midair, locked his muscular arms tightly around his chest, and jerked him away from Nachari, just before his fangs could sink home. "Get a hold of yourself, Kagen!" Nathaniel shouted. His voice was no longer gentle.

The tussle that ensued was monstrous to put it mildly.

The vampires somersaulted across the cave. They slammed into an adjacent stony wall, kicking up dirt, rock, and gravel in their wake, and the mountain beneath them began to groan. They snarled, bit, and traded punches, the unholy blows far more violent than any human could have ever endured.

Finally, Marquis stood up, took one hard look at the twins rolling around on the cave floor like feral animals, and barked an imperious command. "Nachari! Back away from Arielle."

Nachari immediately released her and teleported to the back of the cave, his enigmatic green eyes bulging in their sockets as he watched the scene unfold with horrified shock and disbelief.

"Kagen!" Marquis barked next. "*Look.* He's gone. *He let her go.*"

The healer looked up, glancing beyond his twin's shoulder, and he seemed momentarily disoriented and confused, at an utter loss as to what was happening, or what he intended to do next.

"He's gone," Marquis repeated, rolling his angry eyes in disgust.

Kagen stumbled to his feet. He stared at the empty space where Nachari had just been, then across the cave at Marquis, as if for confirmation.

"By all means," the Ancient Master Warrior snarled, "you may be the one to do it."

Arielle recoiled. She turned on her heels and started to run, not at all sure where she was going.

Nachari looked utterly exasperated as his pleading eyes met hers. "Don't run, Arielle," he called after her. "You'll only make it worse."

Kagen stepped swiftly to the side, blocking her retreat with his formidable body, and in that rare, pregnant moment, Arielle knew that the instinct that drove him was not hunger or the need to save his father, but a fierce, animalistic need to undo whatever Nachari had done.

To claim the other vampire's territory as his own.

She shrank back, and then she nearly fainted as he reached out to take her, swept her up in his arms, and cradled her to his chest like a weightless child.

Before she could scream or protest, he bent his head to her neck, his thick brown locks fanning out like a preternatural veil to give them some privacy, and sank his fangs deep into her throat.

"*Damn!*" Nachari cursed from the back of the cave.

Nathaniel dusted off his clothes, whistled low beneath his breath, and took a tentative step toward them—but he didn't interfere.

And Marquis? He just snorted with derision and turned his back on the whole primitive scene.

And that was the last thing Arielle saw.

Swept up in the intensity of the vampire's emotion, in his fierce, unyielding need to dominate her will, she felt her body go limp in his arms; and then a pleasure she could only describe as unconscionably erotic swept through her body like a firestorm, blazing across a dry, wild prairie. Despite the fact that she had no experience with such things, her body tingled from head to toe, like the two of them were making love.

She shuddered and grasped at his arms for purchase, afraid that she might just spiral into the cosmos, forever lost in a heightened state of unimaginable bliss.

"Gods," she moaned inadvertently, embarrassed to her core by her carnal reaction, yet knowing all the while that the vampire was wringing it out of her, immersing her in pleasure, all in some primal need to prove that he could. When at last her body splintered in his arms, fracturing outward from her womb to her hips and thighs, traveling down her torso to her knees and then her toes, she thought she might just die of shame.

It hadn't been an orgasm, so to speak—at least she didn't think it had been—rather, her soul had come apart, her heart had fractured into a thousand little pieces, and her body had wept for mercy beneath the unrelenting onslaught of sensation. It had been a command, a directive, an imperious yet desperate plea.

A prayer, for lack of any other description.

And Kagen would not have stopped until it had happened.

As the vampire slowly seemed to regain his senses, Arielle held her breath. She could feel his touch—it was much more gentle now, much more controlled and deliberate—snaking through her mind, slowly reaching back in time, farther and farther, until at last, he arrived at the beginning, the memories she herself no longer had access to. And then, one by one, he slowly moved forward, absorbing each one into his own consciousness.

Finally, when Kagen had consumed all that she was—as a child, as a warrior, and now, as a woman—he withdrew his fangs and set her gently down on the earthen floor.

She immediately cowered and covered her body with her arms—she felt positively naked before him—and the look on his tortured face was one of absolute regret and utter humiliation.

"Forgive me," he said, his voice a barren whisper. His mouth dropped open and his arms fell to his sides. "I don't know what happened to me, Arielle. I…I…" He raised a trembling hand, ran it through his hair, and glanced up at Nathaniel. "Brother..." His voice was hoarse with regret.

Nathaniel held up both hands in question, as if to say, *Yeah, please; explain this one, if you dare.*

"There are no words," Kagen said softly. The anguish in his eyes was real. Raw. Guileless. He turned toward the back of the cave, and when his eyes met Nachari's, he slowly shook his head. "Wizard...*Nachari*."

"Mr. Hyde?" Nachari echoed warily. "Are you good?"

Kagen momentarily shut his eyes. "It wasn't *that*, Nachari. I don't know *what it was*... and yes, I'm fine now." He turned back toward Arielle and visibly cringed. "Daughter of my father's heart, please...don't cover yourself like that."

Arielle averted her eyes in humiliation and shuffled a few steps away.

"Just what the hell was that?" Marquis demanded, taking a bold stride in Kagen's direction.

Kagen looked at Arielle and studied her closely. "Show me your arm," he commanded, albeit in a much gentler voice. It was as if he were trying valiantly to maintain his dignity, to repair a hopelessly awkward moment.

"Pardon me?" Arielle asked, even more uncertain.

"Your wrist," Kagen clarified. "Show it to me."

Arielle turned her right arm over and held it up to his gaze.

He quickly shook his head. "No. Show me the other one."

She reluctantly held it forward.

Kagen stared at the smooth, unmarred skin for what almost felt like an eternity, although just *what* he was looking for, Arielle couldn't say. She followed his gaze as he studied her perfect flesh more closely—one line, one contour, one vein at a time—his face a mask of sweeping emotions, from expectancy to confusion...to blank resignation. And then, as if he didn't have a clue, he simply shrugged his shoulders and shook his head. "Then...I don't know." He seemed to be speaking primarily to Marquis. "I just...don't know."

Arielle averted her gaze. The contact was far too intimate,

and she felt like there was something so much deeper going on… She was almost sorry she had been a part of the whole sordid episode—it was almost as if she had caused it somehow—although she couldn't possibly imagine what she might have done wrong.

Much to her chagrin, Kagen took a cautious step forward and cupped her face in his hands. He touched her with such exquisite gentleness and care that a lump formed in her throat. "I swear to you, Arielle Nightsong," he said in a whisper, "in a thousand years, I have never harmed or forced myself upon a woman." He reached into his cloak and withdrew a thin, sharp dagger, the perilous blade polished to a dazzling shine, and then he placed the pommel in her hand. "If I ever do anything like that again, use this to defend yourself."

Arielle drew back, appalled.

She shook her head adamantly, refusing to take the weapon, and her voice quivered with the strength of her resolve. "I could never do such a thing, not to one of Keitaro's sons." She cleared her throat and somehow found a steadier tone. "You didn't harm me, Kagen. I'm not injured. I'm just….just so terribly embarrassed."

He nodded, as if he truly understood, and then he pulled her into the most tender embrace she had ever felt. "Never, sweeting," he whispered in her ear. "*Never.*" He nuzzled her hair with his chin and crooned to her in a lyrical voice, almost as if she were a child, cradled in his arms. "Arielle, I have seen your memories…*your soul*…and you are incomparably beautiful. A rare and unblemished jewel. What you have done for our father…what you have *meant* to Keitaro…" His voice faded into silence, and his eyes clouded with pressing tears, a well of emotion he would never release. "I am honored that you took my passion and returned it, and I will spend whatever short time we have here in Mhier trying to earn your forgiveness. I am *so sorry*, little warrior. I am…*so*…very sorry."

Nachari cleared his throat and strolled cautiously forward, emerging reluctantly from the rear of the cave. "I guess no good deed goes unpunished," he quipped, eyeing Kagen sideways. He seemed to be trying for humor, but it fell just a little bit short.

Kagen looked at him with abject apology burning in his eyes. "Nachari?"

The wizard smiled, however faintly, and then he slowly shrugged his shoulders. "That was *bizarre*, Master Healer," he said. And then he threw up his hands. "Next time, just ask."

Nathaniel sauntered back to his place on the other side of the fire, as if the matter were simply and indelibly closed. He turned his attention back to Marquis and the map. "Never too old to get into an old-fashioned scuffle with your twin," he mumbled beneath his breath. It was clearly his way of dismissing the entire episode.

"Perhaps," Marquis said circumspectly. "However, I think the healer is the one who needs therapy now." If Arielle didn't know better, she would have thought the rigid vampire was trying to make a joke, perhaps an inside jest, but his husky voice lacked the requisite humorous intonation; and she had no desire to ask what he meant.

Nachari and Nathaniel laughed just the same, and the sudden merriment broke some of the tension. Even Arielle tried to brush it off at this point. After all, the deed was done. Kagen had her blood—that fact was indisputable—and he also had her memories. They had much more important things to get on with now.

Still, she couldn't help but think of the white owl and the omen that had occurred just twenty-four hours before at the ternary streams: *a song of blood beneath the moon.*

The white owl had come for her, and whatever the omen meant, Kagen Silivasi had everything to do with it.

She had felt it as clearly as she knew her name to be Arielle.

When his soul had joined with hers.

And hers had responded in kind.

Napolean Mondragon, the ancient king of the Vampyr, strolled onto the veranda at the front of his regal manse and stared at the enchanting sky. His eyes were filled with wonder and trepidation—he could hardly believe what he was seeing—what was happening before his ancient eyes.

The canvass was as dark as pitch.

The moon was as sanguine as blood.

And the northern region of the Milky Way was a virtual cornucopia of intersecting stars and lights, each element blending into a celestial tapestry that reflected a singular, ancient constellation: Auriga, the Charioteer.

Kagen Silivasi's ruling Blood Moon.

Napolean tried once more to reach the Master Healer with telepathy, but the communication would not go through. It was as if he were trying to push a feather through a solid brick wall—there was simply no momentum, no power behind the prod, and the realization was unsettling to say the least.

Turning his attention to the goddess of his birth, he chose to say a prayer for his faithful subject instead: "Great Andromeda, keeper of my soul, protect our native son as he travels through foreign lands. Do not let him die as a result of this Blood Moon. Do not let him perish for failing to claim something he doesn't even know he has."

eleven

Mhier

The silence was nearly deafening in the cave as the Silivasi brothers took their respective positions on their individual bedrolls, surrounding the central fire, and Kagen, at last, shared Arielle's memories with his brothers.

As Keitaro's years in the slave camp finally came into full, vivid view.

As the horrors of the arena played out in real time, up close and personal.

As each of Keitaro's sons finally understood just what life had been like for their beloved sire in Mhier, the horrors King Tyrus Thane had visited upon him out of nothing but sheer cruelty and malice.

It was odd for Kagen, to say the least, being able to *see* his father's face after so many years—and through the exclusive, unique memories of another person, filtered through Arielle's own distinctive and caring perspective. And it was haunting at best to realize just what this precious daughter of Keitaro's heart had meant to him: the joy and the relief, however slight, she had brought into his endless, monotonous life.

Kagen stirred restlessly on his bedroll, eyeing the entrance to the cave for the twentieth time, watching Arielle as she stood with her face uplifted toward the moon, soaking in the lunar rays, almost as if in prayer. He still felt abominable for what had happened earlier, and he knew that she still felt ashamed, vulnerable, and exposed.

When at last the silence seemed like it would linger on forever, Marquis cleared his throat. "So, there we have it then, the truth of our father's life. The question is: what are we going to do about it?"

Nathaniel sat forward, his elbows propped on his knees, and his coal-black eyes glistened with unconcealed anger and resolve. "We are going to kill these lycan bastards, one by one, slowly, painfully, and we are going to take Keitaro out of that damnable slave district."

Marquis's expression hardened, ever the unmovable one. "Yes, but the question is how."

Nachari laid the map of Mhier out on the floor between them, illuminated by the firelight. "I think our greatest chance to get to him will be on Sunday, either right before he's taken into the arena, or right after the games begin."

Marquis stared pointedly at the map. "What is your reasoning, wizard?"

Nachari sighed. He pointed to the various entrances and the U-shaped stands. "There will be a lot of chaos, and Thane will be sitting here." He pointed at the icon drawn to indicate the raised royal platform and inadvertently snarled with disdain. "With all the commotion going on, the inevitable excitement of the crowd, they won't be expecting an invasion, for anything to go off other than as planned. And they won't be in any position to react quickly, to marshal forces in the midst of chaos. I think it all comes down to the element of surprise."

"And what if we are a moment too late? If we misjudge…by even five seconds?" Nathaniel asked.

"We won't be," Marquis said forcefully. "Your plan has merit, Nachari. I was thinking something similar myself." He pointed at the diagram and began to expound on strategy, yet his words drifted into the ether…

"Excuse me, brothers," Kagen said softly, rising from his bedroll. "When I return, you can impart all you've discussed in a psychic stream, so I'll be instantly up to speed. But for the moment, I have some fences to mend."

Nathaniel looked over at Arielle and nodded with quiet understanding. Now that they all knew who she was, what she had done, what her childhood in the slave camp had been like, there would be no objection to seeing to her comfort. For truly, she was the daughter Keitaro had never had, and they were forever in her debt.

"I'll give you this indulgence, healer," Marquis said in an authoritative tone, "but don't take more than a half hour. Your presence is needed here, and not just to hear the briefing, but for your input as well."

"As you wish, brother," Kagen said, declining his head with respect. And then he headed toward the mouth of the cave where the isolated female was waiting.

As he approached, Arielle drew her blanket tighter around her shoulders and sidestepped a few feet away. She fixed her eyes on the ground.

"What can I do?" Kagen asked, not wishing to play any games.

Arielle tried to force a smile, however insincere, and then she looked out, over the ridge, at the beautiful valley below. "What is there to be done?" she finally said. "I am as good as naked before you." Before he could protest, she shook her head and held up her hand to silence him. "And it's not just the…physical piece…what happened. It's the spiritual piece, the emotional exposure." She sighed then, her unique aquamarine eyes growing cloudy with regret. "You know my deepest fears, my greatest regrets, my unvanquished demons…even my unfulfilled longings. You know everything. And I know nothing. I just feel like being alone." She turned to meet his eyes briefly, and her soft gaze was more penetrating than a brandished sword. "If you don't mind."

Kagen exhaled slowly. "I do mind, Arielle. I mind because I'm the cause of it." Strolling to her side, he leaned back against the outer arch of the cave entrance and gazed up at the stars, following her lead. "This is an oddly beautiful land, for a place of such incredible cruelty." He let the words linger, a mere observation.

Arielle nodded, and a piece of her thick, copper-colored hair fell forward into her eyes. Without thinking, Kagen reached out to tuck it behind her ear, and Arielle flinched.

He drew back his hand and frowned. "You fear me?"

Her voice was as hushed as it was hesitant. "A little. Yes."

He swallowed his pride and looked away. And then he crossed one ankle over the other, both arms across his chest, and leaned back, once again, against the stony wall. "Let's see: My deepest fear is letting my family down, my people down, not being able to heal someone who needs it—letting another warrior, wizard, or healer experience what I have endured—the grief or the loss." He angled his body to face her then. "*Right now*, my deepest fear is leaving this land without my father, knowing that I could never live with the outcome." He thought about her words, the various points she had made, and tried to be as candid as he knew how. "And as for my deepest regret, there are two: the fact that I couldn't save my mother on the night the lycans came to our valley, and the fact that I let my baby brother Shelby die at the hands of Valentine Nistor. It would have been so easy to have just been there for him, to have sequestered Dalia until the end of Shelby's Blood Moon…to have prevented the whole thing by being *just a little bit* prepared for the enemy. Not a lot. Just a little."

Now this got Arielle's attention.

She cast a sidelong glance at him and nodded with sympathy. "I was going to ask, earlier, when I only saw the four of you, about Keitaro's blond-haired son, about Nachari's charming twin, but I was afraid to intrude on a matter so personal; and I figured, if he could have been here, he would have been." She looked away and sighed. "I'm sorry, Kagen. I…I'm so sorry."

"Thank you, Arielle," he whispered. "So am I."

Silence seemed to settle between them like dew on morning grass, until finally, she shook her head, raised her chin, and found the courage to continue. "Earlier…when you bit me…you weren't really in control, were you?"

"Not at all," he said, a bit ashamed by the admission. "Not even a little bit, and perhaps that is what scares you the most."

She nodded. "How do I know it won't happen again?"

Kagen looked off into the distance. How could he answer

that? There were simply no words. Besides, he didn't have the answers himself, and that brought him back to her third admission. "You know my unvanquished demons, too. You saw one tonight."

Arielle frowned. "But I thought you said you've never done anything like that before, *lorded your power* over a female."

Kagen tried not to recoil: *lorded your power over a female…*

Damn.

"That's true, never over a female. But…" He tried to find the words to say what he was thinking—he felt he owed her at least that much—after all, she could not take back or hide her vulnerability: Why should he have the privilege of hiding his? "There is something dark inside of me, Arielle. Something that doesn't belong in a healer."

She stared at him pointedly then, urging him to continue with her eyes.

"It's rarely a problem. In fact, it so seldom rears its head that it's almost forgotten…until it's not." He took a deep breath and let it out slowly, trying to collect his thoughts. "And then there are those rare, incalculable moments when it stirs, this darkness, and I know that there is just something so incredibly…broken…at my core that it frightens me." He glanced over his shoulder instinctively. "My brothers call it Dr. Jekyll and Mr. Hyde, this rare but terrible temper, but I just think of it as a demon. And the thing is—the really disturbing part—I don't hate it. In fact, I nurse it. *I need it.* The reason I can function as well as I do is because I know he's always there."

Arielle tucked the same errant locks of hair, the ones that Kagen had almost touched earlier, behind her ear and straightened. "It can't be as bad as all that, not if you're aware of it. Not if you can talk about it."

Kagen chuckled softly then and met her gaze with one of contrition. "I am just over a thousand years old, Arielle Nightsong, and you are the first person I have ever told this to."

Arielle's expression belied her surprise—she looked positively taken aback. "Why?" she exhaled. "I mean, *why me*?"

He took a cautious step in her direction, placed a gentle hand beneath her chin, and lifted her head so that her gaze met his. "Because you are the first person—no, the first woman—I have ever known on such an intimate level."

She inhaled sharply. "But you don't really know me."

"Ah," he mused, "but I do." He became all at once serious. "What happened earlier…*to you*…it was an inexcusable intrusion, and I'm sorry for that. I really am. But for me, it was one of the most intimate moments of my life, and that's not so easy to regret." He leaned in, far too closely, but he just couldn't help it. "I know you felt dishonored, sweeting, but I felt…*privileged.* As crazy as that sounds."

Arielle stared at him intently, as if she could measure the truth of his words by gazing into his eyes. And then, all at once, she turned a deep shade of red, blushing from her head to her toes. "Have you never…*been* with another woman, then?"

Kagen laughed aloud. He didn't mean to. It was just—her question caught him off guard. It was so sweet, so pure…so honest. "I've never *been* with you, Arielle." The corner of his mouth turned up in a smile. "But seriously, *yes*; I have been with other women, many over the centuries"—he thought he might just fall into her eyes and get lost—"but never with anyone as lovely as you. With a soul as beautiful as yours."

Arielle swallowed hard and turned away. She seemed positively flustered. "Just tell me that it won't happen again, and I'll feel a lot better."

Kagen frowned. He wanted so badly to just say *yes,* to tell her what she wanted to hear—and why?—he couldn't say. Maybe it had something to do with how she had cared for Keitaro over the years, or maybe it had something to do with the purity of her heart. Either way, he just couldn't do it. He had begun this conversation with truth, and that was how he intended to end it. "I will tell you this, Miss Nightsong: Nothing physical will happen between us again without your consent, or at least, not until you clearly express a desire…" When she practically tripped over her own two feet trying to back away from him—it wasn't possible; there was a wall behind her—he tried to gentle his voice. "But as for some crazy, impulsive need to claim you, to taste your blood, to feel you beneath me, to mold your passion to match my own, I will try very hard to restrain it, because I don't know where it's coming from; and I don't want to make your life harder than it already is, especially when there is nothing I can give to you long term." He pushed off the cave wall and took several measured steps backward, forcing himself to give her some room to breathe. "But pray that I never meet this Walker Alencion, the human male who placed his hands on you so possessively, without your consent. This *rebel* who forces his affections on you with such callous disregard. Because *that* I would have a hard time ignoring."

As if her throat had suddenly become dry, Arielle swallowed convulsively. "Walker isn't a threat to anyone. He's—"

"It doesn't matter."

"He's my *friend*."

"It doesn't matter."

"But what right do you have—"

Kagen shook his head, repressing the instinct to snarl. "Arielle, it doesn't matter if I have every right or no right at all."

She blanched. "And how is that different from what happened with you…what Walker did?"

This time, Kagen did snarl, low in his throat, and his ire began to rise. "Because Walker has no claim to you, and I do."

Arielle blinked so rapidly she looked like she had dust in her eyes, yet she swallowed her fear and pressed on. "How can you say that? How can you *believe* that? We only just met."

Kagen shook his head in frustration, wishing he could articulate something he could hardly understand. Finally, when the words continued to elude him, he said the most honest thing he could. "*How* doesn't matter."

Her mouth dropped open, and she stared at him blankly, her face a mask of confusion and alarm. "Then you will do whatever you wish, and no matter how much you desire to restrain your impulses, *that* doesn't matter. Because *you* are not in control."

Kagen felt utterly helpless: *Now that had turned out well.* Instead of mending fences, he had pretty much torn them all down. Instead of making the woman feel better, he had made matters worse. Much worse. "That's not true, Arielle." *How the hell did he explain?* He took a generous step forward, cupped her face in his hands, and bent his head until his mouth hovered only inches away from hers. "If I were to do whatever I wished, I would take you into my arms, carry you into the night, and make love to you beneath the moonlight, until you no longer knew your name, until you no longer cared to know your name...until you could no longer speak any name but my own. I would make you feel things and want things, need things and plead for things, you cannot even *imagine* in your lovely innocence." He swallowed hard and backed an inch away. "But as it stands, I will go back into the cave and join my brothers—because *I am* in control." He bent over and placed a chaste kiss on her forehead. "Do not stay out here long, Arielle. The night is dark, and there are shadows all around us. You are safe in our care—*in my care*—perhaps safer than you have ever been before, whether you know this to be true or not."

With that, he turned and walked away.

Arielle struggled to catch her breath as she watched the powerful vampire retreat. Her heart was thundering in her chest; her *good sense* was laid out on the ground; and she was certain that her knees were going to give way any moment. She shivered, trying to come up with an explanation: What had she done to provoke this primitive male so deeply? Surely, she had not led him on...

She watched as he crossed the dark expanse, his lithe form becoming one with the shadows he spoke of, and she tried to control her trembling.

Kagen Silivasi was more than just an enigma—

He was a dangerous, *dangerous* man.

And if she thought Ryder Nightsong had left a hole in her heart, then perhaps she didn't know what true heartbreak felt like, for this male was capable of creating a crater the size of the Mystic Mountains.

She cringed at the very thought of the damage a male like Kagen Silivasi could leave in his wake, at the very idea of being hopelessly in love with a being from another realm. By all that was sacred, a careless moment could leave Arielle pregnant and abandoned, just like her mother, pining away a lifetime of possibility over the memory of a ghost…one who had never been anything more than a thief in the night.

Oh yes, Kagen Silivasi was dangerous, all right.

He was powerful beyond measure; handsome beyond reckoning; and seductive beyond what was safe. And he took whatever he wanted—just because he could.

Arielle Nightsong resolved to remain wary. She would do everything in her power to help Keitaro Silivasi, but she would keep a safe, *safe* distance away from his son.

twelve

For a male accustomed to sleeping on a king-sized mattress, with memory foam and a pillow top to boot, Kagen was sleeping as soundly as he could on the thin, rollaway pallet when he heard soft but distinctly human footfalls approaching the narrow cave opening. His eyes shot open, instantly alert, as he measured the faint patter of gravel shifting beneath heels and toes—they were walking softly, carefully…*deliberately*—and the steady, shallow inhales of breath betrayed no less than four strangers approaching the temporary dwelling.

He immediately sent a gentle pulse of energy into his brothers' minds, all three at once, conveying the imminent presence of the intruders, the presumed number of the entourage, and the obvious need to remain silent as they watched the scene unfold. All four Silivasis rose from their pallets like ghostly apparitions rising from shallow graves. Without hesitation, they rendered their formidable Vampyr bodies invisible and slinked noiselessly into the numerous shadows of the cave, becoming one with the jagged rocks, melting into the shallow crevices, and blending into the stony walls.

They waited.

Perilously alert and listening.

To see what was coming their way.

Kagen swept his eyes across the dimly lit cavern, making note of the single lantern that flickered in the otherwise dark, ominous space, noting how Arielle slept soundly, if not peacefully, on a pile of blankets toward the back of the cave.

Discerning in an instant what would be required to confront the enemy, neutralize the threat, and protect Arielle—all three things at once—he prepared to act with unerring lethality. He had no doubt that Marquis, Nathaniel, and Nachari had just done the same.

As the smell of human sweat and fear drew nearer, he practically held his breath. His fangs slid down from his upper gums, and he prepared to strike in defense of their territory. Their mission. Their unwavering determination to live long enough to rescue Keitaro.

The first intruder to round the corner of the cave entrance was a tall, slender male, about five-foot-eleven, with flame-red hair and pale gray eyes. He held a crude battle-axe in his right hand, and he crouched low on the balls of his feet, prepared to attack at the slightest provocation. Kagen immediately recognized the human from Arielle's memories—it was the rebel called Walker Alencion, the one who had placed his hands on Arielle so crudely. His lips twitched involuntarily, and he suppressed a rising snarl, even as he unconsciously licked his lips like a salivating wolf.

Steady, healer, Nathaniel intoned psychically from across the cave. *Let's see what all awaits us before we dispense of our enemy.*

Kagen blinked several times and nodded. He measured the three strong males at Walker's back: The blond directly behind him, brandishing a heavy sword, was called Kade, and Arielle had described him as forty years old, deliberate in his thinking, and strategic in all his maneuvers. He was a thinker, and he did nothing rash or impulsive. Kagen's eyes darted to the male on Kade's left, a sandy-haired youth of twenty-two years named Echo, with a barbaric, spiked club in his hand. According to Arielle, he was a fierce and unafraid fighter, known for his quick temper and brazen attacks. This one was not afraid to die, and that's what made him dangerous. To the far right was the fourth and last rebel, Neil Potter. His locks were trimmed so close to his scalp, he appeared to be wearing a helmet, and he was, without question, the most experienced fighter of the group. He held a pair of sharpened triangular daggers in both hands, and he had the unmistakable look of a hawk in his dark, brooding eyes.

Kagen regarded Marquis with nothing more than a shift of focused attention, the barest transference of energy toward his eldest brother, their unquestioned leader, to ascertain any immediate orders—if, in fact, there were any.

Marquis felt the probe and responded coolly. *Nathaniel, subdue Walker so that Kagen is not* inclined *to take his life prematurely. Nachari, take the reasoned one with the sword, the one called Kade. I will capture the fierce one, Echo; and Kagen, you will apprehend Neil. At my command,* he added tersely.

So we are to leave them alive…no matter what? Nathaniel drawled lazily in his typical cat-like way, sounding interminably sleepy and more than a little bit bored.

For now, Marquis replied, sounding equally annoyed. His psychic voice relaxed, and he turned his attention to Nachari. *Wizard, what do they want?*

While all vampires could reach into the minds of humans and extract their thoughts with ease, as a Master Wizard, Nachari's touch was virtually undetectable. A pregnant moment passed before Nachari answered his eldest brother circumspectly. *The tall one became worried when Arielle did not return to camp this night; he brought a handful of warriors, including a tracker—I believe Echo has exceptional hunting skills for a human—to trace her steps, and it eventually led them here. They are hoping to rescue Arielle.*

He tracked us by scent alone? Nathaniel asked, sounding mildly surprised, if not slightly impressed. *They could not have moved this quickly by simply studying tracks at night.*

Nachari's voice brightened. *I believe Echo has a small trace of wolf's blood in his veins, although he knows it not. Perhaps that is why he is so wild and fearless.*

Mmm, Marquis replied. *Well, the best laid plans of mice and men…and wolves…*

He didn't finish the familiar refrain.

The approaching rebels drew into tighter formation. They raised their weapons and entered the cave in an organized charge, like warriors hoping to capitalize on the element of surprise, despite not knowing what they were walking into.

"Now!" Marquis barked, this time speaking aloud.

The seizure that ensued was as exact as it was quick and

eventless: Nathaniel descended upon Walker from above with deft precision. He removed the battle-axe from his grip, forced him onto his knees, and fisted his wild red hair in his hand, rendering the human immobile before Walker knew what had hit him. The startled male arched unnaturally forward beneath Nathaniel's pressing knee, his head bent low, and Nathaniel used the opportunity to press the human's face into the dirt. "Do not move a muscle," he ordered with a hiss, as if the human could.

Marquis and Nachari acted at the same time, each male becoming visible in the same instant, as if they no longer felt the need to maintain an element of surprise: Marquis snatched Echo by the back of his collar, lifted him effortlessly off the ground, and shook his spiked wooden club loose from his arms. He held him steady, at eye level, snarled a fearsome warning between gnashing fangs, and then seared an imperious command into his mind, lacing the words in compulsion. "Submit!" There was no need for an entire diatribe, not from Marquis.

Nachari leapt from his position at the back of the cave, practically landing in Kade's footsteps, as if the two males were wearing the same pair of boots. As Kade inhaled sharply in surprise, the wizard paused, waiting for the ensuing exhale, and then he held out his hand, drew back his fingers, and stole the human's breath from his chest, refusing to allow him another breath of air until he clutched at his own throat and dropped his sword in an effort to coax oxygen into his lungs. Nachari watched patiently as Kade folded in on himself, dying from aspiration; and then the wizard kicked the sword away.

Kagen took Neil with as much stealth and ease as his brothers. He plucked both lethal daggers out of the rebel's hands and swiftly tucked them into the waistband of his trousers; and then, with one swift, targeted blow to the male's throat, Kagen dropped him like a sack of potatoes, leaving him agonized and retching on the cave floor, his frantic eyes darting this way and that as if struggling to comprehend what had just happened. Then, and only then, Kagen shimmered into view.

"Welcome to our camp," Nathaniel drawled in a dark, silken

voice, even as all four humans continued to reel from the sudden attack: They scrambled to regain their composure, groped for their missing weapons, and struggled to make sense of what the heck had just happened. "Have a seat around the fire, please," he added wryly.

Just then, Arielle shot up from her repose at the back of the cave. She grasped her bow, as if she had done so a thousand times before, drew a silver-tipped arrow from the quiver beside her bed, and bounded to her feet in one smooth, agile motion. Her reaction was not measured or thought out. She did not assess or identify her enemy. She simply acted with an instinct born of years…*and years*…of training, responding, surviving as an integrated part of a whole: one member of a group coming to the immediate aid of the others, her rebel companions. As she quickly surveyed the scene, her vivid aquamarine eyes heated with fury. She took a cautious step toward the fire, turned her head sharply toward Kagen, and glared at him in defiance. "What is the meaning of this, healer!" Her wild gaze swept to Kade, who was still bent over and gasping for air, and she practically seethed malevolence. "Nachari! Release his throat, *right now*! Let him breathe!" She pointed the arrow directly at the Master Wizard's heart.

"I already released it," Nachari assured her, his own silken voice absent of concern: Either he didn't notice the arrow pointed at his heart, or he didn't feel threatened enough to acknowledge it. Kagen figured it was the latter.

She spun around to face Marquis, who was now carrying Echo to the fire like a puppy being dragged by the scruff, and her face turned three shades of crimson. "Marquis!"

One stern look from the Ancient Master Warrior, and she instantly backed off. Marquis Silivasi was not one to be ordered about by humans, and apparently, the look on his merciless face made that clear.

Arielle took a cautious step backward, lowered her bow, and turned to Kagen, instead. "Kagen, *please*." She sounded so pitiful, so desperate…*so incensed*.

Kagen sighed, but he didn't back down. "Arielle, let us handle this…our way."

She started to nod, albeit reluctantly, and then she caught sight of Walker, still bent over with Nathaniel's knee planted in his back, his face pressed hard into the earthen floor. "Are you kidding me!" she shouted. She immediately rushed to his side. "Walker! Are you all right?" She slapped at Nathaniel's knee, as if the vampire were nothing more than a recalcitrant child, and then she implored him with her eyes. "Nathaniel, stop! *You're hurting him.*"

Before Nathaniel could reply, Kagen snarled deep in his throat—the sound was a feral mixture of warning and surprise. "*Do not,*" he clipped harshly, instantly regretting the harsh authority in his words. The last thing he wanted to do was intimidate Arielle further, or worse, lose his temper and end up tearing Walker's throat out in front of the female. Not only would such a thing likely turn her against him *for good*, but the sight of his animal nature, so unrestrained and primal, might just scar her for the rest of her life.

Yet and still, how could he explain that he had read the male's true intentions within seconds of looking into his duplicitous eyes, that for all of Walker's professed friendship and admiration for Arielle Nightsong, the human was a cauldron of insecurity and raging hormones, as confused as he was loyal, as desperate as he was determined?

How could he explain that Walker was *this close* to crossing the line?

That he had already moved from admiration to stalking, and it was just a matter of time before stalking turned into…rape.

The male may have been her childhood friend, and at one time, he may have truly cared for her like a brother, perhaps even desired her as a man, but her constant denial of his affections had warped him—that, and the untenable life the lycans had forced him to lead. Walker was tired of being the bottom man on the totem pole, and the next step up was subjugating a woman, *taking what he couldn't have.*

Not caring to reveal what was so obvious to his naked, vampiric eye, Kagen sought to find another way to avert disaster—why it mattered so deeply, he just couldn't say—still, he swallowed his anger and tried to soften his tone. "Arielle…"

She looked up at him beneath angry lids, her luminous eyes filled with obvious sympathy for the red-headed human. "What!" Her voice was uncharacteristically clipped.

Kagen licked his lips and suppressed another growl. "Do you remember what happened *earlier*, when Nachari tried to take your blood and your memories?"

Arielle's eyes widened with budding understanding. "Yes." The word was a mere whisper.

Kagen gestured toward Walker with his chin. "Get away from that male." When she didn't respond immediately, he added, "Unless you wish to sentence him to death."

Like someone who had just reached out to pluck a piece of fruit from a tree, only to discover that it was actually a nest of hornets, Arielle froze. She draped her bow over her shoulder, held her hands up in front of her, and slowly backed away from Walker.

Kagen gestured toward the back of the cave, his stark gaze indicating the farthest region of the cavern, well beyond the fire pit.

Shaking her head back and forth in bewilderment, Arielle started toward the back of the cave, heading for the exact spot he had indicated.

And that's when Walker sat up sharply.

His face flushed with righteous indignation, he stared angrily at Kagen and then sneered at Arielle. His insipid gray eyes shot back and forth between the two, and his mouth turned down in a frown. "Arielle, what the hell is going on?" He wiped a smear of dirt out of his eyes and turned to glare at Kagen. "Who are these men?"

"Not men," Echo spat defiantly. "Vampires."

Ahh, so his latent wolf senses serve him well, Nathaniel said telepathically.

"Indeed," Marquis said aloud. He dropped Echo in front of the fire and nudged him with his foot, making it clear that he wanted him to sit exactly where he had planted him, until further notice, assuming *further notice* was given. "Stay as you are, and you may yet live."

Kagen followed suit. He appraised Neil Potter, making sure the human was at least drawing air through his damaged windpipe before he required him to walk, and then he gave him a sharp shove toward the fire pit. "Sit down next to your friend."

Neil did as he was told, flinching as Kagen came to stand behind him.

Nachari held his hand out to Kade like a gentleman. "Sorry about your throat," he said kindly, referring to the clever use of magic that had robbed the soldier of his breath, his dignity, and his sword. "Shall we?"

Kade stared at the proffered hand with disdain and rose to his own two feet without taking it. He shuffled irritably to the fire and sat amongst the circle, showing no emotion at all when Nachari sauntered up behind him.

Nathaniel shrugged as if he hated to be the odd man out. "Walker?"

The human jolted at the sound of his name. He stared at Nathaniel with callous disregard and then turned back to Arielle once more. "Arielle?" he repeated, his voice thick with insistence. "*Who are these men?* And how do they know my name?"

Nathaniel clucked his tongue several times. "You are not a particularly bright boy, nor a quick study, are you?" He inclined his head toward Kagen. "That *unstable* vampire over there is my brother—my twin, to be exact—and he is so much closer to doing you harm than you can imagine: painful, grisly, irreparable harm." He grimaced, and then he shrugged his shoulders. "And while I can't clearly articulate just why that is, I can give you a word of advice: You would be wise to stop talking to Arielle—as in zilch, *nada*, cat's got your tongue." He gestured toward the fire then. "When in Rome..."

Walker scrunched up his face. "What's *Rome*?"

Nathaniel rolled his dark, intense eyes. "Ah, yes; you are not from our world." He bent down to whisper in Walker's ear. "When in Mhier, surrounded by lethal enemies who can *and will* kill you with only a glance, one should get up and have a seat by the fire. Is that clearer?"

Walker stared at Nathaniel, incredulous for several prolonged seconds, and then he grudgingly rose to his feet, stretched his back as if to relieve some lingering pain, and reluctantly made his way to the remaining place at the fire. He didn't appear surprised when Nathaniel followed closely behind and stood directly at his rear.

Marquis cleared his throat and spoke to no one in particular. "Yes. We are vampires, and you are rebels, wanting to rescue Arielle. However, she does not need to be rescued, so we will ask you several questions; you will answer them succinctly, without wasting our time; and then, we will feed from you, erase your memories, and send you home." He snorted as if the entire recitation was beneath him, not to mention taxing his patience, and then he added: "If you do not comply, or you otherwise make things difficult, we will kill you instead. Whatever is most convenient."

Nachari tilted his head from side to side as if weighing the content of Marquis's words against the somewhat crude delivery. Apparently deciding that, all in all, it could have been worse, he nodded.

Arielle was less impressed. "Kagen," she whispered from the back of the cave, knowing he could hear her clearly. She deliberately pitched her voice in a nonconfrontational tone. "These are my friends. *My family*. Don't do this…not the way you are doing it."

Kagen met her troubled eyes, and for a moment, he felt as if he might just drown in the placid depths of compassion, the liquid pools of anguish. For reasons he couldn't explain, her entreaty tugged at his heart, and not because he cared one iota about a group of human soldiers who would have readily killed them all without asking questions first, should the cards have fallen in their favor; but because he cared about her experience, her feelings. He had viewed her memories, and he understood that *this*—these overmatched, mostly well-meaning rebels—were all she had left. All that had given her tortured life meaning. And, on a deeper level, he also understood that Keitaro, *their father*, also cared profoundly about this woman's feelings and her well-being.

Sighing, he made his way to the cave entrance and retrieved each of the rebels' weapons, returning them one at a time to their owners with no more than a nod of his head. He didn't bother to say, *Take care not to brandish this armament, lest you choose the hour and instrument of your own death.* He hoped it was implied, and he assumed they hadn't lived this long by being fools.

When Walker, being the last male to receive his battle-axe, stroked the handle with relish and puffed out his chest, angling his jaw in defiance, Kagen almost regretted the decision. The male was foolhardy at best, unashamedly stupid at the least, and he was going to get himself killed if he wasn't careful.

Arielle seemed to sense the mounting tension and sought to diffuse the situation: Careful to fix her eyes on Echo—not Walker—she spoke thoughtfully. "These are Keitaro Silivasi's sons," she said without preamble. "They are here to try and rescue Keitaro."

Walker's face turned whiter than it already was, but he held his tongue for a change.

"We are not here to *try*," Nathaniel corrected her, his voice thick with inference.

"And we haven't the time to waste on pacifying your friends," Marquis added. He regarded Kagen thoughtfully—at least as thoughtful as Marquis could be—and cleared his throat. "I appreciate your *interest* in this human female's feelings. Unfortunately, I don't share it."

Nachari raised his eyebrows. "She *is* the daughter of our father's heart, brother." His words were as measured as his voice. There was no disrespect intended.

"Perhaps," Marquis said, "and should our father be displeased with me, I will offer a dozen olive branches, every day for the next ten years, seeking his forgiveness. And all the while, I will thank the gods for his disapproval because it will mean that I once again *have a father* to disappoint. It is a trade I will gladly make. So until such time as Keitaro stands before us and makes these judgment calls himself, my word remains your law."

Nachari's deep green eyes darkened with acquiescence, and he immediately inclined his head. "As you will, brother." He could have said more in his defense—he could have tried to explain the subtle nuance in his words, the fact that he was only pointing out that Arielle was important to Keitaro, and her feelings could be taken into consideration without jeopardizing their mission—but he was wise and measured, as always.

Marquis didn't entertain *gray* on the best of days, and in this situation, in this place of so much danger and uncertainty, the world was definitively black and white: They came for Keitaro, and nothing—and no one—would take precedence over that singular focus.

Marquis eyed each of his brothers in turn, and the hardened resolve reflected in his gaze was far more telling than any words could have been. Turning to regard Arielle, he added, "I don't know how much our father has shared with you about vampire hierarchy, but know this, sister of my father's heart: I am the eldest of Keitaro's sons. Both my rank and my life have entitled me to a certain measure of deference and an absolute measure of obedience. While Nachari may have a wise and sensitive soul; while Nathaniel may—or may not—entertain your requests, depending upon his mood; while Kagen may have claimed you as his own, for reasons none of us can fathom, I will not hesitate to put you or anyone else aside that stands in our way. I care nothing about anything—save bringing Keitaro home alive."

Nachari let out a deep breath of air, but he held his tongue.

Nathaniel whistled low beneath his breath and then mumbled, "*Depending upon his mood*?" He sounded mildly insulted.

And Kagen bit a hole through his tongue out of respect for

his older brother: Marquis had no intention of harming Arielle—he was simply making a point—but he was also treading on very thin ice where this female was concerned. No one was going to threaten Arielle Nightsong.

No one.

Walker, on the other hand, jumped to his feet in an impulsive display of outrage. "What the hell does he mean, *Kagen may have claimed you as his own*?" His eyes bored holes into Arielle's. "Answer me, Arielle! *What the hell does that mean*?"

Arielle's mouth flew open, and she immediately turned to gape at Kagen. "It's not like it sounds, Walker. That's not even possible. It just means—"

"It means," Kagen cut her off, "that you don't get to put your hands on her anymore." He was so focused on making his point, so focused on not losing his temper and plucking the male's head from his shoulders like a ripe banana from a tree, that he took several unwitting strides in Walker's direction, not bothering to go around the fire pit in order to get there.

As hot flames licked at the hem of his pants, instantly igniting the flammable material, Kagen continued to advance toward the human. His eyes were as heated as the blaze—he had no doubt they were glowing feral red—and his fangs began to descend even further from his gums, the roots throbbing with the need to draw fresh, human blood.

thirteen

"Brother," Nathaniel drawled in his usual silken voice. "Your pants are on fire."

Kagen heard Nathaniel's voice as if from a distance, but the words didn't register…at first. And then he glanced down at his pants.

Noticing the orange and yellow flames wrapped about his ankles, he blew several shards of frosty air over the nuisance and continued along his path, not bothering to stop until he stood nose to nose with the human. Well, more like nose to chest, as Walker was considerably shorter than Kagen.

The fire went out in an instant.

Clearly stunned by the obscene display of power, Walker took an unwitting step back, his eyes as wide as saucers. "I was speaking to Arielle," he said defiantly, despite the quiver in his voice.

Kagen smiled broadly, but if looks could have killed, Walker would have already been six feet under. He reached out, grasped Walker by the nape of his thin, pale neck, and slowly tugged him forward. The human's resistance was like that of a child's: paltry, faint, and insignificant. As the thrum of Walker's heartbeat pulsed in Kagen's ears, and the blood in the rebel's carotid artery swirled like water cascading through a fountain, Kagen slowly bent his head to the human's throat and his mouth began to salivate.

He struck with fierce precision and primal hunger, his fangs sinking deep, his lips forming an implacable seal over the wound, and he began to draw blood through the narrow openings in his canines. As a deep, guttural moan escaped his throat, he swirled the viscous fluid around his mouth, allowing it to pool on the back of his tongue, before taking the first robust swallow.

And then he bit down harder and drank like a demon

possessed.

Walker trembled beneath him, and his lean body convulsed in a natural reaction to those first acute moments, caught in the vampire's control. His left arm dropped to his side, still clutching his useless battle-axe, even as he pressed his right hand squarely against Kagen's chest and tried to shove him away.

Kagen didn't budge.

He sent a scorching pulse of heat through his fangs, searing the male's skin with his bite and causing him to cry out in agony, even as he continued to take his due. His prey would submit like the inferior being he was: Walker would yield to Kagen's command, willingly, even if he commanded him to die.

When, at last, the final remnants of resistance drained out of Walker's body—he still had enough blood left to live, but his will had been utterly dominated—Kagen withdrew his fangs, left the wound open, unsealed, and watched as blood trickled down the human's neck in two snaking rivulets of red.

Kagen took a measured step back.

And the only thing that stopped him from reaching out and crushing the defiant rebel's windpipe with one powerful flex of his hand was the fact that Arielle was watching, no doubt in utter horror. "Tell me, Walker Alencion..." Kagen spoke in a lethal purr. "Which of these three options do you prefer? Death, quick and clean; to live your life as a vegetable; or to lose so much of your mental capacity that you don't know the difference either way?"

Walker blanched, and his Adam's apple bobbed up and down in his throat, betraying both fear and revulsion.

"Choose," Kagen snarled. His voice was an imperious command. "*Now.*"

"Death," Walker uttered helplessly, clearly appalled that he had answered such a debasing question.

"Kagen!" Arielle cried from the back of the cave; her voice was hoarse with desperation. "*Please...* Please don't."

Ignoring the female's plea, Kagen nodded frankly at Walker. "Very well." He lowered his voice so that only Walker, and likely his brothers, could hear him. "Up until now, you have not crossed the line, but you are wrestling with the decision. When the time comes, *if the time comes*, and you make the decision you are considering, to take Arielle by force, you will take this battle-axe instead"—he tapped the smooth, wooden handle several times for effect, never losing eye contact with the human—"and you will lodge it deeply into your own skull." He tapped Walker on the forehead, right between his eyes. "Right here. At least three inches deep."

Walker gazed down at the battle-axe and began to tremble. Clearly, he knew enough about vampires to realize he couldn't resist a direct order, a psychic compulsion.

"Now give me your word," Kagen said. The command had been laced in vampiric coercion—Walker could no more disobey the order than he could choose to stop breathing or shaking in his boots. And that meant if he ever chose to violate Arielle, he would commit certain suicide instead.

Walker choked out his reply. "You have my word." The syllables came out stilted, rote, and robotic; yet he meant each one to the depths of his soul. It was one promise the rebel would keep.

"Good," Kagen replied, his own voice barely audible. "Now then, speak to her one more time this night, and I will end this tiresome game once and for all."

Walker's eyes literally bulged in their sockets. He nodded like a dolt, lowered his body to the ground in an act of spineless submission, and drew his knees to his chest. Then he stared into the fire like a snake charmed into a trance.

Kagen took a deep breath, reined in his temper, and returned to his place behind Neil. For the briefest of moments his eyes met Arielle's, and he knew that she found him repulsive. Her cheeks were drawn tight with terror; her lips were pursed together in fury; and her overall countenance was stricken, shocked, and appalled. But it just didn't matter.

Marquis was right.

They were there for one solitary purpose, and that was to

bring their father home. The rest was incidental. "I believe my brothers have some questions for all of you," he said, making fleeting eye contact with each remaining member of the group, one at a time. The implied threat hovered in the air like a low-lying cloud, thick, tangible, and impossible to miss. "Now that Walker has decided to behave, shall we all continue?"

Neil Potter, the man sitting on the floor beneath Kagen, peered behind his shoulder and raised his hawkish eyes. He clasped his palm absently over his neck, unconsciously shielding his own exposed artery, and his gaze was absent of challenge. Kagen met his stare head-on, and Neil quickly turned away. He clutched his dual daggers in his hands, as if for reassurance, but he didn't brandish them in a threatening manner. "What would you like to know?" he said, turning his gaze to Marquis. His voice only trembled slightly.

Marquis squared his massive shoulders toward the group. "Tell us all you know about Tyrus Thane and the organization of the lycans."

Nathaniel descended into a squatting position, so that when he spoke, his voice reverberated in Walker's ear, even as it carried to the rest of the group. "We already know the layout of the Royal District and the slave encampment from the information Arielle has shared with us, but what we'd like to know from you is the efficacy of past strategies: raids, rescues, and forced retreats." He began to gesture with his hands. "Assuming your resistance has prevailed from time to time, what do you perceive as the king's greatest weakness? And what are his implacable strengths? Tell us about his alpha generals."

"When and where do they patrol, when and where do they rest, when and where do they take a shit," Marquis clarified.

Nachari spoke up next. His voice was characteristically moderate, but it still held an iron resolve in its depths. "If any man here has intimate knowledge of the arena, then we need that information, too. Not just a description, but an accurate *underground* blueprint—can one of you draw this?"

Although terrified, the rebels waited quietly.

Apparently, they assumed the vampires were going to ask more questions, and not one dared to interrupt.

When the cave remained quiet for more than a few seconds, Neil was the first to speak up. "I can tell you all about the generals," he said, his keen eyes narrowing with focus. "I can even draw you a map of the arena, the seven tunnels underneath, and the passageway that leads to the animal compound, where they keep the beasts."

"Good," Marquis grunted in approval. "Nachari, get a pen and some paper."

The wizard was already on top of it, heading for his pack.

"I know a thing or two about how they run the slave encampment," Echo offered grudgingly. Apparently the hot-headed rebel had made a wise set of calculations: Living was better than dying, and if the vampires were willing to cull their enemy's numbers, then why not let them. "Schedules, routines, weaponry—that sort of thing," he added.

"Do tell, wolverine," Nathaniel purred, rising back to his full height and winking at the male.

Echo stirred uneasily. "What does that mean, *vampire*?" His courage was impressive, however ill-advised.

Nathaniel chuckled low in his throat. "Oh, I think you know, deep down inside. I think your sense of smell and your ability to track vampires *simply by sniffing the air* speaks volumes about your mixed heritage, *human*." Before the angry young man could object, Nathaniel added, "And there is no greater asset for a warrior to have than inside knowledge of his enemy. It doesn't make you one of them—it simply makes you better equipped to confront them. Use it, soldier. Share it this night, and we may all benefit from your lineage, however distant."

Kade shifted nervously against the ground, rocking forward onto one knee. "As the oldest member of the resistance, I know the military history of Mhier like the back of my hand." His voice was steady and deliberate. "I can tell you what military tactics have succeeded and failed in the past. I can even tell you the strategies the lycans have chosen to employ over time against various enemies…against their own kind. What they might be likely to do in the future."

"We would welcome that information," Kagen said graciously, no longer feeling the need to intimidate the visitors. Apparently, the point had been made. He turned to regard Arielle once more, hoping she could see that, while his and her tactics may have been at odds, their goals were in harmony; and on two points, they were unified: They both hated the lycans with a passion, and they both wanted to see Keitaro get out of Mhier alive. The Silivasis would not do anything to her friends, to her rebel *family*, that they didn't have to do in order to achieve that goal. "Will you join us?" he asked, holding out his hand in an offer of friendship, however undesired. He avoided making any reference to what had just happened with Walker, as he knew it would only push her further away: The male was still staring blankly into the fire; and truth be told, Kagen's compulsion had been so strong, so invasive, that it had probably burned out a section of the human's brain. The rebel was incapable of participating in the conversation in a meaningful way at this juncture. Perhaps tomorrow, he would be in better shape, when it no longer mattered.

Kagen dismissed the thought.

He wasn't going to dwell on it.

He had done what he had to do in order to protect Arielle, to see to her safety amongst the rebels long after he and his brothers were gone.

For a moment, the thought unsettled him, and he had to put it out of his mind: The last thing he wanted to think about was that unconscionable moment when the Silivasis would have to leave Arielle Nightsong behind…in Mhier. "Miss Nightsong?" He repeated his request.

Arielle glanced cautiously around the room. She swallowed hard—perhaps she was swallowing her anger or her pride—and then she slowly nodded. She took several unconscious steps in Walker's direction, a behavior most likely born out of habit and misguided trust, and then she stopped abruptly and quickly turned around. "Sorry," she whispered. She strode deliberately to Kagen's side and took a seat at his right, avoiding any further eye contact.

As the warriors began to speak once more, she leaned in toward the fire to listen, and then, when it was clear that everyone was focused intently on the conversation, she risked a glance at Kagen through the corner of her eye. "When this is all over," she whispered, ostensibly believing only he could hear her, "will you feed from me and scrub my memories as well? After all, I'm just an inferior human."

Kagen's heart constricted in his chest, and his airway felt suddenly tight. He took a moment to steady his composure, and then he reached out and took her hand. He rotated his thumb against the center of her palm in an absent, reassuring motion. "No, sweeting." With his free hand, he gestured toward the circle of men in general—and Walker, specifically—speaking with conviction. "*This* is only a means to an end, Arielle." He raised her wrist to his lips and slowly lowered his head to press a soft kiss over her radial artery. "But you? You are much, *much* more than that to me." His eyes swept over her hair, her face, her strong yet elegant shoulders. "So much more than you know."

Arielle stared at him blankly as if at a loss for words. Her face grew impassive, and she closed her shadowed eyes. "Why?" she whispered softly, even as she withdrew her hand and placed it neatly in her lap.

Kagen shrugged, wishing he had the answer she was looking for. "Why, indeed." He spoke with regret. "My heart is far more vulnerable in your hands than these rebels, here, are vulnerable in our presence."

And then he repeated the question once more to himself:

Why…indeed?

Arielle tried to listen to the warriors' words, to the rebels and the vampires alike, as they exchanged vital information. After all, it was critical to the success of their mission, critical to saving Keitaro—if, in fact, he could be saved. But her heart was beating too loudly in her chest; her throat was far too constricted; and the skin on her wrist, where Kagen had pressed that soft, gentle kiss, would not stop tingling.

Her mind would not stop wandering.

Time and time again, her attention came back to the impossible male sitting so closely beside her: the vampire who had insisted upon her compliance, while trying to offer her friendship; the creature who had subjugated Walker with the strength of a lion and the cruelty of a tyrant, while speaking to her in a voice full of compassion; the man who walked through fire, yet wore his heart on his sleeve, who professed vulnerability…as if *anything* could lessen his power.

She couldn't stop thinking about Kagen Silivasi—Keitaro's healer son—and those mesmerizing, penetrating eyes. And, truth be told, a part of her wanted to jump up and run, to do something so blatant and unforgiveable that he would be forced to see her as an enemy.

To abandon their unified cause.

And it wasn't because she no longer cared about Keitaro—she cared more than she could ever say—but a part of her was just so afraid *of everything*.

Of all of it.

Of Kagen.

And she wanted him to cast her away, to send her home with the other rebels when the vampires were finally through with them. Still, she didn't dare provoke him, and that was the greatest enigma of all: Why couldn't she just simply oppose him and be done with it?

Arielle sighed in confusion. She stared into the fire, noticing the haphazard way the flames flickered and cascaded about in the dimly lit atmosphere of the cave, the way it dipped, danced, and inevitably cast shadows against the craggy earthen walls, and she bit her bottom lip, considering her predicament. In the interest of being completely honest, she had to admit there was something else going on, that a part of her soul, however remote, was inexplicably drawn to the vampire's intensity and his feral, carnal need.

A spark flew up from the center of the flames, sizzled a bright, glowing red, and then it popped like a piece of corn, before plummeting back into the dancing flames. She rubbed her hands together anxiously. On one hand, the vampire made statements he couldn't possibly mean—even Arielle knew that every male in the house of Jadon had a *destiny,* just *one destiny*, and they didn't go about claiming random human women in a careless, arbitrary manner. Heck, the celestial gods themselves had to decree their pairings.

So whatever was happening to Kagen Silivasi—whatever was happening between her *and* Kagen Silivasi—was something entirely forbidden.

Something illicit and unnatural.

And it didn't make any sense.

Perhaps he did harbor a dark alter ego, after all.

She only knew that the more possessive he became, the more she felt like a trapped animal. The more he ordered her about, the more she felt like opposing his will. And the more he stared at her with those eyes, the more he touched her with those hands, the more she felt like drowning in his arms, giving in to his contradictory, infuriating nature, and allowing it to take her where it may.

It was perplexing at best, disturbing at the least, how some distant part of her felt inexplicably drawn to his animal nature, curiously intrigued by his inhuman qualities…bizarrely compelled to comply with his demands. And perhaps that was it, precisely what was happening: Arielle was being compelled by Kagen Silivasi, quite literally.

But why?

Why was he doing this?

Why did he insist on avowing that she belonged to him? Why did he behave as if he had the indelible right to stake some claim over her?

Arielle Nightsong was a lot of things, but she wasn't easily manipulated, and she wasn't a bad judge of character. Kagen Silivasi was not a fickle male, nor was he irrational, unduly impulsive, or reckless by nature. In fact, Keitaro had described him as loyal, honorable, and responsible to a fault, yet he had displayed each of the former traits with reckless abandon when it came to his dealings with her. And it just didn't make any sense.

It was irrational for him to keep calling her *sweeting*; impulsive of him to give into some transitory, base attraction; reckless at best to keep insisting that she belonged to him in some strange, barbaric way, knowing that she did not.

That she could not.

And it was slowly wearing her down.

Making her as fearful as she was confused.

And yet, there was something in his voice that seeped past her barriers, something in his soul that reached out to hers, if only for a fleeting instant…now and then.

There was something magnetic, powerful, and undeniable in his soul.

Something that tugged at her heart.

She eyed him sideways, trying to discern what it was, and he met her stare head-on, those damnable eyes illuminating like soft silvery-brown shadows in the sparkling glow of the firelight. *What do you want from me?* she asked him in her mind, half expecting him to answer her in kind.

When nothing but silence met her probe, she quickly looked away.

In truth, she was positively terrified of the male: terrified that he had the power to destroy her, and those of her kind; terrified that he had the means to compel her to do his bidding, whatever it may be; terrified that he could take her life—and her heart—and shred it into a thousand unrecognizable pieces, each one more damaged than the last. And then, he could take Keitaro, the father of her heart, and leave her carelessly behind, alone in a barren world, *broken*, with all she had ever known left in ruins.

From where Arielle sat, Kagen Silivasi may as well have been the devil in disguise, the most dangerous adversary she had ever encountered.

By all the ancestors, please—just leave me alone.

She spoke the words silently, once again, hoping that at least the intensity of her plea would break through.

"Please," she repeated, one last time, not realizing she had spoken the word aloud.

fourteen

The next day

"Are you tired? Do you need to rest?" Kagen asked Arielle, his voice thick with concern.

Marquis had set a brutal yet necessary pace for the team, and they had been walking for hours, trudging their way through the cold Mystic Mountains, headed toward the slave encampment in a furious effort to reach Keitaro in time.

As they continued to climb in elevation, the crowns of the white-bark pines became increasingly dusted with frost; light purple blooms of wolfsbane progressively dotted the land; and the smell of the air grew crisper, strangely bitter, as if the icy chill that surrounded them foretold of trials to come.

Arielle shivered. She fisted her hands in her animal-hide gloves and tried to appear stoic. "I'm fine," she told Kagen assuredly, careful to keep an arm's-length distance between them as they walked. "I've taken this trail more times than I can count. I'll be fine."

"Perhaps," Kagen said thoughtfully, and then he looked up at the sky and frowned. "But does it always snow in May?"

"In the Mystic Mountains?" Arielle laughed in spite of her reticence. "Unfortunately, yes." She stomped some snow off her boots. "In Mhier, it's not so much a function of seasons but surroundings. It depends more on *where* you are than *when* you pass by." She tucked her hands beneath the crooks of her arms and continued to trek forward.

Kagen reached out and grasped her by the sleeve of her heavy parka—late the night before, he had followed the rebels back to their camp, and using Arielle's memories as a guide, he had packed a small bundle of appropriate clothing and food to see her through the journey. He had been back before Arielle or his brothers had awakened. "If it's all the same to you, I'll feel better if you at least allow me to warm your hands."

Arielle turned to face him, which was at least something, but by the cautious look in her eyes, she was weighing the pros and cons of allowing him even that small indulgence.

Kagen sighed. "It doesn't have to mean that we're married." He tried to keep his tone light. "Don't make it harder than it is, Arielle. Just let me attend to your hands."

Arielle puffed out a frozen breath and shuffled in place to stay warm. "Fine," she said, glancing ahead at the trail. "Go ahead. Just hurry." She quickly removed her gloves, tucked them beneath her left arm, and held her hands out in front of him.

Kagen gasped at the sight before him. "Arielle, your fingertips are *blue*."

She shrugged and tried to force a smile. "The color always comes back once I reach the valley."

Kagen bit his lip and stifled a growl. "If you keep acting foolishly, I will insist upon carrying you."

"You will not!" she snapped, her vivid eyes flashing hot with defiance.

The left corner of Kagen's mouth turned up in a grin—the woman was positively adorable. "You're right; I will not." He chuckled softly, unable to contain his amusement.

To his surprise, Arielle smacked him across the arm and glared at him mischievously. "You really do enjoy nettling me, don't you?"

He grinned from ear to ear. "You make it far too easy, Miss Nightsong."

"What?" she said, without thinking. "I'm no longer your *sweeting*?"

Kagen's nonchalance disappeared. He took both of her hands in his, raised them to his mouth, and blew soft, gentle air over her fingertips, his breath as warm as a summer's day. He continued to repeat the process until a healthy pinkish tone reappeared, and then he whispered softly, "Is that better…*sweeting*?"

She swallowed convulsively and tried to look away, but her eyes came immediately back to his, as if drawn by an unseen magnet. She opened her mouth to speak and then slowly closed it, which only drew Kagen's attention to her lips: They were the color of pink pearl roses, as full as they were sculpted, and more tempting than a pond full of cold, inviting water on a hot summer's day. He bent his head, and his hair fell forward to shade his eyes. Still, he managed to hold her gaze through a disheveled curtain of brown locks. He released her hands, placed two fingers beneath her jaw, and gently lifted her head to force her to maintain the eye contact. "I want to kiss you," he said, closing the distance between them slowly, carefully, until his mouth hovered mere whispers over hers.

Again, Arielle tried to speak but failed, and her parted lips were too tempting an offer for Kagen to pass up.

He brushed her lips with his, so softly that the contact was almost imperceptible, a mere grazing of souls, and then he deepened the contact, molding the contours of his mouth to hers with a slightly firmer touch. His tongue swept softly over that adorable pout, and she immediately pulled away, practically jolting from the sensation, as if she had been prodded with a hot iron. *"No,"* she said with insistence. She took a hasty step back and almost stumbled over a fallen branch. "No, Kagen. *No.*"

Kagen watched as various emotions swept over Arielle's face—desire, confusion, and fear, each one in turn, warring for a dominant place—and he rubbed his forehead in frustration. Bewildered, he cupped her face in his hand and gently stroked her cheek. "Very well." He spoke quietly, though no longer in a whisper. "I…I must've misread your signals. I'm sorry."

Arielle shook her head from side to side and gently removed his hand, looking more than a little…*perturbed*? She wrung her hands together in a rare show of nervousness and continued to back away. "I mean it, Kagen. *Please.* Please don't do that kind of thing again."

Kagen Silivasi was not accustomed to this level of rejection, but even if he were, this would have rattled him deeply: There was something else going on with Arielle, something much deeper, much more complex, than a misguided kiss. And he didn't want to leave her this unsettled, this uncertain within herself. "Come to me," he said, gesturing her forward with his hand.

She looked like a frightened rabbit as she shook her head. *"No."*

"Shh," he coaxed tenderly. "Silly warrior, *come*."

She took a tentative step forward, and he met her halfway, immediately enfolding her waist with his arm. He pulled her gently into the security of his chest, and then he kissed her lightly, *chastely*, on the top of her head. "I already told you, I will never force you. You have no reason to fear me, Arielle."

Arielle buried her head in the crook of his arm and shivered. "I have every reason, Kagen. And that's why the answer is *no*."

He ran his hand upward along the small of her back, swept it along the ridge of her shoulders, and buried his fingers in her silky, wild hair. Then he gently grasped a handful of untamed tendrils and wound them through his fingers, allowing the long, curly ends to slowly fall away. "Your words do not fall on deaf ears, Arielle. I am not without compassion." He stepped away from her then and continued to walk in silence.

She quickly fell into step beside him, her face still flushed with heat.

Just then, Nachari Silivasi appeared on the trail beside them, as if emerging out of a mist, and he nodded to Arielle. "Daughter of my father's heart," he addressed her formally and with respect. "Marquis would like to speak with you."

"What about?" Kagen asked, immediately regretting his proprietary reaction.

If Nachari noticed the tension between them, he was too polite to say anything. "He has a few more questions about the medical condition of our father, the serum that the lycans pump into his veins, and the contraption they use to do it." He shrugged, apparently trying to remain detached. "We have all tried on many occasions to reach out to Keitaro telepathically, but the communication doesn't go through, not even as we draw closer to the slave encampment." He cast a sideways glance at Kagen. "Kagen believes that the diamond dust, the many centuries of infusing Keitaro's blood with such a debilitating substance, has rendered his ability to receive the transmissions ineffective, that he can no longer receive our probes; but as you can imagine, it is still a cause for concern."

Arielle nodded, and her voice became all at once firm. "Take my word for this, Nachari. You don't know Tyrus Thane like I do—he's a sadist and a narcissist. He will not take your father's life, or allow anyone else to do it for him, before Sunday. If he wants him to die in the arena, on a grand stage for the entire realm to see, then what King Thane wants, King Thane gets. Your father isn't silent because he's…*gone*."

Nachari's deep green eyes softened with gratitude. "Thank you, Arielle." He gestured toward the front of the trail, pointing in Marquis's direction. "Just the same, Marquis has many questions: Would you mind walking with him for a bit? Besides"—he turned to regard the healer once more—"I would like to speak with Kagen privately for a moment, if you don't mind."

Arielle seemed only too happy to oblige. "Oh, no. Of course, I don't mind." She gathered her coat more closely around her shoulders and hurried forward on the trail. Truth be known, she was probably grateful for the reprieve.

Kagen watched her walk away, sighed in frustration, and then he raised his eyebrows and turned his full attention on Nachari. "Well?" he said. "Speak then."

Nachari fell into easy step beside him, but the awkward silence that followed belied the seriousness of his intent: Kagen could tell there was something important on Nachari's mind, and the wizard was searching for a way to broach the subject.

"Just pick someplace and dive in," Kagen said, prompting his little brother with a smile. "I don't bite, unless your name is Walker."

Nachari chuckled. "Touché." His easy step became an easy

glide, the cat-like stroll flowing in gentle, rhythmic harmony with the natural landscape around them. He rolled his muscular shoulders in an effort to release some tension, and then he simply dove in like Kagen suggested. "Marquis, Nathaniel, and I have been talking,"—he wet his lips, *for courage?*—"and we agreed that one of us should approach you."

Kagen's eyebrows shot up and he groaned. "Damn, that sounds serious."

"A little bit," Nachari agreed.

When the wizard didn't smile to soften his words, Kagen frowned. "What is it, little brother?"

Nachari sighed. "What's going on with Arielle?"

Kagen shook his head. "What do you mean?"

Nachari waved his hand through the air as if to dismiss all the extraneous nonsense. "I mean, what's going on with *you* and *Arielle*, with your overwhelming desire to be with this woman…to get close to this human?"

Kagen smirked. "Are we going to talk about the birds and the bees, little brother?"

Nachari leveled a stern glance at the healer. "I'm not playing with you, Kagen."

Kagen shrugged. "Then what do you want me to say? I don't know. I honestly…*don't*…know."

Nachari shook his head. "Not good enough, healer. I mean, you almost attacked me that first night in the cave—in fact, you would have attacked me if Nathaniel hadn't intercepted you. And you got into a physical altercation with your twin. Not to mention, you practically *took her* right there in front of all of us."

Kagen visibly recoiled. "I didn't *take* her." His tone was defensive, rising with emphasis. "Not like that."

"It was pretty—"

"*Not like that*," Kagen insisted.

"Almost like that," Nachari argued. Before Kagen could object again, he shrugged his left shoulder and shook his head. "I'm not…I don't care to get into an argument. This is not about sexual nuances. As far as I'm concerned, you're a grown male—

what you choose to do is your business. But this is something else entirely, brother." He angled his body toward Kagen's, and his eyes were brimming with concern. "I don't know which is more telling, the fact that you wanted to kill Walker on sight for his past insults to the female, or the fact that you restrained yourself from doing just that, in order to pacify and appease her. Both say something *important* is going on."

Kagen stopped walking then. "We can catch up to Marquis and Nathaniel in a minute. Look at me, Nachari. What are you trying to say?"

Nachari looked off into the distance as if gathering his words from the Mystic Mountains. When, at last, he met Kagen's stare head-on, his jaw was set in an uncharacteristically hard line. "Has it ever crossed your mind that this female might be your *destiny*?"

Kagen chuckled out loud then, although there was nothing humorous in the sound. "Of course it has. You know damn well that was the first thing I checked, but have you seen her wrist lately?"

"I have."

"Then you know that there are no markings on her flesh: *Auriga isn't there.*"

"I realize that."

"And have you seen the sky recently?" Kagen asked. "The plain white moon?"

"I've seen the *Mhieridian* moon," Nachari said bluntly. "I haven't seen the moon in Dark Moon Vale, and neither have you. And trust me, I've tried."

Now this caught Kagen's attention. "What do you mean, *you've tried*?"

Nachari placed his hand on Kagen's shoulder. "Last night, after we all went to bed, while you were out collecting Arielle's things, I tried to send my spirit out of my body in the form of a raven, kind of like I did from the Abyss. I was hoping to enter Dark Moon Vale and, I don't know, see what I could see." He furrowed his brow in consternation. "It wasn't an easy feat to accomplish from the Valley of Death and Shadows, and I didn't expect it to be easy from here; but I just couldn't make it happen." There was a hint of humility, if not outright apology, in his voice. "I think, perhaps, that when I did it before, it was because Deanna's spirit called out to mine—our connection was just that intense—there's nothing calling me now, other than my own desire to know..." His voice trailed off. "Just the same, I tried."

Kagen placed his hand over Nachari's and patted it gently. "You did all that for me?"

Nachari rolled his eyes then, the gesture both playful and serious at once. "Of course I did that for you. And for me. I don't think you quite follow what I'm trying to say...not yet."

Kagen frowned. "Then perhaps you should spell it out, say it more plainly."

Nachari took a deep breath, ran his fingers through his hair, and pushed any remaining awkwardness aside. "I don't care how long it's been since you've *had a woman*, brother. You are a Master Healer, an Ancient, at that; you shouldn't be this tied up in knots over a human female, not unless..." He paused again, only this time, he locked his gaze with Kagen's. "Brother: If, for some strange reason, Arielle Nightsong is, in fact, your *destiny*, and we manage to rescue Father—"

"*When* we manage to rescue Father," Kagen interjected.

"When we manage to rescue Father," Nachari said, "if we leave with Keitaro, if we leave *without* Arielle, you are as good as dead." Although he had tried to speak the words without emotion, his hand began to tremble, and he removed it from Kagen's shoulder and placed it at his side. "Do you understand what I'm saying? Whether or not she's your *destiny* is more than just a little bit significant. Even if there's only one chance in a million, it's not a chance we are willing to take. Not when your reaction to her is this extreme...this *primal*."

Kagen understood exactly what Nachari was saying, and he wasn't about to belittle his concern. Still, he really didn't think it was an issue. "But there's no reason to believe that she is," he said—in a sense, he was playing devil's advocate, trying to get

Nachari to convince him. If the wizard's argument was stronger than his own, he might reconsider the facts. "I mean, think about it, Nachari: The moment we entered Mhier, Marquis and Nathaniel tested all of our vampiric powers, and they work just fine. We've been able to communicate telepathically, at least with each other, if not with the warriors back home, and there has been no Blood Moon. Wouldn't the celestial gods know that I'm here—that she's here?—and wouldn't they be capable of marking my *destiny*, no matter where she was? There are no markings on Arielle's wrist, and frankly, she doesn't seem drawn to me in the least."

Nachari laughed out loud then. "So that's what's going on? *That's* what's clouding your judgment?" He slowly shook his head. "Spoken like a male so caught up in his own infatuation that he can't see the forest for the trees." He eyed the woodland terrain all around them and snickered. "No pun intended. The female is more tied up in knots than you are, Kagen. Trust me, she's drawn to you, so strongly she's about to throw herself off a cliff to get away from it. And as for your other points, just hear me out, okay?"

Kagen waited in silence, listening intently. If Nachari was nothing else, he was incredibly intuitive and wise. He had earned his wisdom through blood and fire and loss; and if he could shed some light on the infuriating situation, then far be it from Kagen to stop him. "Go on."

"It's hard to explain—some of what I learned in the Abyss—but whether or not our powers remain intact is more of a function of density, the dominant vibration of a particular realm, than it is proximity to earth. I was much weaker in the Abyss, but the vibration there was dark, sluggish, and stilted. It's actually lighter here, higher, despite the fact that the lycans are evil." He gestured toward their vibrant surroundings. "That's why the trees are greener and the skies are bluer; it's why all the colors are richer." He clasped his hands together and held them to his forehead as if trying to physically retrieve clearer thoughts. "As for the Blood Moon and the markings on Arielle's wrist—or the lack thereof—I'm not so sure they *would* show up in this realm. Kagen, I'm not so sure they *could* show up in this realm."

"Why not?" Kagen asked, deeply curious now.

Nachari's speech quickened. "Again, when I was in the Abyss, the gods knew I was there—they hadn't forgotten me or abandoned me—yet they couldn't interfere. They didn't interfere. That world, it wasn't their domain. It was under the authority of the dark lords and the demons. What if Mhier is under the authority of a different set of deities? What if the lycans have their own, evil gods?" He tilted his head to the side. "What if the celestial gods know you're here? What if they know Arielle belongs to you, and they're doing all they can to steer you both in the right direction, but they can't directly interfere? This realm is ruled by lycans. Hell, it's their universe of origin, much like the earth and its heavens are ours. Why would beings that hate and hunt vampires as a primary way of life come from a world that was hospitable to our kind? The moon is theirs. The sun is theirs. Hell, wolfsbane grows like dandelions here, and the timber wolf moon never goes away. What if there are no constellations in this galaxy? No way for them to appear? Or maybe they have 'em, but they're just different." He held up both hands. "My point is: This is *their* realm, not ours, and there's just no way for us to know for sure."

Kagen nodded, acknowledging all of Nachari's salient points, and then he continued to argue. "But Arielle is from here—this world—not ours. Why would my *destiny* come from a realm other than ours?"

Nachari shook his head vehemently. "*No*, on that point, we have to disagree. Humans are not native to this land, Kagen. They did not originate here any more than the Vampyr originated in North America. According to Mhieridian history—what we learned from Arielle and the other rebels—they were originally *brought* to this land by the lycans, stolen from earth by their captors. Perhaps they have procreated over many centuries and have no memory of any other realm, any other life, but this is not their native land."

Kagen considered his brother's words carefully, *very carefully*. "There is still the matter of Napolean's law, the covenants that bind us to the house of Jadon, that dictate our interactions with humans."

Nachari practically snorted then, which was so unlike the placid wizard. "Once again, we are at odds in our interpretation of facts, or perhaps we're at odds regarding matters of nuance: It's true, we are not to interfere with *free will*, the religious or spiritual practices of humans, and we are not to play gods in their world—we must let their choices stand, and we must allow them to direct their own futures, without interference—unless it directly pertains to us. But I don't see how this applies to the former."

Kagen's mouth fell open in astonishment. "You don't see how taking Arielle out of the only world she's ever known, against her will, without any proof that she belongs in our realm is in violation of the law?"

"No," Nachari answered empathically. "We're not talking about human matters now—we're talking about vampiric matters. We're talking about our family. The same way you saved Kristina from a Dark One so many years ago—the same way you, Marquis, and Nathaniel *took* Deanna and kept her at the clinic, once you realized she might have something to do with my fate, with my eventual return. The same way Marquis eliminated the biker gang when they threatened the female he *believed* to be his *destiny*." His voice grew heavy with conviction. "Once our worlds collide, and the human's outcome becomes inexorably linked to our own, all bets are off." He raised his brows. "I have already lost one brother, Kagen. Do you think I give a celestial damn whether or not Arielle belongs on earth or in Mhier?" He shook his head sadly. "And as for Nathaniel, he has no idea what it is like to live, to try and breathe, without one's twin. *I do.* And for that reason alone, I would interfere with Arielle's free will."

Kagen stared intently at his little brother, understanding that there was a wealth of emotion beneath his words. He measured his own words more carefully. "Her life is not less important than mine, Nachari. You have to remember that. And if she isn't my *destiny*—"

"*She's human*, with a mortality of what? Perhaps ninety years? You are immortal, with a lifespan that spans thousands of years."

"And that makes my life more important?"

"*You* are my brother."

"And she is the daughter of our father's heart!"

"Yes!" Nachari retorted. "But ask yourself this: When I was in the Valley of Death and Shadows, all those months when I remained in a comatose state in the clinic, what would you have done to save me, Kagen? What would you have traded to bring me back? What would *you* have sacrificed?"

Kagen averted his eyes. The answer was already known…

Anything.

"Everything."

"Then how can you expect less from your own brothers, healer? It just doesn't work that way."

Kagen frowned, realizing for the first time that his siblings had already given the matter a great deal of thought. "What have the three of you discussed?"

Nachari smiled sheepishly then, his deep green eyes alighting with mischief. "Well, we started out with three possibilities: The first, and least intrusive, you already know: I tried to use the body of the raven to travel to Dark Moon Vale—I had hoped we could just come up with a definitive answer." He shook his head with regret. "As you already know, that didn't work. The second idea was Marquis's, so you already know it was unreasonable…and extreme."

"What was it?" Kagen asked, cringing.

Nachari waved his hand through the air and drew in a deep breath of air. "Doesn't matter."

Kagen glanced at him sideways. "*What was it*, Nachari?"

Nachari shrank back, and then he shrugged his shoulders apologetically. "From Marquis's point of view, there was one other way to answer the question, once and for all, to know without doubt whether Arielle was indeed your *destiny*."

"*And that was*?" Kagen repeated.

"Conversion."

Kagen literally jolted. He stared at Nachari with what he knew had to be a blank look of stupefaction on his face, but he just didn't care. "Are you insane?"

The wizard shrugged. "To Marquis's way of thinking, it was logical: There are only two ways to successfully convert a human female to our kind. The first way, she has to be your chosen *destiny*. The second, she has to agree to the change and relinquish her eternal soul in exchange for immortality. The way Marquis looked at it, Arielle would never relinquish her soul, nor would you ask, *or allow*, such a thing. Therefore, if you tried to convert her as she is, she would either live…or die. Either way, you would know for sure."

Kagen shook his head in horror. "So Marquis wanted me to play Russian roulette with Arielle's life, to flip a coin with her suffering? Heads, she's your destiny. Tails, she suffers a prolonged, hideous, and painful death. Is that about right?"

Nachari wrinkled up his nose. "Nathaniel and I talked him out of it. Does that count for anything?"

Kagen pinched the bridge of his nose and tried not to think too hard about his barbaric older brother. The male meant well, and that's what he had to remember. "That's immoral, not to mention savage and inhumane." He had a suddenly bitter taste in his mouth. "Shit, that's *unconscionable*, Nachari."

To Kagen's surprise, Nachari defended the Ancient Master Warrior. "No," he said in a matter-of-fact voice. "That's a brother's love for his sibling."

Kagen couldn't get his arms around it. "Would he really have tried to order me to do such a thing?"

Nachari held a single hand up in the air. "Kagen, would you not trade your very soul for Nathaniel, for Marquis, or for me?"

Kagen didn't answer the question. After all, what could he say? "Gods, we live in a world of insanity."

"We live in a world of nuance and degrees." Nachari spoke softly. "Of celestial gods, dark lords, and lycans. We live in an immortal world of Vampyr—not a human world of frailty—and our code, our honor, and even our choices are sometimes larger than life. Yet we make them without apology because we must."

Kagen sighed. "Yeah, well, that last choice absolutely sucked."

Nachari chuckled softly then. "Agreed."

Kagen crossed his arms over his chest and braced himself for what was to come. "So, tell me then, little brother: What *choices* have you, Marquis, and Nathaniel already made on my behalf?"

Nachari smiled ruefully, his smooth, sculpted cheeks nearly notching with dimples from the mirth, and then his countenance became all at once serious. "If we survive to return home from this place; if we are blessed to find *and free* our father; and if through it all, you are still breathing as well"—he averted his eyes, either unwilling or unable to face the gravity of his words—"then Arielle Nightsong will return with us to Dark Moon Vale. If you are willing to take her, then of course, we will defer to your lead in the matter; but if you are not willing to act in this way, then Marquis, Nathaniel, or I will do it on your behalf. There is no room for debate on this subject, Kagen. Our minds are made up."

"And who is going to tell her this? My *brothers*...or me?"

"Before we rescue Keitaro?" Nachari shook his head. "Neither." Kagen opened his mouth to object, and Nachari cut him off. "Marquis's final word, Kagen."

Kagen tried not to bristle. "Can I ask why?"

Nachari nodded. "Of course. Marquis thinks it's a wildcard, and Nathaniel and I agree. Her emotions. Yours. The danger Keitaro is facing. The whole unfortunate situation is just too volatile already, and Marquis doesn't want any distractions, any side drama." He shrugged his shoulders apologetically. "Look, we understand how sensitive this is—*we really do*—but you have to put each item on a scale and weigh it objectively: Arielle's emotional comfort or our father's *life*." He toggled both hands up and down in the air to demonstrate his point. "Both matter to each of us, but the former can be healed, repaired over time. The latter, if it's lost, it's gone for good."

Kagen tried to process all he was hearing—he really did—yet he couldn't help but wonder: When had his brothers decided all this? "And if, in the end, she is not my *destiny*—which she most likely is not—then what?" He hated to be so recalcitrant, but he wanted to belabor the point one last time.

"Then we will care for her as if she were. She will want for nothing—not ever—and, in time, she may have a better, *freer*, life, just as Kristina has now."

"And as for her world back here? Her friends, the cause she believes in and fights for, her rebel *family*"—he made the last word in air quotes for emphasis, knowing that they were truly not her blood—"as for all she has ever known?"

Nachari sighed. "Whether Arielle is your *destiny* or not, she will live, whether on earth or in Mhier. The same cannot be said for you." He leaned in close and growled his next words. "You are *not* going to die like Shelby in the sacrificial chamber, Kagen. *Not on my watch*. Not when there is something we can all do to prevent it." He stiffened and hardened his voice. "Your world is in Dark Moon Vale: your nephews, your *duty*, your family. My loyalty lies with my brother. My loyalty lies with my house." He placed his clenched fist over the left side of his chest. "My loyalty lies with my heart—it lies with *you,* Kagen. And *that* is the only world I've ever known. You asked me to be honest: Well, there it is."

Kagen placed his hand over Nachari's clenched fist and tightened his fingers around it. "Be at ease, brother. I will not fight you on this."

And then he stood, just like that, unwilling to move…

Until, at last, Nachari stopped trembling.

fifteen

Later that night, Kagen watched as Nathaniel and Nachari pitched two tents at the base of the Mystic Mountains in a shallow ravine, concealed by lush greenery, in the form of blackberry bushes and tall larch trees, their intermingled branches extended and interlocking with one another as if they were soldiers linking arms. The entire narrow gorge was a veritable sea of lavender as the poisonous perennial, the purple wolfsbane flower, carpeted the earthen floor like an absurd welcome mat, heralding the vampires' arrival.

Tomorrow was Saturday.

One day away from the games in the arena.

And they were now less than twenty-file miles from the Royal District, the region where the games would be held.

Marquis believed they could traverse the space in about seven hours, that this would allow ample time for Arielle to rest, but if they had to fly, if they had to take turns carrying her through the air, then so be it. They might just have to take the risk.

They would do whatever it took.

The main thing was to get close enough to survey the layout, to go over their plan one last time *in intricate detail*, to take advantage of the cover of nightfall in order to cement their strategy, once and for all.

There could be no room for error.

Keitaro's life depended upon the Silivasi brothers getting this right.

Kagen hung back by a large, leaning larch tree about thirty yards from the camp. Arielle had retreated inside of her tent to partake of a late afternoon meal of rabbit, nuts, and berries; and she was now getting some much needed rest.

Or so Kagen thought.

When she rounded the bend of the ravine, her thick, coppery locks blowing gently in the wind, her stark, luminous eyes searching the landscape—*for him?*—he stepped away from the tree and practically held his breath, instantly coming to attention.

"It's only me," Arielle called amiably. She emerged from the shadows like a wild goddess, both fiercely beautiful and adorably disheveled at the same time.

Kagen relaxed his posture and leaned back, once again, against the brittle bark of the tree, trying to appear nonchalant.

Only me.

Now that was the understatement of the century.

As she slowly approached him, her customary bow slung over her shoulder, the familiar quiver resting at her back, he couldn't help but appraise her appreciatively: By all the gods, she was one of the most stunning women he had ever seen: so strong, so untamed, yet so clearly vulnerable, even as she tried to hide it. "Did you get enough to eat?" he called. It seemed like a safe enough question.

"I did." She spoke kindly, and then she frowned. "But the rabbit was kind of tough."

Kagen chuckled. "I could have gone hunting, brought you something else."

Arielle flashed him a devilish grin. "We don't share the same diet, vampire."

"*Ha. Ha*," Kagen teased. "I would have found something appropriate for *you*."

Arielle chuckled; apparently, she wasn't feeling quite as apprehensive as earlier. "I know you would have—*thank you*—but I don't want anyone else to do my hunting for me." She tapped her bow and smiled. "It keeps me on my toes, sharpens my skills. I should really use my weapon every day."

Kagen nodded with appreciation, wondering to himself just what her life had been like. Well, in a sense, he already knew, after all, he *had* viewed her memories, but that was not the same as knowing her intimately, sharing her feelings, or experiencing her life. He looked all around him at the looming night sky; the ever-present timber wolf moon; and the inexplicably vivid countryside. It was such a beautiful land, yet at the same time, it was so barren and harsh…so spiritually bereft. There was so little hope. So little freedom.

Arielle's life had been one long exercise of stark endurance and desolate survival.

"What are you thinking about?" she asked, curiously. And then her eyes grew dim and her face grew impassive, as if she instantly regretted asking the question. Perhaps it was just too personal.

"Are we not even friends, that you can ask me my thoughts?" Kagen said. He wasn't sure where the query had come from, but she was keeping such a safe distance between them, ever since he had kissed her on the mountain. She had walked for three straight hours beside Marquis—and that had to be one hell of a stilted conversation—and then she had chosen to follow Nathaniel, and then Nachari, anything, to avoid being close to Kagen.

The realization was infuriating.

Humiliating.

But what could he do? He had no rights to this woman.

So, why then, did he feel like he had every right to every part of her?

She appraised him thoughtfully. "We are friends." A sly smile crossed her mouth. "You are like the brother I never had."

"Brother?" Kagen said, appalled by the chaste terminology. "I am not at all like a brother to you, Arielle."

"I only meant that—"

"You meant that we share the same father-figure, which technically makes us like brother and sister." He shook his head, feeling like a scrawny teenager who had just been picked last for the team. *Hell's bells—enough was enough.* "I know what you meant, Arielle." He pitched his voice lower, in a silken drawl. "But you forget that I am Vampyr: I can hear the beat of your heart, the way it races whenever you are in my presence. I can feel the catch in your throat, sense the chills that race up and down your spine. And I can still taste the honey on your lips." He ran his tongue along the tips of his fangs, willing them to stay as they were. "You may not *want* me for your lover, but it *is* how you see me." The words seemed unnecessarily bold, perhaps even a bit indecent, but he couldn't help but speak them. They were true, and now that he knew she would be coming back to Dark Moon Vale—with or without her consent, with or without *his* consent—he dared to be just a tad more assertive, to explore their connection a little bit further.

She stopped about five feet in front of him and then abruptly gazed at the sky. "It is a beautiful night, don't you think?" All things considered, she had handled it well.

"Come closer," he beckoned, knowing he was no longer playing fair.

She shook her head and dug in her heels. "You know I can't."

"Why not?" he asked.

It was a stupid question, not to mention redundant. He already knew *why not*. Still, it didn't hurt to ask, if only because it might make her reconsider her answer.

She huffed in exasperation. "I just…because…"—and then she appeared to pull an answer right out of the air—"because I have no way of knowing if my actions are my own or if they're being forced…or coerced…you know, due to vampiric compulsion."

He bit his lower lip. *Really?* So this was how she intended to sidestep the issue? He raised one brow: It was clever—he would definitely give her that—but it was also absolute nonsense, and that he could not abide. "What do you mean, Arielle?" He rolled her name off his tongue in a thick Romanian accent, and she almost swayed where she stood.

She swallowed hard, trying to collect her wits. "*I mean…*" The woman had a bit of the devil in her, and it only made him like her more. "That if I simply do your bidding, like a servant, like a puppet"—she squared her jaw to him in an impressive display of defiance—"even in a matter as menial as coming to you when you call, then I will never know if I *obeyed* you out of coercion or came out of free will. And I am nobody's lackey, Mr. Silivasi." She smoothed out the front of her parka, although the gesture made no difference in the wrinkles, whatsoever. "I will never know if I did it because I wanted to or because I had to." She plastered a congenial smile on her face and shrugged apologetically. "You said yourself—you're Vampyr. You have the power to make things as you wish. And I am simply human. I don't even have the ability to know whether or not you are compelling me: a lion and a lamb. Is that what you want?" She batted her long, curly eyelashes without even realizing she was doing it. *Oh, she was really, really good.*

Kagen frowned. "*Arielle…*"

She waved a delicate hand through the air in quaint dismissal. "It doesn't matter, Kagen. I'm sure you're a male of integrity. *I am.* It's just…since I can't be sure whether or not you're compelling me, I don't want to take any chances."

Kagen nodded as if he truly understood. "I have never compelled you to do anything, sweeting," he said softly. "And it troubles me *deeply* to think you might question my abuse of power."

She shrugged and forced a smile. "Okay."

Okay? If redirection, dismissing the subject, was an Olympic event, this woman would win a gold medal. "You don't believe me?"

She sighed. "I don't know what to believe. A lot has happened in a short amount of time." She looked sincerely confused, and that's when Kagen knew that, beneath all the tongue-and-cheek antics, she was genuinely concerned.

He lost the playful tone. "What has happened between us, this far, that leads you to believe I have countermanded your free will?"

"Countermanded?"

"Overruled, gone against it, ignored it, Arielle."

She frowned. "You mean, other than that first night in the cave when Nachari tried to take my memories?"

Kagen felt like an utter heel. "I already apologized for my behavior, sweeting. But if you need to revisit it again, we can. One thing I will tell you, *with absolute certainty*, is this: There was no compulsion involved that night. However inappropriate my behavior may have been, it was unconscious, a reaction, instinct, pure and simple; it had nothing to do with manipulating your free will…or even my own. It just *happened*."

Arielle nodded. "I know that. I do." She appeared to be thinking it over, and then she surprised him with her next question. "And today, *earlier*, on the mountain? When…when you…" She bit the inside of her cheek, blushed a pale shade of pink, and stopped talking. Apparently, she couldn't even speak the words…

"When I *kissed* you?"

"When I kissed you back," she said boldly. "Was that forced? Was it a compulsion?"

Kagen had to suppress a chuckle. He didn't know whether to be flattered or insulted. First, she hadn't really kissed him back—she had pulled away so quickly. And second, her emotions had been so raw, so vulnerable, yet so clearly infused with genuine desire, whether she understood it or not. "That was me being me, and you being you. There was no compulsion."

She nodded and retreated within her shell once more. "If you say so."

If I say so? He didn't respond out loud, and apparently, he didn't have to.

Arielle sighed in apology. "It's not that I think you're lying, Kagen. *Truly*. The point is: I just wouldn't know the difference, either way. And I don't want to take that chance."

Now this bothered him.

If she did turn out to be his *destiny*, how could she ever trust any of her actions with him? How could she possibly trust her words, never knowing if they had been coerced or not? If they had been hers…*or his*?

And if she did not turn out to be his *destiny*, which was likely to be the case, how could she ever adjust to life in a different realm, come to know and depend upon the Silivasi family, if she believed vampires were nothing more than charlatans, supernatural magicians who imposed their will on others by playing constant mind games? In the blink of an eye, Kagen made a decision: He would show her very clearly what compulsion was. He would give her a standard by which to compare the two polarities: free will versus vampiric coercion. Then, whether she was his *destiny* or not, she would never doubt his psychic intrusion again.

"Why are you out here in the night with me, Arielle?" he asked dryly. "Wouldn't you be much safer with my brothers?" Her eyes shot to his in immediate alarm, and that was all he needed. He locked his gaze with hers and infused it with preternatural power. "Come to me," he drawled. He waved her forward with his hand, but the gesture was really unnecessary: His voice was a chilling command, darkly sensuous, and laced with the strength of his will.

She froze.

She looked at him with a passing flicker of understanding in her eyes; opened her mouth to refuse; and then began to march steadily in his direction, placing one foot in front of the other as if some unseen inertia compelled her forth.

Kagen leaned back against the tree and waited, guiding her forward with his eyes.

When, at last, she began to tremble, he knew she felt the full power of his coercion, the magnetic pull that was beyond attraction or mere acquiescence, the irresistible force that demanded submission. But she had feared him before. Compulsion was something much stronger. She stopped about two feet in front of him, and he slowly shook his head. "Closer," he whispered, "until we are touching."

Arielle shuffled forward.

She took two small steps, and then she inched her feet along the ground until her toes were touching his.

"Better," he whispered, his voice still laced with imperious command. "Now, look at me."

Her eyes locked indelibly with his, the soft, iridescent irises betraying the presence of alpha waves, a form of waking hallucination, in their depths. “Kiss me, Arielle.”

She rose up to her toes, as graceful as a gazelle, and pressed her mouth to his. Her eyes were so wide with terror that he almost released her, but then he saw something else in their depths: hunger, need, and longing.

Feelings he hadn’t commanded but simply revealed.

He kissed her with a passion he had no right to display, and she responded in kind, encircling his shoulders with her arms, clutching his hair in her hands. She moaned into his mouth, and he almost felt faint—he hadn’t compelled that either.

Forcing himself to pull away, lest he take advantage of something that started out as a lesson, he reined in his desire and released her from his hold. “Now that is compulsion,” he said firmly, feeling a bit like a lecherous jerk.

Arielle stepped back and blinked several times, as if coming out of a trance. She brought her hand to her mouth, lightly touched her lips, and stared at him with a mixture of shock and confusion in her now-shadowed eyes.

“When you feel like a puppet,” Kagen said evenly, “when you sense that you are being pulled through a dense, indefinable fog, when the words you hear are dreamlike and your body moves of its own accord, *that* is compulsion.” He kept his hands religiously at his sides. “It is very different from inner conflict or battling one’s own emotions. The latter originates inside of you—the former is forced upon you. ”

Arielle clasped her hand over her mouth and shivered. She looked absolutely horrified.

“I’m sorry,” Kagen whispered. “But now, you will never have to wonder. You will always know the difference.”

When a single tear escaped her eye and trickled down her cheek, he felt like more than just a lecherous jerk—he felt like a complete and utter ass, an absolute bully. Okay, so maybe it had been a terrible idea, after all. “Arielle…”

“No.” She took a cautious step backward. “Why would

you?" She cleared her throat. "Didn't it ever occur to you..." She shook her head to dismiss the thought. "Never mind." She turned on her heels and started to walk away; and then, just as suddenly, she stopped in place, glanced over her shoulder, and took a deep, steadying breath. Spinning around to face him once more, she stared at him bravely. "So my coming to you was compulsion, but my *wanting* to do so was not. My kissing you was coerced, but my reaction was genuine. You sought to teach me a lesson, while I succumbed to...need. You must feel very satisfied. You are a good teacher, Kagen Silivasi: I get the difference now. Thank you."

The words were delivered with more bluntness than spite, yet Kagen felt their sting.

For a moment, he almost wished she had just stepped forward and slapped him—it would have been far easier to take. "Once again, you misinterpret my intentions, Arielle." He scrubbed his face in his hands. This was maddening.

Hopeless!

And why he felt so compelled to keep trying remained a mystery.

Surely she had to be his *destiny*—his brothers might be right—why else would he keep putting himself through such torture, stuffing his foot in his mouth, time and time again?

He held up his hands in helpless petition, beseeching her with his eyes. "Tell me what you want from me, Arielle. Name it, *whatever it is*, and I will do it."

She looked momentarily speechless. "*What I want?*"

"Yes," he whispered, feeling more exasperated than ever.

"Haven't you been listening to a word I've said?"

"I have," he replied. He was about two seconds from falling to his knees. "And you continue to tell me what you *don't* want...what you *don't* like...what I keep doing *wrong*. Please, just once, tell me what you *do* want, Arielle. They are not the same thing."

She threw up her hands in frustration. "I want...*I want*...I don't want to be used like a puppet." She was doing it again.

Still, he held his breath and listened.

"I don't want you to come into my life, into my dangerous, impossible world, and turn it upside down, just to ultimately leave it—*and me*—like some broken, used-up toy you've grown tired of. I don't want..." Her voice trailed off.

"You still haven't—"

"I don't want to get hurt!" She rushed the words, and he held his tongue, not daring to interrupt. "There is no room inside me for any more hurt, Kagen. Surely, you can understand this. Could you bear to lose your brother again? To find your father, just to be separated in the end? I know you could not."

Kagen nodded slowly, but he didn't let up. "You are still avoiding the question, Arielle: Tell me what you *want*."

She breathed a heavy sigh. "I lost my mother when I was only ten, Kagen. I have never had a father. I was a *slave* for nearly eight years, and I have had to live hand-to-mouth, week to week, always on the run from a merciless king that would take me, and claim me, and abuse me if he could. I have never had a real family. I have never known true tenderness. I have never felt passion, and I don't want to because there is no place in my world for it to exist. Can you understand that?"

"I can." Gods, he felt abominable for pushing her like this, yet he knew, somewhere deep inside, that if they didn't break through this, here and now, they never would. "Yet again, you tell me what you *don't* want."

"By all the ancestors, you are infuriating!" Her eyes flashed a deeper shade of opal-blue, and she planted her hands on her hips. "What difference does it make, *what I want*, when this world cares not at all for my kind...for women. Why do you push me, knowing that I cannot return your affection? Knowing that we come from different worlds, and we always will?"

Now was not the time to tell her that her last sentence was not entirely true; that, if his brothers had anything to do with it, she would be returning to his world, one way or the other. Besides, he had given Nachari his word. "Because I am utterly helpless before you, Arielle." He spoke softly but with conviction. "Because your every need, your every longing, your every sorrow pierces my heart like a blade I can't remove. Because I want to please you so badly; yet, time and time again, I fail so miserably; and even as you push me away, I am helpless to go… *I must stay. I must try.* It is not a choice."

"Then why can't you just—"

She withdrew from the statement as if the words had been a branding iron that nearly scorched her skin. She concentrated on her breathing instead. "And what if *what I want* is something entirely different than what you imagine? What if it's not something you are willing to give?"

Kagen's heart nearly skipped a beat. Then there *was* something she wanted from him. "What is it?"

"Well, it's not to have a torrid affair with a vampire that is doomed to end badly, a meaningless tryst that will ultimately break my heart."

"Arielle, tell me what you want."

"It's not to walk in the footsteps of my mother, and—"

"*Arielle*, tell me what you want!"

All the air seemed to leave her body as she visibly deflated. "Why can't you just…"

Kagen waited with bated breath for her last word. When it never came, he prompted her one more time. "*Just what*, Arielle? Why can't I just…*what*?"

She averted her gaze. "Nothing."

"*Just what*, Arielle?"

She wrapped her arms around her chest, hugging herself like a child, and her body began to tremble.

"Talk to me, sweeting," Kagen cajoled, forcing himself to avoid the use of compulsion—gods knew, he wanted to take the information from her mind, so badly.

When, at last, she began to speak, her voice dropped to such a low whisper that, even with his hyper-acute hearing, he had to strain to hear her words. "All my life, for me, growing up in Mhier…whenever a man wanted a woman, it was more of a threat than an endearment." She bit her bottom lip and shifted her weight nervously from foot to foot. "A promise of dominance…or degradation…but rarely an act of love. Your passion overwhelms me, Kagen. It both frightens and intrigues me; but the truth is, I am not the beautiful, desirable woman you think I am. I'm just a girl, *a woman*, who has never even been held." She turned a pale shade of what Kagen could only call alabaster. "How can you expect me to respond to you with passion or affection, when I don't even know what it is to feel safe, to feel *wanted*…to just be held?"

Kagen stood in stunned silence as her words settled over him like frost on a winter's day. By all the celestial gods in the heavens, he wanted to go to her, take her in his arms, and never let her go, but he had to proceed with caution. "You *are* the beautiful, desirable woman I think you are, Arielle." His voice thickened with conviction. "And I am not the monster you would make of me: one who could *ever* hurt you, degrade you, or do anything other than worship you. I would *love* to hold you, sweeting. No passion. No desire. No demands. Just once, to show you what it is to *be* safe, to *be* wanted…to be held." He momentarily closed his eyes. "My arms ache with the need."

Arielle drew back in surprise and simply stared at him as both longing and terror warred within her eyes.

"Shh," Kagen coaxed sweetly. "Silence your mind. Let go of your fears. Just *be*." He held out his arms and prayed to Auriga, the god of his ruling moon, *Please, just let her take this one, intractable step.*

Arielle regarded him as if he were a stranger, as if she were seeing him for the very first time; and it was so painfully evident by the look in her eyes that she wanted this more than she had wanted anything in a very long time. She just didn't know *how*…

How to ask.

How to allow it.

How to take the risk.

And Kagen refused to compel her.

"Arielle, come to me, sweeting." It was a request, pure and simple, heartfelt but absent of coercion.

She blinked back tears, and her eyes darted warily around the grove before returning, once more, to his. "You don't have to do this."

"I want to." He almost groaned. "So badly it hurts."

She sighed and took a cautious step in his direction. "And you won't—"

"I won't do anything but hold you. *I swear.*"

She looked down at the ground then. "I feel so…silly."

"There's nothing silly about it," he said. "Come to me, Arielle. *Please.*" When she took two tentative steps forward, stopped in place, and then regarded him warily once more, he thought he might just come apart at the seams from the frustration of it all. "I would kill for you, Arielle Nightsong. I would open my veins and bleed if I thought it might ease your pain. Won't you please just let me hold you? Just this once?"

He knew the moment she capitulated.

The instant her heart stopped resisting and opened up, the second she decided to let him in.

As silent as a mouse, she took the last remaining step in his direction, careful to remain impassive, to look at anything but him. She was determined not to meet his eyes.

She couldn't.

It was just too vulnerable.

And that was just fine with him.

When, at last, she lowered her head to his chest and pressed her ear to his heart, he felt a non-erotic shiver course through his body. He gathered her softly in his arms and enfolded her in his warmth. He clutched her as tightly as he dared, and then he nestled his chin in her hair, refusing to let go.

He refused to breathe.

He refused to cheapen the moment with words.

And as she nuzzled in deeper, her soft, flowing tresses blanketing his chest in glorious waves of bronze, he tightened his hold and finally exhaled.

Arielle was in his arms at last.

Trusting him with her safety and her heart.

And then, to his utter amazement, she wrapped her arms around his waist, burrowed in even deeper, and spoke shyly into his chest. "Thank you, Kagen." Her voice was thick with tears.

"Oh, my sweeting," he whispered. He anchored his hand in her hair so he could hold her even closer. "My sweet, beautiful warrior." He kissed her softly on the forehead—there was nothing more to say.

As a lifetime of tears began to roll down her cheeks, Kagen held Arielle like his life depended on it, like *her* life depended on it, and truth be told, perhaps it did. He blanketed her in his warmth; sent soothing energy radiating throughout her body; sent healing vibrations up and down her spine. He engulfed her in a cocoon of peace, even as he sought to draw as much pain and sorrow as he could out of her spirit and into his.

It was all he had to give, but he gave it to her freely.

Willingly.

Lovingly.

It would have to be enough…

For now.

sixteen

Just beyond the southern pack's district boundaries, General Teague Verasachi threw open the heavy wooden doors of the secluded outbuilding. The old, dilapidated barn stood in virtual isolation at the south end of the Wolverine Woods and was still used from time to time for private meetings and other, *less pleasant* activities…

Such as torture.

The moment he entered the musty structure, he immediately spied his beta lieutenant Jacob Tansy and the three captured prisoners: the rebels Walker Alencion, Kade Burnett, and Echo Morgan. In their search for Arielle Nightsong, they had stumbled across the Rebel Camp quite by accident and managed to capture or kill all but a handful of fleeing humans. Unfortunately, the object of the king's desire had not been present—there was no trace of Arielle anywhere. And so, they had brought three of the fiercest rebels back to the southern lycan district in hopes of *coaxing* further information out of the prisoners.

"Anything yet?" Teague asked Jacob, strolling across the disorderly space in three great strides.

Jacob frowned. He pointed to Walker Alencion, who was hanging from the ceiling, his wrists bound together and attached to a large iron hook. The skin of his back had been flayed raw with a leather lash, and there were several sharp metal spikes protruding through his feet, where Jacob had pierced the limbs through the soles, upward. "Nothing useful," he bit out. "I have questioned this human trash a dozen times, and I continue to get the same answer: The last time he saw Arielle was two days ago, early Wednesday morning. She was heading to the banks of the Skeleton Swamps to collect healing herbs, and he hasn't heard from her since." He interlocked his fingers, cracked his knuckles, and rotated his head on his neck to release some tension. "It's strange because it's almost as if there is something else he wants to tell me, something he knows about her whereabouts, but he just can't access the information."

Teague circled Walker slowly, glaring at him with barely concealed rage. "What do you mean: *He just can't access the information*?"

Jacob shrugged his brawny shoulders and shifted his weight from one large foot to the other. "Don't know. Can't explain. It's like a part of his memory, maybe even his mind, has just been burned away." He pointed at a particularly hideous gash in Walker's left side—the wound was bubbling with thick, coagulating blood and already oozing pus. "I've packed salt, poured alcohol, and even inserted poisonous thorns into these wounds. He screams like a stuck pig, but he still doesn't talk." He grasped Walker by the chin and dug his nails into his cheeks, causing him to gasp in pain. "I don't think he's that strong. It's almost as if he would tell us…if he could. But he can't."

Teague grunted in displeasure and turned his attention to the second male, Echo Morgan. "And this one?"

Echo was bound to a high-backed torture chair—the crude implement was fashioned like any other stool, only there were manacles attached to the base for the ankles; the back was wrapped in thick strings of barbed wire; and the seat itself was a bed of sharp, protruding spikes that jutted upward from the seat. Everywhere an occupant's flesh touched the chair, he or she would be pierced with sharp, rusty stakes.

"Same thing," Jacob said, pausing to hawk some phlegm from his throat and spit it on the ground at Echo's feet. "He's far tougher than the other one. I think he would be willing to take his secrets to the grave, but just the same, I don't think he knows the female's whereabouts."

Teague crouched down in front of Echo and flashed a vicious set of canines in his face. "Ever had your throat ripped out by a lycan?" he whispered. "Ever had your flesh consumed one piece at a time?" When Echo simply glared at him in disgust,

Teague smiled. "It can be arranged, Mr. Morgan. It can be arranged." He reached out and slapped him so hard that the chair fell over, driving two- and three-inch barbs deeper into his sides. "Pick him up," Teague ordered Jacob, sauntering over to the final prisoner. "And what do we have here?"

Kade Burnett was kneeling on the ground, his face hovering over a barrel full of water, his hands and arms bound behind his bloodied back. His dirty-blond hair was soaked from repeated dunking in the drum; the pupils of his dazed brown eyes were dilated with shock; and his skin looked like a checkerboard made of white and red squares, from where Jacob had carved uneven slices of flesh from his body and dropped them in the barrel.

"He says he last saw Arielle on Tuesday night, that she and Walker returned to the camp after midnight. Swears he hasn't seen her since."

Teague held out his giant hand and gestured toward the thin filet knife attached to Jacob's belt. "Hand me your blade."

Kade's eyes grew even wider and he grit his teeth—but he didn't speak out.

"I'm going to carve your spine out of your body, rebel," Teague growled. He held up the five-inch blade and rotated it in the lantern-light. "I will start at your neck, slice down, along your left side, make a cross-wise slash at your tailbone, and then gut you from your waist back to your shoulder, along the right side. When I am done, you will no longer be a warrior, a rebel…or a man. You will be a pile of meat and bones, unable to move your limbs." He slashed him swiftly across the cheek with the tip of the blade, licked the blood off the steel, and moaned. "Is there anything you would like to tell me in order to procure a swifter, easier death? *Where is Arielle Nightsong?*"

Kade trembled where he knelt, his broad, muscular shoulders straining with the effort to hold his damaged body upright. Despite his valiant attempt at courage, his eyes filled with tears, and he shuddered. "I don't know," he bit out angrily. "I swear by the ancestors—I don't know!" He grimaced and squinted, as if suddenly seized by a violent headache, and then he shook his head, as if trying to clear his vision. "Please…" He swayed in a circular motion. "*Please.*"

Teague turned to Jacob and shrugged. *"Please."* He mocked the prisoner callously. "Make the weak one watch."

Jacob strolled across the earthen floor until he stood directly behind Walker, and then spinning his body like a carcass drying out on a rack, he turned him to face Kade. "Watch and learn, rebel," he said, licking the side of Walker's jaw and growling like the supernatural creature he was, even in human form.

As Teague began to carve out Kade's spine, the man writhed and screamed in agony. At first he shouted in defiance, and then he just pleaded for mercy. Until, at last, he slumped over the barrel and died, his face floating morbidly in the tainted water.

Walker shook from head to toe. "Oh shit," he mumbled beneath his breath. "*Oh shit, oh shit, oh shit*! I swear, General Teague"—he addressed the lycan directly—"I don't know where she is."

Teague frowned and took a careful step in Walker's direction, menacing the pathetic human with nothing more than his gait: his smooth, lithe, mongrel stride. He pulled back his lips and snarled, allowing his lower jaw to begin shifting, before he reined it back and, once again, donned the persona of a man.

Walker began to urinate, trickles of pungent yellow fluid streaming down his legs. "Please," he begged piteously. "C'mon, man…*please.*"

Teague turned up his lips in disgust. "I'm going to remove your testicles, Walker." He laughed out loud. "And then, I'm going to make you watch while I feed them to your buddy, Echo."

Echo whimpered mechanically, breaking his stoic silence.

"No!" Walker cried out, blatantly horrified. "No…I swear…I'd tell you if I could. *I swear.*" His mouth began to work in small little O's, like a fish that had just been scooped out of water. He twisted and turned and yanked on his bonds. "I would give her to you if I could. *I swear it.* She's never done anything but reject me anyways. I swear!"

Now this got Teague's attention.

So the redheaded human had a thing for Arielle Nightsong, and he had been spurned by her on more than one occasion. *This* might be something he could work with. "Arielle is a whore," he whispered harshly. "Do you know what she used to do in the slave encampment, during her teenage years? The favors she used to bestow on King Thane's soldiers? I was one of them," he lied, "and I can tell you honestly, she *loved* it."

The human turned the color of ripe tomatoes. In his weakened state of pain and privation, he couldn't discern the truth from a lie, and apparently, he was too stupid to understand that King Thane would have murdered any soldier who had dared to place a single hand on a female he had chosen for a bride.

No matter.

The words were having their desired effect.

Walker writhed in pain, even as he jerked in anger. "That *bitch*," he whispered, nearly biting his own tongue. "She lied to me."

"Of course she did." Teague taunted him. "But all is not lost: Tell us where she is, and we will seek vengeance for you." He smiled as if they were merely having a congenial conversation. "I give you my word as a general." It sounded good anyway.

Walker shook his head sadly, his dangling feet swaying in the air in response to the motion. "I swear to you, General Teague. The last time I saw her was early Wednesday morning, right before she left for the banks of the Skeleton Swamps to pick herbs. But"—he quickly rushed the words—"*but* there is something important that you don't know."

Teague raised his eyebrows and practically held his breath. He brandished the knife in front of Walker's face, dropped it low to hold it between his legs, and snarled. "Do tell."

Walker swallowed hard, causing his Adam's apple to bob up and down several times, before he continued. "She makes regular trips back and forth to the slave encampment. To the royal district."

Teague drew back in surprise. "What? *Why*?"

"To visit the vampire—the slave—Keitaro Silivasi."

Teague's jaw tightened, and he ground his teeth in annoyance. "Tell me more."

"She prepares healing herbs and salves, and she sneaks into his tent at night to try and give him comfort."

"How often does she do this?" Teague asked.

Walker tried to shrug his shoulders, but the weight of his body prevented them from rising. "I don't know. It depends…on a lot of things. Whether or not she can get away. The weather. A lot of things."

"And when was the last time—"

"The last time she was there was Tuesday evening, just after full moonrise. *I think*."

Teague could hardly believe his ears. So Arielle Nightsong had been right under Thane's nose all this time, moving boldly in and out of the slave encampment, only hours from the heart of the royal district, only a full day's journey from the arena, and all for the sake of that degenerate vampire. King Thane would be murderous; perhaps it was better if he didn't know.

Of one thing, Teague was quite sure: The information would lead to her capture once and for all. Now, it was just a matter of placing a sentry outside of the circular clearing, on the narrow path that wound between the Mystic Mountains and the slave encampment. Sooner or later, the woman would rear her arrogant, rebellious head.

And Teague Verasachi would be waiting.

He turned to regard Walker Alencion with fresh, new vigor in his heart. "Is there anything else?"

Walker sighed in visible relief. "No, not that I can think of, but I swear, I would tell you if there was. I *will* tell you if there is. If I think of anything else."

"Very good," Teague said. He turned to face his beta lieutenant and barked out a formal command: "Lieutenant Jacob, I want you to send the third squadron, the elite pack of Omegas, to the circular clearing just outside the slave encampment, on the northern side of the Mystic Mountains, with the mission to set up surveillance in the thick of the woods. To capture Arielle. Tell them to prepare for a long deployment if necessary: I don't give a wolf's damn how long it takes; they are not to leave their post. Tell them the information is classified. The mission remains hush-hush, between you, the squadron, and me." He wrung his hands together eagerly. "How long will it take to get them into position?"

Jacob massaged his brow, thinking. "At least one hour to mobilize and twelve to travel: They should be there by tomorrow, no later than eleven AM—noon, in the worst-case scenario."

Teague nodded his head in approval. "Fine. I want you to position them in the thicket, just beyond the clearing—we can only hope she doesn't know Keitaro has already been moved to the arena." He tilted his ear toward his shoulder in a gesture of chance. "If luck is on our side, she will try to visit him once more, before Sunday's games, and we will be waiting."

"You really think she would be crazy enough to go anywhere near the slave encampment—or the games on Sunday—knowing that King Thane will be looking for her, scouring the countryside to find her?"

"Just do it, soldier!"

Jacob Tansy stood to attention, saluted his general, and took a cautious step backward. "Yes, sir!"

"And hurry," Teague snarled, beginning to lose his composure. They were so close now. He didn't dare risk losing a chance to capture Arielle due to needless procrastination. He pointed brusquely at Echo Morgan. "And cut the defiant one out of the chair. I want the Omegas to take him with them; they may need to use him as bait. She obviously doesn't give a rat's ass about the redhead. Maybe this one, she at least respects."

Walker began to object in earnest, and Jacob started to answer—but Teague didn't hear either one.

He had already shape-shifted into the form of his wolf.

The matter settled, he rose to his hind feet, sprung deftly at

Walker, and savagely tore out his throat.

At least he left his testicles intact.

seventeen

The next morning

The day was overcast and dreary, not quite as dark as the night, but with a thick, inky fog settling over the land like a skeletal hand of mist, it felt just as foreboding.

The Silivasis had packed up their camp in silence, the weight of what was to come weighing heavily on each male's shoulders; the knowledge that they were less than an hour away from the slave encampment, eleven hours away from the arena, had left them all in a contemplative if not downright surly mood. They didn't expect to find Keitaro in the despicable slave hut; but still, to actually see where their father had lived, where he had been kept for so many centuries like a captive animal, was more than any of them could bear.

Kagen hoisted his heavy pack onto his shoulders, careful to check once more around the ravine, to make sure they had left no trace whatsoever of their passing, and then he turned to glance at Arielle. She was kneeling over her bedroll, rolling it up into a neat, even trundle, and her wild copper hair hung loose about her shoulders, several errant strands of red highlights framing her vivid eyes like a crown. She smiled at him and then quickly glanced away.

And his breath caught in his throat.

While the beautiful warrior had not been exactly inviting since their intimate exchange by the larch tree, the change in her otherwise impervious demeanor had been palpable.

Endearing.

She blushed whenever she looked at him, and her heart could only be described as soft…pliable…*open.* The kindness that was rooted at her core, the compassion that defined her true nature, was no longer locked up in a vault, so carefully protected.

It was responsive, available…and subtly exposed.

Kagen smiled inwardly, grateful to have made even the smallest inroads with the beautiful native.

"Are you ready, healer?" Marquis's voice cut through the silence, bringing him back to the present moment.

"As ready as I can be," Kagen said.

Marquis grunted. "What we will see today, at the slave encampment; do not let it linger in your mind. We can't afford to be distracted or off-balance as we head to the arena. We will need all of our faculties, our full concentration, to map a final strategy, to execute as we *must* tomorrow."

Kagen nodded. Now this was a moment worth noting, indeed, Marquis Silivasi warning his brothers not to be irrational. "Whatever I see today, Master Warrior, will only fuel the fire that burns inside of me—my determination to see our father freed."

Nachari sauntered up to the two other vampires. Although his gait was casual as usual, his face betrayed his angst. "Then you do not believe there is any chance our father is still there?"

"No," Marquis said gruffly. "The games are at three o'clock tomorrow, and the arena is at least ten hours away from the slave encampment. Thane would be a fool not to have moved Keitaro already, and while I do believe Thane is a worthless pile of mongrel shit, he is not a stupid adversary."

"No," Nathaniel chimed in, his normally placid features hardening with resolve. "Just a dead one."

Marquis met Nathaniel's stare and sniffed. "Indeed."

Nachari licked his lips involuntarily, his inner panther demonstrating his assent. He purred deep in his throat, and they all took notice.

When Arielle padded silently up to the others, all three of Kagen's brothers turned to glance at her, and then Kagen, appreciatively. He smiled—what else was there to say? "Good morning, Miss Nightsong." He practically hummed the words.

She bit her bottom lip, looked down at the ground, and then deliberately lifted her head to meet his eyes, her cheeks flushing a beautiful pink. "Good morning, healer." In an effort to distract herself, she started fussing with her arrows; counting the brightly colored fletchings; checking and rechecking her bow.

"Is everything in order?" Kagen asked. He couldn't help but rib her just a little.

She smiled so sweetly that her teeth nearly sparkled, and then she simply rolled her eyes and walked away, hurrying to catch up with Marquis.

Kagen chuckled aloud. *What an enigma*, he thought. The female could release three arrows faster than most people could notch a bow; she could hit her chosen target with unerring precision; and she wasn't a rival to take lightly. Yet, she blushed like a teenager in response to a male's attention. *To his attention.* "Arielle," he called after her, unable to resist the urge to needle her some more.

"Yes?" She tried to appear relaxed.

"If there's anything you need"—he narrowed his eyes and then winked, his mouth turning up in a devilish grin—"you know where to find me."

She huffed in exasperation, smoothed the front of her parka—as if an animal hide could be smoothed into place with the swipe of a hand—and turned on her heels. "You are incorrigible, Mr. Silivasi. And I am *fine* for the moment."

He took a deep, appreciative breath. "Oh, believe me; you are that."

Utterly flustered, she scurried away.

The group traveled quickly, making exceptionally good time. They arrived at the outskirts of the slave encampment in less than an hour, and it took only mere moments—listening, feeling, directing their heightened senses toward the hut Keitaro used to occupy—to recognize that it was indeed empty.

Marquis had squatted down on the ground, careful to remain out of sight should any lycans pass by, as he had struggled to control his rage. Fortunately, all of the Silivasis had come to realize by this, their fourth day in Mhier, that emotions did not have the same effect in this strange new land that they had in Dark Moon Vale: While tree branches might sway or rustle, and while the air might grow thicker, the earth did not rumble or split open beneath their rage, and the skies did not open up and pour down sorrow as buckets of rain. And it was a good thing, too, because Marquis had been simply murderous after seeing the conditions of Keitaro's slave hut, even from a distance, after recognizing on a visceral level that this was how their father had lived…for centuries.

Nathaniel, on the other hand, had reacted just the opposite: He had been eerily casual and far too calm. It wasn't that the ancient vampire didn't feel Keitaro's pain, or even his own: Quite the contrary; it was that he could not allow himself to process any of it *just then*. The weight of it would have been too heavy; the breadth of it would have been too vast. So he had locked it up, somewhere inside, relegating his emotions to some internal box, to be accessed and *fed upon* at a later date and time—undoubtedly, he would draw upon it in the arena, when they finally faced the lycans for the first time.

Nachari had been the only one to face the horrors with open sensitivity, to allow himself to cry, even if he had only shed a half-dozen tears. He had bowed his head, retreated for a time in prayer, and then gone about the business of checking his weapons and consuming a quick repast of bagged blood in order to fortify his body for the rest of their journey. He had chosen to prepare himself for the voyage yet to come, the longest trek of their day, a ten-hour hike beyond the Royal District to the gates of the arena.

Kagen had quietly slipped away, retreating back into the thick of the forest, into a small, circular clearing that stood no more than one hundred yards from the outskirts of the slave huts. Despite its proximity to the encampment, the clearing had afforded him some much-needed privacy—it was isolated like his pain, concealed by a large, U-shaped hedge of towering conifers. The trees looked like they had been planted eons ago for just this purpose, perhaps by the gods of the lycans, if in fact, such beasts had gods…

Or souls.

He ran his hands through his hair and tried to focus on his breathing, to simply draw air in…and then slowly let it out. Not only had he gazed upon his father's crude, unimaginable prison, but Arielle had pointed out a similar hut about five hundred yards away, the place she had grown up as a teenager.

The idea of it all—that beautiful little girl, along with their proud, invincible father, being stored away like so much garbage beneath the tyranny of a lycan king—sickened him to his core, and he had just needed a moment…alone.

Now, as he padded softly through the clearing, listening to the discreet snap of branches, the delicate rustle of leaves beneath his feet, he thought he sensed Arielle beside him. He turned to greet her, hoping she had come to be with him in this solemn, intimate moment, only to find that there was no one there. He wrinkled his nose in confusion and turned his head to the left, then the right, in an effort to make sense of what he was detecting.

He drew in a deep breath and discreetly scented the air.

He repeated it a second time…and then a third.

He stooped down on his heels, placed his hands in the dirt, and felt the earth for subtle vibrations: the clear, unmistakable imprint of the energy he was sensing.

Arielle's…

Her distinct genetic footprint was everywhere around him. He tasted it on his tongue, felt it in the soil beneath him, scented it in the air. And just to be sure, he scanned his surroundings once more, half expecting to see her standing right beside him.

She wasn't.

He was still alone.

Kagen sat down on the ground and sought to quiet his mind. He was an Ancient Master Healer, and he had taken Arielle Nightsong's blood. He could track her anywhere—detect her fear, sense her distress, and dial-in on her whereabouts with finite precision—just by homing in on her blood, because he *knew* her DNA. He knew the unique genetic code that made her distinct, that made her Arielle, and the taste of it, the feel of it, the knowledge of it was all around him in this meadow, embedded in the circular clearing itself.

But how could that be?

True, she had lived in the encampment for years, and perhaps she had visited this site several times; but what he was feeling was so much stronger than a passing foray over ten years ago. It was a joining, a cohesion of elements, a fundamental oneness with the chemistry of the land itself.

And then he suddenly understood.

Kagen was picking up on a genetic code so similar to Arielle's that it almost *had to be hers*—because it was. It was an identical pattern of fifty percent DNA, and that meant it belonged to one of three persons: her mother, her father, or a sibling. And it was deeply embedded in the clearing, not a passing impression, not a subtle imprint, but a permanent part of the land itself.

And that meant he was reclining on a grave.

He let out a contemplative sigh. By all the gods, Arielle didn't have any brothers or sisters, and her mother had been killed on the southern end of Mhier, in General Teague's encampment, over a day's travel away. So this could only be one thing. It could only be one person.

Kagen had stumbled upon Ryder Nightsong's grave.

And that meant her father had been within five hundred yards of Arielle's slave hut, at least once. For what purpose? Kagen didn't know. But perhaps Nachari could shed some light on the subject.

He rubbed his forehead in consternation. This was a delicate matter at best, and he needed to proceed with caution. Legend had it that Arielle's father had been killed trying to rescue her from slavery, but the story had only been a rumor, a fable. Now, one way or the other, the information Nachari could divine might be healing…or devastating. Yet he couldn't keep it from Arielle.

Mustering his courage, he called out to his brother on a private, telepathic bandwidth, needing the wizard's help: *Nachari, I am in the thick of the forest, in a circular clearing. I need you to come to me…and bring Arielle with you.*

Nachari's response was immediate. *Is something wrong, Kagen? Is there danger?*

Not of the corporeal kind, Kagen said. *I believe I've stumbled across a grave, and it may belong to Arielle's father. However, I have no way of knowing how he came to be here, how he came to rest here, and I may need you to try and read the energy. See what you can see.*

Nachari was quiet for a moment. When he finally replied, his psychic voice was cautious. *I assume Arielle doesn't know.*

She knows nothing. But the decision will be hers.

As you wish, brother. She just finished eating. I'll bring her to you now.

It felt like an eternity before Nachari and Arielle emerged through the thicket, although it had probably been less than five minutes. Arielle's expression was eager, and her eyes were alight with curiosity. "Kagen? Nachari says you want to see me?"

Kagen rose to his full height and held out his hand. "Yes, sweeting. Come to me, *please*: There is something I need to tell you."

Arielle paused, as if she sensed something amiss in his voice, and then she slowly stepped forward and took his hand. "What is it?"

Nachari followed in her footsteps, stopping several feet away to stand unobtrusively at her side.

"This clearing," Kagen began, "when I first got here, I thought you were right behind me, perhaps beside me: I felt your presence very strongly in the air, in the flora, in the ground."

Arielle frowned in confusion. "I don't understand."

Kagen tightened his grip on her hand. "Remember when I took your blood?"

She nodded. "Of course. I don't think I will ever forget."

He smiled sheepishly. "No, I don't suppose you will. But this is not about our connection…or my insanity." He gently massaged her palm with his thumb, hoping to somehow soften his words. "It is about something much more important."

When she looked up into his eyes, her gaze was so filled with trust—yet foreboding—that it tugged at the strings of his heart. He forced himself to continue. "Arielle, I took your blood in order to have a way to track you, in an effort to keep you safe. As my brothers and I explained that first night in the cave, your specific genetic imprint acts almost like a GPS system—"

"A GPS system?" She frowned, confused.

"A homing or tracking device—information encoded in your specific DNA that allows us to sense you, to find you, to recognize you wherever you may be." He gestured broadly at the clearing. "In a sense, it's like your name or your fingerprint, something that only belongs to you. However, parts of that code, elements of that fingerprint, were given to you by your parents. You share at least half of the same…material." He frowned. "I know it isn't easy to understand. I can only ask that you trust me in this."

Arielle nodded gravely, and her soft aquamarine eyes turned a much deeper opal-blue. "Of course…*I do*."

Kagen smiled warmly then. Her trust was a newfound and welcoming gift. "At first, I didn't understand how I could have such a powerful sense of you all around me when you weren't, in fact, here. But then I realized that the *code* I was reading, the fingerprint that I was seeing, actually belonged to someone else. Someone who shares your unique information, at least in part."

Arielle sighed. "I still don't understand."

"You had no siblings, correct?"

"No." Arielle shook her head emphatically. "No brothers or sisters. My mother swore to that fact."

"Then it belongs to your mother or your father."

Arielle took a moment to process his words. When, at last, she answered him, it was with a simple, reasoned argument. "But my mother has never traveled this far north, and she died in

Teague's encampment."

"I know," Kagen said softly. He drew in a deep breath and waited for her to make the connection.

"My father?" she said calmly; and then her forehead creased with confusion. "But how can that be? You can sense his…*fingerprint*…that clearly? Simply by passing by, standing somewhere he may have once been? I…I don't understand. It doesn't make sense…" Her voice trailed off, and he could almost see the wheels turning in her mind: *Ryder had been in this clearing before*. He had been *this close* to the slave encampment.

Still, she hadn't fully connected the dots.

She still didn't grasp the full measure of what he was trying to say.

"I could not—or perhaps it is better to say *I would not*—sense his presence that clearly if he had just *passed by* so many years ago, not from a fleeting moment in time. But if your father were still here, if he had somehow…*become*…a part of the land, than that would be a different matter entirely."

Arielle released Kagen's hand and gradually turned around, rotating in a slow but steady circle. She gazed up at the trees and then down at the ground. She peered between bushes and scrutinized shadows, searching for something she still couldn't name. "You're saying my father is *here*?" She chewed on her bottom lip. "That's not possible. Legend has it that he died many years ago, when I was still a teenager; and I'm certain that, even if he never wanted to know me, he would not have turned his back on the resistance, not all this time. If he were still alive, the rebels would know."

Kagen nodded, and Nachari looked away.

Her face grew ashen. "What are you saying, Kagen?"

Kagen held her gaze in an unyielding stare. "I believe this is your father's final resting place."

She took a step back, her face still blank, as if his words and her hearing had yet to cross paths—she understood the syntax and even the connotation, but the meaning eluded her because her mind wasn't ready to grasp it. Finally, she spoke softly, in an eerily dispassionate voice. "So…you believe this is Ryder's grave?"

"Yes," Kagen whispered.

"You believe this, but you don't know for sure?"

Kagen closed his eyes, just for a moment, in order to muster his courage. "I am absolutely sure."

"*Hm*," Arielle intoned, as if she had just learned that clothes were made from cotton. "But why…when…*how*?" She stumbled to the side and Kagen reached out to steady her, but she quickly pulled away. She turned to face the direction of the larger slave encampment and clasped her hands over her mouth. "This can't be more than a hundred yards from my slave hut, the place I was kept all those years. Why would Ryder have been here?"

Kagen felt his heart constrict in his chest—*from my slave hut*—the words made him sick. "I don't know, Arielle, but I think it's an awful strange coincidence, don't you?" He reached out for her hand, pulled her forward beneath him, and then encircled her shoulders with his arms. "You were always told that Ryder *left this world* trying to find you, to rescue you, but you never had any proof. We know one thing for certain: He left this world only a hundred yards away from you, and that certainly lends credence to the stories."

Arielle choked back a sob. She wrested her body out of Kagen's arms and stared absently at the ground, her face a mask of both astonishment and dread. "We'll never know."

"Perhaps not," Kagen said gently. "There's no way to retrieve the full memory; however, I asked Nachari to accompany you because he is a wizard with exceptional skill."

Arielle glanced at Nachari and furrowed her brow.

"He can sometimes read the energy of a place, or an object, draw very accurate impressions from what he feels."

Nachari met Arielle's troubled gaze with one of compassion. "I can't choose what information I get—I have no idea what I will or won't find, or even what the impressions always mean—but I can tell you with certainty, if I pick anything up." He bowed his head in deference then. "If it is your will."

Arielle looked positively perplexed. She looked back and forth between Kagen and Nachari, several times in a row; and then she opened her mouth to speak, but nothing came out.

"Arielle," Kagen prompted, "I know this is a lot to process in a short amount of time—it's completely unexpected—but you have to know that we may never pass this way again. This may be your only opportunity to learn more about your father…about his passing." He looked toward the heavens for strength, noticing how the sun was all but absent from the sky, how the deep, heady fog that surrounded the land had grown even thicker, and how the timber wolf moon shone even brighter, more luminescent than he had ever seen it before. "I don't want to pressure you, but we can't remain here all day."

"Keitaro," she whispered softly.

"Yes," Kagen said.

She nodded slowly. She dropped her head in her hands and took a deep, steadying breath, and then she turned to face Nachari. "Wizard, do you think you can do this?"

"I can try," he said quietly.

"Then try," she said.

Her hands began to shake, and Kagen reached out to grasp them. "Step back with me…over there." He pointed toward a nearby grouping of conifer trees—the first ten feet of the trunks were bare—and guided her to stand beneath the branches.

Arielle followed willingly, while Nachari squatted low, near the ground.

He splayed his palms wide, pressed them firmly against the earth, and then slowly closed his eyes. The silence was ominous, nearly palpable, and time seemed to completely stand still as Nachari poured his full concentration into the divination.

He seemed a million miles away.

When at last, he shuddered, ever so slightly, and rose from the ground, it was clear by the look on his face that he had picked up a vivid impression.

Kagen and Arielle stepped forward. "What did you see…what did you hear?" Arielle asked eagerly, her expression a mask of both suspense and dread.

Nachari swallowed, his throat softly churning. He met her aquamarine inquiry with a salient forest-green reply. "I felt the energy of a struggle. The presence of several armed combatants, several humans, the taint of lycans"—he slapped the back of his right hand into the open palm of his left, causing them to make a sharp report—"the force of projected voices: shouts, cries, curses. I didn't get the words. I heard the sound of steel, chiming in the air, like swords being drawn or metal clashing, and I felt the waning…" He paused as if searching for a better way to say it. "The slow abatement of breath, the last moments of sentience, before a body dies."

Arielle rubbed her arms with nervous energy. Then she stiffened her spine and looked him straight in the eyes. "Is that all?"

"No," Nachari said softly. And then, despite himself, he dropped his head and turned away. When he finally looked back, it was clear he was searching for courage. "I also heard three distinct words—they were whispered, but they were clear."

Arielle cleared her throat and absently smoothed her parka. "Who spoke them?"

Nachari shook his head. "I can't say for sure, but I would presume they were Ryder's."

Arielle swallowed hard, and Kagen felt the full weight of her dilemma: Did she really want to know her father's last words? Would he want to know Keitaro's? He pushed the thought out of his mind and waited along with the anguished woman.

Whatever it is, tell her, Kagen urged telepathically.

Nachari declined his head in respect and then he held it bowed in reverence. "Arielle, I'm sorry."

Arielle shook her head. "Don't be sorry, Nachari. Just tell me what he said."

Nachari closed his eyes. "I did. That was it, the man's last three words: *Arielle, I'm sorry.*"

Arielle gasped and staggered backward. Then she took several steps forward, as if to halt her retreat, and spun around in confusion. When her eyes met Kagen's, her face was ghostly white. "Oh gods, Kagen, he knew of me." She stared down at the ground, and her slender shoulders seemed to curl inward. "He came for me."

Kagen nodded, not knowing what else to say.

She stared blankly at Nachari then. "My father tried to save me, and he failed. He was *killed*." She turned once again to Kagen and simply shook her head. "No. Oh…*no*." She dropped to her knees and planted her hands in the dirt, scooping fistfuls of soil into her palms as if she could somehow retrieve the relationship she had never had. "Oh, no, Father…*no*."

Nachari shook his head sadly at Kagen. He nodded one last time and then shimmered out of view.

Kagen knelt beside her. "Arielle…"

She looked up at him, and her expression was so lost, so barren, so indescribably bleak. "He died then…trying to save me."

Kagen reached out and ran his hand through her hair. "Oh, sweeting."

She hugged her arms to her chest and trembled uncontrollably.

He cocooned her body with his, wrapping his arms so tightly around her that it was like encasing her in a shell. "I'm here, angel. I'm here."

And then she wept.

With her hands in the dirt and her face buried in Kagen's shoulder, Arielle Nightsong wept for the father she had never had, for the memories they had never made, for all the years she had spent believing he had never cared.

She wept until there were no more tears left to cry.

When, at last, she raised her head, wiped the moisture from her swollen eyes, and gently cleared her voice, her words were full of strength and resolve. "Kagen, this is my father's final resting place, and while I never knew him in life, I would like a moment alone with him in death."

Kagen nodded. "I'll stand back by the trees."

"No," she argued, her eyes pleading softly. "Please. There are things I need to say that no one else can hear. I *need* to be *alone* with my father…for just a while." She took his hands in hers and squeezed them. "I promise I won't linger long. I know we have to move on, to get to the arena."

Kagen shook his head vehemently. "It's not that, Arielle. It's just"—he glanced around the clearing—"we are so close to the slave encampment, to the Royal District. I cannot leave you alone, unprotected."

She shrugged helplessly, and her pupils narrowed with resolve. "Healer, you are a vampire. You can hear me breathe from five feet away, let alone scream from three dozen yards. Please…the slave encampment is empty. We haven't seen a single lycan, a single member of Thane's guard. They are all at the arena." She held her hands up in frustration. "You have already viewed all of my memories, witnessed all of my pain. There is nothing I have inside of me that has not been laid bare before you, but *this*, *this belongs to me*. Only me. *Please*. Let me have this moment, this time, this private farewell with my father. Just once, do not listen, do not watch, do not hover. Do not treat my most private, intimate moments like they are yours to peruse. He was *my father*—please, just give me the space that I need. I am too tired, too strung out to beg. I can only ask you: Return to your brothers and give me thirty minutes, *one half hour*, to say hello *and good-bye* to my father. *Alone*."

Kagen contemplated her words. He wrestled with his overwhelming desire to be near her, to protect her, and his innate understanding of her request. He knew that there were moments that were meant only for one's soul and the gods. And this was one of them. "Very well, sweeting. I will give you this because I know how badly you need it, and I will not pry or listen in. But should you see so much as a squirrel scampering down from a tree, you must promise to call out to me."

She cupped his cheek in her hand and nodded. "I promise, healer."

Kagen rose slowly. He glanced around the clearing, and then

he checked the sky. "It is nearly ten o'clock, Arielle. I hate to be the one to say this, but if we hope to reach the arena by the same time tonight, we cannot tarry. I wish you had more time."

"I'll be brief," Arielle said firmly. And then she stood and forced a feeble smile. "Thank you, Kagen. Once again, you have made your way into my heart." She stepped forward and placed a soft kiss of gratitude on his cheek. "And please don't worry…I'm okay. I've managed to take care of myself for the last ten years: I think I can handle a half an hour. *I'll be fine.*"

Kagen nodded, and then he quietly slipped away, shutting down his hyper-acute senses in order to give her privacy.

eighteen

"Do not move. Do not make a sound. Do not even breathe—or your comrade dies."

Arielle froze, staring up into the embittered face of the approaching lycan: His eyes were glowing amber with hatred, and she recognized him immediately from her years in the slave camp. It was Lieutenant Jacob Tansy from Teague's regiment, and he had a pack of omega soldiers with him. What was worse; they were holding Echo at knifepoint, and the sharp, hazardous tip of the blade was pressed so deeply into the rebel's throat that blood trickled down his neck, staining his dislocated shoulder.

Echo looked moments away from death already.

His brow was soaked with sweat, and his face was gaunt and pale. His lower torso was littered with festering wounds, gaping, open *holes*, almost as if he had sat on a bed of nails or spikes, and his upper torso was equally damaged: The flesh was torn away from his body in uneven, jagged lines, and his shirt was caked with blood, some dried and brown, some fresh and red. His head lolled forward, even as two guards held him up by his arms, and his feet dragged along the ground as if it were too much effort to walk.

Arielle gasped in horror, and then she became deathly quiet as she quickly assessed the scene, noted the level of danger, and calculated her immediate options: She could fight; she could flee; or she could call out to Kagen and his brothers. *Where had the lycans come from*? she wondered. And how was it possible that they hadn't made a sound? That no one had heard their approach?

She glanced toward the far end of the clearing, in the direction of the slave encampment, and thought about how easily Kagen and his brothers had overtaken the rebel soldiers that first night in the cave. She knew the lycans were an entirely different proposition, *an entirely different kind of enemy*, but she didn't have any doubt that the Silivasis would prevail, eventually.

Only, not before the lycans killed Echo.

Not before they possibly killed her.

Not before the vampires' presence in Mhier was exposed, and their hopes of rescuing Keitaro were dashed.

She stared once more at Echo's battered face and body, and her heart constricted in her chest: He was so close to death already; there was probably little she could do to save him. Whereas, Keitaro? He still had a chance.

"Get up quietly and come with me," Jacob ordered. By the iron set of his jaw and the unmistakable twitch in his lips, Arielle knew that the lycan wasn't playing—Jacob Tansy was *this close* to shifting, as it stood. What she didn't know was whether or not he had any inkling of the four vampires just on the other side of the thicket, the ones she had asked to shut down their senses and tune her out, to allow her complete privacy, just this once, for a half an hour.

She shook her head, making an immediate decision: *No*, Lieutenant Tansy had no idea that he was one hundred yards away from his mortal enemy, or he wouldn't be standing there speaking to her. Still, why was his voice so hushed, and why did he insist upon her silence? Maybe he figured there were other rebels close by. Maybe he wanted to keep her capture a secret, save all the glory *and reward* for himself.

Why didn't really matter.

The only thing that mattered now was that Arielle had only one chance to get this right. To make the correct choice. And whatever she chose, whatever she did in this fateful moment, it would affect dozens of lives, irreversibly, for years to come.

She rose softly to her feet, careful to maintain Jacob's piercing gaze—she was unwilling to provoke him to violence or to alert him to the presence of the vampires: Yes, the Silivasis might save her in time to elude capture—*they might*—the lycans could certainly kill her faster than the vampires could appear, but there was no way, whatsoever, that Echo would be spared in the process. And as deeply as that concerned her, as much as it broke her heart, it was truly the least of her many concerns: If the Silivasis fought the lycans, their presence in Mhier would be known *a day too early*; and that was really the long and short of it.

Word would spread from one district to another, and King Thane would have an opportunity to marshal his forces, or worse, to execute Keitaro before the games, to make sure that his despised prisoner was never found or rescued. And *ancestors forbid*, what if he ended up with another prisoner to torture? The thought of Marquis, Kagen, Nathaniel, or Nachari being resigned to Keitaro's current fate was more than she could bear.

More than she was willing to risk.

Arielle had no doubt that Kagen would fight to save her, *that he would kill for her*, that he would die for her if he had to. But where would that leave Keitaro? Where would that leave Keitaro's sons?

And after all these years…

If even one of the lycans escaped, the Silivasis' plan would be ruined. Their entire mission would have been in vain. For all of it—every part and parcel—relied on the element of *surprise*. The vampires intended to storm the arena while invisible, to get to Keitaro before anyone knew they were there, and they hoped to get out just as quickly, before they had to fight the entire lycan army. Oh, they would do so if they had to, but the odds were not stacked in their favor, not with so many Alphas gathered in one place…at one time. An alpha lycan was an even match for an ancient vampire, and as impressive as the Silivasis were, they were only four amongst dozens. And that wasn't counting the Betas and Omegas.

Staring into Jacob's calculating eyes, she knew that her fate was sealed: If she left this clearing and went with the lieutenant, she would never see Kagen again. She would never see Keitaro freed.

But she also knew that her sacrifice would not be in vain.

She had already lost the father of her blood; perhaps she could still save the father of her heart.

Drawing in a deep breath for courage, Arielle let her hands

drop to her sides as she accepted her inexorable fate: She would rather trade her life for Kagen's and Keitaro's than doom so many to death, *or worse*, than resist for her own selfish gain.

She nodded compliantly at Jacob and held her hands up in the air: "I will not resist you," she whispered, praying the Silivasis were too far away to hear her surrender.

"We have no time to waste," Jacob growled with insolence. "I will shift, and you will ride on my back, without incident or complaint."

Arielle clenched her eyes shut to hide her revulsion: The thought of clinging to Jacob's matted fur, of straddling his disgusting canine haunches with her thighs, of allowing his wolf to take her to King Thane was abhorrent in every way imaginable. Still, she acquiesced. "As you command." The words turned her stomach.

As the evil lycan loped forward, shifting in mid-gait, she couldn't help but think that in the end, she was very much her father's daughter: She climbed onto the wolf's back, anchored her fingers in his fur, and whispered a final farewell to the lover she would never have:

Kagen, I'm sorry.

Five minutes seemed like an hour.

Ten minutes seemed like a day.

An entire half hour seemed like an eternity…

Still, Kagen kept his word.

Arielle had a right to say good-bye to her father in privacy—without Kagen, or any of the Silivasis, really—intruding upon her grief. While his brothers had reluctantly agreed to go along with her request, he'd had to continually remind them, as well as himself, that they could hear her if she screamed; that she was more than capable of taking care of herself; and that soon, they would be on their way to the northern end of the Royal District. Their thoughts needed to remain on Keitaro and the arena, on what was soon to come.

When, at last, the time was up, Kagen placed the last of his gear inside of his pack, disposed of a drained bag of blood, and padded quietly into the forest to retrieve Arielle so the group could move along.

The moment he entered the clearing, the hair stood up on the back of his neck, and he froze. His eyes swept the circular glade in an instant: He scanned the tops of the trees, peered into the shadowed hallows between the various shrubs, and examined every nook and cranny where a human might hide.

Arielle wasn't there.

He took a deep breath, filtering the air through his nostrils, trying to identify her familiar scent, but nothing came back to him, save the lingering traces of Ryder's remains.

His heart skipped a beat in his chest.

He took two agitated steps forward, and that's when he saw the wolf tracks on the ground. That's when he smelled the lycans…

And he knew…

The bastards had Arielle!

He called out on a telepathic bandwidth to his brothers, and then he summoned all the supernatural speed of his kind and tore off blindly into the forest, tracking the scent like a seasoned hound. His heart pounded with a surge of adrenaline, and his feet felt nearly numb against the ground. Still, he homed in on Arielle's scent like an eagle, dipping down from the sky, about to snatch a mouse from the ground. His arms and shoulders shook with the desire to strike.

Marquis was there in an instant.

Heading him off at the pass.

He landed in front of him; dove at his chest; and brought him down to the ground with a powerful lurch.

"*What the devil!*" Kagen saw red.

Marquis thrust a massive hand over Kagen's mouth. "Be quiet, brother. Stop!"

Kagen wrenched the offensive hand off his mouth and

slapped Marquis's arm away in a fury. "Didn't you hear me? *Arielle is gone!* The lycans have her. We have to go after her!"

Nathaniel appeared, as if out of a fog, a forest wraith emerging from a tree. He shoved his hand where Marquis's had just been and snarled. "Be quiet, healer! *Lower your voice.*"

Kagen bit him in a rage, and Nathaniel withdrew his hand. *What the hell were they doing?* He leapt to his feet and tried to continue his pursuit, but Marquis grabbed his waist from behind. "Kagen, *listen.*"

Kagen broke free and spun around, facing both Marquis and Nathaniel like a cornered bear. He was ready to release his claws and swipe at their hearts if necessary—*had the entire world gone mad?* He tried to glide around them, continue his pursuit, but Marquis only sidestepped in front of him.

"*Wait,*" the Ancient Master Warrior snarled.

"The lycans have Arielle! They've taken her, probably to Thane, and possibly to the castle. We have to go after her before the trail goes cold!"

Marquis looked unusually conflicted, more than just a little bit tortured, but he did not give in. He spoke in a clear, even, hushed tone of voice, while his body practically oozed authority. "Brother, you are not thinking clearly right now. Our father is slated to be executed tomorrow at noon. *In the arena.* It is still ten hours away by foot. We cannot teleport across the distance carrying an object over fifty pounds in our arms, and we cannot fly while keeping ourselves *and our armaments* invisible, not for such a sustained period of time, not if we hope to remain undetected, not so long as we are subsisting on bagged human blood. Until we come in contact with more humans, we have no way to fully rejuvenate from any real type of battle, to replenish our strength, and we will need every ounce of it to save Keitaro. We must think about this strategically. We cannot fly off on an impulse."

"Fly off on an impulse?" Kagen could hardly believe his ears.

"They are going to *kill* our father tomorrow, Kagen," Nathaniel cut in. The male spoke as calmly as Marquis, yet his voice still held a perilous edge. His strong, chiseled features were etched with concern.

"I…I know that, but Arielle…we have to go after her. *I* have to go after her." He peered beyond Marquis's shoulders, staring at the vanishing trail, trying to keep the lycans' tracks in his view. "Fine. Then I'll go it alone."

"To what end, Kagen?" Nathaniel asked.

"*To what end*?" Once again, Kagen sounded incredulous.

"You would fight an unknown number of lycans *alone*? And what if you are confronted by Alphas? What if the males who took her are Alphas?"

Kagen shrugged. "I don't know. Then—"

"Then you will surely die!" Nathaniel supplied the answer, his words resounding as harsh as they were true.

Kagen glared at his twin with barely concealed resentment. "Thanks for the vote of confidence, brother." He took a step back and shook his head.

Nathaniel wasn't dissuaded. He held up his hands in an act of supplication. "Kagen, even if you live, then what? Then what becomes of our father?"

Kagen responded to the softer tone of Nathaniel's voice with increased reason. "Then I'll return. I'll catch up with you. I'll run."

"With Arielle?" Marquis asked. "She will likely be hurt. *You* will likely be hurt."

"No," Nathaniel cut in, leveling a stern, sidelong glance at Marquis before turning back to Kagen. "You will likely be *dead*, and so will she if you try to go after her alone. I don't even know that the four of us could get her back right now, not against a large enough contingency of lycans. And even if we have the element of surprise, we will lose it. We will lose it before we go after Keitaro."

Kagen couldn't believe what he was hearing…

On one hand, his brothers were right.

They were thinking and acting as warriors—just as they should—but what did they expect him to do? "And what would you have me do, *brother?*" Kagen finally asked Nathaniel. There had to be another solution. "Leave her to that monster? Forget her…and move on to Keitaro? Choose between the woman I love and our father?"

Nathaniel whistled low beneath his breath. "So you do love her, after all?" He shared a knowing glance with Marquis.

"Even if I didn't…" Kagen's voice trailed off. "I still couldn't leave her with those monsters. You don't understand what she's been through…what she fears."

Nachari stepped forward, emerging from the shadows as if he had been standing there all along, just waiting for the right moment to chime in. Knowing the wizard, he had donned his sword the moment Kagen had called out, and then, he had taken some extra time to walk…and think. "*Kagen…*" He spoke softly, kindly. His voice was low, soothing, and gentle. "We are not asking you to choose between Arielle and our father. We are asking you to choose between life and *death*. To choose the possibility of something over the inevitability of nothing."

"You, too?" Kagen asked.

"Think about it." Nathaniel jumped back in. "Try to be rational for just a moment: If we go after Arielle right now, one of three things will happen: One, we will all get killed or captured in the process; two, Keitaro may be executed tonight in retaliation; or three, our numbers may be so reduced that any chance of rescuing *either one* is made futile. After all, we have no idea what their numbers look like; how they've fortified their district; what Thane is prepared to do in the event that he detects a band of vampires in his realm. No matter how you turn it, we lose the element of surprise for tomorrow; we burn the precious time we need to make it to the arena; and we doom either Keitaro, Arielle, *or both*, to death. If we go after her now, *we can't win*. If we regroup and go after Father first, then there still may be a chance…for both of them." He sighed in frustration and sympathy. "The lycans will all be in one place tomorrow, at the arena. If Arielle is being kept at Thane's castle, you will have a better chance of getting to her after we rescue

Father—"

"You will also have human prey to feed upon in case you're injured," Marquis interjected.

"Exactly," Nathaniel said. "And if she's there, at the games, we may be able to kill two birds with one stone, to get to her during the ensuing commotion and confusion."

"We may still be able to save them both," Marquis added.

Nachari sighed. He captured Kagen's eyes like a snake-charmer might capture a snake's, and held them in his powerful, empathetic gaze. "Kagen, we have already told you our suspicions about Arielle, *about you and Arielle*, the fact that we believe she may be your *destiny*. This makes the situation even more volatile. It makes our plans even more critical. You must know—*you have to know*—that our desire to see her safe, to retrieve her alive, is as great as your own, if only because of our concern for *you*. But what we aren't willing to do is rush recklessly forward with a plan that is doomed to fail from the start, risk losing Arielle—which means we may also lose you, too—risk losing Father, *and* risk losing our own lives in the process. Not when there is still the chance of salvaging everyone. It is a horrific choice. We understand. But it is the only one we can make."

"By all the gods, brother, *think about it*," Nathaniel implored.

Kagen paced in an anxious circle, his fingers digging absently into his scalp, as if by clutching his head, he could make his mind work better. "Do you have *any* idea what the lycans will do to her if we leave her alone with them overnight? What Tyrus Thane will do to her?" He knew it was a cheap shot, but he said it anyway. "And what if it were Jocelyn, or Deanna, or Ciopori?"

Marquis bit down so hard on his lower lip that his emerging fangs drew a trickle of blood that snaked down the side of his chin. "Ciopori was once in the hands of Salvatore Nistor, held captive in the Dark Ones' Colony, being tortured in a chamber filled with snakes, yet I waited for the warriors to gather together, to plan a strategy, and to go in…united. I felt she would be better served by my life than my death. And I'm sure

Nathaniel and Nachari would've felt the same way if it had been Jocelyn or Deanna."

The brothers nodded, and Marquis drew a deep breath. "We have every idea—*I* have *every* idea—what King Thane might do, brother. And I say to you, if there was anything we could do to prevent it, we would; but there is not." He placed his hand on Kagen's arm. "How does your death at the hands of the lycans protect Arielle…or prevent her violation? How does getting captured or killed, or allowing our father to die, protect this female…or prevent her humiliation? How does leading your brothers to their deaths protect her…*or you*? Tell me, Kagen, so I might understand and join you."

Kagen's head began to spin, and his heart began to ache, *literally ache*. This was inconceivable. And, try as he might, he simply could not process Marquis's words. His soul would not allow it.

"We cannot get Father out of that arena as *three*—we may not even be able to get him out of there as *four*," Nathaniel said. "And with the gods as my witness, we all know that our father will need a healer."

"Arielle may need a healer…" Marquis's voice faded into the background.

Nachari said something next, but his words were no longer audible.

There was nothing but space…and pain…and darkness. A void that was closing in on Kagen like an oncoming train in a dark, narrow tunnel. He tried to look up, to meet his brothers' eyes—*any* of his brother's eyes—just to anchor himself in the present moment.

But he couldn't.

I don't know how to leave her, he tried to say, but his voice failed him. *You don't understand—I can't.* He felt something slipping out from underneath him, but he couldn't define what it was. *I want to do what's right, what I must, but it's not within my power*. He tried to convey all of it, but his throat closed up and betrayed him. *I can't breathe!*

He tried to warn them, but he was utterly and completely lost.

Lost to the insanity of the choice…

Lost to a fog of despair, beyond any he had ever known.

And it made no sense—it wasn't rational, and it wasn't defensible.

And his ability to communicate *any of it* simply eluded him.

As the fog that had hovered over Mhier all day began to seep into Kagen's soul, the skeletal, shadowed hands clutching at his heart with cruel, meandering indifference, he felt his arms fall to his sides and his legs buckle beneath him.

nineteen

Kagen Silivasi stumbled like a drunken human, lost in a fog of disbelief and anguish.

The lycans had won…

Again.

They had taken all he valued and claimed it as their own, and he was as helpless as a child swept away in a turbulent stream, tossed relentlessly beneath a rotating current of evil.

It was impossible.

Unthinkable.

Beyond reckoning.

The tragic choice was more than he could bear, and as his body folded beneath him, he sank to the forest floor and wept. Thank the gods emotion did not have the same effect in Mhier, for he was powerless to contain it.

Then, as darkness continued to descend upon him, the strangest thing began to happen: He was swept into an icy tunnel, an unfamiliar void, where the past and the present swirled all around him like an arctic wind, each divergent force seeking to pull him in an opposite direction in order to force his hand. One sought to anchor him in Mhier, to compel him to deal with the present situation, to get hold of his emotions and stay the current course, no matter how reprehensible. The other sought to take him far, far away, back in time, back to Dark Moon Vale.

Back to the night his father had disappeared.

And the origin of his rage had been born.

As his consciousness splintered, he thought he heard his brothers calling his name, hovering above him, shouting and shaking him in desperation. He thought he felt imploring hands on his shoulders, entreaties being made with pleading voices, each one more alarmed than the last; but all of it was waning, fading into a collective, distant dream. He withdrew into the tunnel, traveled back in time, and his brothers became like mere skeletons in the mist as he embraced the ghosts of his past.

The crisp colors of Mhier were gone.

The heavily treed forest was no longer there.

Instead, he found himself in Dark Moon Vale, walking beneath a luminous autumn moon. He looked down at his chest and then patted his arms and legs, trying to reacquaint himself with his body. He was no longer an Ancient vampire, ten months past his first millennium birthday, but a recent Master Healer of 521 years, who had just suffered the loss of his mother.

He was alone and wandering aimlessly in the night.

He was overwhelmed with grief and concerned for Keitaro, afraid that his father might be suicidal: It was two days after his mother's burial, and Keitaro had yet to come home. While all of them were still reeling from the finality of Serena's ceremony, the shock and anguish of losing her in such a horrific way, Keitaro had been absolutely beside himself with grief: heartbroken, inconsolable…teetering on the brink of madness.

Kagen knew that the Ancient Master Warrior needed some time alone—perhaps he had just gone off into the forest to mourn his mate in privacy—but just the same, he had to know how much his sons needed him right now. *How badly Kagen needed him right now.* Marquis was lost in a virulent rage, consumed with an overpowering lust for blood; Nathaniel was only moments away from doing something self-destructive; and Nachari and Shelby—well, the twins were just lost. Broken and confused. On the verge of giving way to despondency.

And Kagen had no one to talk to.

He rolled his shoulders to release some tension and forced his feet to continue plodding forward. Things were…exactly as they were…and no one could go back and change them.

He rounded the corner of the mineral plant, hopped down into the center of the old, dried-out riverbed, and continued to follow the contours of the ravine as he made his way toward the northern forest. Glancing upward as he walked, he couldn't help but notice that the sky was as black as coal. While the moon shone brightly all around him, there wasn't a star to be seen in the sky, and the air—it was so cold it was arctic. The valley floor was as hard as granite.

All at once, every hair on the back of his neck stood up, and he froze in place in order to tune more acutely into his senses. He saw nothing but the thick canopy of trees in front of him. He heard…only silence. He felt no strange vibrations in the atmosphere, save the constant heavy vibration of grief—and death—that continued to hover over Dark Moon Vale like a dense fog rising up from the sea. He closed his eyes and sniffed the air…

And that's when he knew he wasn't alone.

The northern forest was infested with lycans, killers hiding like cowards, hidden amongst the numerous trees, and they were watching his approach.

His muscles contracted involuntarily, the need to draw blood rising up within him like an insatiable hunger, gnawing at his gut, demanding that he fight, kill, and maim. But he held it at bay—if only for a moment—as he fought to employ reason, instead.

He was just about to call out telepathically to his brothers when he noticed a strange, enigmatic ring of light glowing in the forest: Translucent beams of violet and blue flickered in the moonlight, coalescing into a circular pattern like a radiant halo, the center glowing fiery red, and for reasons he couldn't fathom, the word that came to mind was *portal*.

It was as if he were gazing at a doorway to another world.

Kagen blinked several times in quick succession, trying to dismiss the strange, unbidden thought, and then the next thing he saw stole the breath from his body: There were six enormous lycans hovering about the halo, and by all the gods, they each looked like Alphas, angry, formidable, lethal *Alphas*; yet their arms were linked in unison. And, for all intents and purposes, they appeared to be working together like one cohesive unit. No one was fighting for dominance or control, and they seemed to be of one mind and purpose.

He stood for a moment, transfixed by the sight, watching them warily and trying to decide what to do. Despite his calm demeanor, he was a roiling vat of emotions inside. He couldn't help but wonder: Were these the Alphas who had ordered the attack on the valley? Had one of these creatures murdered his mother?

A low, feral growl rose in his throat, and his fangs began to descend from his gums, but he took three deep breaths and forced them to recede.

And that's when he noticed the prisoner.

The vampire.

The broken and bloodied male swaying in the center of the circle. His arms were bound behind his back; the femur in one thigh jutted out at an unnatural angle—the bone had clearly been broken; and his eyes were so swollen they were practically shut, the dark brown centers barely discernible beneath the heavy, distended lids.

Kagen recoiled.

He could not believe his eyes.

The male in the center of the circle was *his father*...Keitaro Silivasi.

Something so primal—so dark, hateful, and venomous—rose up inside of him, he thought he might just shatter from the intensity of it. Every cell in his body was exclaiming the same thing: *I will kill them! I will kill them all! And I will not stop until the rivers run crimson with their blood.*

In the next instant, he heard one of the Alphas speak: The lycan wore a gold medallion around his neck, and he addressed the man beside him as *Teague*. "General Teague, forget the lone intruder. We have what we came for. Along with our Betas and Omegas, we have laid this valley low with devastation, and we are returning with a prisoner worthy of our king."

The general nodded, and just like that, the lycans were gone.

Kagen's father was gone.

Kagen startled at the suddenness of it all, and then

something inside of him virtually exploded with panic. He shouted a harsh, guttural cry; leapt from the floor of the riverbed in one lithe bound; and closed the distance between him and the lycans in an instant, grasping wildly at the space where his father had stood.

But there was nothing there.

There was no one there.

He spun around in wild circles, shouting, snarling, raving like a madman: *"I'll kill them! I'll kill them all! And the rivers will run crimson with their blood!"* He thought he heard a harsh, keening moan in the background, and he whirled to confront the source of the sound before he realized it had come from his own hoarse throat. "No. *No!* I will not lose my father. *I cannot.* I *will kill them. I will kill them all! And the rivers will run crimson with their blood*!"

Somehow, the lycans must have heard him.

They must have either perceived his threat, or registered the insult, because they came back through the portal: All six of them returned.

Without Keitaro.

Kagen knew that he needed to call out to his brothers, right then and there, but there wasn't any time. The lycans gave him no quarter. They stealthily surrounded him in their own garish circle, and in that singular, harrowing moment, he knew he could not concentrate on two things at once: detecting the barest twitch of an enemy's hand—which one would lunge at him first?—and calling out telepathically for help.

So he concentrated on the six hulking males in front of him, instead, praying he would make it out of this alive. And then he summoned the depths of his rage: *I will kill them! I will kill them all! And the rivers will run crimson with their blood!*

The instant the first lycan started to shift, Kagen struck with amazing speed and precision. He caught him by the throat, even as his jaw was beginning to distend, and ripped out his esophagus with his teeth. The swift, immediate kill was as surprising as it was satisfying, but there wasn't enough blood. Not nearly enough blood! As he spat the enemy's spine on the ground, he rocked backward, stooped down into a crouch, and angled his body to face the five remaining Alphas.

In the blink of an eye, there were no longer five intimidating persons in front of him, but five enormous beasts with wicked teeth and jagged claws; and each emitted a rancid, gut-wrenching smell, an odor that could only be described as *rage-filled Lycanthrope*.

He started to call out to Nathaniel, but the lycan called Teague lunged at him so quickly, so savagely, that he barely had time to raise his left arm and block the attack. As the massive, furry jaw clamped down on his wrist, snapping the radius in two, the one who wore a gold medallion maneuvered behind him, sank down on his paws, and tore a quart-sized bite out of Kagen's flexed hamstring. Kagen bit back a cry of pain and wrenched his leg free from the monstrous jaw, watching in morbid fascination as another of the lycans shifted back into human form, retrieved a syringe from the ground, and plunged it into Kagen's neck.

He had no idea what was in the syringe.

It burned like molten lava, and the effects were instantaneous: He immediately began to feel weak and disoriented. As he staggered backward in reaction to the substance, he tried to call out to his brother again—this time, to Marquis—but the communication would not go through.

It was as if the focused thought were a stone slung against a brick wall: It hit an implacable barrier, bounced off with a ping, and then shattered on its way to the ground. There would be no communication with his brothers.

Kagen was on his own

Against an enemy every bit his equal, down to the last, solitary male.

Realizing that death may be imminent—if not *inevitable*—he fought like a vampire possessed. He severed limbs, gouged out an eye, and even managed to rip out a spleen before the red haze finally cleared enough for him to measure the carnage. Lying before him were three dead lycans, sprawled out unnaturally on the valley floor, their bodies a mangled heap of blood and gore and excrement: the one he had killed earlier, right off the bat; the male who had injected him with the syringe; and another wiry beast with a gruesome, ejected eyeball lying near his mouth, still attached to the optic nerve. He spat on the corpse closest to him and turned to face the remaining three. "Where is my father!" he demanded, his voice wild with volcanic fury. "*Where have you taken him? And which one of you killed my mother!*"

In a brazen act of insolence, one of the remaining males took a defiant lope toward him and snarled like a rabid beast. His grotesque mouth was drawn back in a smile; his garish yellow teeth were gleaming in the moonlight, and blood-tinged saliva swung from his jowls, emitting an odor so foul Kagen could taste it on his tongue. The beast's very existence was repugnant. And then, in an act of careless arrogance, the wolf shifted back into the body of a man, flipped Kagen off with his third finger, and mocked him with a scowl. "*We've taken him to hell, and you will never see him again!*"

Kagen took immediate advantage of the idiot's insolent pride.

He crouched even lower, speared his hand through the male's groin, and ripped out his intestines. Then he sucked the blood out of the carnage before tossing it to the valley floor. "*I'll kill you.*" He seethed in defiance. "*I'll kill you all. And the rivers will run crimson with your blood…*"

The wolf named Teague rose to his full height—he must have stood at least ten feet tall on his hind legs—and he glared at Kagen with utter madness radiating in his feral, amber eyes. He opened his mouth, baring a vicious set of canines, and bellowed his rage at the moon.

Kagen hissed in reply, preparing to take him on; but this time, they attacked as a unit.

Pain shot through Kagen's sternum as Teague struck like a viper, sinking his massive teeth into Kagen's shoulders; clamping down as if his life depended upon it; and snapping the large clavicle like a twig. A second set of canines sank into Kagen's neck, tearing through the now-exposed tendons from behind. A forepaw raked across his bicep; another slashed him through the cheek; and a third swipe temporarily blinded his eyes.

As teeth pierced deep into muscle, as muscle gave way to broken bones, as blood splattered and organs rent, Kagen doubled over on the valley floor and then scrambled to his knees.

His enemy was far too strong.

Their numbers had been far too great.

Yet…and still…it didn't matter: his life or his death, his certain passing into the world beyond.

All that mattered was his utter failure to do what he had set out to do—to save Keitaro.

To save his father.

And now, the rivers would never run crimson with blood.

As his mind gave way to defeat, and he tried to brace himself against the coming blow—*his coming death*, a small, distant voice whispered tenaciously inside his head, echoing in his soul: *Vampire, you are a healer, a magician, a practitioner of unparalleled ability. Fight them with what you have left.*

Kagen blinked several times, trying to make sense of the words. *Who had spoken them? And what did they mean?*

He turned his attention inward and assessed the situation: He was kneeling on the ground before his mortal enemy. His arms were broken, his throat was torn open, and his organs were serrated and leaking blood. His left foot was barely attached to his leg, and his shoulder was virtually crushed. Within moments, the lycans would rip his heart from his body, and his mortality would come to an end. What was the point of trying to address his wounds now? Of trying to heal so many injuries? As if he had time…

Where would he even start to use his venom?

To use…

His venom?

For reasons beyond his comprehension, Kagen glanced up toward the sky, and that's when he saw them: the scavengers, the vultures, the vile birds circling all around them, waiting to devour the carrion, waiting to feast on the dead. And although he had never given an imperious command to an animal, tried to use the vampiric power of compulsion on a species other than *human,* he could sense their collective consciousness, the spark that gave them life.

And he understood it in a way he had never understood it before:

All life was one.

And it was connected at a subatomic level.

The vale grew very dark and still—silent, almost dreamlike—as he all at once realized what he had to do: Kagen Silivasi was a healer, a magician, a practitioner of unparalleled ability, and he had to welcome death in order to reclaim life.

A single tear escaped his eye as he focused all of his power in that one, critical moment, as he sought to merge his consciousness with the foreign mind of the birds: *You will do as I command!*

He bent low to the ground and pressed his face in the dirt, almost as if he were kneeling in supplication before the enemy, pleading for what remained of his life; and then, he coaxed as much venom as he could out of his fangs and watched as it pooled beneath him. He left a mound of venom collected at his knees, and then he seared the rest of his compulsion into the minds of the scavengers: *You will wait until the lycans are gone; you will dip your talons into this venom; and then you will retrieve my heart and place it back in my chest.*

Kagen shuddered as an even more horrified thought entered his mind: What if the lycans removed his heart *and* severed his head from his body?

He quickly dismissed the thought.

If that happened, then nothing he was about to do would matter.

He would never save his father.

He would never kill them all.

And the rivers would never run crimson with their blood.

Both Teague and the other lycan had already shifted back into human form, gloating arrogantly while Kagen knelt before them, jeering as he appeared to plead for his life.

Teague kicked him ruthlessly in the side, breaking a pair of ribs. "Sit up, vampire! Face your death—and your superior enemy—like a man."

Kagen swallowed a nasty retort. He swallowed his pride, and he swallowed his fear.

He could do this.

He *would* do this.

And the rivers would run crimson with their blood.

He rose unsteadily to his knees, gasping from the pain in his sides, his torn throat, his crushed shoulder, and his laboring lungs; and he let his head fall forward in a gesture of defeat.

"Link your hands behind your back," Teague snarled, clearly taking enormous pleasure in forcing the vampire to cooperate with his own execution.

Ah, Kagen thought, with resignation, *then they do intend to seize my heart.*

He didn't dare resist, lest they become enraged once again and decapitate him.

He linked his hands behind his back—at least he faked it, considering the impossible condition of his broken bones and fingers—and he exposed his chest to his enemy, using his last ounce of strength to raise his jaw and meet the lycan's stare head-on. *To you, Lord Auriga, I offer my soul, and I pray you will return this sacrifice: Let me live to save my father. Let me return to kill them all. May the rivers run crimson with their blood!*

The one called Teague descended upon him like a thousand hounds from hell.

He lunged at his proffered torso, shifted in midair, and tore through his breastbone with his jaw, wrenching the still-beating heart from Kagen's chest with a force so brutal it felt like his spine had exploded.

Kagen jolted in sudden, inexpressible agony.

His mouth flew open in a wordless shout, and the breath left his body in a whoosh.

As his eyes bulged in his sockets, his once-powerful physique collapsed in on him, and his limp, eviscerated body slumped to the ground.

Silence.

Darkness.

Stillness engulfed him.

He heard a crisp pop, like the sound of grease sizzling in a pan, and just like that, his soul shot upward, ascending into the sky like a comet spiraling in reverse.

No! Kagen's soul shouted defiantly, reaching desperately for the ground. *The rivers must run crimson with their blood!* He repeated the familiar refrain again and again, all the while, seeking his body, holding onto his once-immortal existence by a thread.

Kagen Silivasi haunted his corpse like a ghost.

He clung to his sentience while his spirit hovered about the scene of his death.

He waited like a specter while the lycans gathered their dead and, at last, slipped back through the portal.

He watched while the scavengers descended from the trees, as they dipped their talons in the pool of venom; grasped his heart in their faithful claws; and placed the damaged organ back into his battered chest.

He marveled as his heart began to knit itself back together…

And then he awoke to a pain unlike anything he had ever known in his 521 years—he awoke without any recollection of what had just happened.

He awoke completely absent of memory.

Kagen Silivasi had no idea, whatsoever, what had just befallen him.

He shouted in agony. He tried to draw his knees to his chest, but his ribcage assailed him. He tried to roll onto his side, but his back began to spasm. He tried to bring his hands to his face, to bite into his own flesh in order to counter the pain, but his limp hands and arms betrayed him: His limbs were broken, his chest was saturated in blood, and his throat felt like someone had sliced it open with a razor.

As he writhed on the ground in torment, alternating between retching and extracting his venom, he struggled to start healing his wounds, and he tried—

By all that was holy, he tried!

To remember…

Something.

What?

It had seemed so vital!

"Kagen!" Nathaniel Silivasi stared at his twin in abject horror. He shook him by the shoulders once again and tried to get through to him with his mind. *Brother…please…snap out of it!*

Kagen had been *gone* for at least a half an hour, lost in some sort of trance, trapped in some sort of living hell—ranting and raving like a madman, pulling his hair out by the roots, rocking back and forth like a stricken child, and pounding his fists into the dirt. Nachari had tried every spell he could think of in an effort to pull him out of the nightmare—the vision? *The meltdown.* And Nathaniel had reverted to pleading to the gods on his twin's behalf.

Still, nothing had reached the tortured vampire.

It had been terrifying, ghastly…utterly appalling to watch.

When, finally, the Master Healer had started to vomit and writhe along the ground, as if his body was in unbearable pain, Marquis had rolled him on his side and held him down by his arms and legs. "Kagen, *brother*, stop this at once!" As if an implacable order would get through, where compassion, magic, and pleading had not.

"Wake up, Kagen! Please come back!" Nathaniel tried again.

Kagen jolted upright, as if suddenly hearing his brothers' words. He looked up into the compassionate eyes that were boring into his and blinked with the first, true sign of awareness. "Nathaniel?"

Nathaniel breathed an audible sigh of relief. "Yes, brother."

"Where am I?"

"You're in Mhier, Kagen. We all are," Nathaniel said softly.

"What the hell just happened?" Marquis demanded.

Kagen sat up straighter then. He scrubbed his face with his hands and tried to calm his breathing. He looked around the forest, as if seeing it for the first time, and shuddered. "I don't know. *I don't know.* I just—" His words broke off. "There was something…something I needed to do. *To remember.* Something so very important."

"Something *you needed to do*?" Marquis grumbled, repeating the muddled words. "I believe you just *did* plenty. You have been rolling around on the ground for the last half hour, healer. I thought I was going to have to knock you out."

Kagen furrowed his brow. He looked up at Marquis and shook his head in apology. "I'm sorry, warrior. I don't know what happened." And then all at once, his face went slack, and his stark brown eyes deepened with shadows. "Oh gods, oh gods…*oh gods*!"

"What is it?" Nachari asked, kneeling beside Nathaniel to get closer to Kagen.

Kagen blanched, his skin turning a ghastly shade of white. "I knew," he whispered gravely, his voice lingering like a soft bow drawn across a bass cello—deep, sorrowful, and filled with regret. "All this time, I knew our father had been taken by the lycans. I knew that he needed our help. I knew there was a portal, yet I did nothing. I said…*nothing*." His voice vibrated with anguish, and his eyes clouded with tears.

"What are you talking about?" Nathaniel asked, his own voice rough with insistence. "What do you mean, *you knew our father had been taken by the lycans*? You knew nothing! None of us did." He met Marquis's anxious gaze and shrugged his shoulders in confusion.

Nachari drew back, waiting to hear more.

"I remember everything now—*oh, gods*—I was supposed to save him." Kagen spoke to no one in particular. "Instead, I let them take him. I said nothing. I did *nothing*. For centuries!"

"Brother, we don't understand what you're talking about," Nachari said. His voice radiated with kindness, yet it also rose with fear.

"What do you remember?" Marquis bit out.

"All of it," Kagen said sadly. "Everything. The night Father disappeared from Dark Moon Vale." He fisted his hands and pressed them against the ground to steady his body from shaking. "I was there. I saw it happen."

"You saw what happen?" Nathaniel asked.

Nachari held his hand up as if to silence his brothers' questions, and then he leaned closer to Kagen and gently touched his cheek. "Brother, you say this is a memory, yes?"

Kagen slowly shook his head. "A nightmare."

"Can you share it with us?" Nachari asked softly.

Kagen froze—as if trying to decide—and then he slowly nodded his head. "I think that might be best."

Marquis took a step closer to the circle then. "Send it out in a unified stream, to all of us at once, healer. And we will decide for ourselves if your words make any sense."

"*Marquis*," Nachari chastised beneath his breath.

Nathaniel rolled his eyes before turning to regard Kagen with concern. "Are you strong enough to do that?" he asked.

Kagen nodded. "Of course, the strength I lacked was then…not now."

Nathaniel shook his head, feeling helpless. He placed a firm, reassuring hand on Kagen's shoulder and gave it a squeeze. "Share your experience with us now, and we will discuss the latter in a moment."

Kagen took a deep, centering breath and slowly closed his eyes. "Brace yourself," he whispered. And then he began to send a steady stream of images, thoughts, and feelings to his brothers. He replayed the entire horrific night from front to back like a video streaming in high-definition on a big-screen TV, right down to the very last moment when the lycans removed his heart, the vultures returned it, and he awakened absent of memory, with zero knowledge of what had happened before.

Marquis took three angry paces back, his shoulders heaving in fury and surprise.

Nathaniel placed his fingers in his mouth and bit down hard to stifle a brutal, inappropriate reaction. He wanted to murder every living creature in sight, and since there were only woodland animals and his brothers nearby, it was highly ill-advised. "That night…you came home so late, and you looked so haggard, so lost. *So exhausted.* We thought it was grief. We thought something bad had happened, like maybe you had been in a fight, but I, for one, was in no place to dig deeper, to ask questions. I could barely function myself. We were all consumed with grief and sorrow…and rage. If I thought you'd had a chance to take it out on an enemy, I would have simply envied you. I would have never suspected…" His voice trailed off.

"But why didn't I make the connection?" Kagen asked sadly. "Several days later, when it started to become clear that father wasn't coming home, that something had happened—why didn't I make the connection then?"

Nachari wiped a tear from his eye and cleared his throat. "Grief has a way of catapulting the living into a place of altered perception: The grieved are neither in the spirit world, with the deceased, nor on the earth, with the living, but somewhere in between. That's why individuals always say that it seems so strange, *so wrong*, that life can continue to go on all around them, that the sun still shines and others continue to go about their menial, everyday tasks: Don't others know that the earth has stopped spinning on its axis? That nothing is as it was before? That life has, in fact, stopped moving?" He sighed. "I believe the mind shuts down in grief in order to allow the survivors to heal in their own time…and at their own pace. We were not in a position to accurately perceive your turmoil, and you were not capable of maintaining the memory of what occurred in that *place of limbo* beyond the threshold of death. It's not unusual for someone who *dies*"—he stumbled over the word but pressed on—"to have no recollection of the events that occurred right before their passing. Perhaps it has something to do with the mind, the brain, that suspended time when there's no oxygen flowing to the cells."

Marquis waved his hand in angry dismissal of the whole conversation. "You survived!" His powerful voice clashed like a symbol, resounding in the night. "You killed four alpha lycans; you orchestrated your own resurrection from inevitable death; and you survived! That is all." His harsh, implacable features were drawn tight with fury.

Kagen slowly released his fists. He opened and closed his hands several times in a row, as if trying to gain a grip on the unfathomable. "I walked away from that entire encounter with nothing productive retained. Just enough of my memory left intact to know that a part of me needed to *save*…to heal…to fix something so fundamental…so valuable. And another part of me, absolutely splintered, broken, and destroyed, emerged with an insatiable urge to kill. A burning instinct to forge endless rivers of blood."

"Dr. Jekyll and Mr. Hyde," Nathaniel whispered softly. "Your need to save the world. Your inexplicable desire to destroy…"

"Well, no wonder," Marquis muttered.

"I shattered," Kagen said disgracefully. "I came out of it damaged."

"No," Nachari insisted. "You came out of it *alive*. And I, for one, am grateful."

Just then, Nathaniel shuffled in front of him, still on his knees. He grasped Kagen by both shoulders and gently angled his body to face him, and then he cupped his twin's face in his hands with exquisite tenderness. "Look at me, brother," he whispered. He felt as if his heart might just break into a thousand pieces and become one with his twin's anguish.

Kagen looked up him obediently, his benevolent brown eyes almost pleading for absolution.

Nathaniel's spine stiffened. "When the spark of life that is you—and the spark of life that is me—first came into being, we were together in our mother's womb." He dropped his head forward until his silken mane of blue-black hair fanned out about his face, and his forehead rested on Kagen's, endearingly. And then he spoke in a voice so pure, so intimate, that Nachari and Marquis took several steps back to give the two some privacy. "And we have been together ever since: *except that night*." His voice trembled from the depth of his emotion, and he had to steady his hands, which were now firmly planted on both of Kagen's arms. "The night that my twin died at the hands of the lycans, yet came back to me…somehow. And you have carried this burden, *alone*, for nearly half a century." He tightened his grip on Kagen's arms until his fingers cut into his skin in an effort to maintain his composure. "If anyone has failed anyone, I have failed you." His voice trembled, he felt a fine mist settle in his gaze, and he looked away. When, at last, he had steadied himself enough to continue, he cleared his throat and pressed on. "But I say to you now: You are my brother, you are not to blame, and *you are not alone*. You. Are. Not. Alone. *Never again*."

Kagen clutched Nathaniel's wrists and held on for dear life, even as Nathaniel continued to grasp his arms.

"We will enter that arena tomorrow, *together*." Nathaniel gestured with his hand to indicate all of them, Marquis and Nachari included. "And we will finish what you started. We *will* save our Blood Father; and then we will find Arielle. *Together*." A deep, primal growl reverberated in his throat, and Nathaniel did nothing to restrain it. "And by all that is holy, I make you this solemn vow, as your brother and as your twin: We *will* kill them. *We will kill them all. And the rivers will run crimson with their blood*."

twenty

Later that night

Arielle stumbled into the gaudy bedchamber, trying to catch her balance.

Lieutenant Jacob Tansy flung her into the oversized room with all its garish red furnishings, silk-covered tapestries, and strange, occult-like symbols displayed as tasteless artwork on the tiled walls. It had taken them at least seven hours, running at full speed, to reach the royal castle; and they were still a good three hours away from the arena.

But Thane was on his way.

His soldiers had sent him word through a carrier falcon, and from everything she gathered, he would be coming back to retrieve her. He wanted her beside him tomorrow…for the games.

Arielle grit her teeth and spat in the lieutenant's face as he snatched her by the arm, dragged her to one of the four bedposts on the raised platform in the center of the king's room, and struggled to bind her arms to the column.

"There!" he snarled, his wicked delight barely concealed. He wiped the spittle from his face and sneered at her. "Enjoy your solitude while you can, Miss Nightsong." He grasped her by the jaw and squeezed until his thumbs pressed the walls of her cheeks into her teeth. "I have no doubt our king will break your defiance…and your will."

Arielle glared at him with abject hatred, no longer caring what he said or did.

She had no doubt that Thane would try. But she knew something none of them knew: There was an enemy of equal power and superior cunning in their midst—a band of vampires in Mhier—that would give the haughty king and all his detestable minions a run for their money.

Soon.

Very soon.

The Silivasis would be arriving at the arena. They would begin to dig their tunnels, to hide their caches of weapons, to plot their final attack.

And hell would be unleashed in the land of the lycan tomorrow at noon.

The heavy door to the bedchamber swung open with a fury, and King Tyrus Thane Montego stormed in, his thick golden robe flapping behind him like a dark angel's wings, all six feet six inches of his muscular frame approaching with arrogant swagger. His copious golden-blond hair hung about his shoulders in loose, honey-combed waves, and his piercing amber eyes shone with a fury that could only be described as unholy.

He took several long strides to the platform, leapt the narrow row of stone steps in a single bound, and glowered at Lieutenant Tansy. "Get out!"

Jacob Tansy bowed his head and immediately backed away, careful not to turn his back on the angry monarch as he found his way unerringly to the door and shut it softly behind him.

Thane stared at Arielle like she was a mystical creature from another planet. He paced back and forth in front of her, scrutinizing every hair on her head, every feature on her face, every curve on her body, and then he finally stopped in front of her and reached out to stroke her cheek with a malevolent hand. It was almost as if he had to prove to himself that she was actually there…

She was actually real.

"Arielle Nightsong," he muttered in a harsh, gravelly voice. "The prodigal slave returned. I trust you have enjoyed your years as a member of the rebellion?"

Arielle swallowed her retort. She glared at him with an equal measure of hatred and derision but continued to hold her tongue. What was there to say to a being so foul, so repulsive? Words were pointless when actions could say so much more.

No, Arielle would wait until tomorrow. She would let the Silivasis' actions say it all for her. And she would rejoice when Keitaro was freed.

She closed her eyes and sent a silent prayer to the ancestors: *Please, by all that is sacred, go with the sons of the father of my heart, and see that Keitaro is freed. Do not let my sacrifice be in vain.*

"I will dine with your friend Echo tonight," Thane said, apparently hoping to get a rise out of her. When she kept her eyes closed and simply listened, he snarled. "Mmm, that's not quite accurate," he amended. "I meant to say, I will dine *on* your friend Echo tonight. The warrior Walker is already dead, and so is your companion Kade. We know where the rebel encampment is located now, so it is only a matter of time before all are captured…and killed. You are alone, Arielle Nightsong, save the benevolent whims of your king."

Arielle kept her eyes closed and her mouth shut. Just the same, she began to tremble. She couldn't help it. Tyrus Thane Montego did not speak words that were not true. She felt as if the ground had just opened up and swallowed her whole, swallowed her hopes and dreams, and she held her breath to keep from coming apart, to keep from breaking down and giving full vent to an ocean's worth of tears. *Dearest Ancestors*, Kade, Walker, and soon Echo…were gone.

The room grew deathly quiet as she internalized the full meaning of the king's words.

In fact, the silence became so glaring that she had to open her eyes once more just to make sure Thane was still standing in front of her. While she could feel his breath on her face, sense his malevolent presence all around her, they were both so incredibly quiet that she hardly believed he was there.

"You have nothing at all to say to me?" he finally bit out through clenched teeth.

Arielle took a deep breath and held her tongue.

"Ah," he snarled. "Then I suppose you may listen, instead."

Arielle gathered her courage and tried to find a center of calm.

"Tomorrow, you will accompany me to the arena as my soon-to-be bride: the new queen of this realm. You will bathe this night in scented oils, and you will soften your skin in a milk and rose-petal bath. You will dress in a gown made of silk, and you will appear beside me on the dais more beautiful than you have ever been. I will provide you with several maidservants to see that this is so." He flashed a wicked smile. "But know this, Arielle Nightsong: The only thing beautiful about your life will be its appearance."

Despite her determination, Arielle faltered. She swallowed convulsively, choking down her sorrow.

King Thane raised his angular jaw and peered down at her like she was nothing more than a gnat buzzing about his face. "You will indeed be my slave in every way. You will grovel at my feet; you will beg for my forgiveness; and you will worship me until the day you die—at my hands." He reached out, grabbed a fistful of her hair, and yanked her head back so he could plant a harsh, unyielding kiss on her mouth.

There was nothing tender or amorous about it.

His lips were laced with hatred. His tongue was intrusive and foul. His breath was rancid with the desire to commit violence. When he finally pulled away, Arielle had to struggle not to vomit.

"Is that all?" she asked defiantly, immediately regretting the words. *Why—oh why—couldn't she just control her tongue*?

Thane smiled then, a wide, maniacal, wolfish grin, and the visage was illogically grotesque on his deceptively handsome face. He threw his shoulders back, leapt down from the platform, and began to stroll away in a regal, dismissive manner.

And then he stopped dead in his tracks and turned around. "Oh, there is one more thing." He prowled back to the dais like a lion in his prime, the king of the jungle asserting his claim. He climbed the steps one at a time, slowly placing each foot on the narrow stone steps, as if to menace her with his very approach.

Arielle stared at him, transfixed and waiting. What more did he have to say?

And then he drew back his massive arm, clenched his fingers together in an open palm, and struck her across the face with what felt like the full brunt of his fury.

The full brunt of the last ten years.

She didn't have to respond.

All the lanterns dimmed.

And the world went black.

twenty-one

Sunday ~ the arena

Kagen Silivasi tried to settle into the eye of the storm, to ignore all of the pounding waves, swirling winds, and clashing thunder rattling in his head. He narrowed his focus, instead, into a pinpoint of light: the immediate situation, the conditions directly before him, and *the present moment.*

All four of the Silivasi brothers perched outside the arena walls, careful to remain invisible. They peered through several tiny holes they had drilled into the stones and waited for the optimal moment to enter the dome.

The high, stone structure was more oval than circular, and raised above each supporting column was a lit torch, the golden fires burning like macabre lanterns in a creepy cavern. The day was overcast; the ever-present sun *and* moon were eclipsed by clouds; and the sky was an unusual shade of deep, cobalt blue—it was almost as if the realm itself had prepared to witness the deaths of the combatants.

Kagen heard Marquis grunt as he shifted nervously where he crouched. Now that the crowd had taken their seats, the guards had taken their posts, and the juxtaposition of the players inside the stadium had become definitively clear, it was up to the Ancient Master Warrior to make any final adjustments. Despite the fact that he spoke telepathically, Marquis still cleared his throat. *Nachari, it appears as if all the spectators have been seated on the eastern, northeastern, and west-eastern side of the arena—some in the corners above the pits that will release the beasts, some in the center with the clearest view of the…main event.* He was careful not to say "the execution of our father." *I note four sentries in the stands by the rails and one positioned in front of the northeastern gate. The former are probably there to control the crowds, and each appears to be a Beta. The latter looks like an Omega from here, and he is more than likely poised to open the gate and release the beasts. You will take all five sentries out as quickly as possible, and then you will turn your attention to whatever beasts are released from the northeastern gate.*

Nachari leaned closer to the wall, no doubt scanning for each of his assigned targets, and then he sent an affirmative charge of energy to Marquis across the common wavelength. *I understand.* His voice was as serious as it was calm.

Marquis continued soberly. *Nathaniel?*

Yes, warrior?

You will take the southern end of the arena, parallel to the main entrance. Again, whatever beasts come out of the southeastern gates, you will dispatch; but not before attending to the three omega guards on the ground floor of the arena.

Nathaniel purred deep in his throat—he probably didn't even know he was doing it. *There is a guard posted outside the southeastern gate, probably to release the beasts, as you've indicated, and two flanking the main-floor entrance, one on either side. They are Omegas, and I will kill them as easily as I would slaughter a calf in a field.*

Kagen tilted his head back and forth, ever so slightly, thinking, *Well, that was succinctly put.*

Indeed, Marquis responded to Nathaniel. *But your responsibility does not end there: From the way the rebels described previous games, the king will most likely position our father on the far southern end of the arena, with his back turned toward the royal dais, which means that his opponent, Cain Armentieres, will enter on the southern end with his back turned to you. Needless to say, you will not allow this alpha lycan to execute our father—no matter how compromised or weakened they have made him. While your instinct may be to go for Keitaro first, do not. It is possible that he can hold his own for a time, despite their machinations. We must eliminate the Alphas, or we will never escape with our father.*

Kagen let out a slow, feral hiss, struggling to contain his emotion: Ever since he had absorbed Arielle's memories, he was able to connect Cain's name with his face. Now that he had his own memories back—he could recall that fateful night in the valley, the night Keitaro had disappeared—he also knew that

Cain Armentieres had been there. The lycan had virtually eviscerated Kagen's hamstring and his throat.

Nathaniel placed a reassuring arm on Kagen's shoulder and gave it a firm squeeze. *Do not lose your focus during the battle, Kagen. Your enemy is my enemy. And there will be no vultures to return his heart to his body when we are through.*

Kagen gave Nathaniel's hand a crisp pat and slowly nodded his head, even though his brother couldn't see the gesture.

Marquis seemed to hesitate then, as if he were thinking his next words over carefully. *There is one more thing, Master Warrior*, he said, still addressing Nathaniel.

And that is? Nathaniel asked.

Marquis sighed. *It would appear that these repulsive lykoi intend to launch their ceremony by lighting their own version of an Olympic torch.*

Nathaniel breathed a revolted sigh. *Queen Cassandra, on the raised platform.*

The beautiful yet tortured human was already bound, gagged, and strapped naked to the two enormous posts jutting out of the raised podium at the southwestern corner of the arena; and her quivering body was coated in tar in the most vulgar of places. The fire pit at her feet had been arranged with highly flammable logs in a v-shaped manner in order to sweep the fire upward as quickly as possible.

Are we going to let that spectacle ensue? Nathaniel asked.

Marquis snorted. *Any diversion is a good diversion, but even I have my limitations. If it is at all possible, put the fire out as soon as it is feasible to do so. Whether or not it will be in time to save her, I cannot say. But know this, warrior: You have only one goal today, one priority, one yardstick by which you will measure every choice you make and every action you take, and that is to save our father. If you can spare this evil woman such agony, then do so; but if it interferes with saving Keitaro, then let her burn.*

"*Damn*," Nachari uttered beneath his breath.

Kagen shifted anxiously on his knees, but he said nothing. The woman had been a power-hungry witch according to Arielle, or at least her memories. She was as evil as her husband,

and she had chosen to commit adultery with Thane's top alpha general, one of his best friends, knowing exactly who and what her husband was. While it went against all decency to allow any female to perish in such a harsh manner, to risk Keitaro's safety in favor of hers—well, as far as Kagen was concerned, Marquis was right: If necessary, the bitch could burn.

As for you, Master Healer, Marquis went on. *You will enter the arena on the northern end, directly beneath the royal dais. I am giving you King Thane himself because to give him to anyone else would just be futile and a constant distraction. If Arielle is nearby, then she is also your charge.*

Kagen sighed, a breath of relief. He absently patted the custom leather case at his hip, the pouch containing his silver-tipped scalpels, and he ran his forefinger over the outline of the largest blade: a polished handle made of ivory, with a four-inch precision tip. As a surgeon, he could wield it with uncanny dexterity and accuracy.

However, Marquis added, *do not forget, the vile king may be the least of your immediate concerns; on top of dealing with an alpha monarch and trying to save a woman who may—or may not—be your* destiny, *you will be faced with five other immediate challenges.*

Kagen peered through the peepholes in the weathered stones and watched intently as he listened.

There are four beta sentinels posted on top of the dais—do you see them?

Kagen's eyes swept swiftly over the platform. Oh yes, he saw them. In the center of the elevated platform were two garish, enormous thrones, and on either side of the pair were four guards, dressed in military finery—there were two on the right and two on the left. *I see them,* he snarled.

Good, Marquis said. *Then you also see the two alpha lycans posted on the ground floor of the arena, just beneath the dais—they are probably extra security for the king.*

Kagen nodded instinctively. *I see them, too.*

I will take the Alpha on the western end, just as I will dispatch both of the beta sentinels posted on either side of Cassandra's platform. All will be closest to me on the western side of the arena, but you will need to dispatch the Alpha toward the east before you even attempt to seize the actual dais and dispatch its occupants.

Kagen nodded again, this time, for himself. *Understood.*

And then Nathaniel said what Marquis could not. *Then you will take Keitaro?*

Marquis grew deathly quiet. When, at last, he spoke, his voice was grave with determination. *I will bring our father out of the arena and protect him from whatever occurs around us.*

Nachari shifted where he crouched. *You do know…* He started to speak, but his voice trailed off.

Nathaniel picked up where Nachari left off. *We* all *know that the best laid plans of mice and vampires often go astray.*

Things might get even uglier than we anticipate, Kagen chimed in, *and one or more of us may get hurt…rather severely. Or worse.*

Just the same, Nathaniel said. *You stay at your post, Master Warrior. You protect and defend our father…at any cost. It is why we are here.*

We all have each other's backs, Nachari cut in, *but we are far more likely to succeed with our individual assignments if we know that, come what may, you have Keitaro's.*

Marquis grunted in an affirmative fashion. There wasn't much more he could say.

The Silivasis had chosen him for such a critical mission because he was the harshest and most dispassionate of them all, at least when it came to approaching war as a lethal tactician—without emotion and without compassion. Marquis would fight like a wild beast for their father, and he would let the spectators die, the sky fall in, and the stadium burn to the ground—with everyone in it—if that's what it took to accomplish his goal. If anyone could bring Keitaro out alive, it would be the Ancient Master Warrior who had led their family with such honor and courage for the last 480 years.

We are ready, Marquis said by way of a reply, and to a degree, it was true:

Not only had they planned, prepared, and surveyed every possible inch of ground the night before, but they had moved in and out of the temporary, pre-game encampment, feeding on the abundant human prey all around them. Each male had taken more than his share from an unsuspecting merchant, a carnival peddler, or a soon-to-be onlooker. They had primed their bodies for an epic battle: Their muscles were twitching, and their adrenaline was flowing.

They had waited 480 years for this moment.

Kagen stilled his thoughts and reached out one last time to his brothers, telepathically. *Then this is it*, he said solemnly.

Nathaniel purred like a satiated cat. *Indeed, it is.*

Marquis said nothing, but Nachari reached out and felt for the hands of the males beside him. *Brothers, take my hands.* Without hesitation, each of the Silivasis linked arms with the sibling beside him as Nachari bowed his head in prayer: *To Perseus, the Victorious Hero, god of my reigning moon; to Cassiopeia, the keeper of Nathaniel's soul; to Draco the Dragon, Marquis's eternal guardian; and to Auriga, the Charioteer, protector of Kagen's heart: We offer you homage, even as we kneel before you in supplication: Give us, this day, the strength, the wisdom, and the power to defeat our enemy. Bless our hands, our weapons, and our minds that our every decision will be correct, our every action true. This day, give us back our father, return Arielle to our care, and make us victorious against our rivals. And to Libra, the celestial god of balancing scales and of meting out justice, we ask for this single, supreme blessing: May the rivers run crimson with their blood.*

All four males consummated the prayer by drawing a solitary blade, slicing their wrists, and leaving a joint offering of blood on the ground between them, and then they healed their wounds with venom and stood.

Ready for battle.

twenty-two

The trumpets blared.

The crowd rose to their feet.

And King Tyrus Thane entered the dais, announcing the opening of the games.

He read the final decree for each execution, and then he introduced the realm's newest, soon-to-be queen: Arielle Nightsong.

Kagen's heart nearly leapt out of his chest.

He leaned forward to peer through a narrow hole in the wall, and practically came unglued. *Dearest goddess of mercy*, Arielle was dressed like a high-class courtesan, standing next to the lycan king, and her face was mottled with bruises. He felt his demon stir and struggled to hold it at bay. *Not now…*

Not yet.

Soon.

Very soon.

He held his breath and waited as the heavy set of wooden doors on the southern end of the arena swung open and Cain Armentieres entered the auditorium with a crescent-shaped throwing axe in his right hand and a crude, iron stabbing knife in his left, the weight nestled snugly against his palm. A gold medallion shone at his chest; the circular handle of the blade encased his wrist like a cuff; and Kagen couldn't help but take notice—the last time he had seen that face, the male had stood over him in the northern Dark Moon Vale Forest, wearing that same golden medallion around his neck. Kagen blinked twice to clear his vision. An eerie stillness settled inside him as his senses grew sharper and his muscles grew taut. Every cell in his body was itching to fight.

And then a hushed silence swept over the crowd as several lycan guards exited the doorway, leading a tall, sinewy male—*a vampire*—by the arms.

Kagen drew in a harsh intake of breath.

He practically swayed where he stood.

It was him.

Keitaro.

Their father.

And the male looked like nothing he had remembered: His once shiny black hair was dull and matted; his eyes were narrow with purpose but devoid of life. His frame had to be at least fifty pounds lighter, and his once luminescent skin was scarred with dozens of pocks and blemishes. He walked more slowly than Kagen remembered, and his gait seemed to drag rather than amble, as if he carried the weight of the world on his enslaved shoulders.

He was indeed *nosferatu*—the walking undead.

But not because he was a vampire, because he was a shell of a warrior, forced to endure the unendurable for longer than most beings lived.

Kagen sucked in air through his front teeth and purposefully regulated his breath. He watched with barely restrained fury as a second set of guards approached the raised platform where Cassandra struggled futilely against her rawhide bonds, and casually lit the fire. The gag was removed from her mouth, and she screamed like a woman possessed.

Kagen dialed down the sound. He turned his attention back to the raised dais and studied King Thane and Arielle, and then he simply held his breath waiting for Marquis's command.

Now! The warrior spoke gruffly, even in their minds, and in an instant, all four Silivasis leapt the formidable walls of the arena and landed on the stadium floor, quietly taking their respective places on the circular battle field, primed, invisible, and teeming with adrenaline.

Without delay, Cain charged at Keitaro, and everything seemed to happen at once: Keitaro and the general, who was still in human form, met in a clash of sound and fury in the middle of the stadium, their brutal blows and lethal maneuvers a dreadful sight to behold. For a frozen moment, Kagen watched in stunned fascination as *his father* and Cain Armentieres lunged, trapped, and parried like swordsmen of old, only Cain wielded an axe and a blade, while Keitaro marshaled his fists and his fangs.

And then, Cassandra's fire went out: Nathaniel had blown icy wind over the conflagration, and the two platform sentinels were struggling to rebuild the blaze as the king glared at them angrily from the royal box. Nathaniel turned his attention on the two omega lycans at the main entrance of the arena floor, and although his assault could not be seen, it was swift and lethal just the same. Both males doubled over, and their bodies slumped lifelessly to the ground.

At the same time, Marquis literally twisted off the head of the nearest beta lycan, wrenching the trophy right off the male's shoulders, even as the soldier continued to add accelerant to a dying log.

Nachari struck next.

The Master Wizard sent two blazing streams of blue lightning from his invisible fingertips out toward the crowd, up into the stadium, each bolt searing directly into the heart of a beta guard. Two sentinels clutched their chests and staggered backward, yet Nachari did not let up. The streams grew hotter, more intense, searing through flesh, blood, and bone until, at last, the guards fell to the stadium floor, nothing more than a combined pile of sweltering ash. And that's when Nachari leapt into the stands, his curved sickle clutched tightly in his right hand—it was a bizarre sight to watch, as if the sickle moved of its own accord—as Nachari went from one remaining male to the other, clutched both by their hair, and slit their throats from one ear to the next, leaping back into the stadium before their blood hit the ground.

The wizard finally shimmered into full view.

And it seemed like the crowd would have noticed—*should have noticed*—but they were so caught up by the action in the arena, the epic battle between Keitaro and Cain, that they didn't see the bloody vampire or the fallen sentinels.

At least not right away.

Nachari took the opportunity to stalk toward the omega guard, posted at the northeastern gate. The lycan caught sight of him, threw open the hatch, and then started to shift into his wolverine form. Nachari lunged at the lycan. Still brandishing his blood-drenched sickle, he gutted the male from stem to stern and dropped him to the arena floor, booting him out of the way.

The crowd began to scream.

Kagen watched in macabre horror as two enormous beasts, which could only be described as a cross between a rhinoceros and a velociraptor, stormed through the open northeastern gates, charged into the arena, and pointed their horns at Nachari.

Before he could see what happened next, a loud, thunderous crack drew Kagen's attention to the center of the arena.

Cain had just landed a violent blow against Keitaro's skull, and the vampire had fallen forward onto his knees—it was obvious that Keitaro's ribs had all been broken, long before he entered the battle, and Cain took full advantage of the unfair odds: He shifted into lycan form and lunged for Keitaro's throat.

Marquis was there in an instant: enraged, determined, and no longer invisible.

He hurled his massive warrior's body onto the wolf's back; pounded him three times in the back of the head with his wicked, spiked cestus; and then thrust the same hand, like a dagger, through the wolf's thick haunches, burrowing deep beneath his wiry fur in an effort to tear out his heart. Marquis looked positively rabid as the lycan somehow managed to dislodge his murderous hand.

A shrill horn-blast resounded from the royal dais, a formal sounding of alarm: as if the people didn't know they were in peril…by now.

And once again, Kagen was forced to turn away.

The alpha lycan beneath the dais, along with the remaining beta guard who had been tending Cassandra's platform, rushed to the center of the arena to aid Cain in the sudden, unexpected battle, to assist in the execution of Keitaro. At the same moment, the omega guard at the southeast end of the arena opened the gates before Nathaniel could get to him, released two more of the hideous beasts, and joined in the maniacal fray in the center of the arena. Nathaniel shimmered into view and dove into the mix; Nachari shifted into panther form and sprinted toward the beasts—apparently, he had escaped the first attack—and Kagen was left to take on the remaining Alpha beneath the dais, all four Betas on the top of the royal platform, and King Tyrus Thane himself. Not to mention, he still had to rescue Arielle.

In short, he could not stop to watch his brothers.

There was no time to play spectator in this life-or-death sport.

Luckily, he was still invisible.

He turned his attention toward the alpha guard who was making his way toward the center of the arena, wholly unaware that a vampire stood less than ten feet in front of him. Kagen immediately recognized the loathsome mongrel: It was Teague Verasachi, the male who had killed Arielle's mother and given her to King Thane as a slave, the male who had broken his arm as well as his clavicle, kicked him in the side, and ripped out his heart so many years ago in Dark Moon Vale.

The male who had murdered him beneath a waning moon.

Something wicked, buried, and too-long controlled swelled up in Kagen's soul, something that had waited 480 years to be released: the fury, the rage…

The rivers of blood.

"Here, puppy," Kagen whispered in a sadistic, disembodied voice. He snapped his fingers two times. "Here, Fido. *Come*!"

Teague spun on his heels and sniffed the air. He was immediately aware of Kagen's presence, although he still couldn't see him. "Who are you? What are you?" He dropped low to the ground in a defensive posture.

Kagen moved like a bolt of lightning, striking out of a clear blue sky. He lunged for the general's arm and tore it out of the socket, tossing the offensive limb into the middle of the arena as he swiftly retreated to his original position. "Bad doggy. Very bad doggy."

Teague snarled in pain and fury. He grasped at the space where his arm had just been and howled in outrage. His eyes flew open with shock, and he started to shift into his superior, lykos form.

Kagen withdrew a silver-tipped scalpel from his belt, sliced sideways across the lycan's chest, then downward along his sternum, before the male could shift or even sense it coming. And then he took a generous step back, sliced the palm of his own hand crosswise, and slowly dripped blood along the arena floor. "Come, Fido," he taunted wickedly, "follow the blood. Use that canine nose."

Teague howled in fury. Despite his serious injuries, he shifted as fast as Kagen had ever seen a lycan shift and rose to his full ten-foot advantage. Spittle dangled from his fangs as he snarled in the direction of the invisible attacker.

Kagen toyed with him.

He flashed quickly in and out, displaying his human form before the enemy like a matador parading a red cape in front of a bull, and then once again, he disappeared into the overcast day.

The lycan lunged, just as Kagen expected, and as he flew in midstride through the air, in the vampire's direction, Kagen careened like a batter sliding into home plate, landing right beneath his outstretched form, directly beneath the beast's hind legs. He slashed at his jewels, neutering him in midstride, before landing once again on his feet and spinning around to face him.

"What's the problem, lycan? Can't you face your death—*and your superior enemy*—like a man?"

Teague's rage-filled, dark eyes lit up with recognition.

"That's right," Kagen whispered. "At last, we meet again."

Teague howled like a wild thing. He gnashed his teeth together and swiped blindly at Kagen with a vicious paw, drawing a deep, painful line through Kagen's right cheek.

And that's when Kagen saw red.

That's when he released his cloak of invisibility, withdrew a thinner scalpel, and began to stab and slice, to dice and chop, like a crazed banshee, alternating between using the tool and his teeth, his claws and his fangs.

That's when he leapt off the mangled pile of meat he had left on the arena floor, flew onto the raised dais, and smashed his forehead against the skull of the nearest beta lycan. That's when he gouged out the male's eyes and ripped out his intestines, turned to the guard beside him, and began to skin him alive in crisp, clean, uniform layers, stacking each new filet in a pile at King Thane's feet. Kagen's surgeon hands moved so quickly—perhaps at the rate of twenty to thirty strokes per heartbeat—that the entire filleting took place in mere seconds.

King Thane was enraged at the insult.

He booted the pile of discarded flesh away from his feet and lunged wildly at Kagen, swinging with a huge, iron fist. Kagen ducked out of his reach and back-handed him across the platform, sending him careening into the monstrous throne, watching as it splintered into a dozen pieces…as Arielle dove out of the way.

And then he turned his attention on the two remaining beta lycans.

His shoulders hunched, his biceps twitching, his eyes undoubtedly glowing bloodred, Kagen crept down low, distributed his weight evenly between his back feet and his front right fist, and looked up at his enemy like a hungry jackal. A rabid snarl escaped his throat, and he slowly licked his lips, releasing his fangs to their full, lethal length. "Come," he whispered softly, "join my river of blood." He stroked the familiar scalpel in his right hand like a long-lost lover and waited.

The coercion didn't compel them—they weren't exactly human—but the desire to dispatch him quickly elicited the same effect: The first of the two lycans started to shift and lunge at the same time, his sinister yellow teeth gnashing together in fury, even as he drooled in anticipation, practically salivating over his prey.

Kagen met the Beta's lunge with equal force, thrusting his entire body upward and shoving his left arm, hard, into the lycan's throat. He gave it an extra thrust on impact, crushing the windpipe with ease, and then he followed the blunt maneuver with a razor-quick stab—a fierce, neat plunge into the lycan's left ear—impaling his brain with the full length of the scalpel, before swiftly pulling it out.

There was a one-second delay…

The lycan's eyes stared fixedly ahead, as if he thought he was still in a fight, and then his pupils dilated, lost their focus, and his eyeballs rolled back in his head, completely absent of…*life*.

Kagen caught the dead lycan by the arm as he fell.

Like a child toying with a wishbone on Thanksgiving, he snapped the useless appendage out of its socket; drew it up, behind his shoulder, like a baseball bat; and widened his stance, preparing to swing. Just as Kagen suspected, the remaining lycan went for his jugular: With his jaws open wide, his gnarly teeth bared, he tried to rip out Kagen's throat; and the vampire could not have asked for a better pitch.

Kagen swung the macabre club with all of his might, and the bat hit home with a thud. Teeth shattered; the lycan's tongue rolled back along the roof of his mouth; and the entire contents of his oral cavity lodged in the back of his throat. As the lycan hacked and wheezed, choking on his own teeth and gums, Kagen sliced his carotid artery open and kicked him off the dais with a brusque shove of his foot. *Let him bleed out on the arena floor*, he thought, reveling in the fresh scent of *more* spilled blood.

He was just about to turn his attention to Arielle and King Thane when the explosive sound of gunfire, erupting from the center of the arena, drew his eyes to the battle, and to his brothers, once more. He turned in the direction of the rapid echo, *pop…pop…pop-pop-pop*, one long series of firecrackers following another, and gasped.

Nathaniel was emptying his AK-47 into the side of a rhino beast from no more than three yards away; and the moment the monstrous creature fell, Nathaniel leaped over his enormous carcass and began to unload a fresh clip into another one. The omega guard who had tended the southeast gate was nothing more than a pile of twisted skeleton and serrated flesh, and by the telltale position of his dislodged bones—they were protruding from his *hind parts*—there was no doubt that Nathaniel had done the nasty deed.

Nachari—well, the panther that was Nachari—had a third rhino beast on its back and was making exceedingly messy work of its throat, while Marquis twisted the head of the fourth creature in his brawny hands, trying to wrench the three-horned abomination from its bloated body.

And Keitaro…

Keitaro was lying, nearly lifeless and still, at the feet of the second alpha lycan, the one who had been standing in front of the dais on the arena floor. Cain Armentieres was lying next to Keitaro, and his torn, bloodied heart was still resting in their father's open hand—no doubt, the Ancient Master Warrior had ripped it from his chest, even in his weakened state. But now, another Alpha was bending over him with a crude thrusting-dagger clutched in his right hand: His innards were oozing out of a wicked gash in his right side; his left arm was dangling morbidly, like a broken tree branch along the bloodstained trunk of his body; and his legs were barely holding him upright. Yet and still, he was about to avenge Cain by taking Keitaro's life.

Kagen could not look away.

He opened his mouth to shout to his brothers, but no sound came out.

In an instant, he gathered two radiant balls of fire in the palms of his hands and hurled them in quick succession, one right after the other, at the alpha lycan, at his gaping wounds. The missiles struck their target and the male stumbled back, just in time to meet the broken horn of a rhino beast as Marquis Silivasi plunged it through his back, impaling him through the heart.

Kagen breathed a sigh of relief, and then he heard a deep, menacing growl behind him.

He had only turned away for a moment…

But it was a moment too long.

Tyrus Thane Montego had shifted into his magnificent lykos form. His thick, tawny hair was bristled and standing on end. His enormous pointed ears were tucked back and erect, literally twitching with anticipation. His vile, jagged teeth were brandished, and they looked like three-inch knives jutting from his bloody gums.

Thane lunged for Kagen's throat, and as Kagen sidestepped to the right, the king caught his left arm by the bicep and wrenched at the muscle, tearing through the tendons as if they were nothing more than raw, tenderized meat. He spat out the flesh with disgust, opened his jaws wider than any jaws should ever open, and sprang once again at the vampire, this time, at Kagen's head, trying to crush his skull in one lethal bite.

Kagen raised his good arm to block him. He kneed him in the ribs and fell onto his back as the lycan landed on top of him, the wolf's vicious teeth sinking deep into the cage of Kagen's skull.

Kagen grunted in pain, trying to maintain his focus.

He reached blindly for his largest scalpel, trying to feel for the blade at his hip, hoping it was still tucked inside the waistband. When at last he felt the familiar implement slide into the palm of his hand, he began slicing and stabbing wildly, going for every vital organ he could find.

The pain in his head was debilitating. Still, Thane clamped down harder, trying to crush Kagen's skull with his powerful jaws. Based upon the overwhelming sensation of pressure, the sound of ligaments stretching and cartilage collapsing, it would only be moments before Thane succeeded if Kagen didn't get out from beneath the lethal bite.

Why the hell didn't the asshole respond to pain? To Kagen's scalpel?

He didn't even flinch!

And great celestial gods, there was so much blood in Kagen's eyes—he couldn't see a thing.

Kagen dropped the surgical instrument and grasped Thane

by the throat instead. He clutched him by the windpipe and squeezed as hard as he could, until he finally felt the knobs of the lycan's spine, tight against his fingers, and then he tried to crush the vertebrae with his hand.

They wouldn't snap.

What the hell was this lycan made of?

"Kagen!" Arielle screamed his name. She shot forward on the dais, bent over in her ridiculous gown of blue and white silk, and scooped the scalpel up from the platform. And then she began to stab the king, over and over and over, thrusting wildly into Thane's shoulders, his sides, and his neck, screaming all the while in bloodthirsty passion.

Thane roared in fury and surprise, and the effort cost him his iron grip.

He released Kagen's forehead, leapt back from their entanglement, and shifted back into human form. Swatting Arielle away like a fly, he reached beneath the rubble of the broken throne and retrieved his royal broadsword. "I will kill you as a man, vampire; and you will know the true strength of your enemy."

Kagen blinked his eyes several times, trying to bring his vision back into focus. The dais was spinning around in dizzying circles, and his head felt like it was about to explode.

He was just about to black out from the pain when he noticed a thick blade of steel plunging toward his chest. Thane held the iron broadsword in a wrathful, primal grip and was mere seconds away from impaling Kagen's heart, if not slicing the vampire in two, in his furious rage. He put the full weight of his enormous body into the thrust even as he bellowed a bone-chilling, guttural war cry, half human, half beast.

Kagen didn't have time to stop Thane's momentum, and he didn't have time to get out of the way.

He was at the mercy of the lycan.

All he could do was *react.*

In that solitary, critical moment, as his life flashed before his eyes, Kagen drew on all the rage inside of him, the alter ego, Mr.

Hyde, his long-repressed and conflicted core. He slammed the back of his right hand against the palm of his left and raised his arms like a shield. And then he called on the part of his soul that had been dormant, like a sleeping volcano, for 480 years, just waiting to erupt, just itching to unleash its molten power. He drew on the pain and the grief and the need—the absence of his father and the absence of his sanity. He drew on every instinct he had ever had as a healer and harnessed it, as one…

Kagen funneled the energy of his alter ego into the palm of his right hand. He used the power of his mind to pack the molecules tighter, to compress the bonds, and to increase the electrostatic attraction between atoms. And, in the process, he made his own hand into an iron shield of impenetrable steel rather than flexible flesh and bone.

When the tip of the sword hit his palm, instead of piercing his flesh, it vibrated wildly with resistance—*and then froze*—almost as if it had been thrust into the side of a concrete wall.

Kagen pushed back with everything he had, with everything he was or ever would be.

And the steel gave way to the vampire's power.

The blade rolled back like a scroll, folding in on itself in the direction of the hilt; and as the metal wheeled into an improbable round ball, Kagen wrapped both hands around it and thrust back at Thane.

The king's eyes flew open in shock as the vibration forced his hands from the grip and the pommel shot back at him, reversing directions, striking him squarely between the eyes. Kagen gave the trundled sword one more mighty thrust, and the pommel sank deep into the king's skull, driving through his flesh and bone, penetrating his frontal lobe and his gray matter, like a battering ram piercing a castle wall.

It finally halted, lodged opposite of the cross guard, a twisted sword…impaled backward.

Thane slumped forward onto his knees, trying to extricate the massive projectile from his skull. His mouth fell open as sluices of blood gushed in crimson streams through his teeth.

They looked like miniature *rivers of blood…*

Crimson, thick, and beautiful.

Kagen wiped his eyes with the back of his hand, stumbled to his knees, and watched as King Tyrus Thane Montego drew his last breath on the royal dais. Just to be sure, he withdrew a silver-tipped scalpel from his waistband and carved out the lycan's heart. He tossed it over the side of the platform and then reached out blindly for Arielle, swiping at empty air. "Sweeting? *Angel.* Come to me."

A shadow of blue silk appeared at his side as Arielle rushed to be near him, dropped down on her knees, and threw her arms around him. "I'm here, Kagen. *I'm right here.*"

He ran his bloodstained hands along her back, her arms, and her sides. "Are you all right?"

She actually chuckled then. "I think I'm in better shape than you are."

He forced a faint smile. "Yeah, well, you might be right about that, Miss Nightsong." And then a feral growl rose in his throat. "What happened to you, sweeting? Did Thane…did he—"

"No," Arielle rushed the word. "He did not. *That…*didn't happen."

Kagen sighed with relief, and then he began to choke on a glob of blood, most likely Thane's, before spitting it out on the dais. "Would you mind cleaning off my eyes while I try to heal my cheek, my hands, and my head with my venom?"

Arielle nodded emphatically. "Of course." He heard her rip the hem of her dress, tearing a long, silken strip upward, and he winced in pain as she began to dab at his eyes with the soiled cloth. But there was no time to complain or dally.

He needed to heal his wounds, and quickly.

He needed to get to his brothers and Keitaro…if it wasn't already too late.

He could hear howls coming from wolves deep beneath the dais; snarls and growls outside of the stadium; rage-filled battle cries rising in the stands, and he knew that the king's soldiers were amassing in force—those who had remained outside the stadium to guard the realm; those who had stayed in the underground tunnels to orchestrate the games; and those who were not on official duty, who had taken a seat in the stands.

There were dozens of lycans converging, and they were no doubt incensed at the murder of their king. Lycans were already fearsome vampire-hunters by nature; only now, they would be fevered in their rage.

Kagen and his brothers needed to get the hell out of Mhier.

And now!

They needed to gather their father, collect Arielle, and escape.

There was no point in staging an all-scale war they couldn't possibly hope to win.

He turned to Arielle and cringed, wishing he had the time to explain things, wishing he had the privilege of diplomacy. In truth, he could afford neither one. "Oh, sweeting, this is not how I wanted to tell you, *to do this*, but we have to get out of this realm. And you are coming with me to Dark Moon Vale."

twenty-three

Arielle clung tightly to Kagen's back, her arms locked unerringly around his broad shoulders, her legs wrapped indecently around his waist, her head burrowed snugly in the crook of his neck as she struggled not to empty the contents of her stomach in his hair.

They were flying through the air at dizzying speed, trying to escape the lycans.

Marquis had slung Keitaro over his right shoulder, nestling the male between his blue-black wings in what Kagen referred to as a *fireman's hold*; Nachari had taken point, leading the vampire pack just above the tree line, all the while hurling neon bolts of fire at the lycans down below; and Nathaniel was bringing up the rear, spraying the ground furiously with repeated bursts of silver bullets.

And all of them were flying.

Flying.

Covering the entire twenty-two-hour journey from the Royal District to the south side of the swamps in what would ultimately amount to less than one hour.

Arielle took a deep breath, trying to make sense of what had happened: Now that the vampires no longer had to worry about detection—they no longer required the element of surprise; they no longer needed to remain invisible; and they no longer needed to heft heavy packs of bagged blood, ammunition, and camping supplies—they had opted for the most expedient *and nauseating* form of travel, taking to the air like a flock of migrating birds.

They had dumped everything but the weapons and ammo they carried on their persons, fought their way out of the arena like a well-oiled machine, and taken to the air like wild birds of prey; and Arielle was going with them. She was returning with the Silivasis to Dark Moon Vale.

Arielle replayed the jarring moment in her mind:

Kagen had told her, in no uncertain terms, that he was sorry to break it to her so abruptly but they were fleeing the realm of the Lycanthrope, and she was coming with them. There was a chance, albeit slim, that she might be his *destiny*. "Get on!" he had barked from the dais, dipping low to heft her onto his back. She had started to object, but his severe glance had brought her up short: *Now was not the time.*

Although she'd had a dozen or more questions, a hundred or more objections, talking them out in the arena, with the enemy converging like a swarm of nasty flies, had simply not been an option. Trying to locate remaining members of the resistance—if, in fact, there were any—had also seemed fruitless, at best. From what Thane had told her, her rebel family was either dead or on its way to being captured: One way or the other, the members were beyond saving.

Feeling frustrated, shell-shocked, and utterly lost, Arielle had climbed on Kagen's back like a dutiful, disheveled equestrian mounting a wild steed—she'd figured she could think about the meaning, the repercussions, and the healer's decision later.

"What if I lose my grip?" she had asked Kagen, feeling ridiculous for posing the least important question at the most important moment, but truth be told, it had been at the forefront of her mind. Arielle was human, and she couldn't fly. Hurtling to the ground at lightning-fast speed, just to become a red dot, embedded in the earth, was not her idea of a well-versed plan.

Kagen had laughed out loud in that annoying yet endearing, roguish way he had of displaying his amusement. "Don't worry, Miss Nightsong: I'll catch you before you hit the ground."

The thought had been too unsettling to contemplate, so she had gone with him without argument; and now, all she could manage to do was hold on, try to decipher which way was up in light of the overpowering vertigo assailing her, and pray that the ancestors would be merciful and keep her from slipping off his back.

"Are you okay?" Kagen spoke into the wind, his guttural words echoing past her ears like fragments of Nathaniel's bullets ricocheting off the trees.

She tried to mumble an answer but couldn't quite manage it. "I think I'm going to throw up in your hair," she finally whispered.

He heard her. And he laughed again, that musical, infuriating sound. And then he stroked the outside of her thigh far too lovingly.

Far too intimately for the situation.

Arielle gulped and burrowed her head even further between his shoulder blades, between his magnificent outspread wings. If she vomited now, it would go down his shirt. Her stomach turned over in a fresh, violent wave as he dipped an outstretched wing toward the ground in order to get a better look at the wolves running beneath them, the lycans struggling to keep up with the vampires' pace. From such a high elevation, they looked more like tiny ants scurrying along the ground than the fearsome, deadly creatures they were.

Her stomach roiled.

The contents heaved.

Oh well…so be it.

Arielle gagged three times in an effort to quell her retching, and then she simply let it fly.

"Open the portal, Braden!" Marquis shouted in frustration, punctuating the sentence with a string of Romanian curses. He glanced over his shoulder to glare at Nachari. "You sure you can't get it open?"

All four Silivasis were standing back-to-back in a tight, defensive circle, with Arielle and Keitaro wedged protectively in the center, as they awaited the arrival of their enemy—they could hear them coming, dozens more lycans, dispatched from the southern pack's keep, arriving from General Teague's stronghold. The vampires were hovering in the exact same position they had arrived in the morning they had entered Mhier, waiting to exit through the portal; only this time, the lycans knew they were there.

"It's not going to open from this side." Nachari spoke in a clipped, solemn voice.

"How is Father?" Nathaniel asked, directing his question to Kagen.

Kagen peered behind his shoulder. "He's still unconscious, but his heart rate is steady. We need to get him out of here and back to the clinic."

Marquis grunted again. "Where is that boy? What time is it, Nachari?"

Nachari sighed in aggravation. "It's coming up on *two*—Braden knows to open the portal *every hour on the hour*."

Marquis snorted. "All of this—our fate and our father's welfare—resting on the shoulders of that silly, impetuous boy. What the hell were we thinking?"

"He'll be here," Nachari insisted.

Kagen patted his waistband reassuringly, checking for the familiar feel of the custom-made belt and his trusted scalpels. He also had a silver dagger tucked into a sheath and an LC9, loaded with silver bullets, strapped to his ankle in a holster: He would use whatever he had to if the lycans came too close. As he watched a pack of five wolves approach slowly from the west, he reached behind his back to gesture at Arielle. "Get directly behind me, sweeting."

Arielle placed a gentle hand on his shoulder from behind. "Give me my bow, Kagen. I can at least cover you from here."

Kagen glanced at the determined female and nodded. He had completely forgotten that the simplistic weapon, and its associated quiver, were still strung over his left shoulder, that he had been carrying both since they left the arena. "Do what you must, Arielle, but do not leave the center of this circle, no matter what occurs. And even if I fall; when the portal opens, you must go through it with my brothers."

Arielle looked momentarily surprised. "But I thought all of this"—she gestured toward the clearing; the primed, resourceful Silivasi brothers and the approaching werewolves, now twenty yards away—"was about *your* Blood Moon, *Auriga*. The possibility that I might be your *destiny*. If you are gone—"

"The rebel resistance has been broken. Your friends are dead or captured. Your parents are gone, and the lycans will be seeking a terrible blood vengeance. There is nothing for you here, Arielle, no way for you to survive. At least, in Dark Moon Vale, you will have a chance at a life, the hope of beginning again. *Promise me*."

Arielle started to answer, but Kagen never heard her words.

All five lycans attacked at once.

twenty-four

Braden Bratianu drew a crude circle on the ground.

He placed the bark from a tree in the north and stones from the eastern cliffs in the east. He emptied a vial of clear water from the Winding Snake River in the south and tossed a chunk of uneven rock from the Red Canyons in the west. With each placement, he repeated the rhythmic Latin phrase he had heard Nachari speak five days ago; and then he placed a piece of Tristan's hair, one-half of the lock Nathaniel had ripped from the lycan's dead scalp, in the center of the haphazard circle, careful to bury it just below the surface, exactly as Nachari had done before. He had to admit, the hair was getting extremely filthy and gnarled; after all, he was burying it *and digging it up* over and over again.

He surveyed his handiwork and sighed. *Yeah, yeah, yeah…*

Open the portal—again—every hour on the hour.

Been there, done that, hoping to toss the T-shirt.

And it wasn't like he didn't take the duty seriously. On the contrary, he was both honored and humbled to be chosen for such an important task. It was just…

It was just that he had done this over four dozen times already; the Silivasis were never there when the portal opened; and everyone in Dark Moon Vale was growing restless and concerned. On some level, he wondered if they doubted his ability to handle such an important assignment, if they didn't suspect him, already, of screwing it up.

He sighed, biting his lower lip as he went through the familiar motions like a robot. He understood his duty, and he would do it: Contact Napolean the moment the portal opened to give the king a report—up until now, the report had always been the same: *nothing to report*—transmit a telepathic summary to Ramsey Olaru and then Saber Alexiares, of all vampires, if he saw anything at all. In the event that there were werewolves bold enough to follow the Silivasis back into Dark Moon Vale, Napolean had wanted some badass warriors ready to greet them, prepared to fight…

Just in case.

Yeah, Ramsey and Saber could handle that assignment.

Braden fingered the smooth, leather scabbard at his side and smiled, imagining the amazing thrusts, downward slashes, and lightning-quick parries he could wield with the small dagger if he had to—well, okay, so he wasn't all that good with the ancient weapon quite yet—but still, he could fight like a crazed lunatic if he had to.

He *would* fight like a crazed lunatic if he had to.

As blue and violet light began to rise from the ground, the pale, luminous beams radiating outward like a halo, the center of the circle began to glow, and once again, the portal opened.

Braden began to count backward from ten to one—it was how long he usually waited before closing the gateway—when all of a sudden, he saw the most primitive thing he had ever seen: Nathaniel Silivasi, drenched in the blood of an enemy, the head of a lycan still dangling in his outstretched hand; Nachari's sword, slashing perilously through the air, slicing a werewolf in half; Marquis's fangs, bared to their full, lethal length, stained with cherry-red chunks of flesh; and Kagen Silivasi, slicing the heart out of a werewolf with a fine silver scalpel, his crisp, clean movements too swift to be seen. On the ground, at the brothers' feet, was an unconscious male lying next to a beautiful woman. She was standing over him protectively, dressed like a warrior princess, releasing arrow after arrow into the frantic melee with amazing speed and precision.

Braden stepped back and gasped. "Nachari!"

And then he remembered what he was supposed to do.

Napolean! The telepathic call was frantic. *They're here. And they're fighting lycans!* He turned his attention to Ramsey and Saber, calling out on a universal warriors' bandwidth. *Saber! Ramsey! The portal is open and the Silivasis are here…with lycans.*

All three vampires shimmered into view instantaneously, faster than Braden could spit out the last word. Without hesitation, Napolean Mondragon shot into the portal—his eyes were narrowed with purpose; his pupils were burning flame red; and his jaw was set in a wicked hard line. Instinctively, Braden just knew: The ancient monarch was channeling the sun. He assessed the situation in an instant—counted the lycans, measured their strides, made lethal note of their various positions—and then, as if the sun were simply his to employ, he gathered the hot, roiling gases, sent a single stream of fire blazing from his eyes, and cast it outward in a wide arc, saturating the remaining lycans in intense, poisonous light.

His body never moved.

His face never hardened.

The only sign of his toxic wrath was a subtle but uncontrollable twitch in his upper-left lip.

It was enough.

The sweltering radiation engulfed the werewolves with agonizing results—it sizzled, hissed, and hummed on contact—consuming the beasts in a preternatural fire, leaving nothing in its wake but a pile of steaming ash.

The king stumbled backward and staggered out of the portal; Ramsey stepped forward to catch him. As Braden understood it, the king's rare radioactive powers were as dangerous as they were lethal: Every time he used his *solar ability* on a grand scale, he risked his health; and in extreme cases, he even risked his life. Luckily, this had been a minor use of his power: short, sweet, and effective.

"Milord, are you all right?" Ramsey, one of the valley's most-revered sentinels, was not taking any chances: Releasing his fangs, he tore a long, vertical gash in his wrist and pressed the offering to the king's mouth. "I offer freely. Drink."

The king didn't hesitate.

He latched onto Ramsey's arm like a viper, sucked what had to be a pint of blood in under thirty seconds, and then casually sealed the wound with his venom, appearing instantly revived and alert.

Braden swore beneath his breath, wishing he were as strong and brave as Ramsey. He turned his attention to Saber Alexiares, watching as the brutal soldier extended a long, muscular arm into the portal and grasped the first wrist that met his. He pulled Nachari out with a sharp tug, and then he reached back in for Nathaniel. Marquis came out on his own accord. His thick black hair was drenched in blood; his face was a wild mask of fury; and his arms were heavy-laden as he cradled the limp, unconscious body of a male vampire close to his chest.

Before Braden could study the vampire more closely, Kagen emerged with the wild-looking woman clinging to his arm. He fixed his gaze on Braden and practically snarled. "Close the damn portal, son. *Do it now*!"

Braden struggled to remain calm and focused. He waved his hand through the air three times, weaving a simple spell as he closed the portal. And then he stepped back and gawked at his newly arrived companions. "Holy shit!" The words left his lips unbidden: The Silivasis had returned *with their father*!

Napolean turned his still-blazing eyes onto Kagen, and the fiery red centers flashed back to haunting black. "Do you have her?" His voice was rough with demand.

Kagen met the king's gaze with an equal amount of intensity, and something in his gaze spoke of such hope…*such desperation*…such need that Braden could hardly comprehend the question. *Did Kagen have who?*

"I have Arielle Nightsong with me," Kagen said brusquely, even as he genuflected in a slight bow to the king. "She was a warrior in the land of Mhier, a healer, and a friend. I could not leave her behind."

Napolean sighed in obvious relief. "Then you know?"

Kagen swallowed hard. "I know nothing." He seemed to consider his next words carefully. "However, I *suspect*…" His voice trailed off. "Tell me, milord. By all the gods, *tell me what I am waiting to hear*."

Napolean nodded. He raised his right hand and gestured

toward the sky. "The first night you entered Mhier, the moon turned as blood, and the celestial constellation Auriga, the charioteer, appeared in the night sky." He reached out to take Arielle's arm, and she drew back in alarm. Napolean placed his hand at his side.

"Shh, sweeting," Kagen soothed the woman softly. He gently grasped her left arm on his own and slowly turned over her wrist, staring longingly at her sun-drenched skin. And then he nearly groaned in surprise—and relief—at the sight of the strange, enigmatic symbols etched so plainly in her flesh. "Dear Gods…just like that."

Braden leaned forward to get a better look.

Sure enough, Auriga, the Charioteer—the entire constellation—was stamped on the wild-woman's arm. "Holy cow," he said. "Your *destiny* was in the land of the werewolves?"

"Braden," Nachari chastised, shaking his head back and forth to silence him.

"Sorry," Braden whispered. He turned to stare at Napolean, wondering what would happen next.

As if an enormous weight had just been lifted from his shoulders, Napolean's entire bearing relaxed. His face lit up with an unexpected light, and he declined his head in deference toward Arielle. "Greetings, Daughter of Auriga. Welcome to Dark Moon Vale." He shook his head in wonder. "You have no idea how many prayers have been said on your behalf."

The woman took a cautious step back and turned to gape at Kagen, her eyes like that of a frightened deer. "Healer?"

Kagen met her unspoken query head-on. "Do not fear me now, sweeting. All is well. All will be made well." With that, he turned his attention to Marquis—and to the male who was still lying limp in the Master Warrior's arms. "As long as we can save my father…our father."

Napolean appraised the unconscious vampire carefully, and while his eyes seemed to reflect a subtle recognition, there was also a hint of dread…and doubt. "Then this is *Keitaro*?"

Marquis nodded. "It is our father."

"Is he—"

"Barely alive," Kagen interrupted. "We must get him to my clinic, *immediately*." He turned to face Napolean directly then. "Milord, I know such things are considered sacred—they are rarely done. But I must ask—"

"My blood and my venom are yours, healer." Napolean spoke without hesitation. "Whatever we must do to heal this warrior, we will do."

Kagen breathed out a heavy sigh and nodded his head. "Thank you, milord." Then he turned to his brothers and gestured in the direction of the clinic. "Let's go!"

twenty-five

Kagen sat on the edge of the hospital bed, staring intently at Keitaro.

At his father.

He appraised the outward signs of his physical condition in the space of a second: the increased flush of color in Keitaro's skin; the gentle rise and fall of his chest as he breathed with less difficulty; the heat emanating from his forehead, indicating that his current body temperature was rising; and the smooth set of his brow, indicating an absence of the terrible pain that had plagued him…up until now.

Kagen had been at it for twenty-four hours: operating, mending, healing…

Intervening.

And there was little more the healer could do at this point other than to watch. And to wait.

Much like the human process of dialysis, Keitaro's blood had been siphoned from his body, no less than four separate times, and strained of vile poisons. Kagen had treated the plasma with venom to clear the offensive toxins and reintroduced it into Keitaro's bloodstream, along with a pure mixture of critical healing agents, not the least of which consisted of Napolean's ancient, powerful white blood cells. In addition, Kagen had injected Napolean's venom directly into Keitaro's heart so that the potent, regenerating liniment could travel as organically as possible throughout Keitaro's body, healing and restoring his vital organs in a natural process. Each wound had been cleaned, treated, and repaired with more of the king's venom; and fresh, human blood had been infused directly into the ducts beneath Keitaro's fangs so that he drew in constant vital nourishment of his own.

He had been bathed.

His hair had been washed.

And Kagen had even trimmed and filed his nails, for lack of anything more constructive to do.

He had wanted to make his father as comfortable as possible; moreover, he had needed to make him look more like the male he remembered: the handsome, powerful, vital warrior who had always loomed larger than life.

Yet and still, he waited like a helpless child for the faintest sign of awareness.

For his long-lost father to just…*wake up.*

Marquis had finally taken to pacing the hall, just outside Keitaro's room, with Ciopori at his side. Nathaniel had finally fallen asleep in an oversized armchair in the front lobby of the clinic, while Jocelyn softly stroked his uncombed hair.

And Nachari?

He had practically sequestered himself in Kagen's office, refusing to feed or come out, as he prayed to the celestial gods and offered sacrifices of his own blood on Keitaro's behalf.

Deanna was never far away.

In fact, it seemed like half the warriors in Dark Moon Vale had stopped by the crowded clinic to offer a word of encouragement to the family. Or a prayer. Their massive vampiric bodies had quickly filled up the otherwise spacious waiting room, overflowing into vacant exam rooms, and even filing up the narrow staircase toward the upper levels of the clinic, until Kagen had finally asked them to go home.

In short, everyone's presence had been felt, except for Arielle's.

The beautiful, independent female—*Kagen's newfound destiny*—had chosen to wait alone in one of Kagen's private guest rooms, sequestered next door in the healer's private residence like a captive bird, albeit by choice. She was confused by her sudden change in circumstances; overwhelmed by the sheer volume of family *and potential friends* who stopped by to wish them well; and her senses were drastically overloaded by all the foreign sights and sounds: computers flashing, appliances buzzing, apparatus humming or beeping at every turn. So she had retreated into herself, insisted upon being left alone, while the Silivasis worked feverishly to try and save their father. She had even refused to let one of the brothers' mates keep her company while the critical rehabilitation dragged on.

And Kagen had never felt so frustrated or helpless in all his life.

Under normal circumstances, he would have been with his woman. He *should* have been with his woman, reassuring his *destiny*, slowly…gently…introducing her to the strange new world she now inhabited, making her feel wanted, safe, and secure. Helping her understand her unexpected fate.

He should have been teaching her about the Curse, giving her options, and choices, and answers—*lots and lots of answers.*

He should have been showing her how deeply she was loved.

But nothing could happen until Keitaro was out of the woods, until the patriarch of their family was finally stable and no longer in danger of being lost. While Arielle had seemed to understand this intimately—she had even insisted upon this exact order of priorities—she had also seemed so lost and alone, so bereft and confused, and the knowledge of her distress weighed heavily on Kagen's heart.

"Please, Father," he whispered, staring at Keitaro's unconscious form. "We need you to come back. The *daughter of your heart* needs you to come back. You are all that remains familiar to her in this terrifying new world." He let out a plaintive sigh. "Please, just open your eyes."

He thought he saw a flicker of response, the barest twitch of an eyelid—it wasn't exactly a resounding reply, but it was something.

Rising to his feet, he moved closer to his father and bent over his slumbering form. "Father?"

Keitaro's eyelids twitched again.

Marquis! Nathaniel! Nachari! The telepathic communication was instantaneous. *I think he's waking up!*

All three brothers shimmered into view at the exact same

moment, each one hovering over the bed like an overeager ghost, their dark, luminous eyes filled with stark anticipation and need.

"Father?" Nachari spoke first.

Keitaro blinked two times, and then, like the sun peeking out from beneath a dense cloud after a long winter's storm, his brilliant, deep brown pupils appeared beneath his lids, illuminating the room like glorious beams from the luminous star. "Nachari?"

The wizard practically fainted. "Yes, Father."

"Then you are dead, too?" Keitaro's voice was raspy, deep, and laced with sorrow. He slowly turned his head to look around the room, but he didn't appear to focus on anything in particular. "Then this is the Valley of Spirit and Light?" He slowly licked his lips as if testing his tongue for function. "Where is Serena?"

Nachari took Keitaro's hand in his and squeezed it gently. "You are not dead, Father. You are in Dark Moon Vale."

Marquis stepped forward from the end of the bed. "We found you in Mhier, Keitaro." He held his father's gaze with an expression of unusual compassion. "We brought you home."

Keitaro tried to sit up but faltered. It was as if the room had started to spin, and he reached out to steady himself on the lowered rail.

"Easy, Father," Kagen murmured. He braced one hand on the rail, another on Keitaro's shoulder, and helped him lie back onto the thick, down pillows. "Don't move too fast."

Keitaro furrowed his brow. He stared one by one at his sons, and his face grew more confused. "But I died in the arena." He looked off into the distance. "I killed Cain Armentieres, the male who murdered your mother, and then…and then I saw my sons as I left this world. You were beside me…a final escort…as I died."

Nathaniel shook his head, his long blue-black locks swaying from the motion. "No, Father. We *were* there…with you…in Mhier, but not to escort you to the spirit world. We came to get you, to take you out of that gods-forsaken place, and we found you in the arena. We fought alongside you, and we brought you back home. You are safe in Dark Moon Vale. *You are home.*"

Keitaro drew back against the pillows in burgeoning surprise. He patted his chest, stared down at his arms and legs, and then reached up to feel his cheeks. "I'm alive?"

"You are in my clinic," Kagen said. He couldn't take his eyes from Keitaro's. He couldn't believe this moment was actually happening.

Then all at once, as if a dam had broken, a blockade forged from confusion and slumber gave way to the weight of truth and awakening; and Keitaro's ancient eyes filled with tears. He turned to his eldest son and smiled. "Marquis."

The warrior held his breath. He bit down hard on his lower lip, drawing a trickle of blood, perhaps to quell his emotion, perhaps to convince himself that he was truly awake and the moment was finally happening. "It is with great respect that I greet a fellow descendant of Jadon, an Ancient Master Warrior, my beloved, honored father and *friend*, whom I have missed with all my heart. We welcome you back to Dark Moon Vale." He spoke with unusual eloquence, relying on formal protocol to help him through the moment.

Keitaro planted one hand against the mattress and pushed up with all of his strength. Throwing formal protocol to the wind, he reached out with a trembling arm and snatched Marquis, pulling him into a fierce embrace. "*Marquis.*"

Marquis enfolded him with both arms, at first squeezing so hard that Kagen was concerned for Keitaro, and then he buried his face in his father's shoulder and began to weep.

Keitaro stroked his thick, downy hair and simply repeated his name, over and over. "Marquis…Marquis…*Marquis. My son*…my firstborn son."

When the ground began to shift beneath them, Kagen placed a soft hand on Marquis's shoulder. "Emotions, brother." The reminder was gentle: How in Hades could any of them hope to contain the emotions they were feeling in this moment?

Marquis pulled out of Keitaro's embrace, cupped his father's face in his hands, and gave him a gentle kiss on the forehead—it was the most tender act any of them had ever seen Marquis perform, outside of his occasional tender exchanges with his own son, Nikolai.

Keitaro looked up then and reached out for Nathaniel. Nathaniel stepped forward, taking Marquis's place. He took his father's hand in his, raised it slowly to his jaw, and cradled the strong, perfect palm against his cheek. It was almost as if he simply wanted to feel Keitaro's skin against his own, to become one with his own flesh and blood. "*Father.*" The word was choked out as Keitaro embraced him, and the two powerful males rocked in a strange, rhythmic motion, their hearts beating as one.

Keitaro clung to his second-born son. "How old are you?" he finally said, and all four brothers chuckled—the break in tension was welcome.

"I'm one thousand years old, Father," Nathaniel said softly, "but today is truly my first birthday."

Keitaro brushed a tear from the corner of his eye, and then he turned to regard Kagen. "So you, too, are an Ancient? An *Ancient Master Healer*...my curious, intelligent son?"

Kagen blinked away his own tears, but he couldn't stop from trembling. He palmed the back of Keitaro's head and brought him forward to his chest—*to his heart*—where his memory had always lived. "My father," he whispered, nearly breaking into a sob. "*My father.*"

Keitaro inhaled deeply as if reveling in Kagen's scent. He nuzzled his chin in an intimate gesture, not caring if the display wasn't manly, and then he sat up straight, appearing to gain strength from the love of his family, and brushed Kagen's cheeks with his thumbs. "By all the gods, I never thought I would see you again"—he turned to glance around the room—"any of you." He met Kagen's gaze and held it warmly. "Thank you for coming for me."

It was more than Kagen could bear.

The centuries, the guilt …the regret.

He felt his emotions slipping, the tears about to give way, and he pulled back momentarily to regain his composure.

Understanding, Keitaro turned his attention to the other side of the bed, where Nachari sat patiently beside him, waiting. His entire face lit up with joy. "By all the gods, you are more handsome than I remembered. And you were utterly *perfect* back then."

Nachari smiled that stunning, breathtaking grin he was so famous for, and the entire exam room lit up with the magnificence of his joy. "Father…" The word came out with the barest hint of hesitance, and Keitaro took his hand.

"You were only…what were you, Nachari? How old, when I disappeared?"

"Twenty-one," Nachari said solemnly.

"And now?" Keitaro asked.

"I will be 501 in three months' time."

A fleeting mask of grief—indescribable, inconsolable, acknowledging *so many* lost years—flashed over Keitaro's face before it was quickly replaced with wonder. "What discipline did you choose?"

Nachari swallowed hard. "I'm a Master Wizard, Father." There seemed to be the barest tension between them, not an absence of love—*never that*—but the silent awareness that in an immortal lifetime, they had only shared twenty-one years.

Keitaro nodded, regarding Nachari with a fierce, glowing pride. "Of course you are, my sensitive, alchemist son." He raised Nachari's palms to his face and breathed into them as if wanting to impart his life force, and then he deeply inhaled as if taking in the wizard's hopes, dreams, and heart. "I have missed you with every ounce of my being, Nachari," he whispered.

Nachari shifted anxiously on the bed—he looked like he might fall apart.

And then, as if the awareness suddenly dawned on him, Keitaro looked up, glanced around the room, and frowned. "Where is your twin?" he asked eagerly. "Where is my most mischievous son, the one with his mother's golden hair?"

Nachari cleared his throat, even as he drew from a waning well of courage. "Shelby is…no longer with us. He is with our mother in the Valley of Spirit and Light." He absently clutched his beloved amulet, the one that always hung around his neck, the one that Shelby had given him when Marquis made the Dark Sacrifice of his unnamed son. "He lives…always…in our hearts."

Keitaro drew back in anguish. "What happened?"

"Later," Kagen interjected, not wanting to jeopardize the vampire's health.

"*What happened?*" Keitaro repeated, his grief-stricken voice deepening with command.

"Valentine Nistor happened," Marquis cut in.

"He got to Shelby's *destiny* before they could fulfill the demands of the Curse," Nathaniel added, before he dropped his head in his hands.

Keitaro visibly wilted. "My son? My loving, happy-go-lucky, compassionate son died in the *sacrificial chamber?*"

Nachari stiffened and raised his jaw. "*Father…*" The word was a mere whisper.

Keitaro held out his hand to silence him. "My son…and *your other half,*" he lamented. He leaned toward Nachari and gestured him forward with the slightest bend of his hand. And in that barren moment, as the two males closed the distance between them, a lifetime of grieving was shared.

Keitaro clung to Nachari like he was the last soul on earth, and together, they mourned a loss too great for words. "Oh, Nachari. My boy…my son…*my son.*"

The wizard wept unabashedly, not caring that the mountains rumbled and the sky opened up, pouring down buckets of rain. When, at last, he regained his composure, he sat back and tried to force a smile. "But there is much to celebrate." He gestured toward Marquis, Nathaniel, and Kagen. "All of us…we're mated now. We have *destinies*…and sons of our own." He inclined his head at Marquis. "And Marquis—he's married to one of the original princesses."

"One of the original princesses?" Keitaro echoed, his voice disbelieving. "As in the sisters of Jadon and Jaegar?" He looked positively dumbfounded. "How can that be?"

Nathaniel filled him in on the story, the CliffsNotes version, explaining everything in succinct, sequential order, and Keitaro practically reeled in astonishment. "Where are they now—your *destinies*, your sons?"

"They're just outside the room," Kagen said. "We didn't want to—"

"Nonsense," Keitaro interrupted. "I want to meet them, *right away.*"

Marquis nodded, and Nathaniel rose to make his way to the door. He opened it, peered into the hall, and said something softly to Jocelyn. Within moments, the women and children were gathered at the door.

They walked in quietly, their arms filled with their precious bundles, and the look on Keitaro's face was one of pure, unadulterated bliss.

The moment was too precious for words, too priceless to cheapen with casual banter.

It could only be handled with formality.

As the eldest son, Marquis extended his hand to Ciopori first. "Princess, come forward. I would like you to meet my *father.*"

Ciopori positively radiated with love.

"Ancient Master Warrior, honored father, and fellow member of the house of Jadon"—he rolled the words off his tongue with pride—"I present to you my mate, the daughter of Cygnus, the royal offspring of King Sakarias and Queen Jade, the sister of our revered patriarch, Jadon Demir. Father, I present to you my *destiny*: Ciopori Demir-Silivasi."

The princess placed Nikolai gently in Marquis's arms in order to free her hands, and then she quickly strolled to the side of Keitaro's bed, where she curtsied in an old-world gesture. "Beloved Father." She spoke eloquently, musically. "It is both an honor and a privilege to meet you." She bent over, kissed him on the forehead, and took both of his hands in her own. "Oh dear goddess." She hiccupped a sob, losing the stilted formality. "I can't believe you are finally home." She embraced him, and he encircled her in his welcoming arms.

Marquis beamed with pride and satisfaction. He waited until the two pulled apart and then he set Nikolai in Ciopori's arms. The child wriggled restlessly, his face betraying his discomfort, as if he had no idea what all the fuss was about, and Keitaro laughed, openly and heartily. He took Nikolai and held him up in the air. "You are a strong little vampire." The child bobbed up and down in his arms and gurgled.

Ciopori laughed. "Honored Father, this is your second-born grandson: Nikolai Jadon Silivasi."

Keitaro declined his head with respect and appreciation. "Nikolai *Jadon*…of course."

After a few moments of watching them play, watching as Keitaro bounced the happy child up and down, Nathaniel reached out for Jocelyn's hand, took Storm from her embrace, and hoisted him onto his hip, and then he led her to the side of the bed, where Ciopori quickly retrieved Nikolai and shuffled out of the way. "Father," he said proudly, his voice literally vibrating with adoration, "this is my mate and the love of my life, Jocelyn Levi-Silivasi. She is the daughter of Cassiopeia, an esteemed warrior in the human culture, and the mother of your firstborn grandchild."

Keitaro looked up at Jocelyn and smiled, his keen expression filled with love and acceptance. "Jocelyn, daughter; come closer."

Jocelyn hurried to his side. "Oh hell," she huffed, "I don't know how to do this with any measure of finesse. Just give me a hug!" She plopped down on the bed, wrapped her arms around him, and rocked back and forth with exhilaration. "Keitaro!" She buried her head in his shoulder, wiped her nose on the sleeve of his gown, and chuckled apologetically. "Welcome home."

Keitaro laughed in earnest, and then he reached out for

Storm. "And who is this little ball of fire?"

Jocelyn rolled her eyes in an exaggerated parody of angst. "This little ball of *mischief*, fire, and vinegar is your grandson and your namesake: Keitaro Storm Silivasi."

Keitaro grew instantly quiet. He looked from the child to Jocelyn, then from Jocelyn to Nathaniel, as if for confirmation, and then he let out a deep breath of air. "Keitaro Storm Silivasi?" He repeated the words like a prayer.

Nathaniel's deep emotion was reflected in his eyes. "Yes, Father. We named him after you."

Keitaro shook his head in awe, and for the first time, he appeared completely overwhelmed. "Well, hello there, little Keitaro," he murmured, bouncing the child on his knee.

Kagen took a deep breath: As a healer, he did not want to see Keitaro exert himself—*just yet*—but to his credit, he held his tongue.

"He is quite the spitfire, is he not?" Keitaro observed, watching as the child flexed his nimble legs, trying to extend and enhance each bounce.

"Oh, you don't know the half of it," Nathaniel said, an authentic twinge of angst ringing in his voice.

The entire room laughed, knowing full well the trials and tribulations Storm put Nathaniel and Jocelyn through, with his constant explorations and mischief.

Keitaro was just about to place the child back in his mother's arms when Storm reached out, grabbed a handful of Keitaro's freshly washed hair, and tugged for all he was worth. "Papa!" he exclaimed with a squeal. And then he giggled and gave it another tug. "Papa Su-vasi!" He began to tug in earnest, giving Keitaro's hair three hard yanks in a row, before pausing, and then going after it again.

Nathaniel rushed to Keitaro's bedside and gently pried his son's fingers loose from the vampire's hair, before his scalp began to bleed. "Sorry, Father." He picked Storm up and handed him back to Jocelyn.

Keitaro laughed. "He reminds me of Shelby at his age," he

said, forgetting to censor his words.

The room grew quiet with painful regret.

At last, Nachari broke the silence. He rose from his perch on the other side of Keitaro's bed, sauntered to the back of the room, took Sebastian from Deanna, and ushered the exotic beauty forward, leading her gently by the arm. "Father…" He spoke softly. "This is Deanna Dubois-Silivasi, daughter of Perseus, the Victorious Hero, and mother of your third grandchild."

Keitaro glanced up at Deanna, inhaled sharply, and then slowly let out his breath. Not that all the women weren't beautiful in their own right—*they were*—but Deanna was particularly stunning, with an exotic set of features that were very hard to place. "Greetings, Deanna," he said warmly.

Deanna smiled from ear to ear, her breathtaking countenance lighting up the room. She strolled forward and grasped his hands. "Keitaro," she whispered with unabashed admiration. "*Father*." She sat down on the bed and cupped his face in her hands; and then she bent over and kissed him on the cheek, first the left, and then the right. "Welcome…welcome…*welcome*." It was almost as if she were at a loss for words.

Keitaro blushed and playfully stroked his cheeks, touching each spot where her lips had just been, deliberately acting flustered. She paled, and he laughed. "Thank you, Deanna. I am pleased to see my wizard son has found a mate with a soul that shines as bright as his own." He turned toward Nachari, who was sitting once again on the other side of Keitaro's bed, and gestured toward the handsome bundle in his arms. "And who might this little guy be?"

Deanna sat up straight, her eyes brimming with love. "This is your youngest grandson: Sebastian Lucas Silivasi."

Keitaro regarded him fondly. "Sebastian." He held out his arms, and the child practically leapt from his father's embrace, trying to get to the ancient vampire.

"Gan-pa!"

Keitaro jolted, startled. "Oh my, you are an eager sort, aren't you?" The child grinned with pride as if he had done something truly remarkable, and Keitaro laughed aloud. Finally, he passed the baby back to his mother, turned to Kagen, and regarded him squarely. "You are yet to be mated?"

Kagen sighed. *Where to begin*? "I am…*soon* to be mated."

Keitaro raised his eyebrows and waited. When Kagen didn't elaborate—in truth, he had no idea what to say next—Keitaro urged him on with his eyes. "Explain, healer."

Kagen flashed a faint smile. "I met my *destiny* in Mhier. We brought her back to Dark Moon Vale." He gestured thoughtfully with his hands. "Once I am sure you are out of the woods, I will go to her, and see to…the conclusion of my Blood Moon."

Keitaro frowned. He glanced around the room, eyeing each of his sons in turn, as if he could garner further information from their eyes. When no one spoke, he cleared his throat. "*Well*, who is she? Have I heard of her?"

Kagen smiled broadly then. "Yes, I believe you have. The daughter of Auriga is also the daughter of your heart, Arielle Nightsong."

If someone could actually jump out of their skin, Keitaro would have done it. His surprise and delight were exuberant and unrestrained. "*Rielle?*" He glanced around the room, his eyes darting wildly back and forth between spectators, as if he could somehow pick her out of the crowd, as if he had overlooked her presence before. "Where is she?" he demanded, his voice thick with impatience.

"She is in my private residence," Kagen said candidly. "She didn't want to be here while we were still working to…*revive you*. It is all too overwhelming…too new and confusing. There was too much to process at once."

Keitaro considered Kagen's words. "Of course; she must feel like a fish out of water."

Kagen nodded. "She does."

"Then why aren't you with her?"

Kagen drew back in surprise, feeling immediately defensive.

"Because I'm with you."

Keitaro frowned, and the paternal flash of disapproval on his face was unmistakable. It was as if his eyes were saying, *What the hell are you doing, boy!?*

"Father, I…I—"

"Belong with your *destiny* right now," Keitaro interrupted.

"Of course, but you were in pretty serious need of a healer."

Keitaro tilted his head from side to side as if weighing the healer's words. "And now, I'm fine."

"Well—"

Keitaro's stern glance cut him off abruptly. "You do have a nurse, do you not? An acolyte…a healer in training?"

"Of course," Kagen said. "Katia Durgala and Navarro Dabronksi, but I would like to see to your care, at least for a couple more hours, make sure you don't regress or take a turn for the worse. And I'd like to write up clear orders before I hand over your chart to an *acolyte*."

Keitaro shrugged with indifference. "Nonsense. I'm a vampire. Once we heal, we heal. What do you think is going to happen, cardiac arrest? I'm not that old, son."

Kagen shrank back, his ire rising in spite of himself. "You *are* that old, Father. But that is not the point. As you say, you are Vampyr, so age is of no consequence. I would just like to be sure that all is well before I turn my attention to other matters—it's taken a lot of years to get you home."

"I understand that, son. Believe me, *I do*." Keitaro spoke respectfully, and then he simply pulled rank and dismissed Kagen's concerns offhand. "Yet as your father, *I have spoken*, and we will not revisit this again: You will go to your *destiny*; you will see to her needs; and the *two* of you will not come to see me until your bond is cemented…until it is unbreakable. Do you understand?"

Kagen's mouth dropped open, and the room fell silent.

And then Storm offered his two cents: "Unka Kagen go to time-out?"

Nathaniel burst out in laughter, and Kagen shot him a

sidelong glare. He opened his mouth to speak and then closed it, feeling like a complete idiot. Had his father—and his nephew—just put him in his place? And in front of the entire family? *Gods in heaven*, they had to know there was nowhere he would rather be than with Arielle, but Keitaro had nearly died.

Realizing that Arielle would want to see Keitaro immediately, he decided not to argue with his father but to seek clarification instead: Clearing his throat, he ventured forward: "By *cemented*, you mean what?"

"Once she is soundly in love with you," Keitaro said firmly.

"Mmm," Kagen said. "Small order, *that*."

Keitaro chuckled. "Perhaps not, but an *order* nonetheless."

Kagen winced.

Wow...

So this was what it was going to be like, having Keitaro back home...

He swallowed his pride and considered his next words carefully. "I know how much Arielle means to you, *how much you mean to her*, and I will try to be delicate, to honor that bond."

Keitaro laughed heartily then, catching Kagen off guard. "Rielle is as free-spirited as a wild stallion, as beautiful as the prairie on a summer's day, and as independent as a lioness, accustomed to hunting for her pride. As your father—as *her* father—I wish you to be gentle and kind with each other's feelings. As a male of honor, I wish you to take all the time that you need. As a man who is also a vampire, who understands the Curse, I simply wish you luck. You're going to need it." He chuckled then, and Kagen's brothers joined in.

When Nathaniel continued to laugh, long after everyone else had stopped, Kagen shot him another heated glare. And then he reached out on a private bandwidth, hoping to garner some brotherly sympathy from his twin. *Yeah, because I would have just grabbed her by the hair and dragged her to the nearest cave. Damn. What the hell?*

Nachari laughed out loud. "I heard that, *Twinsies*."

"Would you quit doing whatever wizard-ly thing you're

doing then?" Kagen snapped.

"I heard it, too," Marquis chimed in.

Nachari smiled. "You spoke on the wrong frequency, brother."

"And thank you for saying that out loud," Kagen replied.

They were just about to take it up a notch, really get the banter going, when Keitaro raised his hand and waved it through the air to silence them all. His eyes grew narrow; his expression hardened; and all three sons halted in their mockery…at once.

And then, as if he had never been absent from the valley, Keitaro Silivasi switched into paternal mode, becoming the supreme, unquestioned leader of his family once more. His eyes swept over Marquis, then Nathaniel, each male in turn, and he lowered his voice. "Master Warriors."

The warriors stood up straight and waited.

"Considering what happened with *Shelby*"—he almost stumbled over the word, but he quickly regained his momentum—"you are not to leave your brother unattended, *unsupervised,* for even a moment until this Blood Moon is complete. Do you understand?" He didn't wait for a reply. "You will each take turns guarding both Kagen and Rielle around the clock—you can trade off standing watch in twelve-hour shifts—and I do not want to hear that either of you, for any reason, were ever more than two hundred yards away, not until the sacrifice is complete." He crossed his arms in a gesture of finality.

Nathaniel whistled low beneath his breath and turned to face Keitaro as an equal. "The sentinels will also be close by, and—"

"And you are family. It is a different obligation, a sacred duty."

"Of course," Nathaniel said respectfully, bowing his head in deference. "I make no objection. I just wish to point out that there will be *extra protection* at hand."

Keitaro nodded. "Two hundred yards," he repeated.

Nathaniel shared a knowing glance with Marquis and turned away. "As you will, Father."

Kagen cleared his throat. Apparently, he wasn't the only one

Keitaro was willing to take to task, and for a moment, he couldn't help but wonder: If memory served him well, had the Ancient Master Warrior always been this stern? This abrupt? Nodding his head, he smiled. Indeed, he always had. Perhaps, with four strong vampires to raise, he'd had no choice. And now that he was back, his authority was music to Kagen's ancient ears. That said, Kagen also remembered how he and his brothers had handled their father's many dictates: by appealing to the male's compassion and wisdom…and sometimes digging in. "Um, I think that's all very well and good," he said, careful to keep his voice pitched low and respectful, "but there is the element of privacy…and intimacy." He stared at Marquis and cringed. "Somehow, I don't think staring up into that one's brutish mug is going to be comforting or *bonding* for me…or Arielle."

"His mug is not brutish," Ciopori cut in, flippantly. When they all stopped and stared, she huffed and rolled her eyes. "I'm just…*saying*." She smoothed Nikolai's already impeccable hair. "He's rather handsome in my opinion."

Keitaro snorted with laughter. And then he waved his hand in a dismissive gesture so similar to the one they were used to seeing from Marquis that Jocelyn and Deanna had to do a double-take. "Two hundred yards can be interpreted many ways," Keitaro said. "If you're inside your home, your brothers can be outside. If you're strolling through the forest, your brothers can hide behind a tree. I don't expect them to stand in your bedroom with you. Just the same, they will be within a stone's throw at all times, ready to respond to the threat of an enemy in the blink of an eye."

Kagen bit his bottom lip and nodded.

Well, so much for digging in.

He looked up at Ciopori and then Jocelyn, trying to register how they felt about giving up their mates, *every other twelve hours, possibly for the next twenty-four days*, but they seemed just fine with the idea. Or at least, if they weren't, they were not about to express their objections.

Nachari sat forward. "I could help, if you like." He held up his hands in jest. "After all, I'm a wizard, not a fledgling. I do have a few…unusual…skills that might prove helpful."

"He's a panther…at times," Marquis offered gruffly.

Keitaro stared pointedly at Marquis; he gaped openly at Nachari; and then he simply shook his head, apparently deciding to leave it alone. "Great celestial gods," he murmured. He redirected his attention to the wizard. "I have no doubt that you are more than capable of looking after your brother, Nachari—I did not mean to imply otherwise." He sighed then. "It's just that I would like to work with you on a different, more pressing matter, something more befitting of a Master Wizard."

Nachari cocked his eyebrows.

"You do know how to create energetic wards?" Keitaro asked.

Nachari nodded. "I do."

"Good. Then there are some things I saw in Mhier, things I learned about the lycans, things we can employ here at home—and the sooner the better."

"Like?" Nachari asked.

"Like wolf traps," Keitaro said succinctly. "Using what we know of their species to create specific, energetic wards to repel them, to craft alarms and detectors that we can place throughout the forest. I would like to make certain that they never attack our valley again…that they never again go undetected."

Nachari's deep green eyes lit up with curiosity and interest. "Of course, Father."

"Very well," Kagen said, his gaze fixed on Keitaro's intelligent eyes. "So now that we've settled things—I will go to Arielle, and Nathaniel and Brutus will follow me around—I'm afraid I do have to insist, *as a healer*, as your doctor, that you remain in bed for the next forty-eight hours. At the least, you need to remain under observation." His tone brooked no argument. "If I agree to devote all of my attention to my *destiny*—which is truly what I want—then you must agree to take it easy for a couple of days, to devote your full attention to your recovery. Deal?"

Keitaro looked at Kagen like he had cow dung smeared on his face and laughed. "You *will* agree to devote all of your attention to your *destiny*—because it isn't a request—and as for what I *must* or *must not* do? Let me get this right; *you insist*?"

Kagen visibly wilted. "I…I highly recommend that you remain in bed for the next forty-eight hours."

Keitaro tilted his head to the side, and his top lip twitched, almost imperceptibly.

"I honorably request that you consider—"

His lip twitched again, only this time it was accompanied by a faint, guttural snarl.

Kagen collapsed on the edge of the bed, just to the left of Nachari, and buried his face in his hands. "Oh, hell. *Please*, Dad."

Keitaro chuckled then, and his expression relaxed into a teasing scowl. He reached out and leaned forward to muss Kagen's hair, rubbing his head far too vigorously for comfort. His teasing eyes alighted with joy. "Of course, healer," he said, grinning. "I would not place an undue burden of worry on your shoulders at this time. And for what it's worth, I know that you both honor and desire your *destiny* with every ounce of your being." He winked at him and smiled.

Kagen shrugged and held up his hands in question. "Then what was all of this about then?"

"Your *destiny*, your safety, and your undue fear." Keitaro's voice was suddenly serious, and Kagen frowned, confused.

"Son, I know that you love me. You don't have to prove it every moment of every day. You came to Mhier to rescue me, and now, you can go to Rielle with my blessing…and do what you must." He turned to regard Marquis and Nathaniel. "And warriors, I can feel your anxiety—it's like a bolt of electricity pulsing in the air—following Kagen around will relieve some of that stress and help you to bring the last week into perspective. I am home now, and I am not going to disappear again—but you won't know that until you have tested it, until you leave and come back, and leave *and come back*, again and again. And again.

Twelve hours, for the remainder of Kagen's Blood Moon, should be just about right." He turned to regard Nachari next, and he visibly wore his heart on his sleeve. "And wizard, in some ways, you carry the heaviest burden of all because your soul is by far the most sensitive, and you were only twenty-one when I went away. Right now, you need me more than your brothers. You need me to know who you are, to see the male you've become; and *I will*, as we work on this project together." He regarded all four of his sons with unconcealed affection, and his voice was a balm to their hearts. "I love you boys more than life itself. I know what you risked in Mhier, and I know what you achieved. And I'm home now. *I'm home. I'm not going anywhere.*"

Damn it all to hell! Kagen did not want to cry.

He could not *afford* to cry.

For the sake of Auriga, he was one thousand years old!

Yet, his father was home, and he still knew each of his sons intimately. He still knew what made each male tick and what each vampire needed…above all else.

As the realization set in, the tears began to fall.

And they fell in endless rivers.

twenty-six

Kagen knocked three times on the guest room door before gently turning the handle and pushing the heavy wooden panel open. He dropped a small blue duffle bag on the floor and stepped gingerly inside the room. "Arielle?"

His *destiny* was seated in a soft leather armchair, facing a large, open window. She was staring out at the wooded hills that surrounded Kagen's estate, and her legs were tucked up to her chest, her arms hugging her knees. She wore a heavy white bath robe in lieu of her soiled animal-skins, and she turned to glance over her shoulder in response to his approach. "Healer." The word was formal and stilted, and by the drained look on her face, her swollen, puffy, and red eyes, Kagen could tell she had been crying. Again. "How is Keitaro?"

"Sweeting," he said in response, strolling directly to the chair. He placed his hand on her shoulder, careful to move slowly, to act cautiously, and he gazed out the window with her.

"Is the father of my heart still alive?" she asked, her concern mounting as the moments passed.

"He is," Kagen reassured her, unable to restrain the smile that curved along his lips. "He is alive *and awake*, and he would like to see you soon."

"Of course," Arielle said. Her voice brightened for the first time. "Will you take me to him now?"

"I will…take you soon," Kagen said. "As soon as you and I have had a chance to talk, to reconnect." He steadied his resolve. "Right now, Keitaro is visiting with my brothers, meeting his new extended family, and greeting his grandchildren for the first time. If you are comfortable waiting—"

"Yes…*yes*…of course." She rushed the words. "He should have this time with family…uninterrupted. I understand."

Kagen sighed. He had done it again, placed his foot squarely in his mouth. "That didn't come out right, Arielle. *You* are his family—there can be no doubt. He loves you."

She smiled faintly. "Of course...*always*...I just meant..." Her voice trailed off, and she drew back to appraise him more thoroughly. "Why are you here?" she asked him bluntly, her voice rising with curiosity. "I mean, shouldn't you be with your father and your brothers? Your in-laws? This is a rare and precious moment, Kagen. It has been 480 years. You should not be away from Keitaro."

Kagen sank down into a squat so that he was practically kneeling in front of her, their gazes meeting at eye level. "You are a rare and precious gift, Arielle. This moment is divine to me. And I should not be away from your side."

She inhaled sharply, her resplendent eyes narrowing with censure. "Kagen..."

He reached out and tilted her head up by the chin, his fingers trailing softly along her jaw. "You do know, Arielle, that the time for objections has passed. You *are* my *destiny*. My heart. My life. My desire to know you and to please you, to see to your comfort, is greater than any other concern right now. I cannot stay away, not a moment longer, not even if you ask me to. We need to...talk. *We need to reconnect*. To begin to work through this blessing...and this Curse." If Kagen hadn't known better, he would have sworn that the look in her eyes was one of subtle fear as well as hesitation. Arielle felt like a trapped animal, and the realization stung him as much as it broke his heart.

They had made such inroads in Mhier.

However small, however brief, their connection had been powerful, intimate, and real. He ran his hands gently along the outline of her shoulders, then up and down her arms, as if to quell a chill. "Talk to me, sweeting. Please."

Arielle blinked back moisture from her eyes and pursed her lips. Her eyes darted around the room nervously, taking in the furniture, the décor, the architecture—anything but him—before she reluctantly met his eyes. "Throughout the years...in Mhier...times I spoke with your father, he told me about this land, about Dark Moon Vale and the Blood Moon. He told me about the Curse and all that it entails: the conversion, the sacrifice, the…pairing." She cleared her throat several times, even though there was nothing wrong with her voice. "I will…try…to comply, Kagen." She steadied her resolve and repeated the words with more insistence, with forced determination. "I *will* comply—I give you my word." She looked off into the distance then, staring out the window. "I will not let you die, Kagen. I owe you my life; and I could not do that to Keitaro."

This time, Kagen cleared his throat. He hung his head and raised his brows. "I see." He stood up then and took a few paces away, moving closer to the window, in order to give her some space. "First of all, to be clear: You owe me nothing, Arielle. But I thank you. And I am truly grateful." He smiled, his voice settling into a patient but challenging tone. "When you say you will *comply*: Do you mean the way you *complied* near the shallow ravine in Mhier, the night you kissed me with such passion and abandon, beneath the Mhieridian moon and stars? The night you thought I was compelling you, when I wasn't? Is that the compliance you speak of?" He turned to face her and tilted his head. "Or are you referring to later, that same night, when you asked me to hold you in my arms, the night you cried so many unshed tears? Was that, too, a form of compliance? Did you open your heart to me for our *father*? Or for Arielle?"

Arielle seemed to wilt where she sat. "As always, you are so *direct*. That was different, healer."

"Healer?"

"Kagen." She shut her eyes. "That was different, Kagen."

"How so?"

She shrugged, placing her hands in her lap. "We were in a different place. It was a different time. There was so much going on, and I was so afraid for you and your brothers, for Keitaro, for—"

"No." He placed his finger over his lips to stop her—they could not go forward with untruths. "You were afraid to risk your heart—or your love—to lose either one to a male who might abuse you. You were afraid to give yourself to a vampire who was sworn to a *destiny* other than you, to a woman chosen by the gods." He held her gaze in an unforgiving stare. "You forget, I was there, sweeting. You were afraid to give *yourself* to me because you feared I would leave you, abandon you, when the affair was over. You told me quite plainly: You were afraid of being hurt." He spoke with deep conviction. "Arielle Nightsong, if you have heard nothing I have ever said to you, hear this now: *You* are my chosen *destiny*. You are that rare, priceless gift bestowed upon me by the gods. *You*. And I am grateful beyond measure—I cannot regret this fate—because I wanted you the moment I first saw you; I could not conceive of giving my heart to any other woman; and now, I will never have to." He took several steps toward her, linked his hands beneath her arms, and gently lifted her out of the chair. As a large section of her robe slid down her shoulder to reveal her flawless skin, he bent to place as gentle a kiss as he could on the exposed flesh and then he nuzzled her neck, just below her ear. Trying to restrain his passion, he drew back. "What we share is *not* an affair. What I will give you will be more than you ever imagined: my love, my loyalty, my commitment. The promise you required is right here—it is yours for the taking, for always…for eternity." He tilted his head to the side to gain her full attention. "Look at me, Arielle."

She met his gaze with reticent trust.

"I will not hurt you. I will not leave you. I will not abuse you…ever. You have nothing to fear."

Arielle swallowed so hard Kagen felt the vibration deep in his own throat. She grasped the fallen corner of her robe, slid it back over her shoulder, and wriggled out from beneath his arms. "I…I…" She seemed too flustered to form coherent words. She burrowed her face in her hands and struggled to breath. "I remember the first night in the cave." Raised goose bumps appeared on her arms. "I know what you can do to me…what you can make me feel…if you want to. I also know how territorial and possessive you can be when you are provoked." She peeled her hands away from her face and peered up at him. "And it isn't even that." She seemed so unsettled. "It's just…*it's just…*"

"It's just what?"

She huffed in exasperation, as if she were unable to find the right words.

"Shh, sweeting," Kagen implored. He smiled lovingly and slowly backed away in a demonstration of respect and good faith. "I am all those things and more: territorial, passionate, perhaps even domineering at times. I *am* Vampyr. But even the most primitive of instincts can be tempered with love. You are right when you say, *That isn't it…* That isn't what troubles you so deeply. It's *just* that you're completely overwhelmed. You're scared out of your wits. Not only by me, but by the entire idea of the Curse, the conversion, the sudden reality of a family, something you've never really had…and perhaps even of bearing a child…so soon." He felt more than just a little empathy for her situation. "You have no idea where you are or whether you can even adapt to a world such as ours." He pointed at the modern, solar-powered clock hanging on the wall, and the digital, cordless phone resting on the nightstand. "You have no idea what many of these things are, and you feel lost without your familiar surroundings, your usual routine, your rebel family. By all the gods, you are grieving the loss of everything—and everyone—you ever knew, no matter how hard and desolate life might have been in the world of the lycan. But you are not alone in this experience. Both Princess Vanya and Princess Ciopori have stood in your shoes. They've been where you are, and they will gladly help you make the transition." He held out his hands, palms facing up. "Arielle, we will take it one moment, one step, one touch at a time. I will teach you all there is to know about this modern world, and it won't be hard for you to learn because I can simply transfer my memories, impart my knowledge, into your mind, as if it were your own. But more important, we will ease into…*us*…together. I will ask nothing from you that you are not ready to give. I will take nothing from you that you are not *willing* to concede."

Arielle nodded with appreciation, and then she stared into his eyes as if trying to gauge his next reaction. "And what if I'm not ready…in time?"

He smiled warmly then. "You are my true *destiny*. There is much between us that cannot be explained. There always has been." He slowly nodded his head. "You will be ready—I'm not worried about that." He walked toward the door, bent over, and picked up the small blue duffle bag, unzipping it with one fluid stroke of his hand. He reached inside to retrieve a simple but elegant garment. "Now then, this is a bathing suit—you can wear it under your clothes." He reached back into the bag to retrieve a rugged pair of shoes. "These are hiking boots. The tread helps stabilize your footing on uneven terrain." He reached into the bag one last time and pulled out a pair of khaki pants and a warm, long-sleeve shirt. "And this is supposed to be a comfortable outfit for exploring. Jocelyn, Nathaniel's mate, packed it for you. You two are about the same size." He flashed a hopeful, entreating smile. "Get dressed, get your bow, and I'll be back for you in five minutes."

She furrowed her brow in curiosity. "Where are we going?"

"Someplace more familiar, more comforting." He walked to the window and pointed at the top of a nearby mountain. "There's a natural hot springs just beyond that peak. The water is decadent; the scenery is breathtaking; and you can hear dozens of birds singing in the trees. You can feel every subtle shift in the breeze and smell over a dozen scents of pine. I don't live in the city or the local town, Arielle. The world you knew in Mhier is much like the world I embrace on earth. Let me show you my world. Let me take you someplace familiar, and we will talk and get to know one another better…at our own pace."

"And what about your father?" she asked, sincerely.

"Keitaro is well and truly healed. He will still need to build up strength and acclimate to a whole new life, free of captivity, but he is no longer in danger of dying. While I want nothing more than to see the two of you reunited, my greatest desire is to bridge this gap between us right now. Come. Spend the afternoon with me, and later, we will visit Father together, once our own bond has been mended." He left out the fact that these were also Keitaro's orders.

Arielle raised her eyebrows. "And why do I need my bow?"

Kagen smiled impishly then. "When was the last time you felt safe without it?"

Arielle paused to consider his words. "I guess…never."

Kagen nodded. "*Exactly*. Besides, you and that weapon are like one fluid entity. Perhaps I can show you where the rivers meet in Dark Moon Vale, much like they converge in Mhier, and you can teach me how to hit a target at one hundred yards, *on the first try*."

Arielle shook her head and rolled her beautiful eyes playfully.

And then she did the most wondrous thing of all…

She smiled with abandon.

twenty-seven

Arielle held her fingers in front of her face and peered down her nose at the shriveled skin and ghastly white flesh. "My hands are turning into prunes."

Kagen clasped one of the outstretched hands in his own and gently kissed the center of Arielle's palm, causing goose bumps to rise on her arms. "Mmm, your hands are beautiful."

She snatched it away and laughed, making light of the ever-persistent advances of the amorous vampire. By all the ancestors, Kagen Silivasi had to be the most affectionate, tenacious, and let's face it, utterly distracting male she had ever known. He was worse than a badger when it came to his tenacity, far more focused than a hawk, and way more enthralling than a serpent.

And way, way more convincing.

She bit her lip, sank down into the hot, bubbling pool, and tried to mask her rising intrigue, her growing contentment in his presence.

Kagen had started the afternoon by taking her to a beautiful outdoor cathedral. It had been magnificent, gloriously inspired, with an enormous, rushing waterfall and a peaceful, rolling river. He had shown her a den of red foxes and pointed out where a cougar had made his home last winter, all of which had made her feel more at home in Dark Moon Vale and more at ease in her new surroundings. He had challenged her to several games of skill, catching trout in the local river with nothing more than a homemade spear, and tossing rocks with a slingshot at pine cones lobbed into the air, the latter being a game she was sure he had let her win on purpose. After all, as a vampire, his aim, speed, and accuracy were far superior to hers. Just the same, his easy, playful nature had gone a long way toward breaking down her walls and making her feel more at home.

But what had really touched her heart was when he had stopped to point out several native healing herbs growing wild in the vale: He had shown her three types of sage intrinsic to the Rocky Mountains, and he had gone on to explain how the plants were used internally to treat inflammation, how they were used externally as a compress for wounds. He had taken her to his own personal herb garden, the one he had planted behind the clinic; and he had helped her pick peppermint, elder, and yarrow, all the while describing how the medicine was extracted into tinctures, or mixed into herbal teas, in order to treat fevers in the human population. He had explained how he used his garden to assist the few loyal families that had served the Vampyr for generations, the ones who still lived in the valley today. And he had listened *attentively* to Arielle's own ruminations about the plants, poultices, and ointments she had often used in Mhier.

He had commented on their similarities or differences, adding his immense, almost mind-blowing repertoire of medicine and history to her current understanding, and then, to her great delight, he had begun to explain the basics of modern pharmaceuticals: how compounds, bacteria, and molds were secreted from plants or grown in labs, how they were chemically synthesized into antibiotics or other medications. He had complimented her on her vast array of knowledge and shown an amazing willingness to share as much information as she cared to learn with the naturalistic healer, to add to the base of her already extensive cache of knowledge.

Arielle had to admit, the idea of being able to *absorb* Kagen's memories, once she was converted, was beyond her wildest dreams. While she was too terrified to even think about the possibility of conversion at this point, the idea that the Ancient Master Healer could simply transfer all that information about medicine, all that information about healing herbs and plants, into her mind through a free-flowing stream of thought was intriguing to say the least. She was already relieved to learn that she could simply absorb his familiarity with modern household appliances, the automobile, and even that funny-looking silver thing he called a laptop, without having to spend a century learning about modern technology. The prospect of acquiring his mental medical library, along with a thousand years of proficiency, gained through systematic trial and error, was virtually intoxicating in its allure. And when Kagen had mentioned the possibility of Arielle taking over his human patients, those rare human loyalists who so willingly served the Vampyr, Arielle had nearly shed a tear. It was her dream, reawakened. But more so, it was the highest compliment she had ever received: Kagen took his duty to the human servants very seriously. He was bound by a deep sense of ethics to care for them—and to care for them *well*. Trusting Arielle with such an important responsibility showed an enormous amount of faith, honor, and respect.

Granted, there was a lot more to being an Ancient Master Healer than knowledge. Kagen possessed far more than book-learning and technical skill: He had spent four hundred years at the Romanian University, honing his craft, and nearly nine centuries, in total, becoming adept at every skill. She would be a novice, even with the knowledge he imparted. Still, she had spent her life trying to help humans in Mhier—perhaps the learning curve would not be so bad. The point was: Kagen Silivasi had managed to make Arielle feel important, *needed*, like there was a sacred world they shared, neither Dark Moon Vale nor Mhier, but a magical place, somewhere between the two, where visions could be realized, dreams could be lived, and the future could be so much more than it had ever been before. Perhaps there was more for Arielle than just hiding, rebelling, and surviving…

Perhaps there was an enchanted world all around her, just waiting to be embraced.

And at every turn, with every word, sentence, or gesture, he had punctuated his promises with a stolen glance, one that spoke of something so *intimate*; a gentle touch, one that spoke of something so *passionate*; or a feather-light kiss, one placed so softly on the back of her hand, pressed so lovingly on the top of her head, or planted so tenderly against the rise of her shoulder that it touched her heart and stirred her soul, reverberated in a place she didn't even know she had.

Arielle had been caught off guard by the depth of Kagen's kindness and his gentle spirit. By the sincerity in his words, the interest in his eyes, and the conviction in his heart. It seemed implausible—if not impossible—that this strange Curse, this bizarre fate, chosen so long ago by the celestial gods, could truly be that profound…or *real*.

Yet here it was.

Front and center…

Staring right back at her in a pair of the most stunning liquid-brown eyes she had ever seen: the truth of her purpose, her past, and her future. And all of it was wrapped up in the flesh-and-bone package of one powerful vampire.

Kagen Silivasi.

She arched her back against a soothing stream of natural jets and sighed. "This really is an amazing place," she whispered. She glanced around the outdoor theatre, watching as the sun finally dipped beneath the horizon and the sky settled into a deep, sparkling blue. "Is it safe here at night?"

Kagen paused before speaking, as if carefully considering his words. "That's a somewhat layered question." He laid his head back against a smooth, polished stone, the indentation fitting his form like a pillow, and a lock of his thick brown hair swayed gently in the water. "We are safe in as much as Dark Moon Vale is ever safe, considering our many enemies." He turned to meet her gaze. "But don't be alarmed. I can assure you, there is at least one warrior fairly close at hand the guardian angels are out in force this night. The forest is not empty."

Arielle wrinkled up her brow. "What do you mean?"

Kagen shrugged his shoulders, and a crystal stream of water sloshed off his muscular back, creating extra ripples in the tub. "My father has taken it upon himself to see to our safety, one way or another. He is more than aware of the potential hazards that exist in Dark Moon Vale, and he has made *adjustments* for the possibility that the lycans may react poorly to our invasion of their land."

Arielle's eyes grew wide with alarm. "Do you think they will? Attack, I mean. The lycans?"

Kagen shook his head. "No. Not tonight. Not even tomorrow or the day after. I think they will be licking their wounds for some time to come. I think they are going to have to regroup, reconstitute their government, and live to fight another day."

Arielle sighed in relief. "I think so, too." She settled back into the soothing springs. "And what about Keitaro? Do you think he's upset that I haven't come to see him yet? We should really get back to the clinic soon."

Kagen laughed out loud, although Arielle had no idea why. He shook his head with conviction; his eyes lit up with some inner knowing; and then he smiled, that damnable mischievous grin that made him look like a devious child. "I think my father appreciates our situation…intimately. And I think he is far more eager to see us *connect* as a couple than visit him in his room." He waved his hand in a casual gesture. "Don't get me wrong, he is dying to see you, but I think he would like to see us both, *together*, as one."

Arielle gulped.

It wasn't intentional.

It was just that Kagen always had this way of making her feel like a mouse caught in a trap, wedged between the paws of a cat, even when he wasn't trying. "So, what's next?"

Kagen sat up straight and leaned in closer.

She cleared her throat. "I mean, in terms of the Curse."

He smiled again, like a wayward wolf: *Damn him.*

"I mean"—she wrung her shriveled hands together—"I mean, in terms of the Blood Moon. You know…like…should we talk more about the conversion?"

Kagen shook his head slowly…far too slowly. "*No.*" He practically purred the word. He moved softly through the water until his body was facing hers, *framing hers*, his powerful arms enclosing her in a rock-hard cage, his fingers splayed flat against the rocks on either side of her head.

"Oh." She glanced around the mountain, her eyes darting to the left, then the right, anywhere but on Kagen's piercing pupils. "So then, I should probably know more about the sacrifice. I mean, the Curse…the pregnancy…what to expect." She winced, realizing she was acting like a terrified child.

"Shh, sweeting," he whispered. He leaned into her until his lips hovered barely inches away from hers. "There is always time for talk…later."

Her eyes shot open and her spine stiffened, but he didn't seem to notice.

He reached out to twirl a lock of her hair and studied it with undue interest. "You, Arielle Nightsong, are beautiful beyond description." He wound it between his thumb and his forefinger and exhaled slowly. "I have never seen hair quite this shade, even wet. It's not brown or red, but the color of polished copper, and the highlights, when it's dry…" He bent over to brush the tendrils against her cheek. "They're as fiery as you are."

Arielle tried to relax…and failed.

She dipped down in the water in a misguided attempt to gain some personal space and ended up plunging beneath the surface.

He let go of her hair, seized her by the shoulders, and swiftly pulled her back up, looking utterly amused. "You cannot breathe under water, sweeting," he chided playfully. "Not even once you're Vampyr." He slid his hands down the contours of her arms to her waist, along the curve of her waist to her thighs, and then along her thighs to her knees. He cupped her knees in his large, powerful hands, and with one short thrust, he shoved her back in her seat, forcing her body upright so that her head was safely above the water. The corners of his mouth turned up in a devilish grin. "If you prefer to be submerged…or overwhelmed…if you wish to be out of breath, I can think of a far more pleasant way to go about it." He bent to her mouth and brushed his bottom lip against hers.

That was it.

Just his bottom lip…in a slow, erotic slide.

It hadn't been a kiss.

It hadn't been a bite.

Just a mere brush of his mouth against hers.

Arielle coughed spasmodically, expelling a mouthful of water she didn't remember taking in. "Sorry," she groaned, feeling like a bumbling idiot.

It wasn't so much that the contact had *overwhelmed* her—it was the stolen glance at his rock-hard shoulders as he'd made his approach. For the sake of all that was holy, his chest was like a medieval shield, forged in iron yet wrapped in silk, and the muscles in his stomach cleaved to his bones like someone had carved them from clay. His thighs were like cords of steel: taut, lean, and bulging with strength.

And that was to say nothing of his eyes…

They were like endless pools of moonlight, reflecting silver in their dark, haunting depths, and he used them like weapons of seduction: taunting, hypnotizing, beguiling his…prey.

Arielle shot up straight and gasped. "*Kagen*," she cried in alarm, trying to get control of her emotions. "I don't think I'm ready for all of this."

He studied her like a jeweler appraising a rare, priceless gem; his face was an unreadable mask. "I don't think anyone is ever ready for *all of this*, Arielle. Not even those of us who spend a lifetime preparing for it." He cupped her cheeks in his hands and caressed her jaw with his thumbs. "We just take it one moment…" He traced the contours of her lips with the pad of his forefinger. "One touch…" He released his fangs and bent to her throat, stopping just shy of pressing the ivory tips to her skin. "One taste…at a time."

She exhaled slowly and held her breath.

He purred in her ear like a primitive cat, and then slowly, expertly, sank his fangs into her throat.

She jolted and grasped at his shoulders, and then she felt an unbearable heat—*an undeniable pleasure* like nothing she had ever known—seep into her veins.

Was he drinking her blood or enthralling her with venom?

Was he making love to her mind or possessing her soul?

She tried to remember, to flash back to that first night in Mhier in the cave, the night he had sent her *spiraling* into the cosmos, writhing in his arms in ecstasy, drowning beneath his perilous claim, but she just couldn't latch on to the memory. Not fully. She was too overwhelmed, so incredibly confused, so undeniably, uncomfortably *aroused.*

And it was all the invitation he needed.

Kagen withdrew his fangs, sealed the wound—if there was one—and gazed hungrily into her eyes, his breath coming in harsh, shallow pants. "I want you, sweeting," he whispered, his eyes growing molten with need. "Like I've never wanted anyone, or anything, before. I don't just want to taste you—I want to *feel* you. I want to bury my body inside of yours until it's no longer clear where you begin and I end." He groaned. "Great gods in heaven, Arielle; I want to devour your soul."

She blinked several times, trying to process his words, trying to gather her courage, and then she opened her mouth and revealed her longing, as her heart gave way to his thrall: "Yes, Kagen. *Yes.*"

He shuddered before her. His chest visibly shook for a moment, and then his mouth descended upon hers and his kiss was like a wild desert wind, sweeping her up in unfettered passion, blowing away all previous resistance, whisking her away in a gust of desire.

His tongue swept over hers and he growled like an animal.

His hands clung, caressed, and cajoled with maddening expertise.

And his hips rocked forward, revealing his straining manhood for the very first time: He was hard, thick, and ready, iron wrapped in silk.

His left hand found a purchase in the thick of her hair, and he broke the kiss long enough to breathe her name before he bent once again to her neck. Only this time, he placed soft, gentle kisses along the slope of her ear; took harsh, teasing bites along the length of her throat; and swirled mind-numbing circles with the tip of his tongue, directly above her carotid artery.

And then he slid his hands over her shoulders, removed the straps of her suit, and lowered his mouth to her breasts.

Arielle trembled at the glorious sensation of moisture and heat as he teased her nipples, each one in turn, his tongue performing an intricate dance with her flesh.

She fisted her hands in his hair as he sealed his lips around a taut areola and drew her sensitive peak deep into the warmth of his mouth. He suckled like a man possessed; he nipped like a playful pup; he tormented her like a languorous lover who had nothing but time on his hands. And all the while, she trembled and groaned and writhed beneath him.

When at last he encircled her waist, drew her to his chest, and laid her gently back along the smooth, natural bench, she felt the first real pangs of fear. His shaft jerked against her belly, and she stiffened. "Kagen," she whimpered, her voice betraying her angst.

He raised his head and smiled warmly, his eyes piercing deeply into hers. "Do not think, my love…only trust…*only feel.*" He slid his hand down her back to her hips and kneaded her flesh with his palms, watching attentively as she slowly began to relax…again.

He splayed his fingers over her stomach and simply held his hand there, resting in place, as he kissed her with feeling—slowly, tenderly, passionately—placing all the love he felt into the kiss. Finally, when she returned his passion, ardor for ardor, need for need, he slid his hand lower and began to tease her heat with his thumb.

She squirmed in response, and he added more pressure, kissing her deeper still.

She moaned, and her hips began to rock beneath his, as if on their own accord. The vampire responded with practiced skill, applying all the right pressure in all the right places, as if he knew her body better than she did—and truth be told, he probably did—because the more he stroked her, the more she ached. The more magic his fingers weaved between her sensitive thighs, the more she began to feel faint, dizzy, and light-headed, as if she were spinning inwardly, out of control.

Finally, when the pleasure began to approach pain, when the *want* in her belly grew to an unappeasable *need*, she arched her back, straddled his hips with her thighs, and moaned.

She didn't know when *or how* he did it, but he somehow removed the rest of her clothes…

And his.

Their suits fell away, floating off into the swirling pool, and the deliciously warm water picked up where his hands had left off. He drew back and glanced at her, admiring her naked form beneath him like a tray of exquisite delicacies laid out at an annual feast, and his ragged breath hitched in his throat. "Oh…sweeting…" His voice was guttural and raw. *"My love."* There was nothing—*and everything*—in those simple words of endearment: a request, a command…a plea. And all of it spoke intimately to the most feminine place in her soul.

Then just like that, he shifted his weight onto his powerful arms, lowered his hips to hers, and placed the tip of his manhood against her veil, pushing ever so gently into the threshold of her core.

"Kagen!" she gasped. She felt like she was falling.

"It's okay, sweeting," he murmured. "Tell me what you're feeling."

"I feel…*I feel*…I feel like I'm falling."

He chuckled deep in his throat. "It's okay, baby. That's what you're supposed to feel. I need you to trust me, Arielle. I need you to just…let go and follow my lead."

She tried. She really did. With everything she had inside her, Arielle tried to relax and let go, just like Kagen had instructed. But she couldn't help but think about the massive erection straining against her core. She couldn't help but calculate the length and the width of that flesh-and-blood *spear* in her mind, and the moment she did, she was assailed by terrifying images of...impalement.

Kagen Silivasi wanted to put *what...*

Where?

Everything inside her said *no.*

That was not going in.

No way. No how.

It simply wouldn't fit.

In fact, it seemed like a biological impossibility, and *ancestors help her*, as much as she wanted him, the thought made her queasy: She would never be able to please this male—or to take pleasure from him—her body was simply ten sizes too small. She gritted her teeth, winced, and held her breath, turning her head to the side. "Go ahead."

"*Arielle...*" Kagen's voice was practically dripping with honey...and mild alarm.

She blinked up at him, feeling utterly foolish and hopelessly desperate, feeling like she just might pass out.

"Oh, baby, just breathe for me. *Relax.* I am not going to take you like this."

She thought about the Curse, the conversion, the necessity of a pregnancy—at least, before the end of the Blood Moon—and she nodded blankly as she forced her next words: "It's okay, healer. It really is. I'm ready." She closed her eyes and gritted her teeth. "Go ahead."

Kagen laughed, almost unconsciously, although there was no real humor in the sound, no mockery or disrespect. He raised his hips, rotated his pelvis to the side, and gently settled the massive erection against her hips, instead. "Look at me, Arielle," he entreated. His eyes were virtual pools of compassion.

She opened her left lid and slowly peeked up at him through her peripheral vision, allowing him the corner of one eye. "W...w...why?"

He smiled endearingly and murmured: "Because I'm going to help you through this, and for that, I need you to look into my eyes."

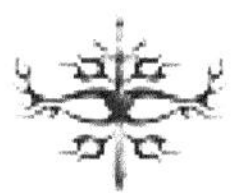

Kagen kept his voice steady and his expression calm, even though his body was about to explode.

Arielle was as tight as a drum, as frightened as a mouse, and it didn't help at all that they were immersed in a pool of *water*. He knew that he could spend the night, a week—hell, a month if he had the time—on foreplay and her arousal, yet none of it would be enough. The demons she had inside were internal, not physical. They were based on a lifetime of knowing only fear and brutality; terror and angst; self-reliance and independence. She simply did not know how to give her well-being over to another person, let alone how to submit her body to a man.

He sighed in contemplation: He had promised her he would never use coercion—and he wouldn't—but that did not preclude making full use of his powers in order to see to her comfort, in order to tend to her soul.

He said a silent prayer, asking for guidance, self-assurance, and wisdom. It would take all of that and more to bring the two of them together. In fact, at this point, he was even willing to rely on a little plagiarism if it helped, maybe a well-placed verse from a song or a famous poem, something that he couldn't mess up.

"Look at me, Arielle," he said. He hoped his eyes were brimming with compassion.

"W…w…why?" she said, reluctantly.

He smiled and murmured, "Because I'm going to help you through this, and for that, I need you to look into my eyes."

With that said he began to sift through his memory, searching for the perfect poem or song, scanning for just the right stanza or melody with soulful words or a soothing pitch; until, at last, he retrieved an old Bob Dylan tune from his subconscious and began to hum the refrain…

Both of Arielle's eyes blinked open—and wasn't that a vast improvement in and of itself?—and then they slowly alighted with curiosity as the melody began to drift to her ears. Kagen added a deep, haunting resonance to his voice, cocooned her body in the vibration of the song, and began to *sing* warmth into her soul, using his tone to gently caress her skin: "*When the rain is blowing in your face; and the whole world is on your case; I could offer you a warm embrace, to make you feel my love…*"

He began to trail his fingers along her stomach in slow, hypnotic strokes, first the pads and then the backs, each touch, each caress, each note infusing more warmth and comfort. "*When evening shadows and the stars appear; and there is no one there to dry your tears; I could hold you for a million years, to make you feel my love…*"

Her breath hitched and her stomach quivered, even as her eyes grew molten with desire. When her tongue snaked out to wet her bottom lip, it took all the self-possession he had not to bend over and taste the offering, but he managed to maintain control. Trailing his fingers along the ridge of her pelvis, he twirled a gentle circle just above the apex of her soft curls and pressed on. "*I know you haven't made your mind up yet, but I would never do you wrong. I've known it from the moment we first met; no doubt in my mind where you belong…*"

His hand dropped lower and his pressure grew more insistent as his fingers began to arouse her peak. Still, he held her gaze with his, sending wave after wave of unconscious reassurance into her spirit, funneling her fears into fantasies, weaving her dreams into desires. "*I'd go hungry; I'd go black and blue; I'd go crawling down the avenue. There is nothing that I would not do…to make you feel my love.*"

She reached up to cup his face in her hands, and then she strained to kiss his lips. As tears of joy—and blissful release—began to roll down her cheeks, he devoured her mouth with his. When, at last, she pulled away and tilted her head ever-so-slightly forward, as if straining to hear more words, he deepened the thrall of the song and obliged her, singing directly into her ear. "*The storms are raging on a rolling sea; down the highway of regret. The winds of change are blowing wild and free; you ain't seen nothin' like me yet...*"

She slid beneath him, almost unconsciously, her beautiful thighs wrapping around his waist in escalating need, and he shuddered, then rotated his hips to the side so their bodies were perfectly aligned.

"*There is nothing that I wouldn't do; go to the ends of the earth for you. Make you happy, make your dreams come true...to make you feel my love.*"

He slid his body into hers and groaned with deep contentment. "*To make you feel my love.*"

Arielle felt her body stretch impossibly.

She felt her core yield to Kagen's invasion, and she felt the walls of her sheath tighten around the staff that still felt ten sizes too big—but there wasn't an ounce of pain.

Kagen watched her like a hawk as he began to move his hips. He controlled his thrusts, adjusted the pressure, and slowly pulled back—or gently pushed forward—based upon her every response.

And still there was no pain.

At least not in her.

Though stoic, his face reflected the truth of what he was enduring: Kagen was shielding Arielle from pain by taking all of the unpleasant sensations into his own body. He was experiencing her discomfort so she didn't have to.

Slowly, gradually, he began to move more freely, and her body began to adjust to his: to stretch, to open, to take him in...as if he had always been there. As if he somehow...*belonged.*

His face eventually relaxed.

His brow finally smoothed.

His tense shoulders became pliant, and Arielle shuddered with relief, pleasure, and anticipation.

As sensation began to return, one small ache, one tantalizing current, one surprising twinge at a time, Kagen dropped his head forward and moaned—it was a deep groan of pleasure, his hair falling into his eyes.

Arielle arched her back at the sound. Her thighs drew back, as if by their own accord, and she wrapped her legs, seamlessly, around his waist.

He took the invitation as the signal it was, meeting her entreaty with his first, hard, uninhibited thrust.

She gasped. "Oh, gods!" Her womb felt like it was on fire, but it was not a painful, searing blaze; rather, it was a slow, burning ember…about to ignite.

He thrust in and out several more times, pulling back so far he almost withdrew, then plunging forward with the same amount of force, burying his body to the hilt. Her stomach quivered; her womb contracted; the muscles in her thighs grew taut. She grasped at his shoulders for purchase, trying to ride out the strange sensations…and he thrust again…and again.

Only this time, he clenched his fists and arched his back.

And then he picked up the pace and changed his motion, *his rhythm*: He rocked his hips and rubbed against her, rotating in smooth, maddening circles until Arielle thought she would scream. He alternated between fast, hard thrusts and long, smooth strokes, all the while, reciting her name.

Arielle bit her lip and dug her fingernails into his powerful, masculine shoulders. *"Kagen!"* She threw back her head and moaned.

His mouth descended upon hers as he continued the erotic assault.

He dipped to taste her breasts and to suckle her nipples. He slid his hand above her belly and began to delve into her curls, caressing her heat with his thumb. He raked his fangs beneath her ear and, finally, sank them deep into her jugular, teasing the wounds with his tongue.

Arielle squirmed like a worm beneath him.

She clenched her hands into fists and tried to control her breathing.

Her eyes shot open, and she stared at the brilliant night sky, trying desperately to find something to focus on, to grab hold of, *anything* to keep her from spiraling into the cosmos in a startling wave of flight. She ground her hips wantonly against his pelvis and drew back her legs…further…wider…begging, pleading, needing him to fill her deeper…

Now.

Tears rolled down her cheeks, and she whimpered in utter helplessness and confusion. Every nerve in her body was alive, singing, and weeping.

It was excruciating, overpowering, and exasperating…all at the same time.

"Kagen. Kagen! *Kagen.*"

He withdrew his fangs. "That's it, baby. Just let go." He growled like an animal in her ear, and she thrashed wildly in reaction. He grasped her hips and held her firmly beneath him, restraining her fevered need for movement, even as he continued to thrust.

Unable to take a moment more, she began to sob. "Kagen, I…I can't…I'm going to break…I can't take it." She nearly screamed.

He growled deep in his throat then, a lion's purr of dominance and satisfaction. Rising up onto his arms, he gazed down into her eyes and met her frantic gaze with a carnal stare of his own. He was magnificent, beyond imagining, stunning beyond compare, with his ivory fangs gleaming in the moonlight, and Arielle felt her body begin to take flight.

"Don't fight it, Arielle," he groaned, his voice nothing more than a guttural rasp. "Come for me, sweeting. Give me all of you." He dropped his head to her neck, ran his fangs along her jugular, and whispered in her ear. "I want to hear you cry out my name in pleasure."

Arielle scored his back with her nails.

She fisted his hair in her hands and screamed his name as her body came apart in violent waves of ecstasy.

And Kagen quickly followed suit.

He bit her again, his fangs sinking deep into her throat as he trembled—his thick, pulsing manhood pumping stream after stream of passion deep into her womb.

When, at last, it was over, Arielle tried to stop her heart from racing. She tried to stop her body from trembling. She tried to catch her breath.

Hell, she would have tried to catch her heart, but it was much too late for that—it was hopelessly and eternally *gone*. It belonged to Kagen Silivasi, every chamber, every vessel, every strong, steady beat. Who knew that making love could feel *like that?*

Rolling onto his back, Kagen sank down into the pool and pulled her gently on top of him. He enfolded her in his arms, nuzzled her sweat-dampened hair, and kissed her softly on the forehead. "Penny for your thoughts?" he whispered in her ear.

She smiled inwardly, trying to think of a way to respond to his query: *Penny for your thoughts…* She couldn't help but remember the last time she had seen Keitaro Silivasi in the slave hut in Mhier; the ancient vampire had used the exact same phrase to get her to talk. Apparently, the leaves didn't fall that far from the tree.

She smiled and opened her mouth to answer, but no words came out. How could she possibly express her thoughts in mere words, the feelings that were swelling in her heart, the contentment that was coursing through her veins? She shook her head and peeked at him through the corner of her eye, and then a sheepish smile crossed her lips. "Can we…could we… possibly…"

"Yes?" Kagen prompted, his right eyebrow raised in question.

She giggled like an impish child. "Could we possibly do that again?"

The Ancient Master Healer drew in a sharp intake of breath. His eyes turned positively molten with desire, and his lips turned back in a devilish hiss. Finally, he smiled like the glorious, mischievous vampire he was and groaned deep in his throat. "Oh dear goddess, *yes*!" He nipped her behind the ear and purred like a satiated cat. "Yes." He placed a soft, tender kiss on her lips and repeated it a third time: "*Yes.*"

And then he laughed with utter male satisfaction and gathered her deeper into his arms.

"Yes, Arielle, the answer will *always* be *yes.*"

twenty-eight

The next morning

Arielle smoothed the front of her thigh-length tunic, glanced down at the comfortable black leggings she was wearing beneath the cascading frock, and drew in a deep, cleansing breath for courage. Kagen had promised to take her "shopping" for new clothes at the first available opportunity, and in the meantime, Jocelyn had offered to lend her several outfits from her own wardrobe. She reveled in the feel of the soft, pliable fabric and tried to still her racing heart as she reached for the doorknob outside Keitaro's room and gently turned the handle.

"Hello," she called softly, taking her first step into the room.

Her breath caught in her throat.

Standing ten feet away in front of an open window was the male, the vampire, she had known since childhood. Only, this man—this dashing, robust creature—looked nothing at all like the captive slave she had come to know over so many years in Mhier.

Keitaro looked positively vigorous.

His thick black hair shined with a light she had never seen in it before, the long, smooth locks gleaming with an almost purple-ish glow, and his chiseled features, so bronzed and etched with intensity, were smooth and relaxed, no longer beleaguered with pain. He stood to his full, imposing height and eagerly held out his arms, the threads of his modern clothes hugging his dynamic form like armor adorning an ancient knight. "Rielle…" He breathed her name like a prayer.

Arielle's eyes filled with pressing tears, and she lost all sense of decorum. She darted across the room and flung herself into his arms, laughing joyously as he embraced her with zeal. "Keitaro! Oh my lords, look at you!" Her voice was positively giddy.

Keitaro chuckled low in his throat and spun her around, the power in his arms, the vigor in his back, the strength in his chest as stark as the radiance in his eyes. "Rielle," he repeated, pressing a soft kiss on the top of her head.

Finally, she stepped back from his embrace and regarded him with unconcealed appreciation. "You look amazing. You look…*healthy*."

He smiled warmly and nodded. "As do you, daughter of my heart."

Arielle glowed inside. She could hardly believe this moment was real. "Thank you."

He gestured toward a soft armchair at the back of the room, strolled languidly toward it, and patted the cushion, encouraging her to take a seat; and then he sank down on a black-and-metal stool, opposite of the chair, and leaned in toward her, his eyes narrowing in rapt attention. "How is my son?" he asked eagerly. "How are you *and* my son?"

Arielle felt her face flush with heat, and she lowered her gaze to the floor. "We are…well…for now."

"Well?" Keitaro pressed.

She bit her bottom lip and fidgeted with her hands. "*Very*…well."

He smiled an ingratiating grin. "Good. *Good*. That's what I wanted to hear. Then you are adjusting?"

She sighed and began to tug on her sleeve, turning the hem in and out several times before grasping it in the palm of her hand. "Oh, I don't know if I would say that. I'm taking things one day no, *one moment* at a time."

Keitaro nodded. "The gods could not ask anything more of you right now, Rielle—and neither could Kagen."

She released the hem of her tunic, folded her hands in her lap, and practically vibrated with emotion. "Keitaro." Her eyes filled with moisture once more, and she struggled to blink back the tears. "You are home…*free*…with your sons." She held her hands up in wonder. "Can you believe it? Does any of this seem real?"

The dark brown irises of his eyes lit up with pleasure as he responded to her genuine joy *for him* with a healthy dose of his own. "I still have to pinch myself occasionally," he said. "Sometimes, I think I'm dreaming—or I'm afraid that I'm still in Mhier—or perhaps I've died and gone to the spirit world."

Arielle shook her head. "You're not dreaming, Keitaro. And you're not dead, either."

"No," he said with conviction. "I'm not." He interlocked his fingers and shifted forward in his seat. "So, tell me everything."

She shrugged and shook her head in wonderment. "I hardly know where to begin." Deciding to start at the beginning, she took a deep breath and thought back to the last day in Mhier, the battle in King Thane's arena, and the flight that led back to Dark Moon Vale. "How much did your sons share with you? About the events that took place in Mhier?"

"Quite a bit," Keitaro said. "We haven't had a lot of time to talk, but we've exchanged a great deal of information in the time that we've had."

She nodded, relieved to hear it. "Then you know that the lycans found the Rebel Camp." She looked away and tried feverishly to concentrate solely on the facts—the last thing she wanted was to imagine her friends' demise. "Walker, Kade, even Echo…they're gone."

Keitaro declined his head in a solemn nod, and then he used his feet to propel the stool forward on the tiny black wheels. When it came to rest in front of her, he reached out and took her hand in his. "I do know this, Rielle. And I'm sorry. I'm so sorry."

She let the words linger, taking them into her heart. Squeezing his hand, she said, "Thank you. *Thank you.* It's just…it's hard to believe…after all these years, the resistance is gone."

"Indeed," Keitaro replied. He waited in companionable silence, seeming to understand her need to process as they talked, and then he whispered in an eerily savage tone: "And

King Thane, he is dead as well." His eyes turned the color of liquid lava, and she literally felt a flash of heat shoot through his hand before it, once again, returned to a normal temperature. "But not before he took you…for a night." There was no accusation in his voice, not even the hint of inflection; nevertheless, his meaning was clear: *What did that vile monster do to you?*

Arielle quickly shook her head. "He did not," she said, her voice trailing off. "He never…" She met his eyes with a rock-hard stare. "Your son is the only man I've ever *known*." She swallowed hard, feeling a bit like a teenager having a *birds-and-bees* chat with her father, but she knew that the information was important.

Keitaro squeezed her hand in reassurance. "But he hurt you…Thane did?"

Arielle raised her left shoulder in a show of disinterest. "Of course," she whispered. "But it's done." She leaned forward and pitched her own voice in a lethal, feminine purr. "Kagen impaled him through the skull with the pommel of his own sword, and then he carved out his heart with a scalpel and tossed it on the ground like the garbage it was. It was a good death for a worthless hound."

Keitaro's jaw tightened. "Very fitting, indeed." His own eyes blazed with contempt, and he ran his tongue along his upper teeth, as if to repel his fangs. "And Cain—the maggot that took my wife's life—his heart ceased beating in the palm of my hand." He stared off into the distance as if reliving the moment. "I am beholden to my sons, grateful for all that they did, but I will forever thank the gods for giving me that exquisite moment, for allowing my hands to be the ones that ushered that bastard into the underworld."

Arielle *felt* the truth of his words and shivered. "And Teague is gone as well…the male who murdered my mother"—she sat back to consider her words carefully—"let's just say that Kagen eviscerated him on the sands, but not before he neutered the worthless cur where he stood."

Keitaro nodded with approval. "And Xavier?"

Arielle frowned. "I never saw him in the arena."

"Nor did I," Keitaro said. "Although the entire experience seems more like a dream, I'm afraid that General Matista lives on—although, I can assure you, if he does, he does not reside in the same world he used to."

"No, he doesn't," Arielle agreed, grateful for that small concession.

"And General Gavin Morel?" Keitaro asked.

"Killed…by Marquis's hand."

"That's what I thought," Keitaro mumbled. He let out a deep breath and simply resided in the moment.

A pregnant silence settled over them then, as pure and unassuming as the driven snow, and then Arielle finally asked, "Will you or your sons go back to Mhier? Will you try to exterminate the lycans that are left?" She tried to conceal her dread, her fear, the thought of Kagen and his brothers going back into harm's way—of Keitaro, yet again, returning to that cursed realm, just to take care of unfinished business. She knew that they were warriors at heart, that they lived by an unyielding code; yet and still, she'd had enough of lycans to last her ten lifetimes, and she prayed the Silivasis would just…stay home.

Keitaro shook his head emphatically. "No. I don't think so." His lips twitched in a reflexive scowl, and he let out a deep-throated snarl he didn't appear aware of. "Nachari has already tried to reopen the portal, just to assess our options, determine our vulnerability, and from what he says, the spell no longer works."

"What do you mean, *The spell no longer works*?" Arielle asked, frowning.

"It means that the lycans have already sealed the gateway, altered the threshold; somehow, they've changed the energetic configuration so we can no longer get in."

Arielle knitted her brow in dismay. Although she didn't want the Silivasis to go after their common enemy, she didn't like the idea of the lycans taking defensive action so quickly. It meant they were already reorganizing. She sighed, wanting to change the subject before she became too morose. She was no longer a rebel living in Mhier—what the lycans did or did not do was no longer her concern. "So"—she made her voice as cheery as possible—"tell me: What will you do next? Where will you go? Where will you live?"

Keitaro chuckled at the sudden change of subject, and the deep, melodious sound cut through the tension like a magic blade. He arched his back to stretch. "Eventually, I want to visit my old dwelling, the place where I lived with Serena, the home where the boys grew up. Marquis says it's still standing and in fairly good condition. Although it's empty, the boys have kept it clean and aired out." He sighed heavily. "But it will take some time to work up the courage….even for a visit."

Arielle considered Keitaro's words and smiled—there was nothing she could say to lessen his pain, to make the transition easier—but she couldn't help but react to his endearing choice of phrasing.

"This makes you smile?" he asked, curiously.

She shrugged. "I'm sorry, Keitaro. It's just…"

"It's just?"

She laughed aloud then. "It's just that you keep referring to the biggest, scariest, most intimidating males I've ever met as *the boys*." She waved her hand and nodded. "I guess it just makes it all so real, who they are *to you*, who they've always been. *Of course*, these fearsome vampires are your boys." She shifted in her seat, tightened her grip on his hand, and met his seeking gaze with one of compassion. "I'm sorry about Shelby," she whispered. "That your reunion does not include your wife…or your youngest son."

Keitaro nodded gravely, and then he squeezed her hands as if to draw strength from her touch. "Thank you." He looked off into the distance. "This life has certainly been harsh—I dare say cruel and unfair. When I am ready, when I am able, I will also visit Shelby's grave…" He blinked back a tear and stiffened. "But there is much to celebrate: I have three grandsons"—he cocked his eyebrows and smirked—"soon to be four, and I have three beautiful daughters and a lifetime of new memories to make with my sons."

Arielle felt her face grow pale. It was as if all the blood had rushed out of her body as she thought about Keitaro's words: *soon to be four.*

"Arielle?"

"Where will you live, then?" she asked, quickly changing the subject before he could delve any deeper.

He measured her warily, scanned her eyes like a hawk—no doubt, seeing entirely too much—and then he released her hand and sat back on the stool. "For now, I will take turns staying at Nathaniel's estate, Marquis's farmhouse, and Nachari's brownstone. Jocelyn, Ciopori, and Deanna have made it abundantly clear that they expect me to spend all my waking hours recovering, and visiting with my grandchildren."

Arielle's eyes widened in alarm. "Recovering? Are you still ill? Is there still any danger—"

"No, Rielle," Keitaro reassured her. "*I'm fine*, but my kids seem to think I should hobble along, taking slow, measured steps for the next century or so."

Arielle laughed and tilted her head to the side. "Well, you can't really blame them, *us*. We just want you here for a very, very long time."

Keitaro smiled. "Indeed." He grew quiet again, and Arielle let the moment linger.

"So," she finally said, "that still doesn't answer the question: What will you do?"

Keitaro patted her softly on the knee. "Not sure. At first, I think I will take the kids up on their offer—spend every waking moment getting reacquainted with my family—learn all there is to know about my sons' lives and their mates…my grandsons. But, I don't make any pretense that it will be enough to sustain me: I will speak with Napolean about taking a role in the valley's protection, in the security of our people. Doubtless, I will want to help with matters pertaining to the lycan: their capture, our defense, their eventual extermination."

Arielle held her tongue. There was really nothing to add to that statement—the world, *every world*, would be better off without the Lycanthrope.

"Now then," Keitaro said, interrupting her thoughts. "Enough with the small talk. As I understand it, you still have twenty-three days left in Kagen's Blood Moon: How are you handling all of this? What is happening with you and my son?"

Arielle winced. She loved Keitaro dearly—and that was truly the understatement of the decade—but she didn't know if she could discuss something so personal, so intimate and vulnerable, with the father of her heart. She thought back to her days in Mhier, to all the many hours she had spent in the slave encampment, looking up to the vampire, clinging to their bond like a lifeline. She remembered all the nights she had snuck into his tent, after escaping her own enslavement, in order to treat his wounds…in order to tend his soul. "Do you remember when I was still a child, maybe ten or eleven, and I worked in the slave camp? When I carried all that water and food?"

Keitaro snarled in a knee-jerk reaction, flashing his fangs unwittingly, and then he quickly reined it in. "Of course."

Arielle ignored the flash of temper. "Do you remember the song the kids would sing, sometimes at the campfire at night?"

Keitaro frowned, trying to recall... "Something about an omen," he said. "Ancient *superstition*, Mhieridian mysticism…the white owl."

Arielle leaned forward. "Exactly." She softened her voice and began to speak in a lyrical, singsong tone. "When the white owl soars in a midnight sky; friends and foes alike will die. When the white owl dips his snow-tipped wing, hearts will weep, and tongues will sing: a song of grief, lives lost too soon, a song of blood…beneath the moon."

Keitaro listened carefully, but he didn't respond.

Arielle sighed. "The night before I met your sons in Mhier, a white owl dipped low out of the sky and nearly clipped my cheek with his wing while I was crossing a river, and I remembered the

Omen. I just knew somewhere deep inside that it was coming…*for me*." She held out her arm, showing Keitaro the enigmatic etchings, the mystical dots and lines that replicated Auriga, the Charioteer, in her flesh. It was the first time she had openly, *eagerly*, showed someone the markings. "Echo, Ryder, Walker…King Thane, Cain, and Teague…*friends and foes alike will die*." She shivered. "I learned that my father, *that Ryder*, actually perished while trying to save me; and you learned that Shelby…that he is now living in the spirit world. Yet, we were delivered from Mhier: You still have your family, and we still have each other. *Hearts will weep and tongues will sing*." She pressed on. "*A song of grief, lives lost too soon; a song of blood…beneath the moon*."

She pointed at her wrist, sat back in her chair, and crossed her arms. Hugging herself, as if to provide internal, moral support, she shut her eyes. "So I tell you this, as the one I name as my father"—her eyes filled up with tears, and she didn't hold them back—"as the best friend I have ever known. I am terrified, Keitaro. I feel like a fish out of water, a drifter with no home. I don't know how to be a mother or a mate or a member of a tight-knit family; hell, I don't even know how to love. And I'm a wimp…" She nodded her head to emphasize the confession. "Because I want to go through the conversion like a rebel wants to sit down and have tea with a lycan. I know the pregnancy will be uncomfortable but tolerable, yet I still flinch every time Kagen reaches out to touch me, even though we've obviously made inroads." She opened her eyes and sighed. "I just want to run deep into the forest and keep on running, until my legs will no longer carry me. And I know that it's crazy, it's wrong, it's insane; but I swear, that's how I feel."

Keitaro sat in silence, clearly weighing her words. After several tense moments had passed, he rose from his seat, knelt before her on the floor, and leaned into her sheltered body. He cupped her face in his hands with exquisite gentleness and held her gaze with a compassion that could only be described as fatherly *love*.

"Oh, Rielle," he breathed out. "You would be less than human if you felt any other way, and my heart goes out to you." He stroked the inside of her wrist in a paternal gesture and smiled. "But daughter, you must know, you are the bravest, the kindest, the purest soul I have ever known."

Arielle warmed at his words.

"And you will get through this. You will come out on the other side, better, stronger, wiser." He punctuated his words with a nod. "Look at me, Rielle. Look at me and trust my words."

Arielle forced herself to meet his gaze and hold it—his eyes were so full of benevolence and wisdom, just like a father's should be.

"As a male who sees you as my own child, the daughter of my heart, you must know that I would do anything—*everything*—to protect you, that I would guide you, shelter you, and provide for you like no other…except for one." He raised his eyebrows. "Kagen. My son." His voice grew hoarse with conviction. "He loves you, Arielle, from a place much deeper than you can imagine. It's written all over his face. Nay,"—he waved his hand through the air—"*este scris in stele*: It's written in the stars. You knew it from an omen in Mhier, and he knew it, without the omen he needed from Dark Moon Vale. And I know it as surely as I know my own name." He kissed the back of her hand tenderly, a father's kind caress.

"Daughter, I am asking you to trust me, to be brave, to put one foot in front of the other and follow Kagen's lead. You don't have to feel everything right now; you don't have to understand it all in a day. All you have to do is trust your heart…trust your father…and trust my son."

Arielle nodded slowly. She knew Keitaro was right.

"And Rielle," he added solemnly. "Kagen needs you. Our people need you. *I* need you."

"You think so?" Arielle asked, a hopeful note in her voice.

Keitaro smiled. "Nathaniel shared something very transformational and *important* with me; and in time, it is something Kagen will share with you also. The night I was taken from Dark Moon Vale, Kagen encountered the Lycanthrope. He saw them take me into Mhier and tried to stop them, but he was too late to save me. They tortured him, Rielle. Ultimately, they killed him, yet he returned from the grave through tenacity alone to avenge his mother's honor, to try and rescue me, but his memory was impaired—it was just *gone.* And all these years—all these long, painful years—he has lived with this secret inside him, an unbearable darkness, an indefinable impulse to heal, *to save*, and to destroy, all at the same time. He is freer than he has ever been, or at least he will be, now that this demon no longer haunts him from the shadows, but it will take time for him to heal, to integrate, to become all that he was meant to be, without this dueling energy. And there is no one who can help him more profoundly than you."

She took a deep breath, trying to wrap her mind around Keitaro's words, what they meant for Kagen and what they meant for her. "He did mention something, back when we were in Mhier: something about unvanquished demons and darkness, something that didn't belong in a healer…something he feared."

"Yes," Keitaro said. "And I know that he has plans for you, *for the two of you*, with regard to your healing arts: You are both such a gift to the people, but I also think you may be a gift to each other, two healers who need to be healed. Perhaps, in time, you can help heal each other." He let his words settle before moving on. "And as for me? I, too, feel overwhelmed, a bit afraid, and more than just a little confused." He laughed, but it was a distinctly hollow sound. "But the thing that anchors me here, the thing that compels me to get up, to go on, and to learn to live again—without Serena, without Shelby—is the knowledge that while I was away, while I was yet a slave, the gods saw fit to give me the most precious gift in the world to a vampire, to one such as myself, bound by an ancient curse that makes siring female children impossible: They chose to give me a daughter. *You,* Rielle. And it is the knowledge that I will teach you all that I taught my sons, that I will hold your babe in my arms at his naming ceremony, my own flesh and blood, that we will walk through the forest *together* as *free* souls that inspires me to go on, to rebuild…to continue. Do not deny me this gift, daughter of my heart. I need you as much as my son does, just in a different way."

Arielle could hardly believe her ears.

It was as if something in her heart, something buried, missing, and frozen in time, finally stirred and came back to life. *Yes*, Kagen was showing her what it meant to love. Slowly, gently, *ever so tenderly*, he was teaching her the ways of passion, commitment, and union; but Keitaro was showing her a different hope entirely, a chance to be reborn. They had survived Mhier together, and they would thrive in Dark Moon Vale, if she could only have faith.

Scooting forward to the edge of her chair, she pressed her thumbs to the corners of her eyes to hold back her tears and nestled her head against Keitaro's chest. "Father," she whispered softly. "Will you hold me?"

As his strong arms enfolded her, as he gathered her to his heart, she knew that she was truly home at last. When he sighed and uttered a familiar phrase—"Yes, Arielle. The answer will always be *yes*"—she couldn't help but laugh out loud.

By all that was sacred, Keitaro and Kagen were cut from the same cloth: They were two males of honor and strength and compassion…

And they both loved her dearly.

She would get through the conversion and the pregnancy.

She would get through the Curse.

And for the first time in her tumultuous life, she would have a lover who adored her, and a father who would never turn away from her again.

twenty-nine

Two weeks later

Kagen Silivasi stood on the arched stone bridge that led to his property, the clinic, and his private residence, and he closed his eyes in order to take in the moment. As he listened to the soothing sounds of rushing water winding its way through the wide creek beneath his feet, he couldn't help but think that his life was a lot like that winding river: rushing, flowing, ever-turning in unpredictable ways in reaction to the hidden elements below the surface…

Yet always remaining true to its predestined course.

He sighed and opened his eyes, and then he drew in a deep, approving breath at the sight of his *destiny*, Arielle Nightsong, standing before him in a beautiful yet simplistic gown of pale green linen and ivory lace.

She was magnificent.

Breathtaking.

The most beautiful sight he had ever seen.

He smiled as she fidgeted restlessly from nerves and bunched the front of her gown in her fists, rolling the delicate fabric in the palms of her hands. Truly, the female was a rare, hidden treasure. She had come to him the afternoon after her visit with Keitaro, bravely announcing that she was ready to undergo the conversion, that she didn't want to wait, and she had approached the entire process with uncommon courage and strength. And, while there was no such thing as a painless conversion, Arielle had been unusually lucky in that regard. As an Ancient Master Healer, Kagen possessed the rare ability to enhance biological processes within the human body; to manipulate energy at a cellular level, acting as an active catalyst; and to speed up the process of change, transformation, and healing with his mind. Arielle's entire conversion had taken no more than forty-five minutes from start to finish, and the beautiful free-spirited female had come through it without incident.

While he had insisted upon slowing things down, taking the next week or so to get to know his mate, to explore Dark Moon Vale as a couple, and to help acclimate Arielle to her newfound powers and abilities, eventually, they had both agreed it was time to move forward with the forty-eight-hour pregnancy. Once again, Arielle had met the challenge head-on with both courage and staunch determination. He laughed inwardly, remembering how she had insisted that they listen to several audiobooks together: *What to Expect the First Year, Helping Your Child Sleep Through the Night,* and *Raising a Happy and Healthy Child from Birth to Adolescence.* Even now, he had to admit the process had been extremely beneficial to both of them. Not only had they learned a lot about child development—which had then given Kagen the opportunity to explain all the ways in which it would *not* apply to a vampire infant, all the ways in which a vampire developed far more quickly than a human—it had given them an opportunity to discuss their hopes and dreams as a family, as parents, to clearly define their values and expectations. It had given them a chance to come together as a team, to draw even closer as a couple.

When the baby was born, Arielle had been positively amazed, not just by the mystical, painless process, but by the sudden appearance of an undeniable angel, the precious little gift from the gods that Kagen had placed in her arms. And she had been nervous at best, stoic at the least, as he fulfilled the demands of the Blood Curse, returning the unnamed one—the dark, soulless twin who would surely grow up to murder, maim, and destroy—to the icy Chamber of Sacrifice and Atonement in the required ritual that always ensued. While the concept of the sacrifice was both foreign and abhorrent to her sensibilities, Arielle had grown up in Mhier, in the land of the lycans, and she had seen evil in all of its various forms, firsthand. While she had been appalled by the cruelty of the Curse, disgusted by the evil, misguided vengeance wrought by the Blood—the original females who had spawned the Vampyr race—she had also understood that it could not be altered: The soul was the seat of all potential; and pure, unadulterated evil could only grow up to wreak pure, unadulterated havoc on the world.

She had understood that the Vampyr had not chosen this blight; they were helpless to remove it from their lives; and raising a demon-like being to become like King Thane was not the answer to their plight.

Now, as she stood on the sturdy, archaic bridge before him, looking more like a goddess than a woman, Kagen could only stare in bewilderment…and love.

"Are you ready, sweeting?" he asked, reaching down to pry her fingers loose from her dress before it became an unsalvageable, wrinkled mess.

Arielle shook out her hands. "I am," she whispered.

As if on cue, Marquis, Nathaniel, and Nachari stepped closer to the couple, taking preordained places at their sides, their beautiful mates forming a loose outer circle behind the pair, even as Braden Bratianu and Kristina Riley-Silivasi joined them at the back of the throng.

Napolean Mondragon shimmered into view, standing all at once before the newly mated couple, and all the air in the valley seemed to coalesce around him, to settle upon his broad, muscular shoulders as it hummed with electric energy. The bridge grew instantly quiet as all the attendees shifted their gaze to the powerful lord, watching as his long black hair rustled in a preternatural wind, the translucent silver highlights framing his face like a halo.

The king smiled warmly at Kagen and Arielle, and then he gently nodded his head. "And where is the precious babe?" His voice was like a warm summer's breeze.

"He's here." The deep, husky burr sent currents of electricity sizzling through the atmosphere as Keitaro Silivasi strolled languidly toward the center of the half-circle, stood just to the right of Kagen, and nestled the peaceful infant tight against his chest. "He's sleeping soundly."

Kagen regarded his father—*his father*—with a look of utter amazement and gratitude, and then he turned to appraise Marquis. Under normal circumstance—*no*, under anything *but* normal circumstances—as the oldest living male of the family, Marquis would have been the one to hold the child, but now that Keitaro was here, now that he was *alive*, the mantle had returned to him.

Marquis straightened his shoulders and inclined his head in a gesture of solidarity, and then he did something highly unusual for the hardened, ancient warrior: He winked at Kagen with unrestrained delight in his eyes. Clearly, the Ancient Master Warrior was thrilled to be standing in his rightful place as the firstborn son, not the *head*, of the family; and as he glided noiselessly to the right of Keitaro, Nathaniel and Nachari quickly followed suit, each male taking his honored place, based upon the order of his birth.

Kagen laughed out loud.

By all the gods, he felt *complete*.

Napolean turned to Kagen, and his face grew all at once serious. "It is with unspeakable joy that I greet you this day, my subject, a fellow descendant of Jadon, an Ancient Master Healer, mate to the daughter of Auriga, father to this newborn son of Ophiuchus, the serpent holder, who makes his home above the celestial equator." He shook his head in awe, his deep voice resonating with reverence. "As your sovereign lord and an Ancient Master Justice, I must point out that it is not lost on me that this child was chosen by this god: For eons, Ophiuchus has been identified with Asclepius, the Greek god of medicine, who has the power to revive the dead."

Kagen shuddered, and he felt deep chills pulse all the way down to his toes. Surely, he knew this, about Ophiuchus and Asclepius—he had studied all the celestial deities in great depth at the University—but now, it suddenly made sense. That fateful night in the valley when he had heard a faint voice urging him to fight his enemy, to resist and survive—"*Vampire, you are a healer, a magician, a practitioner of unparalleled ability; fight them with what you have left*"—it had been the voice of Lord Asclepius, the ancient god of medicine, the one who had the power to *revive the dead.*

"What name have you chosen for this male?" Napolean's melodious voice pierced the silence, interrupting Kagen's thoughts, and he immediately came back to attention.

His eyes alighted with pride, and his heart swelled with love. "Should it please you, milord, and find favor with the Celestial Beings, the son of Ophiuchus is to be named *Shelbie Ryder Silivasi.* And we will call him Ryder."

Keitaro shifted his weight from one foot to the other, and Marquis and Nathaniel let out a collective exhalation of deep regard. Nachari's eyes met Kagen's, and while they glistened with crystalline tears, there was a powerful gleam of gratitude in their depths as he slowly nodded his head.

Napolean reached out to take the baby from Keitaro's arms. "The name pleases me, healer, and there is no objection from the Celestial Beings."

As the sovereign lord bent his head to the child's wrist and his fangs began to elongate, remnants of Kagen's alter ego stirred; but this time, he recognized it for what it was: an unconscious impulse, one that instinctively reared its head in reaction to any perceived threat to his family, and he did not have to react. He definitely did not have to save the child *from Napolean*, and he most certainly did not need to *kill them all.*

He chuckled, took a deep, cleansing breath, and simply watched, dispassionately, as Napolean pierced the child's vein vertically, along the inner arm, and Ryder's soft teal eyes blinked open for the first time. The babe did not flinch in alarm, nor did he protest the intrusion or cry out in pain. He simply stared, mesmerized, at the magnificent being before him and cooed when the king sealed the wound with his venom.

Napolean held the child out in front of him and smiled. "Welcome to the house of Jadon, Shelbie Ryder Silivasi. May your life be filled with peace, triumph, and purpose. May your path always be blessed."

He gave the child back to Keitaro, who kissed him soundly on the forehead and nuzzled his hair with his chin. "Welcome to our family, Shelbie Ryder Silivasi, and to the house of Jadon. May your life be filled with peace, triumph, and purpose. May your path always be blessed."

Marquis took the child next and repeated the refrain.

Once Nathaniel and Nachari had done the same, the child was handed back to Keitaro, who gestured for Jocelyn, Ciopori, and Deanna to come forward and waited as each of the *destinies* took a turn holding the baby and repeating the familiar chorus. Braden and Kristina followed last, and the first part of the ceremony was complete.

Napolean cleared his throat and turned his attention back to Kagen and Arielle. "By the laws which govern the house of Jadon, I accept your union as the divine will of the gods and hereby sanction your mating. Arielle Nightsong Silivasi, do you come now of your own free will to enter the house of Jadon?"

Arielle began to sway on her feet, her lean, agile body rocking ever so slightly to the left. She took a hurried step to the right to regain her balance, and then she reached out for Kagen's hand and squeezed it for all she was worth.

He sent a soft, gentle wave of calming energy into her hand and flooded her body with warmth. *All is well, sweeting*, he whispered telepathically.

She nodded and relaxed her hand. "I do," she said fervently.

"Hold out your wrist," Napolean instructed, the corner of his mouth turning up in a grin.

Arielle held out her arm, no longer bothered by the strange sight of the enigmatic markings and lines, and if Kagen hadn't known better, he would have sworn she seemed almost eager to give her blood to the king. She was definitely willing to give her life to the Vampyr.

Napolean took her arm with exquisite gentleness. He bent his head, long locks of shimmering silver and black falling in a royal curtain around them, and then he pierced her vein cleanly, his teeth sinking deep, his lips forming a tight, unbreakable seal over the wound. As he took long, dragging pulls from her vein, his mouth working in an easy rhythm, Kagen marveled at the sensation of *peace* that flooded his body. There was no hint of possessiveness, no impulse to *kill them all*—

The rivers were finally absent of blood.

Napolean released his hold, removed his fangs, and sealed the wound with deft alacrity, and then he turned to regard Kagen and his *destiny*. "Congratulations," he said with a smile, and then just like that, he shimmered out of view.

Ryder was formally named.

Kagen and Arielle were formally mated.

And the noble king was gone.

Arielle stepped back from the crowd, needing to get some air.

She found a comfortable perch alongside the stony wall that bordered the bridge, and leaned back to rest her legs, grateful that the ceremony was finally over.

As she watched Kagen interact with his family, *Keitaro interact with his sons*, she couldn't help but feel blessed for having been part of this family's journey.

Her family's journey.

It seemed like only yesterday that she had been a child growing up in Mhier, a daughter weighted down by the yoke of a distant and lonely mother; a slave, estranged from her father, with no foreseeable future, save to one day become the bride of a tyrant king; and a rebel, entrenched in a cause that could never be won.

She shivered and ran her hands along her arms to avert the chill.

That was then…

And this was now.

Suddenly, feeling lighter than she had felt in years, she

stepped away from the wall, stretched out her arms, and spun around in a wide, dizzying circle. As the crisp mountain air swept through her hair, teased her arms, and fanned her elation, she laughed out loud with abandon.

Her new family might think she was crazy, but she just didn't care.

How could she do anything but dance—or sing?

If someone would have told her, just two years ago, that *this* would be her future, she would have told them they were crazy, that heroes only existed in fairy tales, and life was a long exercise in survival, brutality, and pain.

But now?

Now she knew different.

When Kagen approached her on the bridge and held up his hands in question, she had an overwhelming impulse to launch herself into his arms, and she did just that.

He staggered back and caught her, laughing. "I take it this is happiness?"

"Oh yes!" She laughed, burying her face in his chest, and then she just as suddenly pulled away. She gestured at the water, the sky, and the valley; and then she spun around again. "But Kagen, it's so much more."

His stunning brown eyes brimmed with joy as the deep, dark pools of splendor narrowed on her face. "Tell me," he urged her softly. "That is…if you can find the words."

Arielle struggled to articulate her feelings, to find a way to express the overwhelming lightness of being that was radiating in her soul: How could she possibly tell him that the ghosts of the past, the unrelenting hounds from hell, no longer haunted her like prey?

That they would no longer plague her dreams?

How could she possibly express that what had once been corporeal was now as mist, that what had once been ethereal was now…simply gone. That what had always—*always*—been too ever-constant to outrun no longer nipped at her heels?

There were simply no words…

So she cupped his face in her hands, rose to the tips of her toes, and kissed him softly on the lips. "I love you, Kagen Silivasi," she whispered earnestly, and then she brushed the backs of her fingers along his cheeks, hoping he would understand: There were few things more elemental to the journey of a soul than the ability to claim one's destiny, than the right to determine one's future, than the chance to reach one's potential.

And Kagen had made all of them possible…

For her.

Though the words failed to come, she felt it in every cell of her being—

Arielle Nightsong was free.

Epilogue

Six months later

Tiffany Matthews cleared away the remaining scattered toys from the front parlor of Prince Phoenix's suite of rooms. She took several steps back and skimmed the wide-planked, hardwood floors, her eyes searching up and down each slat of wood, one at a time, scanning for the missing *Bobee*, a stuffed purple dragon that Phoenix clung to like glue. The child needed the dragon to sleep—or at least he thought he did—and as of three o'clock that afternoon, Bobee had gone missing.

It was an utter catastrophe in the making.

She furrowed her brow and glanced beneath the formal settee. Nothing there. She spun around and checked beneath the mission-style end tables. Nothing there, either. She got down on her hands and knees and tried to view the room from a child's point of view—still nothing reared its dragon-head.

She sighed. She had two financial reports to *peruse* before morning, a ledger full of new accounts to enter into the computer database, and here she was, on her hands and knees like a ninny—or a nanny, to be exact—searching for a purple dragon.

"Still nothing yet?" Brooke asked, stepping quietly into the room. The queen was as tired as she looked, considering the fact that Phoenix had not taken a decent nap all day. "Napolean says he picked up the dragon in Romania the last time he was there to check on things at the University—he can't possibly get another one here in the States."

Tiffany rolled her eyes and huffed in annoyance. "Great. Just great. I don't suppose the child would settle for Barney?"

Brooke drew back, appalled. "Oh gods," she uttered. "Just the thought of it. I think he would have a royal meltdown."

Tiffany laughed, and then she clutched at her forearm. "Agreed." She scratched her wrist and stood up from the floor. "I swear; I have looked everywhere, even in the most ridiculous of places, like the refrigerator, the bathtub, and the pantry, just to rule it out. Where the heck is Bobee?"

Brooke rubbed her tired eyes and slowly shook her head. "You looked in the refrigerator?"

Tiffany squared her shoulders and leveled a warning glare at her best friend. "Don't go there, Brookie."

The queen looked off into the distance. "I think Bobee's dead."

"No!" Tiffany nearly shouted, spinning around on her heels. "Watch your mouth, *milady*." They both giggled at Brooke's formal title. "To even speak of it is treason."

Brooke held up both hands in surrender. "*Sorry*. Hey, why don't you go ahead and make your way to the guest house. It's already going on six o'clock, and I know you have a lot of work to do for DMV Prime. I'll keep searching for the missing toy, and I'll let you know if I find it." She breathed a plaintive sigh. "Who knows: Maybe someone will send a ransom note, and we can pay for Bobee's safe return."

Tiffany laughed wholeheartedly. "Oh, if only we should be that lucky." She tucked her arm to her chest, rubbed it against her shirt, and headed toward the front door of the parlor. "Now, if I could only find my car keys."

"You lost them *again*?" Brooke asked.

Tiffany moaned. "I swear; I would lose my head if it wasn't firmly attached to my shoulders." She squeezed her left forearm with her right hand and began to rub absent, tight circles over her wrist with her thumb.

"What's with your arm?" Brooke said, frowning. She gestured toward the cradled limb.

Tiffany frowned. "I don't know." She held it up and turned it over in order to take a closer look. "I think I must have bumped it against the furniture." She noticed several red welts, swelling near the junction of her elbow, and winced. "Or maybe it's an allergy of some sort, a really bad rash. Maybe I came in contact with some dust or pollen, trying to hunt for Bobee."

Brooke gave her a mock look of insult. "Are you saying my house is filthy?"

Tiffany chuckled. She waved her hand around the room and smirked. "House, Brooke? Your son has a *suite* of rooms. This is a mansion, not a house." She angled her chin in a playful, haughty manner.

Brooke sneered at the amusing gesture. "Don't change the subject. Are you saying my *less than humble abode* is dirty?"

Tiffany curtsied. "No, *milady*." She laughed. "Although I might be saying it would help if you would quit firing your cleaning staff."

"Who?" Brooke demanded in a surly voice. "Please tell me you are *not* referring to MaryAnn, the so-called human servant?" She made disdainful air quotes around the words *human servant.*

Tiffany regarded her with mirth.

"Oh dear gods," Brooke clipped, "the woman was trying to seduce Napolean."

"You don't know that for a fact," Tiffany quipped.

"She was dusting the furniture in the nude!"

Tiffany burst out in laughter and tucked a lock of her short blond hair behind her ear. "Well, maybe she was just being *organic*." She snickered then. "Besides, can you blame the poor woman? She's human. It must have been like being restricted to a really bad diet of celery and tuna, and then all of a sudden, you stumble across a huge chunk of meat, filet mignon: fresh, juicy, and right off the grill. What was the poor woman to do?"

Brooke stepped forward and punched her friend playfully in the arm. "Yeah, more like filet Mondragon." She winked conspiratorially and laughed. "Besides, Carlotta is still with us."

Tiffany knew the human servant well. She belonged to a kind, loyal family, one who had served the Vampyr for almost nine generations, and she was an invaluable asset to the house of Jadon. "Yes, but she's a governess and an all-around magician, not a housekeeper."

Brooke rolled her eyes, apparently refusing to take the conversation any further. She was just about to turn away, start searching for Bobee again, when she eyed the raised ridges on Tiffany's wrist *again*. "Tiff, that is really flaring up. Let me see."

Tiffany held out her arm and grimaced. *Yikes, it did look bad.* Well, not in a gruesome sort of way, but there were dozens of little lines crisscrossing along her skin like a cryptic diagram, parallel points that intersected in such a way that it almost looked like two dancing kids linking arms. "Maybe I should take some Benadryl."

All at once, Brooke's mouth shot open, and she took an unwitting step back, still grasping Tiffany's arm.

"Hey, that is attached, you know," Tiffany protested.

Brooke gazed up at her friend in blank stupefaction, looked down at her wrist once more, and then gulped. *"Tiffany…"*

"What?" Tiffany's voice rose in alarm. "You think it's something serious, don't you?"

Brooke ran her fingers over the bright, mysterious lines and blanched. "I think…I think…" She covered her mouth with her hand.

"*What*?" Tiffany insisted, staring down at her arm in concern. Holy crap, there really was something funky going on.

"That's not a rash or an allergy, Tiff. It's a constellation. *A celestial deity*."

"What do you mean?" Tiffany said, her voice rising with distress.

Brooke slowly shook her head as she took another look. "Correction. That would be celestial deities, as in plural. That's Gemini, the twins."

"Gemini who?" Tiffany shrieked, squeezing her arm with her hand. Her face suddenly felt hot, and her stomach felt queasy, although she didn't quite know why. Well, other than the fact that she was dying of the plague. "Oh, God. How do you catch Gemini? Is there a medication for it?"

Brooke held both hands out in front of her and toggled them up and down as if to say, *Okay, let's just calm down*, and then she gaped at Tiffany's arm once more. "You are so not following me right now, Tiff." She began to speak slowly and evenly, measuring her speech as if she were talking to a child, while over pronouncing her words. "The-mark-on-your-arm-is-the-sign-of-a-Blood-Moon. It's a replication of a deity, one that belongs to a male from the house of Jadon. A vampire. Tiffany, it's the mark of a vampire's *destiny.*"

There was no need for the moron's version of CliffsNotes, nor the repetitive explanation—Tiffany heard her friend loud and clear—although, the full meaning of the words did not quite sink in. And not because Tiffany was too slow to process the English language. On the contrary, she heard it, understood it, and moved right past understanding to *denial.*

No way.

No how.

Not today.

Not even tomorrow.

She marched very calmly to the nearest window, pulled back the blinds, and peeked up at the moon. As her eyes struggled to focus on the bloodred orb that hung like a neon sign in the heavens, her mind swirled around in a dizzying maelstrom, trying to dissect the far-too-obvious clues: mainly, the brilliant cluster of stars and meteors, the complex network of lines and planes, all coalescing in a unified pattern to form the image of a set of twins, two young children, linked at the wrist, staring off into space at a blackened sky.

Gemini.

Tiffany looked down at her arm.

Then she looked back up at the moon.

Then she looked back down at her arm—

And she let out an appalling string of curse words.

"Who is it?" she demanded, all hints of good nature gone from her voice. *This wasn't funny, not in the least.* This was beyond upsetting. It was horrific.

Impossible.

It simply was not happening.

Brooke strolled to Tiffany's side and glanced at the sky.

For a moment, the beautiful brunette simply stared at the stars in awe, and then she fell into immediate formal protocol. "We need to go find Napolean." She spoke softly and deliberately. "Whoever the male is, he has to be close by. Close enough to find you…if he searches."

Tiffany spun around on her heels, her eyes darting back and forth across the room like frenetic lasers—she half expected to see Count Dracula himself hanging from the ceiling. "No!" she exclaimed, to no one in particular. There was absolutely no way they were going *to go find Napolean* in order to offer her up as the virgin sacrifice to a vamp. Okay, well, not necessarily a virgin, but a sacrifice just the same. "That is not going to happen."

Brooke nodded gravely and lowered her voice. "Okay, so what would you like me to do?"

Tiffany glanced around the room and shuddered. "Give me your keys, Brooke. I need to get out of here."

"And you want to take my car?"

Tiffany glowered at her best friend, and if looks could kill, Brooke would have been six feet under, with rigor mortis already setting in. "Damnit, Brooke! I'm not playing around. The guest house is three miles away! Do you want me to walk?" She spun around again, and eyed the back door of the parlor, the passage that led to Phoenix's private portico. "*Give me your keys.*"

Brooke took a slow step backward and sighed. "Sweetie," she nearly crooned, "I get it—you're scared. Believe me, I understand. But you and I both know that you can't run away from this. What we need to do is—"

"We?" Tiffany cut in. "Seriously, Brooke? *We?*" She took several steps back, gravitating toward the door. "No. There is no *we* in this. And I get it, too: You're in love with the vampire king, and your life has been a thousand times better since Napolean claimed you, since you came to Dark Moon Vale. Bully for you." She sighed, trying to catch her breath. "And so has mine—I'll be the first to admit it—but *that* is as your graphic designer, your best friend, and your son's impromptu nanny. Not as some creature's *destiny*."

"Some *creature*?" Brooke looked mildly offended.

"Don't do that, Brooke," Tiffany said. "Seriously, not right now. That's not even fair. You know I have supported you…and Napolean…and Phoenix." Her voice rose in proportion to her angst. "Hell, I've committed myself to living in Dark Moon Vale, knowing full well that I can never go back, not now that I know about the Vampyr, not now that I've placed myself under their protection and care. But"—she held up her hand to silence any protest before one could be made—"but *this*, I cannot do. I will not do. I'm not you, Brooke. These guys scare the hell out of me on a really primitive level, if you know what I mean. So please. *Please*. Just give me your keys." She held out her hand and waited.

Brooke looked positively ill. The turmoil in her eyes was unmistakable, the angst on her face, excruciating. "Oh, Tiff," she whispered. "You are my best friend in the entire world." She straightened her spine and raised her chin, although her confidence didn't register in her voice. "And there is nothing I wouldn't do for you, but what you're asking…" She glanced at the door to the hall and then the door to the portico, each one in turn. "As your friend, as someone who *loves* you, I know that you're in danger if you go off alone." She sighed. "And as Napolean's mate, a member of the house of Jadon—hell, *as the queen*—I also know that whoever this male is, if I help his *destiny* escape—"

"His *destiny*?" Tiffany interrupted, hardly able to believe her ears. "So is that what I am now…*his* destiny?"

"No," Brooke argued. "I mean, *yes*, obviously, but—"

"Don't, *milady*. The indecision does not become you." Tiffany knew she was being cruel, but she just couldn't help it—she was also running out of time. Gritting her teeth, she stilled her resolve and changed tactics. "At least tell me this: Who's here, at the manse, right now? Which of your *subjects*? Which one of the males?" She instantly regretted the sarcasm, but it was too late to take it back.

Brooke looked momentarily stunned, perhaps even hurt by the sharp delivery, but to her credit, she collected herself and tried to answer honestly. "Um…I don't know." She shrugged her shoulders in exasperation, her soft blue eyes clouding with distress. "There's no one…no meetings…no counsels." She dropped her head and ran her hands through her hair, as if physically seeking the answers from her mind. "The only one who stops by this time of night, unannounced, is Ramsey Olaru, the sentinel. He sometimes drops in to compare notes with Napolean, but it all depends on what's up."

Tiffany felt her knees go weak beneath her. "Ramsey? *Olaru*? The six-foot-five walking pit bull? The one who fights with a *pitchfork*?"

"It's a trident," Brooke mumbled weakly, "an archaic weapon that—"

Tiffany leveled a spiteful glare at her friend. "The guy who spit out a toothpick on Napolean's floor, the one who smashed his enemy's head into smithereens by bashing it against the side of a cave wall?" She winked at her friend sardonically. "That's just…lovely." She nodded her head in quick, short bursts. "Remember, Brooke—*it's me*—the one you tell all your secrets to." Her eyes glazed over with tears, and her voice hitched in her throat. "Just give me your keys, Brookie. I'm begging you."

Brooke turned the color of stale, curdled milk. "Tiffany, *listen*."

"No."

"Please, just listen. Let's you and I go somewhere *together*, anywhere you'd like. I'll tell Carlotta that I'm going out, so she can look after Phoenix; and then I'll get my car and come around the back. You can meet me by the trellis. We'll go to a hotel or a cabin—hell, we can go to another town—and I won't call Napolean until you tell me you're ready. At least this way, someone will be with you."

Tiffany pursed her lips and nodded her head derisively. "Yeah, because Napolean Mondragon can't just reach into your mind, or follow the trail of your blood, or just beam himself into any room you're standing in like Captain Kirk, right? Because his queen can just walk away undetected…" Her voice trailed off. There was no point in exploring this angle any further.

Tiffany was out of time.

She wiped a single tear from her eye and reached for her jacket, a soft, form-fitting cloak hanging on a polished bronze hook beside the portico door, and she quickly shrugged into the garment.

"What are you doing?" Brooke asked, her face an ashen mask.

"I'm leaving."

"On foot?"

"Can't fly. I'm human."

Brooke lunged forward, and in that terrifying moment, her unnatural vampiric speed as well as her supernatural agility completely caught Tiffany off guard.

"Don't!" Tiffany shouted, raising her hands to ward off her friend as if she were about to tear out her throat with her fangs.

Brooke drew back in surprise and gasped.

And all the tears Tiffany had been holding at bay began to stream down her cheeks in desperate rivers. Her voice caught on a sob. "You're stronger than me, Brooke, and you're faster. You could stop me, but it would kill me. Do you understand what I'm saying? This is a line you can't cross." She swiped at her tears with the heels of her hands and sniffled. "I'm not asking you to break an oath, to help me get away, just turn your back and—"

"Brooke!" Napolean's deep voice rose in a thunderous crescendo as the ancient king began to make his way down the hall. Undoubtedly, he had sensed his mate's distress and was on his way to investigate the cause.

Shit, shit, and more shit! Tiffany thought, glancing at the door. She had to get the hell out of Dodge…and now.

As Brooke turned around to answer the king—her lethal, vampiric husband—Tiffany dashed for the door. She wrenched open the handle in a fevered rush and flew out onto the patio, frantic to make an escape, flinching as the door slammed shut behind her. She immediately eyed the trellis and gave it less than a moment's thought before leaping over the rail and dashing down the steep hill toward the open meadow below.

Oh, thank the gods of horses and war!

She breathed a sigh of relief as she eyed the majestic Percheron still searching for patches of grass in the snow-covered meadow at the base of the hill. Nearly eighteen hands of muscle, strength, and speed awaited her devotion, and she couldn't help but marvel at her sudden good fortune: Prince Phoenix had wanted to see *da pwetty pony* earlier that day, if that's what one could call the magnificent, intelligent beast, and the king's gift to his son was still saddled and neatly tied beneath a temporary shelter, awaiting Napolean's private trainer to return him to the stables.

Tiffany was not much of a rider—okay, so she could barely sit straight in the saddle—but what the hell: Desperate times called for desperate measures. She eyed the Percheron cautiously, approached with gentle ease, and slowly raised an outstretched hand, careful not to frighten the horse away: "Here, horsy. *Here, horsy*! Come, *please*. Just…come."

The horse looked up at her with luminous, haunting eyes. He tossed back his head and pranced in place, as if showing off his power and pride.

And then he went back to eating.

Tiffany's heart sank into her stomach. *Not now, Mr. Horse. Please…not now.* She held out her hand, palm side up, as if she had a delectable piece of sugar resting in the center, and she tried again. "Here, beautiful prince"—maybe he preferred an appeal to his ego—"here, you gorgeous, magnificent gladiator. Come see Auntie Tiff…*please*."

She waited with bated breath.

And to her utter surprise, the horse trotted over in her direction. Truth be told, he probably came out of pity.

She waited until he was within an arm's length before slowly reaching up to stroke his neck, just beneath his mane. "That's a good horsy," she murmured, feeling more than a little foolish. She sauntered up to his left side and eyed the dangling stirrup, marveling at the barely leashed power emanating from the horse's breast, and praying all the while that he wouldn't trample her, or worse, take off running while she tried to mount. She reached for the reins and softly slid a foot into the stirrup. Okay, so she had to jack her knee up to her chest just to reach the perilous leather hoop, but she did it as gracefully as she could. "Okay, Mr. Horse, I'm counting on you to save me," she whispered.

The stallion snorted in reply, and she took it as a *yes*.

With that, she grabbed the shoehorn, pulled herself into the saddle, and kicked him in the flanks.

Napolean Mondragon burst into the parlor in a maelstrom, his glorious long hair whipping behind him as if stirred by a mystical wind. His eyes were narrowed in concentration; his face was a mask of concern; and his no-nonsense tone made it abundantly clear: He wasn't playing around.

Brooke opened her mouth to speak, but she didn't have a chance.

"What's wrong?" he demanded, staring at her with unconcealed concern. He reached out, took her hands in his, and then quickly released them. He ran his palms up and down her arms, while perusing her body from head to toe with a dark, penetrating gaze, his eyes scanning for gods-knew-what. "Are you hurt, my love?"

"No," Brooke answered. She tried to speak in a calming voice. "I'm…I… It's just—"

"Where's Phoenix?" He immediately strode toward the back of the parlor.

"He's in his room. He's in his crib. *He's fine.*"

Napolean turned back around and visibly eased up. "Then why are you so distressed?"

Brooke took a deep breath and answered bluntly, "It's Tiffany."

"Tiffany?" Napolean furrowed his brow. "Has something happened to your friend?"

Brooke shook her head in denial. "Have you seen the moon, milord?"

"Milord?" Napolean frowned, and then he reached out to gently stroke her cheek with the back of his hand. "That's rather ominous, *rather formal*, coming from you."

"Have you seen the moon?" she repeated.

"Of course," he answered sternly. "A Gemini Blood Moon. It belongs to Ramsey Olaru, but his *destiny* is yet unknown. I was with the sentinel just moments ago in the living room, trying to figure it out. We were about to search for Carlotta when I felt your distress…"

"It's not Carlotta," Brooke whispered cautiously.

Napolean's dark eyes alighted with instant understanding. *"Tiffany?"*

Brooke bit her bottom lip and nodded in a barely perceptible gesture.

Napolean drew back in surprise. "Where is she?"

Brooke took a deep breath and shook her head. "Gone."

"What do you mean, *gone*?"

Brooke turned to face the back of the parlor and pointed toward the still-open door. "I mean, *she's gone.* She ran off. I couldn't make her stay."

"And why is that?" Ramsey Olaru's deep, husky tenor reverberated through the room as the huge, fearsome male sauntered into the parlor. "Forgive my bad manners, milord, but I felt the circumstances warranted the intrusion."

Napolean nodded. "Ramsey," he said by way of greeting. "Then you heard?"

Ramsey inclined his head. "I heard."

Brooke shuddered, recognizing the precarious situation for what it was: Not only had Tiffany taken off into the valley like some kind of escaped convict, but Ramsey Olaru was an Ancient

Master Warrior, a dangerous and hard-nosed sentinel of Dark Moon Vale; and he was standing on the precipice of a perilous cliff, where his life hung in the balance beneath a centuries-awaited Blood Moon. The male was not only hyped up on adrenaline—if not downright feral—he was more dangerous than ever before, and his eerily calm exterior only emphasized that point.

Brooke sought to diffuse the situation as tactfully as possible. "I'm sorry, Ramsey," she whispered. "Tiffany was terrified, and I tried—"

Ramsey held up a large, rugged hand to silence her as he turned to face the king. "Milord, have you taken Tiffany's blood?"

A low growl of warning rumbled in Napolean's throat, and the king's nostrils flared in disapproval. "What the *hell* was that?"

Ramsey lowered his gaze, as respectfully as he could. He glanced up at Brooke and declined his head in apology. "Forgive me, milady. I meant you no disrespect." Then he set his jaw and turned to Napolean. "Milord, by all rights, I should not even be standing here right now. A Blood Moon trumps all other protocol. So please, just tell me: Have you taken Tiffany's blood?"

Oh gods, he really sounds…upset, Brooke whispered to Napolean telepathically. She didn't want to aggravate the situation, but she was growing increasingly concerned for her friend.

It's okay, angel, Napolean replied in a gentle but confident psychic tone. *He is dealing with an overwhelming sense of urgency. It is to be expected.*

Of course, Brooke said. *I understand. I just…are you sure he's okay?*

Napolean nodded, and then he cleared his throat. "Miss Matthews is under the protection of the house of Jadon," he said to Ramsey. "She has been initiated as a human loyalist. Of course, I've taken her blood."

Ramsey shifted his weight from foot to foot and slowly stretched his back. "And?"

Napolean shut his eyes, as if trying to maintain his cool. His hand twitched almost imperceptibly, and his face grew taut—but his expression remained composed. "And she's about three-quarters of a mile into the northern forest…on a horse. She's heading due east."

"On a horse?" Brooke cut in, immediately regretting the irrelevant outburst.

Ramsey's top lip twitched several times in a row, and the tips of his fangs began to extend from his gums before he quickly caught the involuntary reaction and reined it in. His eyes deepened to a darker hue, the hazel tones deepening to amber; but otherwise, he showed little reaction. "Phoenix's Percheron?" he asked, incredulous.

"Yes, on Viking," Napolean confirmed.

Ramsey nodded solemnly, and then his entire body stiffened; his spine grew straighter; and he appeared to grow two inches taller. "If that is all, milord."

Napolean inclined his head, and Brooke nearly swayed where she stood.

Oh gods, Napolean; will she be okay? For the first time that night, she truly feared for her friend, and not because of the Dark Ones or any other supernatural creatures that went bump in the night. Brooke was afraid of Ramsey.

She will, Napolean replied in her mind. *He will find her and retrieve her…*

Faster than she can say his name, Brooke uttered, swallowing her fear. A blind man could see Ramsey's determination—the sentinel would not be denied.

Indeed, Napolean replied. And then he turned to face the powerful vampire before them. "Warrior, do you want—"

Ramsey clenched his fists at his side and then slowly released them, but he held his tongue out of respect…and waited.

"Julien…our tracker?" Napolean persisted.

Ramsey sucked his teeth and exhaled. "Nope."

"Your brothers, Saxson or Santos?"

He rolled his shoulders and popped his neck. "*Nope.*"

When Napolean held out both hands, palms facing down,

parallel to the floor, and then gently splayed his fingers as if to calm a wild beast, Brooke's heart nearly skipped a beat.

"You are one of only three valley sentinels," Napolean said ceremoniously, "a member of my private guard, a warrior entrusted to protect this vale. So I need not express to you the many dangers that could arise."

Brooke clung to Napolean's hand and shuddered. By all that was holy, Ramsey's eyes were like hot, focused lasers as he locked them unerringly with the king's. He didn't interrupt him and he didn't cut him off, yet his silence spoke volumes: He was itching to get on with the search.

"Very well," Napolean said. "Then you also know I can only give you so much time before I interfere. Until we see you *both* home safely."

Brooke's stomach did a tiny flip. *See them both home safely?* Oh gods, the reality was truly sinking in, and she didn't like the implications: Both Ramsey and Tiffany could be in very real danger—perhaps she should have tried harder to stop her friend…

Ramsey cleared his throat with a raspy inflection. "If that is all, milord."

Once again, Napolean declined his head in a regal gesture of formal dismissal. "That is all, warrior."

"That's it?" Brooke squawked out loud, forgetting to hold her tongue. *No please be gentle? Try not to frighten her out of her wits or yank her arm out of its socket? Maybe you should take another vampire along—like Braden or Nachari?*

"Milady?" Ramsey inquired solicitously, although his voice was as hard as stone.

"Nothing," Brooke said quickly. "I was just thinking out loud." When Ramsey didn't reply, Brooke ducked beneath the safety of Napolean's arm, nestling closer to his chest.

Perhaps she was just imagining things.

Perhaps Ramsey was just on edge…

Or perhaps the warrior was truly miffed by the fact that Tiffany Matthews was supposed to be one of them: While human, she understood the Curse and the consequences of failing to fulfill it. She worked in Dark Moon Vale for the royal family, and she also knew Ramsey personally, if only through passing interactions; yet and still, she had chosen to run away, to risk the sentinel's life.

She made no such conscious choice, Napolean said telepathically. *She simply reacted in fear. He knows this.* Having revealed the fact that he was reading her thoughts, he tightened his arm around her waist and pulled her closer. "This male will not hurt his *destiny*, my love." He spoke aloud for Ramsey's benefit, and then he turned back to regard the keyed-up vampire. "Fifteen minutes to find her; thirty to retrieve her; and then…your brethren will step in."

Ramsey nodded in obeisance. "As you will, milord."

Brooke watched in angst-filled suspense as the ruthless sentinel stalked to the back door of the parlor; threw open the panel, using only his mind to do so; and drew some sort of crude weapon from a sheath at his belt. "And just what the hell is that for?" she whispered beneath her breath.

"We have many enemies, my love," Napolean answered calmly, shifting his hand to the small of her back, where he could rub it softly. "And Ramsey is a sentinel. He hunts Dark Ones. He protects the people. He dispatches enemies, of all types, *at my command*. He is not an ordinary member of the house of Jadon. He must take extraordinary precautions."

Despite her mate's explanation, Brooke Adams-Mondragon cringed.

It had only been fourteen months since she and Tiffany had first come to Dark Moon Vale to attend a routine conference. It had only been fourteen months since the two of them had been hurtled into a world beyond comprehension, into the realm of the Vampyr, against their will. And as she thought about it, she had to admit: Napolean had been rather *intense* when she had *met* him as well. For heaven's sake, he had stopped a cab with the palm of his hand, ripped the door off the hinges, and ordered Brooke to get out of the backseat, while Ramsey had driven the "getaway" car. Well, no wonder she still feared the male like the grim reaper…with fangs.

She drew in a deep breath of air and tried to calm her racing heart.

In the end, it had all worked out, and Brooke had found happiness beyond her wildest dreams. She had been gifted with peace, security, and love—surely, Tiffany would find the same.

But with Ramsey Olaru?

As she stared at the open door, shivering from the cool, ominous breeze that wafted in, in Ramsey's wake, she marshaled her courage and summoned her hope. And then she said a prayer to the celestial god Gemini: *Please let Tiffany be okay, and please don't let Ramsey…harm her sensitive soul.*

She knew her best friend well, just as she also knew the vampire…

And this was not going to be an easy Blood Moon.

About The Author

Tessa Dawn grew up in Colorado where she developed a deep affinity for the Rocky Mountains. After graduating with a degree

in psychology, she worked for several years in criminal justice and mental health before returning to get her Master's Degree in Nonprofit Management.

Tessa began writing as a child and composed her first full-length novel at the age of eleven. By the time she graduated high-school, she had a banker's box full of short-stories and books. Since then, she has published works as diverse as poetry, greeting cards, workbooks for kids with autism, and academic curricula. The Blood Curse Series marks her long-desired return to her creative-writing roots and her first foray into the Dark Fantasy world of vampire fiction.

Tessa currently splits her time between the Colorado suburbs and mountains with her husband, two children, and "one very crazy cat." She hopes to one day move to the country where she can own horses and what she considers "the most beautiful creature ever created" -- a German Shepherd.

Writing is her bliss.

Books in the Blood Curse Series

Blood Destiny

Blood Awakening

Blood Possession

Blood Shadows

Blood Redemption

Blood Father

Blood Vengeance ~ Coming Soon

If you would like to receive notice of future releases,

please join the author's mailing list at

www.TessaDawn.com

CPSIA information can be obtained
at www.ICGtesting.com
Printed in the USA
LVHW01s1746220418
574444LV00001B/66/P